BELL' ANTONIO

VITALIANO BRANCATI was born at Pachino, near Syracuse, in 1907, and was educated at Catania where he
took a degree in literature. In 1924 he joined the Fascist
party, but after being "Fascist to the roots of his hair",
as he said, he repudiated it completely, and *The Lost
Years*, started in 1934 and published in serial form in
1938, were the first fruits of his conversion. From 1937
he was a schoolteacher in Catania and Rome, but he
turned to full-time writing after the war. *Don Giovanni
in Sicilia* was published in 1941 and in 1949 came the
present novel, *Bell' Antonio*. It won the Bagutta Prize
and was made into a celebrated film. Brancati also wrote
short stories, plays and a considerable number of articles
for the press. He was married to the actress Anna
Proclemer, and in 1954 he died in Turin.

Vitaliano Brancati

BELL' ANTONIO

Translated from the Italian by
Patrick Creagh

HARVILL
An Imprint of HarperCollins*Publishers*

First published in Italy by
Valentino Bompiani, Milan, 1949
under the title *Il Bell' Antonio*
First published in Great Britain in 1952
under the title *Antonio: The Great Lover*
This edition in a new translation
first published in 1993 by Harvill
an imprint of HarperCollins Publishers,
77/85 Fulham Palace Road,
Hammersmith, London w6 8jb

9 8 7 6 5 4 3 2 1

BRITISH LIBRARY CATALOGUING IN PUBLICATION DATA

Brancati, Vitaliano
Bell' Antonio.
I Title
853 [F]

ISBN 0-00-271327-6 paperback

Set in Linotron Bembo by
Rowland Phototypesetting Ltd,
Bury St Edmunds, Suffolk

Printed and bound in Great Britain by
Hartnolls Limited, Bodmin, Cornwall

To my wife

I

OF THE BACHELOR SICILIANS who settled in Rome around the year 1930, eight at the very least, if memory serves aright, rented furnished flats in quiet, out-of-the-way parts of town, and almost all of them by chance in the neighbourhood of famous monuments; of which, however, they never learnt the history or lit upon the beauty, and often they never so much as noticed them. But then, what ever *did* fail to escape the notice of eyes straining to catch a glimpse of the woman they lusted after among the scrum of passengers alighting from a tram? Domes, portals, monumental fountains... Works which, before they were achieved and accomplished, had for years furrowed the brows of Michelangelo and Borromini, could not for a moment catch the attention of the black, roving eyes of these guests from the South. Age-old bells with their mellow, solemn voices, celebrated in the lines of Goethe and of Shelley, earned themselves a "*Chi camurria, 'sta campana!* Damn those bells!" for vibrating with their dawn chorus through the wall against which the young man was resting a brow but recently surrendered to sleep and still red with the imprint of a pair of lips.

The respect which as a chronicler I owe to truth impels me to own that these Sicilian bachelors were not much of an eyeful; except for one, Antonio Magnano, who was an Adonis. In saying this I should not like you to imagine the ugly ones were unattractive to women. On the contrary many of them, despite being of bantam size, with Semitic noses and little-finger nails left long to pick their lugholes clean, appeared to be linked by some deep complicity to the whole of the female race. You might think that between them and all the women under the sun a disgraceful act had somewhere and at some time taken place. There was not a woman but on first setting eyes on these men seemed to pale and to acknowledge herself bound to them by long-standing and unspeakable moral lapses. Hence their conquests always had a shabby air of blackmail, although (and this I can swear to) these fellows of twenty-five to thirty were of a peerless tenderness and courtesy towards the opposite sex. But upon this earth, for all its mysteries, there is perhaps no more mysterious being than your truly ugly man.

Of quite different stamp were the triumphs of Antonio Magnano. Back in 1932 he was twenty-six years of age, and photographs of him on show in Piazza di Spagna would halt even middle-aged women in their tracks, though laden with shopping and dragging along toddlers in floods of tears with the very hand just used to box their ears. Instant bewitchment streamed from his olive-skinned visage, powerfully blue-tinted on the chin but of extreme sensitivity; the eyes seemed to glint with tears that sat on the uppermost curve of the cheeks, where the shadow of his long lashes would oftentimes abide. In his reticent presence the most jittery, hysterical woman could be seized by one of those yawning fits that discharge nervous tension, prompting her to rise from her chair and stretch out on the sofa, to rise from the sofa and stretch out on the bed. A jaundiced and superficial observer might have consoled himself by saying that women were bored in Antonio's company. What a gross error! Women felt dominated and at the same time perfectly and completely at their ease. When in his presence they sweetly burned, and suffered agonies, and went mad with a pleasure so intense as to make them think themselves possessed by some severe aberration which jumbled up pleasure and pain in that utter lack of discrimination which is the sole state of mind wherein anyone dares to be overheard pronouncing the words "I am happy!"

Antonio's ugly friends looked up to him, and would have envied him too, or perhaps even hated him, had they not (inspired and influenced by the women they knew) unwittingly fallen in love with him themselves. The secret of those conquests so different from their own, and in fact the exact opposite – since their successes with women seemed wrung from the latter as a result of dirty doings, whereas Antonio's appeared to emanate from some mysterious balm which he conferred on his victims – the secret of those conquests, I say, so greatly intrigued them that they would set the alarm for five to be up and out early, and catch Antonio in the shower. Here they were in for a bitter harvest. Faced with those athlete's limbs tempered by a touch of mild and melancholy pallor, as if, whatever the circumstances, that body were invested by some mystic light, his friends – and first and foremost Luigi d'Agata and Carlo Fischetti – would be assailed by a malaise that cloaked self-loathing. "You know what you look like?" they would ask, to come straight out with a catch-phrase that might otherwise have festered in their bosoms and turned to spite: "Like a fresh-baked biscuit!"

And they would start to thump his bare shoulders, tweak the hairs on his chest, grab him by an ankle and hoist up a foot... but only to find themselves possessed and disconcerted by the vibrations of a body so infinitely strange and undeniably superior in quality.

It has to be admitted that Antonio had provoked similar perturbations from his youth up. It was on April 5th 1922 that his mother and father, Signora Rosaria and Signor Alfio, were compelled to take note of the fact. That was the morning on which the maidservant, a country girl, entered their bedroom with her face all scratched and tear-stained.

"In pity's name, what have you done?" cried the good lady, removing the tray from the girl's trembling hands. "What's been going on? Speak up!"

The poor girl sank her chin on her chest and looked asquint like a goat. Eventually she said, "It wasn't me."

"Then who was it?" demanded the mistress of the house, more flustered than ever.

"It's your son!" whimpered the girl.

"Antonio?" bawled his father, extracting from the bed two legs which by dint of wriggling under the bedclothes he had managed to sheathe in longjohns. "Right! I'll soon settle *his* hash!"

There ensued a moment's silence. The girl then flung herself on the floor and began writhing and foaming at the mouth, seizing Signor Alfio by the legs as if to deter him from some crime. Just then in came Antonio with an air so sweet and innocent that you could scarcely credit it. The girl at once released her hold on Signor Alfio's legs, rolled across the floor and grabbed the ankles of Antonio, who appeared genuinely astonished, looking questions at his parents: what on earth was all the fuss about? The girl in the meantime pressed her face to Antonio's feet; subsequent, however (and this detail particularly struck his parents, offending them and practically sending them into fits), to tearing off and hurling away his slippers so as to weep and rub her cheeks and nose upon the naked skin.

"Forgive me!" she cried. "I'm a liar, a filthy liar!"

It was with great difficulty that Signor Alfio prized Antonio from the clutches of that twenty-year-old, her chin by now entrenched in the hollow of his shoulder.

Once alone with the girl, Antonio's mother at last learnt the truth. For five nights now this simple country lass had left her bed and gone to rend her bosom and her cheeks outside Antonio's door, caught betwixt her craving to open it and her reluctance to commit a base act.

"What's set me all on fire, what's making me burn?" whimpered the girl as she gnawed at her knuckles.

The good woman was much affected by this piteous tale, and repaired at once to her confessor at the church of Our Lady in Via Sant'Euplio. She told him the circumstances and, on the verge of tears, "Padre Giovanni," she cried, "would it not be wiser to take on a serving-lad and send the girl home?"

The old priest tapped twice with his fingertips on the lid of his snuff-box and peeked out of the confessional.

"If your son's intentions are not honourable," he said, "he will always find a way of making trouble for women." Clearly Padre Giovanni had no intention of admitting that Antonio was completely blameless.

"But could these women not be urged to. . . ?"

"To. . . ?" snapped the priest.

"To behave more decorously towards him!"

"Can you even imagine all the women whose acquaintance your son will make? Will God every time be able to send an angel to warn you that your son is. . . is. . . Well I might as well say it: coming over all randy?"

"So what must I do?"

The priest was well aware that with regard to Antonio he harboured sentiments not immaculately Christian; but alas, once embarked upon the slippery slope of wrath he was unable to resist the delectable sensation that opens a yawning chasm beneath the feet, and that drags inexorably down.

"What you must do," he informed the mother, "is pray to God that He may soon take your son to His bosom."

The good lady nearly fainted away with horror, and the painted wooden angel on whose plinth she had leant her head began to wobble with her sobs.

"When I am preaching my sermons," said the priest, "and your son is there at the back of the church, the women are always putting cricks in their necks to look at him. It's a scandal!"

It is perfectly true that Antonio, seated by the first column in the nave, had only to shift his chair or clear his throat for the pulpit to be robbed of the attentions of all the finest eyes in the place.

"Death," continued the priest, "is for the true Christian no misfortune: rather, when it harvests us in the flower of youth, it is a gift of heaven. But it is not in our province to make suggestions to God as to the best way of placing a young man such as Antonio in the position of sinning no more and. . ." – he raised his voice and added – "of not inciting others to sin.

For to consign our own selves to perdition, dear madam, is *not* the worst thing we can do. No. It is to bring damnation upon *another* of God's creatures over whom we have no rights whatever! Pray to God, dear madam, and in his infinite wisdom he will find ways and means of mitigating your son's satanic beauty without reducing him to dust and ashes!"

The lady rose, not without having made the sign of the cross at the moment when the priest uttered the word "satanic". If the church had not been aglow with gilded and golden light the extreme pallor of that poor woman's face might have softened even the heart of the priest.

"In what way," she said heavily, "do you think my Antonio might be changed by God?"

The priest answered never a word, and she walked by his side and listened to his footsteps with the numbness of one utterly crushed. When they reached the church door he raised a hand still dripping with holy water and murmured:

"He might even lose his sight. . ."

The poor woman flung up an arm across her mouth to suppress a cry. "Come this way," said the priest, with a return of his wrathful glower. And having led Signora Rosaria down to the forecourt and three times over yammered some incomprehensible word, drawing back his lips in such a way as even to distort the shape of his nose, he burst out as follows:

"Are you aware, madam, are you aware that out of twenty girls of good family who make their confessions to me, ten – yes ten! – have given offence to God by thinking too often about your son, and in a manner scarcely in keeping with their upbringing? Monsignor Cavallaro, three days after hearing the confession of my niece, said to me, "Brother in Christ," he said, "try to keep Rita's eyes off young Magnano!" "My friend," I enquired, naturally concerned, "do you *know* anything?" "Nothing whatever," replied the monsignor. "How could I, a simple priest, *know* anything? But the Lord inspired me with these words, and I have reported them to you. . ." A most worthy person, Monsignor Cavallaro! Your husband

6

really should put in a word for him with the archbishop...
But I ask you," – and here his voice rose once more in a
crescendo, "is it right that in church on Sundays the girls of
good family find the High Altar to be wherever Antonio is
sitting?"

Signora Rosaria reached home at her wits' end, wringing
her hands in anguish as she waited for Antonio's return, as if
her son had been jousting with the Archangel Gabriel. Her
terror scaled the heights when in he came wearing a pair of
spectacles.

"You're losing your sight!" shrieked the poor lady.

Antonio replied with the cheeriest smile in the world, and
explained that his glasses had plain lenses and he was only
wearing them to give himself an air of respectability.

His mother hugged him to her bosom, praying in her heart
to the saints in heaven that all members of the sex she belonged
to, and now went in fear of, should in future hug that boy
only with sentiments such as she was feeling at that moment.

Woe and alas, her plea was not vouchsafed her. Towards
Antonio women continued to nourish a sentiment so far at
variance with those maternal feelings that they unanimously
judged it to be a calamity, a horrendous and well-nigh intolerable tribulation, to be either mother or sister to Antonio, and
obliged in consequence not to tremble to the roots of their
being at the mere touch of his hand.

With so much in his favour in a field of activity that in Italy,
and especially in the South, is thought of as heaven on earth,
any other young man, not blessed with Antonio's good-
heartedness and candour, would have become sceptical, indif-
ferent, even cynical; but Antonio never lost his essentially
provincial sweetness of nature, even when he had gone
through university, come away with a Law degree, moved to
a flatlet (furnished with old Sicilian furniture which his father
had shipped from Catania on a slothful cargo boat) within
view of the Villa Borghese gardens, and started to watch the
autumns – the first, the second, the third, the fourth – fading

out upon the trees of this park dotted with converted shooting-boxes, in the expectation, totally unjustified by the facts, of being employed in the Foreign Ministry; though why by that particular ministry is not really clear.

In 1932 it was no rare thing for a young man to become a consul or a minister for a reason deemed all the more acceptable, indeed admirable, the less obvious it was. "That chap didn't sit the exam," people would say. "He has no qualifications and can barely stammer a few words of French... Yet he's been posted to the Legation in Vienna as First Secretary. Evidently he's well thought of in High Places and will go far."

But the "young hopefuls" blessed with this kind of luck had to knuckle down to it in no uncertain manner, and school their hearts so thoroughly that, try as they might, they were no longer able to fall in love with a woman who was not "influential", or make friends with a fellow who wasn't "a power in the land". The least thing smacking of weakness, self-abasement, misfortune or poverty stirred these lads to feelings of the utmost repugnance.

Antonio, on the other hand, had remained as candid and lackadaisical as any waiter in a Sicilian café who, of an August afternoon, bereft by the implacable sirocco of the least power of dissimulation, of conscious tact or any other species of consciousness, tells his customer he would be well advised not to select anything from the ice-cream list; and if the customer then, despite this warning, should proceed to order a lemon or an apricot sherbet, the waiter, jaded and job-ridden, neglects to bring it.

Thus Antonio had let the years roll by, emitting a "brrr" of pleasure at every first whiff of anthracite from the basements, announcing that the heating had been put on for the coming winter. "Gosh!" he'd say to himself, "this'll be the year, eh? This is going to be it!" Then, rubbing his hands vigorously, he'd cup them, blow into them, go and take a peek at himself in a shop window – and unfailingly discover that at his side was some woman gazing doe-eyed at him... Antonio, beautifically half-closing his eyes, would mutter, "Ah yes, this year we'll make a go of it."

But in the autumn of 1934 a melancholy, strange as it was sudden, had descended on him, and by late November had taken on all the signs of downright depression.

"You really get my goat," said his friend d'Agata while they were having a bite to eat together. "What's wrong? What's the great grievance? Has your dad cut off your allowance?"

"The poor old boy would get it to me," murmured Antonio, "even if he had to forge the stuff."

"Bad news about the job prospect?"

"I don't give a damn about the job!"

D'Agata then, point-blank: "Have you picked up some disease?"

Antonio: "No, I'm perfectly healthy." A pause, then "Perfectly. . ."

"Then for God's sake stop pulling that long face and making us all miserable!"

"Oh, give over, the lot of you! Just stay out of my hair!"

"Not another word do I say! Good Lord! So it's none of my business, eh?"

And his friends agreed among themselves to ask him no more questions.

On the 2nd of December a certain Miss Luisa Dreher, daughter of a diplomat and the most gorgeous foreign girl in the whole of Italy at that time, called on Antonio at ten in the morning. This visit had been neither solicited by the recipient nor announced by the caller. During the strolls he had taken with Luisa Dreyer, Antonio had not so much as dreamt of inviting her back to his place. Such an invitation, indeed, would have struck him as improper conduct towards those who were supposedly going to procure him a position he didn't deserve.

In the meanwhile there she was, this splendid girl, seated on a stool and twisting a cambric handkerchief with dainty fingers still bronzed by a summer of sunshine.

9

Antonio said nothing.

The girl, tilting her face sideways, stared at the toe of her shoe as it nervously tap-tapped the floor.

Antonio still remained silent.

The telephone shrilled in the other room, and Antonio dashed to answer it, closing the sitting-room door behind him.

"Hullo?"

"It's me, d'Agata. Is Luisa Dreyer at your place?"

"How did you know?"

"Ah then, it's true: she's there!"

"What of it?"

"Listen here. The day before yesterday there was a reception at the Embassy. The girls all got drunk and pissed in the flowerpots."

"What of it?"

"Just don't make an ass of yourself."

Antonio hung the receiver sharply back on the hook and returned to the sitting-room.

He found Luisa brushing the corner of her mouth with a fingertip to deviate a tear about to dribble into it.

"Why are you crying?" enquired Antonio.

Luisa shot to her feet, hurled her arms around his neck and nestled a cheek against his chest. "I love you," she sobbed. "I love you!..."

Antonio patted her head, gazing vaguely the while out of the window at the intense green light which the trees of the Villa Borghese cast up against the sky.

"I ask nothing of you!" Luisa went on between sobs. "I don't want to get married! But... you happened to leave a letter from your father at my house, and I've read it."

"What letter?" asked Antonio, horror-struck.

"A letter from your father telling you to get back at once to Catania to meet the young lady they mean to marry you off to."

"I don't believe you managed to decipher my father's handwriting!" stammered Antonio. "I can't even make it out myself..."

"But that's not what I'm crying for... I've already told you I don't want to marry you. I'm all right on my own and... and don't want to marry anyone."

"So what are you getting at?" said Antonio, panic-stricken.

"I love you I love you! In heaven's name can't you understand? I love you!"

Antonio's face took on the pallor of death and he slumped, he practically collapsed, onto a sofa.

The girl glided to his side, bringing with her the tender fragrance of her angora woollies and powdered neck. Shaken with sobs, she insinuated beneath his chin that fair brow on which, at Embassy receptions, there always glittered a small diamond crucifix. With her little frightened hand she sought for the heart beneath his dressing-gown, as if to see whether such a thing as a heart could ever beat there.

Far from just beating, Antonio's heart was at full gallop. Astride this runaway steed he sped towards the blackest anguish.

Luisa no longer knew what she was doing, she had lost all control of herself, she was aghast, ashamed, to discover her hand wandering frantically beneath Antonio's robe.

"I won't make any demands!" she sobbed. "Don't worry, I promise that! I won't make any trouble for you... I'm an honest woman, I'm not like the others!"

"On the contrary," said he, clutching at the desperate expedient of playing it tough and nasty, grabbing her by the wrists to hold her off a little and looking her straight in the face. "You *are* like the others!"

Luisa frowned, scattering attractive, kittenish wrinkles around her eyes and nose: "What do you mean? You don't know what you're saying!" Then, all in a rush, "What are you thinking of? I'm a virgin, I tell you, I'm a virgin!"

Antonio forced an ironic smile, something that came with difficulty and caused him displeasure, because he was a simple-hearted young man and could distinguish a truth from a falsehood.

"Even if I married the most bigoted and ridiculous of you Sicilians," continued Luisa in a more muted, a more measured voice, "he would have nothing to reproach me for. I know that when your women go to hotels in Taormina for the first night of their honeymoon they squawk like hens having their necks wrung. I wouldn't squawk even if you killed me, but anyway... I'd have a right to... But why have you gone all pale? What's the matter? Are you expecting someone? Is there someone at that door?"

A spot of colour crept back into Antonio's cheeks. A faint noise had come from the bedroom door, as of a bodily weight falling against it.

"Is there a woman in there?" demanded Luisa in a hushed voice.

"Yes," answered he, casting down his eyes.

Luisa regained her poise, rose from the sofa, retrieved her handbag from a table, extracted a compact, peered at a pair of eyes that had turned to steel, dried them, then erased all traces of tears with two dabs of a powder-puff.

"Goodbye then," she said. "Forgive me."

And she made her exit.

Antonio sped to the bedroom door, flung it open, and was kissed almost smack on the mouth by his poodle which, impatient of release, leapt up at him with a strangled yelp.

He fondled its ears, tried to calm it, rocked its head to and fro as from among its riotous curlicues it shot him adoring glances. He then stretched out on the sofa, plopping the dog down on top of him, muzzle between front paws, while now and again it darted out its tongue to lick his chin and he, throwing back his head, skilfully evaded it.

In this way passed some hours. The sky over Villa Borghese darkened... A crow flapped in and out of the clouds, emitting at each wheel of its flight a muffled caw.

Tenderly Antonio lifted the dozing dog and deposited it on

the carpet. He then stretched himself lavishly and got up. A glance at the window, and beyond the Pincio the mist had thickened, as if the Tiber were filling the air with the vapour of its breath. The buildings glimpsed through the trees of the park had taken on a yellower tint. Down below in the street, at the corner of Via Pinciana and Via Sgambati, in the guise of a young man waiting for his girl, stood the inevitable plain-clothes policeman, motionless, bare-headed, hat in hand: and hidden in the hat the inevitable love-story he was reading to allay the endless tedium of protecting the life of a man whose car flashed by only once every couple of months.

"Lord, how dreary Rome is!" thought Antonio. And donning his overcoat and giving a rub to the tummy of his dog, which in expectation had already rolled onto its back with its legs in the air, he left the house.

Thus ended the first part of a day which Antonio was destined to remember for many a long year.

Either that same day or (as is more likely) the next, Antonio paid a call on his uncle, Ermenegildo Fasanaro, his mother's brother, who lived in one of the new suburbs.

This said uncle strode up and down the sitting-room, his silk shirt hanging out and his unknotted necktie beforked onto a paunch plumped out by his fifty years.

"Best thing for you to do is get back to Catania," stated this uncle, pausing every so often by the window, his bulk blocking out now the bend in the Tiber around Villa Glori, now the slopes of the hill.

"What d'you think you're doing here in Rome? Trying to find out if there's any end to 'that business'? Well let me tell you, there isn't. You're on the job night and day, you're burning the candle at both ends, your cheeks get hollower and hollower and you're always dropping off like a cat that's been out all night on the tiles... Hell and dammit! Where women are concerned you have to ration it out, lead 'em up the garden path. It's easy enough to take them in if you use a bit of gumption. I'm pretty sure you're one of those fellows who'd give a fortune to make a good score every night, eh? Or am I wrong."

"Well, to tell the truth I..."

"In one way, mind you, you're right. Women stroke you with one hand while they tot up the sums with the other. But what the deuce! it's so easy to spin 'em a yarn. All it takes is a spot of technique. Not that there aren't some pretty crafty ones who haggle over details, but that's the cunning of a fool, because your clever woman knows she has to keep on her toes in other ways. Your job is to know when you've had enough. That's all there is to it... It's the clean contrary of what we're told by the Pig who rules over us... Incidentally, is it true that he has a stomach ulcer?"

"Uncle, I have no idea!"

"Word has it that he has a stomach ulcer... In fact yesterday, sitting in a café, I heard a naval officer at the next table whispering behind his hand to a colleague of his, 'We're home and dry: it's not an ulcer, it's cancer!' I'm pretty sure they were talking about him. No? Do you say not?"

"I didn't say a word."

"For heaven's sake, you've no interest in politics at all! You don't give a fig for it. I bet you've never read Karl Marx..."

"No, I haven't."

"Well don't. If you haven't read him by the age of thirty, don't start now. Just leave him be. In our day we used to read him. That is, we didn't *read* him either, but we talked about him as if we had... Socialism! Abolishing private property! What's your opinion, eh? Would it be possible to abolish private property? I don't think so. But on the other hand we've become slaves to everything produced by the masses: electricity, wirelesses, telephones, railways, trams... As we are slaves to such things, it follows that we are slaves to the masses. And these same masses, hell and dammit, only become as good as gold and work with a song in their hearts under either

Fascism or Communism. As soon as you give them freedom they start to sulk, grow churlish and rowdy, and throw their weight about so rudely that they rip this famous freedom to bits and trample it under foot. You agree?"

"Oh yes, uncle."

"On the other hand, if the majority of the human race wants Socialism, the world will inevitably become Socialist."

"You may be right."

"Maybe yes, maybe no. It wouldn't be the first time the majority of the human race wanted one thing and history took another turn."

"That may also be the case."

"*What* may be the case?"

"That history will take another turn."

"So what's this turn then?"

"Don't ask me."

"On the other hand the rich, among whom I personally number myself, are disagreeable."

"But uncle, you personally..."

"Believe me, we are disagreeable, we are block-headed, we are spoilt, we are bored stiff. Impossible to persist until the end of time with the rich on one side and the poor on the other! I am well aware, hell and dammit, that we can't go on like this!"

"Who am I to say...?"

"On the other hand, in whose hands do you wish to place Capital? In the hands of the State? The State, to put it mildly, is a bunch of civil servants and officials, from whom the good Lord deliver us! Apart from the fact that here in Italy all officials are bandits... No, it's no good shaking your head like that, they're bandits to a man!"

"But uncle, I didn't move a muscle!"

"...Officials, the world over, whenever they are invested with absolute authority, become such tyrants that in comparison the Roman emperors cut the figure of babes in arms... No, Socialism would be the Dark Ages!"

"Doubtless. . ."

"On the other hand, seeing that the Dark Ages occurred once, so they might occur twice. . ."

"Possibly, possibly. . ."

"On the other hand, why should there be a new Dark Ages? Who has set it up? Who has decreed it? It's us who've done it, by getting certain ideas into our own heads and taking them for gospel, like when people got the notion that New Year's Eve of the year One Thousand would be the end of the world – which obviously didn't happen. . . No, I don't believe there'll be a new Dark Ages."

"Neither do I."

"On the other hand, what we have today in Italy, isn't it a kind of Dark Ages?"

"I couldn't say. . ."

"Yes, it certainly is! Dear nephew, only that cancer can save us, if it gets a move on."

"What they say is that he's got a syphilitic ulcer, not cancer."

"Now he tells me! Hell and dammit, we're ruined. Two injections and your syphilitic ulcer goes kaput. . . On the other hand what happens if he dies? Who seizes power? His bunch of cut-purse henchmen? They'd slit each other's throats while they were carving up the spoils. So then, it's the Communist gaolbirds? Worse than the Fascists! At least the Fascists are incompetent scoundrels, and whatever crimes come into their minds they make a hash of, whereas the other lot are stern and upstanding, and make a clean job of 'em."

"Yes, true enough, but. . ."

"On the other hand, I am speaking lightly of Communism. What if it were something reputable and practical?"

"What they say is. . ."

"What they say is a load of bollocks! Even if Communism were to be workable – and I assure you it isn't – I would rebel all the same, because it's immoral, insomuch as it suppresses freedom. . ."

"That's what I was sort of meaning."

"On the other hand, who can take over the reins if *he* dies? The old fogies who now stay snug at home and flatter themselves that they're in no trouble just because they don't read books or newspapers and spend all day around the card table? They're too decrepit to know how to govern the masses."

"Of course... no doubt about it..."

"On the other hand, to hell with the masses! If they care to put their heads in a noose, well I don't! And I can have something to say about it, can't I, at least on my own account? On the other hand what I've been saying may be quite wrong, because in 1922 (you won't remember it) the workers were already going quietly back to work and strikes were becoming rarer and rarer when along came the Pig and took away our freedom, took it from the working classes and from us. No, Antonio, the Italian workers are like the middle classes – they love freedom. It's him, the Pig, who's trying to bully us into thinking they don't. Tell your mother to pray for his death, instead of praying for you not to get chilblains! Pray for him to kick the bucket as soon as possible, before I kick it myself from sheer vexation and nausea. I was told something yesterday that, if it's true, makes life no longer worth living. They're going to make Lorenzo Calderara the local Party Secretary of Catania. *Can* this be true?"

"I believe it is."

"Calderara, son of Poxface, nephew of Chaffbelly! Lord save us! A city that has had its De Felice, its Macchi, its Verga, its Bellini, its Angelo Musco, its Giovanni Grasso, its Capuana, *plus* my good friend De Roberto, bends the knee in this manner to Lorenzo Calderara, commonly known as Blockhead. A hypocrite to boot, and a worm so yellow-bellied you can't stand the whiff of him, such a brainless bloody idiot that his friends once managed to kid him he could buy himself iron gauntlets at the chemist's."

"Iron...? Gauntlets...?"

"Come off it, Antonio! 'The Iron Hand'... But on the other

hand, he'd scarcely have known what to do with them. A drip like that who. . ."

Antonio turned white as a sheet and his head flopped back against the sofa. He gawped at his uncle with pathetically lustreless eyes.

"Hey, what's up?" asked the uncle. "What's biting you?"

Antonio screwed his eyes up tight, leant forward and rested his eyelids on the thumb and first finger of one hand while flapping the other at his uncle to entreat him to keep quiet, not to worry. . . that he was getting over it. . .

"You, my lad," that gentleman resumed as Antonio raised his head and laid it carefully, eyes closed, on the back of the sofa, "must pull up your socks and get back post-haste to Catania. If you hang on here the women will eat you alive, they'll pick you clean. . . I'm an old man now, but even so they don't give me a moment's peace; so imagine someone of your age and your. . . Yes, quite, your genial personality!. . . That face of yours, though it may be cadaverous, they lick at like a lollipop. . . But enough of that. Let's turn to serious topics. I know this Barbara Puglisi, the girl they want to marry you off to. I heard her play the violin the evening her uncle the monk was celebrating his silver wedding to the Church. I'm not saying she played superlatively, mind you. . . On the other hand, what's that to you? She's rich. She owns half Paternò! She went to boarding-school. . . Mind you I'm not saying she's a genius. . . But on the other hand a woman doesn't need to be a genius. Just as long as she's not brainless. And even if she *is* brainless, what's that to you? That's life, isn't it? So come on, buck up a bit!"

Three days later Antonio set off for Catania, shadowed by a lanky, skinny, droopy dog which, despite suitcases thumped against its nose, kicks from people struggling against the tide and whacks from the umbrellas of exasperated old ladies, unflinchingly persevered in tailing Antonio's white poodle, with whom it had struck up a lightning friendship in the booking hall. The poodle, firmly on the leash and hauled swiftly along by Antonio, never ceased – he himself so handsome and sprucely groomed – from turning longing backward looks at his hideous though courteous friend.

At the carriage door was waiting Luigi d'Agata, who embraced Antonio with tears in his eyes, and uttered in tones of reproach, "In the name of God! Do you have to up sticks right now when things are looking a bit brighter? Just imagine, yesterday, round at the General's place, they'd invented a new game. If you tell them about it in Catania they won't believe you even if you fall dead at their feet. They call it 'Nothing but the Truth'. You can ask any question you like and the others have to answer it truthfully. Just listen what they put to Signora Pollini: 'If armed bandits broke in here and forced you to go to bed with one of those present, you've got to tell us in all truthfulness whom you would go with.'"

"And," replied Antonio, climbing into the carriage with his dog and then reappearing at the window, "what was the lady's answer?"

Calling up from the platform d'Agata continued: "She went as red as a beetroot, and God knows who she was thinking of in her heart of hearts, but so as not to make a scandal and let the cat out of the bag and – with that mouth of hers that anyone would have nibbled right down to the teeth with kisses – she said, as demurely as could be, 'Why, the General himself!' Well she could tell that to the Marines... Go to bed with the General, forsooth! But then they got round to me: 'And how about you? Which of the ladies present would you like to take to bed?'"

"So what did you say?" enquired Antonio, lifting up his poodle so that it could make its adieux to the doggy friend stationed beneath the train window as if it had forgotten exactly what reason had brought it there and couldn't think of another for going away again.

"I..." began d'Agata, though as the train had begun to

move he was now trotting beside it, with the dog galumphing awkwardly at his side. "I said, 'With Signora Bertini and Signora Gallarati.'"

"What, both at once?" screamed Antonio.

"Yes, both!" yelled d'Agata, puffing to a halt and waving his hanky, laughing fit to bust and winking now one eye and now the other in quick succession, so that the one wink or the other must surely come to the notice of the friend steaming off this instant for the South, where nothing exciting ever happened.

II

A NTONIO'S FAMILY HOME hovered on the third and top floor of an old building in the centre of Catania. A number of its windows overlooked the courtyard all a criss-cross of cords which, issuing from the caretaker's cubby-hole, were used to wield the clappers of a dozen bells attached to the railings on the various storeys, in readiness to summon a maid, or the lady of the house.

There was a slip of a terrace jammed between their dining-room and the wall of the house opposite, a loftier building at one time totally blank and windowless at this level, but now pierced by French windows at which it was the custom of a certain Stately Elder to appear; to wit, Avvocato Ardizzone. Avvocato Ardizzone who, in spite of his flowery eloquence and the billowing folds of his *peignoir*, and his tendency to flaunt his gown in court, and his forefinger levelled point-blank at his adversary, and – the decisive stroke, thought he – his portrait in oils occupying half a wall in the Great Hall of the Bar Association, in which he was depicted with that celebrated forefinger (though here, from *noblesse oblige*, directed at the ceiling), his other hand resting on a highly-coloured Fascist symbol, the so-called Lictoral Fasces... despite these merits and high deserts, and the despatch of hundreds of boxes of oranges to influential people in Rome, and a plaintive, ranting, suppliant, peppery correspondence with ministers' secretaries... had never secured a place in the Senate. And talking in his sleep at night, "Great God!" he would cry, "there's so many coppers have hung up their handcuffs because thanks to my connections they got appointed Chiefs of Police, now toasting their arses in the Senate House, leaving me here behind them like a fart in the dark... Three cheers for Giolitti!" he added – risking arrest had his neighbour happened to be a dyed-in-the-wool Fascist. "At least this sort of thing didn't happen in *his* day!"

This terrace, on the one side, looked onto the two-mile-long Via Etnea ("the Corso"), rackety with old trams, the lash of whips on the rumps of skinny horses; flurries of talk and of laughter, cries of newsboys; a place awhirl with hat-doffings, back-slappings, gesticulations, collisions, bowings and scrapings... On the other it gave onto a short side-street running straight as a die to the façade of a church in the topmost niche of which shone the Madonna, clad in her blue mantle, her fingers ten rays of light, her head haloed at night by electric bulbs which lost their dazzle in the haze of the sirocco.

On this terrace, on August nights at the dawn of the century, Antonio would fall asleep, face buried in his mother's lap, hearing the comfort-sweet murmur of her fan above his head, while his father, seated nearby, smoked cigar-butts in his pipe and spat continuously; or else gulped noisily from the rim of a jug and then, smacking his lips with pleasure, was wont to exclaim, "Ah, there's nothing on earth to beat cold water!"

This same terrace saw his mother and father greeting Antonio on his return from Rome: here he was hugged and kissed, and here brought coffee and biscuits, raw egg and milk; here, with tears in his eyes, he told them how his lovely white dog had dashed out at the open carriage door never to return... And here his mother gave him his first tidings of the city:

"... Dipaola's son is dead of pneumonia; poor Aunt Santina's pulse-rate is down to thirty beats a minute but the doctor maintains that she could live to a hundred just the same; and don't even *think* of using the word 'whore' while you're talking to Avvocato Palermo! – I know you swear too much, just like your father..."

"Why's this?"

"His wife ran off last Sunday with a young man on his staff... Give the cold shoulder to young Baron Benedettini: he was gambling at the Coronets Club and they spotted a card up his sleeve... Zuccarello's son died, just like that, in a couple of days. No time even to cross himself. Professor Callara hasn't eaten for a week, because (heaven preserve us!) he finds that every morsel he puts into his mouth tastes like a turd. If he goes on like this he'll be a goner..."

"Ye gods and little fishes!" exploded Antonio's father. "Can't you think of anything jollier to talk about? Come along inside, Antonio, and we'll have a bit of man's talk."

Signor Alfio led Antonio to his study, plumped down on the sofa, the high, shelf-laden back of which was set a-jangle with dozens of knick-knacks in peril of falling.

Then, with a sigh, he said: "I think I've got *angina pectoris.*"

"God in heaven!" observed Antonio with some bitterness. "You call that jolly?"

"No, it's not a jolly subject, but it's one I can't avoid bringing up."

"But Dad, how many times have you been convinced you had angina and then the doctor declared you as sound as a bell?"

"Well, maybe it's not angina, but it's certainly something!... In any case, I have diabetes – there's no two ways about it! That was discovered by your – what-d'ye-call-it? – your uncle, the evening I went to dinner with him and drank water endlessly. 'Friend,' said he to me, 'd'you realize that's your sixth glass of water? Get a blood-test done, at once, tomorrow, and no shilly-shallying!' Next day I had the test and they found more sugar in me than in a candied orange. Come on, don't pull that long face at me! I'm still full of beans, and if it weren't for the fact that your mother takes it so much to heart... Good Lord, in a word, I'm still a *man* in the matters that count... I say this so you realize there's no reason to feel ashamed of your father..."

Antonio blushed to the roots of his hair.

23

"Why've you gone all red?" continued Signor Alfio. "I've never minced my words with you. I'm perfectly certain you wouldn't like your father to be a damp squib, just as I didn't like it the day I was told your grandfather was in the habit of paying a pittance to gape at some woman in the nude, mop his face with a hanky, and go off again without so much as a lick or a promise... But then he *was* almost eighty..."

He paused a moment.

"Good Lord, I'm rambling... rambling... It's the one affliction I simply can't bear! Always escapes me, what I started to say... Ah, yes!" (picking up his thread). "I've been going on about all this because it's time you got married."

"But Dad..."

"None of this but-dad stuff! If you don't marry this... what's her name? Hell! Oh yes, this Barbara Puglisi, it'll mean you're your own worst enemy!"

"But I've never set eyes on her!"

"And why? I ask you that! Because when you like the look of a girl you turn your back on her, as if she'd called you a son-of-a-... well, let that go. You're a nitwit. I can read your thoughts like the back of my hand. You're ashamed of yourself because you fancy well-built girls with sturdy ankles. But why be ashamed of that, you nincompoop. If you want to know, your grandfather fancied them too, not to mention me, and they're still favourites with... umm... umm... who was I thinking of?... Ah yes, me! Yes, I still fancy them. Come off it, this... what's her name?... this Barbara Puglisi is a girl with every button where it ought to be. What's more, she's rich, she's taken with you, she's respectable... Lumme! what more d'you want?"

"It's just that I'd like to put it off for a year or two."

"Listen here my friend, you're nearly thirty. You soon won't be able to make it any more... I speak loosely, of course, because we come of good stock, and we unfailingly make it. But it's one thing to marry at thirty and quite another to marry at forty. Add to all this that I can no longer afford to keep you in Rome..."

"But where's all the money gone?"

"In ten years' time we'll have an orange-grove worth the best part of a million. But as things stand today we're down to your mother having to cadge a spot of cash off the caretaker. I've sold all I had to buy this orange-grove, I've raised a loan from the bank, and – I've planted ten thousand young orange-trees... It'll be worth a fortune, tomorrow! But as things stand today what it costs me is this" – and he stretched his arms wide – "and what I get out of it's this" – and he narrowed the span to a slit. "But there! The darling could steal the very bread from my mouth..."

"What darling?" enquired Antonio, with a touch of rancour.

"My darling orange-grove... O Antonio, if only you could see her – she's such a beauty! Even more beautiful than you are... eh, what? That's to say... The fact is that it's bleeding us white! What fiend was it that made me tie this millstone round my neck?... No, no... what on earth am I saying?... Blessed be the day I thought of buying it, and blessed be the notary who signed the Deed! But I'm rambling, I'm rambling again..." He clutched his temples with his right hand, raised his eyes, and all in one breath and like someone forced to walk a tightrope and taking a sprint at it rather than fall, cried, "In the five years you've been in Rome you haven't managed to get your arse moving at all! You've already frittered away a hundred thousand lire, and my heart bleeds to think of it!"

"It's not my fault," mumbled Antonio. "Lots of young chaps have got into the Diplomatic without exams or anything. But me, I've been promised the sun, moon and stars, then whenever I check in to see how my application is going along they seem to wake up with a start, as if they'd never set eyes on me before!"

"But Whatsit... feller there... the minister, calls himself a Count (my foot!), didn't he put himself out for you at all?"

25

"Let us not speak of the minister! He has behaved the worst of the lot."

"You bet!" cried his father, knocking the pipe in his hand against his leg and smothering his trousers with an avalanche of ash and glowing embers. "If you go and poke his wife!"

"That's simply not true," said Antonio mildly.

"I don't need *you* to tell me if it's true or not!" retorted his father. "But what I do say is – Great God, what is his name? – that Count feller – he has more horns on his head than a trugful of snails. They all do it right under his nose and he's never noticed a damn thing. It took my fool of a son to go all the way from Catania to make *him* jealous!"

"But it's not true he's jealous!" roared Antonio, puce in the face this time from sheer vexation. "It's not true I'm his wife's lover! What more do I have to say? It's just not true!"

His father tilted his chin and looked down his nose.

"Be that as it may," he said. "I have no wish to pry into your affairs. That notwithstanding, how do you explain the fact that a man like Blockhead, a damp squib if ever I saw one, who, if I were his father, would have me kneeling in the dirt for shame, has become Party Secretary of Catania, while you've been incapable of getting one of your little tarts to procure you a chair at the Foreign Ministry let alone the desk to go with it?"

At this point a masterful voice was heard intoning from the direction of the terrace.

"Signor Alfio, my dear Signor Alfio, I am informed that your son has arrived from the capital. . ."

Avvocato Ardizzone. And the Lord alone knows how grandiose were his gesticulations from the balcony, since a flock of birds fled in panic past the study window.

"Let's get back to the terrace," said Signor Alfio, and hastily added: "Bear in mind that the Avvocato thinks you're the lover of the whatsit. . . ummm. . . ah yes, the Countess. . . If he asks you if it's true, don't say either yes or no. In any case don't say no as definitely as you did to me: he'd end up believing you!"

Out on the terrace they found Antonio's mother whipping up another egg for her son. The Avvocato was leaning over the balcony, draped in his *peignoir*. At his side, his daughter Elena, a thirty-six-year-old spinster who, following her trip to Switzerland (or so the story went in Catania), was eager at all costs to make it known that her "misadventure" had been "put to rights."

"What account have you to render to us concerning the Eternal City?" apostrophized the Avvocato. "What is afoot in that fetid sewer which the *Duce* would be well advised to raze to the ground? We Sicilians ill thought-of as ever, I presume? It's all because we have brains, brains and to spare. We could hand 'em out to that lot, *and* enough over for the other Party that acts so high-falutin!"

This harangue was interrupted by Elena, bursting through a thicket of simpers to cry, "Signora Rosaria, *do* take a look at the length of your son's eyelashes! How *can* he have such beauties. They're not lashes at all, they're *fans*! Isn't it true, Daddy, they look like ostrich-feather fans?"

"A pox on the woman!" muttered Signor Alfio under his breath, wheeling back indoors without a word to anyone.

But Antonio had to wait until the Avvocato's complexion had ebbed from puce to pallid, betokening that the vein of his eloquence had, at least for the moment, run dry. Thereafter he had to allow himself to be kissed on the forehead and the eyelids by his mother, acting under the direction of the mature spinster who with nervous little giggles thus urged her on from the balcony:

"*There*'s where you must kiss him! Lower, lower... Let's see if it tickles him *there*... Higher up, higher up! Heavens, what a bristly chin! Rasps like sandpaper, I'd say!"

But Antonio was left to himself at last, to gaze at leisure at the much-loved roofs of Catania: the black rooftops, the flowerpots, the skeletal fig-trees and the washing also, around which, at sunset, the March wind carried the kick of a mule; to gaze at the church domes glittering on feast-day evenings like golden mitres; at deserted tiers of open-air theatres and pepper-trees in the Public Gardens; this very sky, low and homely as a ceiling, in which the clouds arranged themselves in old familar patterns; and Mount Etna crouched between the sea and the heart of Sicily – upon its paws, its tail, its back, dozens of black townlets that had contrived to struggle up.

He went into his own room, where what was left of his odours of five years before bade him welcome like a dog faithfully waiting with its nose to the crack under the door... Here, in the two bookcases, were the sturdy volumes in which he had done his earliest reading, from which he had derived fabulous pleasure, until amorous daydreams abruptly put a stop to that. Here were the walls submerged in pictures, prints, hangings, crucifixes, holy-water stoops... and here, in the middle of the room, was the wash-stand with its swing mirror which (watch it!) you had to take care not to tip too far back in case the bottom came shooting forwards and knocked over all the pots and bottles: and here was the quilt, the hot-water bottle, the hand-warmer, the bed-warmer... Antonio stretched out on his back, fell asleep, and two hours later woke up with a tear on his cheek. What had he dreamt? It didn't come back to him, but he felt an overpowering urge to give full vent to a flood of tears that someone seemed to have choked back in his throat.

"Come now!" he said to himself, 'I swear to my crucifix there on the wall that I'll never come over all moody and morose again."

The same evening, in an effort to overcome his moodiness, he accepted a bizarre invitation from a cousin and good friend of his, Edoardo Lentini.

Just arrived from Rome to install Lorenzo Calderara in his post as local Party Secretary was the Deputy Secretary-General of the whole Fascist Party in person, a man with a chest entirely smothered with medals and a penchant for prostitutes. Having been apprised of this foible of his, a bunch of sycophants had strained every nerve to arrange a night out in the manner most agreeable to a personage so highly provided with power both for good and for ill. As a result of these efforts, at eleven o'clock precisely the "Pensione Eros" shut its doors in the face of its regular customers, who immediately began to howl insults, boot at the doors and hurl stones; with the result that a squad of policemen, disguised as raw recruits, turned up pretending to be so drunk as playfully to stroke the cheeks of the crowd with their revolver-barrels, and chivvied the customers from the alleyway. Half an hour later these same cops, fed up with playing drunk and getting curses and worse from every youth who came round the corner, rose up in the full strength of their officialdom, ordering all and sundry to "Move along now, move along!"

"Watch it! I've got your number!" was the retort of several of those addressed, their coat collars turned up high to conceal their faces.

Meanwhile, in the dining-salon of the "Pensione Eros" blazed many hundreds of candle-power, porcelain and crystal sparkled behind the glass doors of dressers, marble-topped tables groaned beneath heaps of officers' coats and cloaks and caps and fezes.

Antonio was introduced to the Deputy Secretary of the Party as "a friend of Countess K".

"So Comrade," said the bigwig, "the stories we hear about you are true, eh?"

"Stories, what stories?" mumbled Antonio reddening, as Lorenzo Calderara whispered in his ear, "For heaven's sake don't be too familiar with him! Address him formally. And incidentally, why the hell aren't you wearing your Party Badge?"

"The story goes," continued the bigwig, "that you have prodigious success with women. What about you, now?" he added, turning to the four girls ringed around him, the two taller resting their elbows on the shoulders of the shorter, and each through gossamer veils displaying her particular pussy, "let's hear *your* opinion. Could you fancy this sort of specimen?"

The four women allowed their gaze to rest for a moment upon Antonio, and despite the fact that they scarcely thought this the most propitious moment for frankness, two of them – the prettiest and the least endowed – in that one moment managed to fall in love.

"So, what d'you think? D'you fancy a specimen of this sort?" And with a swift, insolent movement he thrust back Antonio's cuffs revealing the delicacy of the wrists. "Or d'you go for a man like me?" And he rolled up his own sleeves, displaying two hairy, bulging forearms.

The girls, unwilling to admit the truth, gawked wide-eyed at such wrists as his, crying out in a superfluity of wonderment. One of them plumped herself down on his lap, and fishing around among his medals, through his shirt and beneath his vest, drew forth a tuft of hair which with deft fingers she formed into a tiny plait. All the girls were keen to give it gentle tweaks, and all the men, with the sole exception of Antonio, vied with each other in cracking jokes about it that but thinly, yet brazenly, veiled their intended flattery.

"No one could take *you* for a woman!" declared a sycophantic Lorenzo Calderara.

At this point in came large trayfuls of brandy and gin. Eyes began to glisten bibulously amid the fog of cigarette smoke. The Deputy Secretary-General twice rose to his feet to go upstairs with the same girl, then once again to go with the madame of the Pensione; she however, politely but firmly, refused.

"My dear Nedda, are we going to have to banish you to some backwater?" said Lorenzo Calderara, his voice pitched midway between ribaldry and reprimand, leaving it uncertain which of the two was a fake.

"Right then, arrest me!" retorted Madame, trying to make a joke of it.

The Deputy Secretary-General for his third sortie, had to make do with another of the girls, whose pleasant face had previously, though briefly, been disfigured with pique on seeing the middle-aged madame given preference.

When the Deputy Secretary-General made his reappearance in the room, his bemedalled chest open to the winds and one arm round the bare flanks of the girl, he was hailed with applause.

"If it is not an indiscreet question," said Antonio's cousin, Edoardo Lentini, "may I enquire how old you are?"

"My dear chap," replied the bigwig, "I'm pretty long in the tooth... Go on and guess!"

"Twenty-five! Twenty-four!" cried those who thought it opportune to butter him up by assuring him how young he looked.

"Forty! Forty-two!" wagered those wishing to bestow on him a contrasting pleasure – that of publicly denying any possibility that, in his case at least, it had required long years to rise to such heights in politics.

"Thirty-two!" was his curt reply.

"Heavens!" exclaimed the first lot. "You're such a wow with the women we'd never have thought you a day over twenty-five!"

"By Jove!" ejaculated the others. "Only thirty-two and already Deputy Secretary-General of the Party?"

They went on to speak of Youth, which under the new regime had taken over the "helm of the State". The ministers, the mayors, the Party Secretaries, were all without exception youthful, and the most youthful of all was... Whereupon they all lowered their voices, with a painful effort removed the sozzled smirks from their faces, stiffened in their chairs at the memory of how many times they had sprung to attention as they pronounced that title; and they named the name of Italy's most potent and powerful personage.

Such conversation had become insufferable, not least because it demanded a sort of earnestness that was riotously banished from their faces by the flush of exhilaration and liquor.

To create a diversion a young police inspector snatched up one of the girls and dumped her on the lap of Lorenzo Calderara, who enjoyed what was (in Catania) the mortifying reputation of never having gone with a State prostitute.

They all set to a-clapping and a-shouting, while the girl poured a host of come-hitherings into the ear of Calderara, who contrived to give a sickly smile as he turned red as a turkey-cock.

"Get a move on!" bawled the Deputy Secretary-General (to whom a few hasty words had been addressed by a bony individual whose dismal species of diplomacy – known with a fantasy to match its aptness as hunchback-heartedness – had, from his constant whispering in people's ears, resulted in a perpetual stoop). "Get a move on, Lorenzo, do your stuff! The Party Secretary of Catania has to be a *man*!... You take my meaning, I suppose?... And you, comrade Elena, will thereafter report to me in person!"

The company, with the exception of Antonio, leapt to their feet to heave Calderara out of his chair and spur him from the room along with the girl.

"Don't push!" objected Calderara. "Hey there, that's enough of that. I'll go on my own two feet! Stop it!"

All present thereupon turned their eyes to the Deputy Secretary-General. Had they overstepped the mark with the man who from tomorrow onwards would have all their destinies in his hands?

"Let him alone," said the Deputy Secretary. "He'll go on his own two feet."

"He's not going anywhere!" This sudden shriek from the madame.

An outburst that caused all faces to swivel in her direction, and little by little to drain of their hilarity.

"He's not going!... Mother of God, are you trying to force me to use foul language?... He's not going!"

"What do you mean, not going?" enquired the Deputy Secretary. "On whose orders?"

"On mine!" retorted the woman, clapping a hand to the copious bosom a-quiver beneath her quivering bodice.

Laughter was general and hearty.

"No laughing matter this, you fools!" The Deputy Secretary-General rose from his chair, retracting his chin onto his chest, flaring bloodless nostrils; a pace away from the woman he raised his head, gave her a sidelong look, as a matador sidesteps before thrusting his sword into the heart of the bull; then, like lightning, he delivered a whacking backhand that sent her crashing against the wall.

Arms milling, the woman clutched at a tapestry that instantly ripped from its moorings and fell, entombing her in a number of the edifices of ancient Rome and a considerable stretch of the Tiber.

She slithered to the floor. The girls flocked to her aid, disentwining her from the hangings. One of them put a glass of water to her lips and tipped it gently into her mouth as into a lifeless vessel.

Having drunk, the woman gave a shake to her head, scrubbed her eyes energetically with the backs of her hands and scowled, one after the other, at the men, now resettled in their places.

"Cooled off a bit, eh?" enquired Lorenzo Calderara sarcastically.

"I did it for your sake, you oaf!" the woman said brokenly from where she sat slumped on the floor.

In imitation of the Deputy Secretary a few moments before, Calderara rose from his chair, though in a far more ludicrous manner and, hand raised, advanced in his turn on the woman.

"Oh, give over now, that's quite enough of that!" broke in one of the girls, the tallest and most splendid of them all. "Lay off!" And she gave a shove that sent him tottering backwards. "What a bloody awful evening this has been! What a lot of dead-beats! Give us a break, do!..." And here she addressed

Antonio in the accents of one relinquishing a tiresome role and giving voice to her true tastes. "Come on now, duckie. 'Cor, do I ever want to get a breath of fresh air!"

These words struck the company like the blow of a mace to the midriff. They could not have been more cogently informed that they were unlovable, and that without exception all their conquests of the evening had been but a snare and a delusion.

The girl had clasped Antonio to her side, and while the involuntary undulations of her bare hips, and the equally involuntary sportings of her right hand, manifested a warm and plentiful ardour, at the rest of the company she directed a cold and haughty stare.

"It's been a bloody awful evening for us too, I'll have you know!" declared the Deputy Secretary-General, hefting himself out of his chair. "Let's get out of here!"

Edoardo Lentini, anxious lest such a conquest, by making the others look small, might get his friend into trouble, amiably remarked, "Antonio'll be coming along with us. He's not going to stay and waste his time here..."

"*Here*," retorted the girl, "he would *not* be wasting his time. He'd be wasting it with you lot, with all that daft rubbish you get up to just so as to get on everybody's nerves!"

"Antonio, we must go. We shouldn't stay here a moment longer," said Edoardo, now with a resolute ring to his voice.

"Leave him alone!" commanded the Deputy Secretary, carefully pressing his fez down onto his glistening hair. "We're not such tyrants as to wish to chastise the taste of tarts..."

At this Antonio freed himself from the girl's grasp and, with a motion as indolent as it was self-assured, removed the fez from the Deputy Secretary's head and – O unheard-of thing! – began to toss it nonchalantly from hand to hand while eyeing the open window as if he had half a mind to bung it out into the street.

Every man-jack of them went green about the gills. Lorenzo Calderara puffed up like a drowning man gulping water, his breath coming ever more laboured and spasmodic. Edoardo

Lentini mouthed the paternosters he was mentally rattling off to invoke the aid of God for his friend in peril. The women alone gazed upon Antonio with emotions which (since their very natures prompted them to play it strong) ended in their making some lewd remark.

The Deputy Secretary grabbed Antonio's arm with his brawny hand and held it fast. He raked all present with a stately glare. He glared at Antonio... Then, seized by a sudden impulse of liking for the young man, he burst out laughing.

Sighs of relief all round, except from Lorenzo Calderara, ever slow on the uptake and incapable of lightning switches from wrath to mirth without risking a veritable seizure.

"Good luck to you, young man!" cried the bigwig, re-adjusting the fez on his hairdo and rapping his riding-crop on Antonio's chest. "Would you care to go to Bologna as local Deputy Secretary? Only too glad to oblige. The women there will skin you alive... Anyway, give it a thought in the course of the night, if that girl of yours gives you a chance to think... She looks like giving you the works. A year from now you'll be a local Party Secretary! Right, comrades, let's make a move!"

And as in the meanwhile he had snapped shut the clasp of his cloak, impetuously he swept from the room.

Boisterously summing up the events of the evening, all the officials tumbled away at his heels.

III

THE EVENING SPENT at the "Pensione Eros" was not without consequences for Antonio. Signor Alfio learnt all the details in a dark corridor of the Law Courts, where the mice were producing deafening havoc in the great presses stuffed with old documents.

"Do I make myself clear?" he asked later, at table, addressing his wife and pretending not even to see Antonio. "Your son comes here to get engaged, and the very first evening he lands up in a whorehouse!"

"He's a bachelor," retorted the mother, with a bitter allusion to those who did likewise despite being bound by obligations of conjugal fidelity. "He doesn't have anyone to answer to."

"All you ever do is make nasty cracks about me! Don't you realize that if such a thing comes to the ears of Father Rosario, the uncle of this... er... yes, this Barbara, the wedding will go up in smoke?"

The following day the aforesaid monk paid a visit on Signor Alfio, who at the mere mention of his name was seized with a fit of nerves and had to drink three glasses of water in quick succession.

"I have heard the good news," began Father Rosario, as soon as he had taken his seat opposite Magnano Senior.

"What good news?" queried the other suspiciously.

"I have been informed that your son is in the good graces of the Deputy Secretary-General of the Party..."

"I couldn't say," replied Signor Alfio, all the more fearful that this priest was out to trap him. "Don't even know if they ever met..."

"It appears they met the other evening. . ."

"Father, let's not beat about the bush," snorted Signor Alfio, already as testy as if he had received a reprimand, "let's talk in plain terms."

"Very well, plain terms it shall be: I would be highly grateful if Antonio were to beg the Deputy Secretary to put a damper, once and for all, on the Union boss in Viagrande, who, I assure you, subjects me to every sort of vexation, to the point – last October – of sending me all the thieves in the province to harvest my grapes! I can't tell you what they didn't steal from me. . . everything, including my night-cap!"

"Oh, if that's all you're on about. . ." exclaimed Signor Alfio with relief.

"Why, whatever were you expecting?"

"Nothing, nothing!" declared Magnano senior. "I thought, er. . . nothing, in short. . ."

This conversation with the monk was passed on to Antonio amid a series of grunts which rendered it incomprehensible.

Antonio listened, his thoughts wandering, until his father, hawking up the phlegm which had thitherto engulfed his words, clear and true came out with "My boy, for some time now you've had a bee in your bonnet I don't much care for. What is it?"

"Nothing special," answered Antonio, getting up from the table and edging towards the door.

"So I'm a Dutchman!" grumbled the old fellow, minutely observing his son's receding back and the listless way in which he pushed open the door and left the room.

That evening Antonio and Edoardo Lentini went strolling up and down the short and infinitely beautiful Via Crociferi. The three churches and two convents between which the street sloped away were deserted and silent; the gates in the high wrought-iron railings which embraced the brief, steep flights of steps leading to the church doors were bolted and barred.

The two young men were gripped by a romantic nostalgia more troubling and unhappy to them even than to a real, genuine Romantic who might have trodden that same street a century earlier.

"It's shaming to have to suck up to a man like that Deputy Secretary!" said Edoardo. "Times were when we'd have had to avert our gaze rather than return the least nod from such a man. Ugh! How I'd have liked to kick him..."

"He's very virile," observed Antonio. "He managed to go with three women in less than an hour!"

"I might have done the same myself if I hadn't realized something that he, crude brute that he is, didn't notice at all: the women despised us."

"D'you really think so?"

"The way the madame said 'You oaf!' I could have kissed her feet!"

"Sorry to have to disappoint you, old boy, but the madame was beside herself because she hadn't been able to receive a client of hers who brings her some narcotic or other every evening. After you all left she swore to me, tears in her eyes, that she'd give ten years of her life just to spend a single night with Mussolini."

"What depravity! Makes you weep! To think that I, this very morning, learnt by heart a chapter in the *Annals* of Tacitus. I'll quote it to you. 'Nero bethought himself of Epicharis, and, not believing that a woman was capable of bearing pain, ordered her to be tortured. But nor rod nor fire nor all the fury of the executioners made her confess; and so she won the first day. Borne the following day to the same torments, and incapable of standing on her lacerated members, she drew from her bosom a sash, tied it to the chair, secured a noose around her neck and drew it tight with the weight of her own body, thus extracting what little breath remained in it. A memorable lesson this is to us, that a prostitute, inflicted with so much agony, was prepared to save the lives of strangers; while men – knights and senators – and this without torture, would denounce even the persons dearest to them.' These days, in Italy, not even the women... When a society can no longer rely even on its prostitutes, it's done for. There's nothing more to be hoped for! Personally, I have resigned myself. In fact, I'm going to ask you a favour."

"What is it? Go ahead."

"Since the Deputy Secretary-General has taken a liking to you, do ask him to have me appointed mayor of Catania!"

"What!... I don't follow you..."

"Antonio, my friend, I'm thirty-two and in need of a job. I'm not going to salve my conscience by sitting at home earning nothing and getting dirty looks from my father-in-law. This regime is going to last at least a hundred years, so no need to feel guilty about what we do. But even if the regime falls, I'm not out to make excuses for myself. If I bothered about cutting a figure as an upstanding man with posterity I'd be a fool, and be giving undue importance to pomp. Because becoming a Party official, or not being enrolled in the Party at all, is all a lot of hogwash compared with the black misery we'll be forced to live through, whether we're Party officials or we stay at home and mind our own business. But I must say I have every intention of being an honest man, and my honesty will take the form of not stealing, of treating everyone courteously, while wishing all manner of ill to the regime I serve as punctiliously and conscientiously as is only made possible by being firmly inside and knowing its secrets!"

If Antonio had lent a more attentive ear, and if the channels of his intellect had not been more or less obstructed for some time now, he would certainly have considered his friend's effusion very strange and incoherent. As it was, he confined himself to stating that he never again, for any reason whatever, wished to set eyes on the Deputy Secretary-General.

Edoardo's determination flagged – he had no come-back to that one; and the two friends continued their walk in silence, unaware that the emaciated white face of a nun had stationed itself behind the grating of a high window, and had fixed on the person of Antonio a long, disapproving stare, which she had not the slightest wish to tear away.

"Heavens alive!" exclaimed Antonio out of the blue, "I simply must get back to doing some reading. Do you know that for ten years I haven't read a single book right through to the end! I feel positively doped with ignorance. Books keep you on your toes!... Hey d'you think it's really true that Lorenzo Calderara has never been with a prostitute? Some people even claim that he's never been with a woman at all. What do *you* think? After all..."

"After all," took up Edoardo, "not everyone can be like you!" And he gave a wink, that left his fine brow as unfurrowed and inexpressive as the sole of a foot.

The thought that women existed, their tiny hands, their pink feet, their white throats, their enticing skirts, dispelled all melancholy. Edoardo let out a yell that caused that glimmer of female face behind the window-grating to vanish, blown out like a candle in the wind.

"Three cheers!" he cried, taking advantage of the empty street. "Others may have freedom, but Italy has women!"

A day or two after this promenade Antonio, having learnt that the Deputy Secretary-General had returned to Rome, paid a visit to the headquarters of the Fascist League to have a word with Lorenzo Calderara. As the telephone had summoned the usher into the interior of a phone-booth, and since he had already been sitting in the waiting-room for an hour, he walked up to the Party boss's door and pushed it open. He caught a glimpse of Calderara's head nose downwards on a divan, the brow aflame, the veins taut as whipcords... The penny dropped, he wished to see no more, but tiptoed away with the air of one who has asked a question and received a brutally downright answer, when a few casual words would have more than sufficed.

"Kindly tell him I'm positively glad not to have set eyes on him these last ten years!"

This was the message Antonio received via the pharmacist

Salinitro from his old schoolmate Angelo Bartolini, who lived like a hermit in the environs of Catania, close to a tiny railway station where every other day passed the little chugger-train on its tour of Mount Etna. This was the only noise likely to disturb the meditations of an amiable fellow whose kind-heartedness now found its sole outlet in cherishing his loathing of the times he lived in.

"Why's he glad not to have set eyes on me for ten years?" asked Antonio, pausing with the pharmacist on the pavement of Via Etnea. "Personally, I've always been particularly fond of him."

"Because he's heard you're going to be made Party Secretary of some place or other."

"It's a lie!" cried Antonio. "Tell him it's four years since I paid up for my Party Card, and that one of these days I'm going to shut myself away in the country and..."

At that moment who should emerge from a side-street but Barbara Puglisi with her mother. The girl was bearing a missal and walking with a slight stoop, hugging to her bosom, and concealing in the sweetest manner possible, the exuberance and surge of her youth. A gentle nudge from her mother notified her that she might allow her gaze, albeit attenuated by modesty, to recover both perception and alertness. Barbara permitted her oval face, lapped in violet lace, an imperceptible movement to the left; a more noticeable movement she imparted to her eyes, revealing their dazzling whites; and she espied Antonio gazing at her. A slight stumble detached her from her mother and led her very close to the young man. He inhaled the sweet scent of her veil, of her skin warmed by a swift rush of blood, of tortoise-shell hairpins, of clothes which had long kept company with a pot-pourri which no woman in Rome had ever possessed: it stung his flesh, it pricked him to the quick. He stood stock-still, tracing the course of that species of serpent which had penetrated his nervous system and was biting at its very roots.

"My God!" he muttered. "Could this be..."

"You're leaving me in the dark," said the pharmacist.

Antonio's answer was to throw his arms around the man's neck and hug him.

"I'm still more in the dark," exclaimed the other.

"Tell friend Angelo," cried Antonio in tones of elation "that in no time at all I'm going to marry that girl you saw passing just now... and that I'm delighted at the prospect!"

So saying he rested his eyes upon the statue of the Madonna up there on the church of the Carmine, and retained them there devoutly, as one who, in an act of thanksgiving, presses his forehead to the ground before an altar.

"And what about your political opinions? What shall I tell friend Angelo about those?" enquired the other.

"Oh, *those*... What do they matter?" replied Antonio, grasping the pharmacist's hand in both of his.

That very same evening he entered his parents' bedroom and announced that he was all agog to marry Barbara.

His father, beside himself with joy, rushed in his long johns out onto the terrace and summoned Avvocato Ardizzone to announce the gladsome tidings.

"*Rara avis!*" replied the old lawyer, actuated merely by the wish to pronounce, in open air and cavernous voice, the phrase he had learnt two hours previously; the which, there in the darkness, amongst the jumbled encumbrance of chimney-pots and the glint of star-lit balustrades, was perfectly meaningless. "*Rara avis!*" My most hearty congratulations and felicitations thereupon!"

But his daughter Elena, who had heard Signor Alfio's words from her place of concealment behind the shutters of the French windows, clutched at a heart that writhed like a fish in the net, and was by no means of her father's opinion.

"He's been and gone and done it!" she murmured, at first in a tone of voice that struggled to appear bantering, but that gradually gave place to rage. "He's gone and done it! That's the way they carry on here in Catania! Go off and marry a girl they've never clapped eyes on and take not a mite of notice of their next-door neighbour!"

"Elena, my dear!" exclaimed her father, administering a great shove with his shoulder to get her back behind the shutter from which she was elbowing to emerge.

"Yes, it's true, it's true! When you have a young girl right under your nose, you might at least glance at her, before committing a bloomer in another neighbourhood!"

"But Elena!..."

"The fact is that I'm hapless, hapless, I was born hapless! The stars do not favour me, the saints do not sweat for me, it was not my lot – and my father, instead of hankering after the Senate, might have..."

"Elena, Elena, Elena!" shrieked the old man in three different keys, going wildly off pitch on the last *Elena!*, as if clappering a cracked bell. "You don't know what you're saying. Elena, come now, Elena, Elena!"

Another crack in his voice. Then he turned to Signor Alfio with, "Do forgive me, kind friend. Please have the condescension to pardon me and once again accept my... my... Good night, dear friend."

And the old lawyer flung the French windows to with a tremendous clatter.

Quite early next morning Elena hurled down onto the Magnano terrace three bulky volumes of love-journals in which, along with sketches, pressed butterflies, violets, palm-leaves – all things which had lived and flourished fifteen years before – was pasted a photograph of Antonio astride a wooden rocking-horse: the only copy of that photo, the loss of which had saddened Signora Rosaria.

These journals plummeted onto the terrace while Antonio was engaged in watering the pots of cacti. He did not lose his composure but continuing to sprinkle water among prickles and petals, he turned the pages with his toe, his eye lighting here and there upon a sentence containing words in capital letters. For example: "I would let HIM walk on my FACE," or "From three o'clock until eight always thinking the same THING," or else "What RINGS under his EYES today." He then peeled off the photograph so long sought by his mother and threw the remains in the dustbin.

Two days later these fervent phrases were the playthings of the caretaker's kids in the entrance to the courtyard. Elena, who, we must suppose, felt the beating of those fragments of her heart wherever they chanced to be, rushed headlong down the many flights of the building and swooped like a vulture on those unwitting urchins who were passing around paper hats and boats adorned with words which, could they but have read them, might have put a sudden end to their innocence. Elena, in every case with one quick snatch, succeeded in yanking away the paper and tweaking the fingers holding it; then she flew back up the stairs, wails and caterwaulings in her wake.

That night she knocked back a glass of water in which she had dissolved a couple of dozen sulphur match-heads, and at dawn was convinced she was at death's door. However, it sufficed for her to vomit into a terracotta pot while her poor mother supported her head, and her father, in an agony of fright, delivered harangues to Death, Life, Honour and Madness – all of whom he most likely saw drawn up in front of him – for her to be as right as rain again.

Same day, at lunch at the Magnano's... Signor Alfio to Antonio, having of course recounted the occurrence in their neighbours' house: "What is it you *do* to these women, eh?"

His mother: "He doesn't need to do a thing. It's they who have the hot pants on 'em, not him!"

To forestall further troubles, the engagement to Barbara Puglisi was hastened on, and in the course of one week Antonio found himself up to the eyebrows in the traditions of an old-established Catanian family.

The residence of the foremost notary in Catania, Giorgio Puglisi, was situated in Piazza Stesicoro, opposite the old law-courts, above the roof of which Mount Etna, looking almost next door in the absence of anything to obstruct the view, spreads her enormous wings, white as a swan's in the winter time, and mauve throughout other seasons of the year. This section of the piazza has been subjected to a deep excavation which brought to light the arches of a Roman theatre, rimed with mildew and pierced by passageways that vanish into the entrails of the city. These diggings, approached down a narrow flight of grass-grown steps, are fenced off by cast-iron railings along which any urchin who passes by at the trot will jaggle his stick with a clangour akin to that of shop-front shutters hauled down in a hurry.

This eastern part of the piazza keels over like the deck of a ship which has latterly received a broadside, conforming as it does to the shape of a crater which opened up here in ancient times. It is the starting-point of a road that scrambles, strident with the screech of tram-brakes (so fearful is the incline), towards the upper and more salubrious zones of the city. Tilted thus, it abuts, with its well frequented cafés, its pottery shops, on Via Etnea; beyond which, flat as a pancake, stretches the other half of the piazza, its pavements supporting the most precious of all the burdens with which the soil of Catania is weighted, to wit, the marble statue of our much venerated Vincenzo Bellini, in which he is depicted seated and smiling and surrounded by four of his celebrated protagonists, all with their mouths wide open in the process of scattering to the four winds the divine music of their creator. Here converge various alleyways, some lined with market stalls, some with brothels; and here also are the station approaches. And here more than anywhere the sirocco rubs his sweaty belly, and keeps the cobblestones covered with slithery mud.

But the Puglisi residence rose in the most lofty and luminous part of the piazza, so that in wintertime its window-panes admitted the dazzle of the snows of Mount Etna a-shimmer in the sunlight.

Barbara's mother, Signora Agatina, a vast, vociferous, dil-apidated woman, had a dread of the cold, so often the cause of a nose blocked to suffocation-point, and when she discerned a draught of cold air she turned upon it the look of a trapped game-bird facing a gun-barrel. For this reason she had cajoled her husband into installing central heating – the first ever in Catania.

This was the object of much criticism by the friends of the family, particularly because Notary Puglisi was considered the most respectable and level-headed man in town, related by ties of blood to other highly estimable notaries and to priests, all persons who for at least a century past had, along Via Etnea, been recipients of those obsequious salutations which the citizens of Catania bestow upon integrity, decorum, and absence of vices or debts.

And indeed, to take a closer look at the first and only eccentricity of a respected gentleman, and to glean personal knowledge of it, almost every day these family friends came flocking, with their nannies and their suckling infants, to spend a couple of hours in that insufferable heat; which they left with faces all splodged with red, as if one and all, from grand-dad to grandchild, had suffered a volley of slaps. But in the end they found it quite the normal thing, and one or two of them even installed this "central heating" themselves. "We ought to have know that a man like Puglisi could never have done anything irresponsible," they said.

Barbara spent her girlhood in this summer-and-winter hothouse, singing and skipping along the corridors, but never out of earshot of a voice down the passage: "Don't you go getting too close to them radiators!" Or alternatively, when she dared to set foot on the wooden steps that led up to the attic, a second voice: "DON'T YOU DARE GO UP TO PAPÀ FRANCESCO!"

Papà Francesco, Signora Agatina's father, was of course the grandfather of Barbara, but was called "Papà" on account of the respect owed to his wealth and blue blood. It was not known which king had created him Baron of Paternò, because he himself had a hatred of books, even those which, blazoning

46

forth all the fesses and hatchments of heraldic science, discoursed upon his family coat of arms.

Once Agatina was married off he was left with one decrepit old retainer, alone in his ancient palazzo with its marble pillars and statues supporting wrought-iron lanterns, fronting on an unfrequented piazza in the middle of which the old man could observe the rearing equestrian statue of one of the "continental usurpers", King Umberto I.

His forehead pressed against the window-panes, this nobleman devoted a great deal of time to detesting that statue.

"Tell me, Paolino," said he, addressing the old retainer, long since punch-drunk from having obeyed, though with the utmost respect, so many practically insane commands, "is it that I can't think straight, or does that chap there really have the mug of an ill-bred colt?"

"His visage is that of an ill-bred colt," was the man's invariable reply.

But came the time when the municipal authorities had plane-trees planted all round the piazza, and right in the face of the palazzo sprouted burly trees which went into transports of joy at growing up into the most luminous sky in the world.

The baron succumbed to blacker and blacker rage, as the rooms of his palace were shrouded in ever densening shadows. He protested, he wrote screeds to the papers, he pestered the authorities, both lay and religious: the Hon. Carnazza MP and his rival the Hon. De Felice MP, although he blushed to the core at having to mount the stairs of these men who spoke from the standpoint of fishmongers, janitors and such. . . But the trees were stronger than he was, and continued to soar upwards without a care in the world.

There came a night, however, when the old retainer, furtive and muffled up to the eyes, slank forth from the palazzo, approached the trees and, one by one, subjected them to certain occult treatments known only to him. This ceremony was repeated for a month; and lo, those sturdy, waving fronds which only a thunderbolt could prevent from seeing the year

2000, started to yellow at the very tips through which they imbibed the light.

The glee of the baron at these signs of enfeeblement, which he was the first to notice, from his central balcony upon which the trees were wont to rest their lovely heads, knew no bounds. The ill-starred vegetable matter gradually languished and, beyond the window-panes which on windy days reflected the myriad frolics of their foliage, they espied a human face growing ever more joyous as they themselves crept nearer and nearer to death. . .

The scandal, on the brink of explosion, was quenched with infinite difficulty and expense. The tree-poisoner was obliged by his son-in-law to leave his palazzo and remove to Piazza Stesicoro to live with his daughter and himself. It would seem that something must have been gnawing at the old man's conscience if he, who had always slept in a bed dating from the reign of Ferdinand II of the Two Sicilies, developed a penchant for garrets, unmade beds, poky little windows, and a view of church towers over rooftops. . .

He also became devoted to intense noise, for which reason, every time he closed a window, he rammed it to with all his might and stood there wide-eyed, ecstatic, harkening to it as if he had elicited the sweetest of sweet echoes. One day he bought a drum and (his grand-daughter hopping and skipping in a frenzy of joy) within the narrow confines of the room he perpetrated a tattoo that would have done honour to any parade-ground. But the neighbours complained, and his own dear daughter, her eyes awash with tears, implored him to relinquish this type of performance.

A compromise was arrived at. The baron would, for six days a week, restrain the tormenting urge to beat upon his drumhead. Every Sunday, however, he would have the horses harnessed, step up into his carriage, with his old manservant cradling the drum ceremoniously swathed in a scarlet cloth, and take leave of that tiresome Catania, a city which didn't turn a hair at the screeching of trams, but threw up its hands in horror at a perfectly pleasing paradiddle.

On reaching one of his country properties in La Piana, he would alight from the carriage and, amid bowings and scrapings from his peasants, stalk in amongst the trees, faithful servitor at heel bearing the drum still wrapped in its scarlet cloth. At length he would halt, disenrobe the instrument, sling it on his shoulder, and raise skywards the two ebony drumsticks quivering with all the fervours of a week-long-thwarted drummer. Then, slap-bang, with terrible fury, the old gentleman bombarded the thing time and time again, the drumhead quaked and hollered, the hens went squawking off in all directions pursued by dogs, and the bulls slouched away, furtively eyeing the red rag lying on the ground... and the servitor yawned.

For three hours would the old baron batter his ears with his tremendous onslaught. Then he would have the instrument swathed once more in its scarlet cloth and climb into the carriage to return to Catania. The door open, and one foot on the step, he would pause for an instant and enquire of his servant; "How did it go today?"

"Magnificent," replied the other ancient; and, holding in his left hand the exhausted drum, he extended his right to aid the exhausted drummer.

But one night the old servant rose from his bed, laid himself down on a chest in the hall, and passed away.

For a quarter of an hour the baron gazed upon the inert form of a man who had for so long obeyed his every command, whose life's work was now done for ever and a day.

"What the hell did he do that for?" he muttered. "What the hell made him do it?" And he asked Father Rosario, his son-in-law's brother, to pay him a visit in the garret which he had no intention of ever leaving again.

"Is there any such thing as heaven?" was his point-blank query as soon as the monk appeared in the doorway.

Father Rosario took a seat and gave a detailed description of how the kingdom of heaven was, in all likelihood, constituted.

"You're a bunch of swindlers!" retorted the veteran, and told him to clear out and never come back.

But the very next day he started crossing himself every few seconds, secreting holy pictures under cushions, falling on his knees every time the word "death" chanced to flit through his mind, and combining hatred of the clergy with a bigotry bordering on second childhood. He believed more than the Church's dogma required of him, but he rejected the Church itself. Simultaneously he was a rebel and a pitiable fanatic: a condition perfectly natural in one entangled, without hope of escape, in a mesh of rage and terror. His bedroom window never opened again, and therein the foul stenches stagnated at will until the time should come for them to cleanse and sweeten themselves with the fermentations of their own decay. The old man's body grew callused with that hard, cold, fibrous matter which invests the legs of fowls. One of his eyes remained permanently shut as if the lid were glued down, the look in the other was as watery and irresolute as a lantern in a rainstorm.

He never spoke a word or gave trouble to anyone. But his brain, especially at night, was a tempest of storming thoughts, words of command, shrieks, Ave Marias, sobs.

Barbara was very much drawn to this grandfather who looked for all the world like an oversized rag doll – and, that her footfall might not reach the ears of her mother, who had forbidden her to visit him, she took off her shoes to climb the wooden stairs to the attic. There she put her face to a crack in the door, and there she stayed for ages with her crafty little eye fixed on that ancient wreck which had neither sound nor motion, not even that of breathing... and who, withered and spent as he was, still had twenty years of life left in him.

This eccentricity of Barbara's was not popular with the family, and absolutely infuriated our good notary, who was always on the lookout for eccentricities. His people had always been prudent, responsible administrators of the Municipality or one or other of its institutions, peerless notaries, keepers of the most delicate secrets; the faces of whom (graced with pointed goatees), imprinting themselves on the retinas of dying men already immured in frivolity and cynicism towards the things of this world, recalled them to feelings of duty towards such matters as properties, livestock, houses, and money in the bank.

The women had always been beyond the reproach even of their confessors. Their eyes were as cold as they were beautiful, and fledgling preachers, launching into their tirades against women, would by hook or by crook avoid them, for fear of losing the thread and wandering off at a tangent. One of these women, simply by turning up at her country place after dark, had caused a knavish farmhand to hurl himself into the water-tank. Mistresses in their own house they were, to the extent that not a few ovens, asthmatic in their habits, consented to draw only if *they* were present. Women capable of sitting up night and day by the bedside of an old, sick maidservant, and performing for her the most menial of services. Men and women, then, of the most out-of-this-world normality.

Except that when they were born "different" (something that had occurred three times in a hundred years) they were not content with becoming artists or layabouts or playboys or scientists, like most who are not run-of-the-mill, but became raving lunatics apt to do some damn-fool thing from one moment to the next.

This lack of intermediate stages and nuances between those three unbridled Puglisis and the infinite number of other Puglisis, prudent and decorous, saw to it that the propriety of the family was in no wise tarnished. Those three constituted the exceptions that proved the rule. The vital thing was that such an exception should not occur again; and for this reason all the Puglisi clan would eye the earliest actions of their children with suspicion, and were unable to love them until that mysterious medley of mewlings and kickings gave place to the first signs of the future notary or the future mistress of the house.

In marrying the daughter of the baron of Paternò, our good notary Giorgio Puglisi was aware that he was marrying into the family of a man slightly out of the ordinary. But at that time the baron differed from others only in that he told people to their faces exactly what he thought of them; wealth, on the other hand, which was the greatest proof of respectability a man could offer, spoke highly in the baron's favour. Thus did the notary comfort and console himself. On his wedding day, however, in church, as he knelt before the altar with his bride at his side, the baron leant towards him and spoke into his ear: "I'll burst if I hold it in a moment longer: you look to me exactly like a turkey."

Our good notary blanched; but his common sense immediately suggested the following line of argument: "It's no use crying over spilt milk, and an irreparable mistake should not be thought of as a mistake, since that would be not only useless but harmful. God forbid that I should judge this old fellow to be an eccentric! What he said he said out of affection for me – and in any case, no one heard. As for my descendants... God will surely come to my aid.

And in this connection he remembered how frequently the priests had beamed upon him and said, "May God reward you!"

The first few years of this marriage were very happy. In 1914 Barbara was born, and in 1920 the baron withdrew into his garret, leaving the notary to administer his entire fortune; a circumstance which would have filled the latter's cup of joy to the brim had not Barbara, in that same interval of time, manifested signs of this strange mania for spending hours on end peering through the door at her silent, immobile grandpapa. What depths of curiosity could, in a six-year-old child, be appeased by staring for so long at an old gargoyle? What emotions were there in that small eye glued to the door: gratification, mockery, fear, cruelty, compassion?

One day the monkish uncle, seating himself with solemnity,

drew her between his knees and attempted to probe her with questions as subtle and almost imperceptible as the corner of a handkerchief removing a speck from an eye. But he got nothing out of her. Some years later Barbara developed a similar fascination for the sound of swallows accidentally trapped in the chimney stack. Thoroughly battered by the swinging cowl at the top, they were powerless to resist the suction which drew them down the flue until, after endless struggles, it laid them in the spent ashes of the grate, where Barbara grabbed them up more dead than alive.

This new eccentricity on his daughter's part alarmed the good notary. At this rate, where would it all end? He donated two thousand lire towards the foundation of an orphanage, and only a few years elapsed before God sent his thank-you letter. For that same Barbara, on whose account they had nursed so many and great apprehensions, had become the most normal, respectable girl you could possibly hope for, to the extent of resembling, at one and the same time, about a dozen of the notary's female forebears.

"Do you remember, dear," asked the notary of his wife, as he shed tender looks upon Barbara, "when my mother used to sit there knitting away? Just that same expression on her lips!... Remember Aunt Mariannina winding her alarm clock? The very same pout!... And when my sister Maria laid the table? Why, she'd pick up the glasses four at a time with her fingers inside 'em, exactly like Barbara!"

Barbara learnt to paint and to play the violin; she frequented the theatre, concerts, lectures, and all this without compromising herself one jot or tittle either with art or with ideas of which she remained as innocent as the day she was born.

But strangled as she was by this sedateness, she too was unhappy-happy, as all young people are: she too was breathless to know her future; when she looked at the sky at night, and heard neither sound nor voice vouchsafed her from it, she too was dismayed to think that the cosmos was a barren waste;

she too, doucely or in desperation, prayed to God; and at sixteen years of age, when nature's aesthetes, devoured by the passion for beauty that torments their senses, already have hollow cheeks, pinched noses and bags under their eyes, she was a picture of all that is fresh and fair.

IV

IN 1933 THE PUGLISI FAMILY were threatened by a
legal manoeuvre which would have trimmed their riches
by three quarters. A mayor who was no respecter of
persons had taken it into his head to commandeer the waters
of the River Pomiciaro (which belonged to the baron), for the
use of the municipality.

On learning this scandalous news the notary packed his wife
and daughter off to the theatre, sent the maids to do the shopping, shut the windows tight and gave vent to the following outburst: "Thieves! Blackguards! They're stealing my
stuff!"

He then set off helter-skelter for Rome, and in this city
destitute of persons to treat him with due respect he languished
whole days in anterooms, until it dawned on him that only
one particular minister, Count K., could possibly rescue him,
using the technique of bawling down the telephone – as he was
wont to do in moments of wrath – a torrent of oaths directed
at this mayor. Thus it came about that he reached the conclusion, the moment he returned to Catania, that Antonio, a
close friend of that minister, was a handsome young chap
indeed, and an excellent match for his daughter.

As for Barbara, scarcely had she been informed that she was
to marry Antonio, and that to think about him was consequently now quite proper, than she began to dream about him,
as if in the flesh, although she had set eyes on him only once
or twice, and that very fleetingly; and to suffer strange emotions when her girl-friends came to call... For on such
occasions her mother exhorted her to flaunt in the sunlight of

the balcony the very sheets in which she would henceforth be enveloped by night with the Adonis of the city.

The betrothal was celebrated strictly "Family Only", so Antonio's pal d'Agata had to rest content with making his presence felt over the telephone:

"Is your fiancée with you there?"

"No, 'cos the telephone's in a room miles away from the drawing-room, and Mr Notary is dead-set against Barbara and me going off on our own."

"Have you kissed her yet?"

"Good Lord no!"

"God preserve us! And when are you going to do it?"

A smile crept over Antonio's face: "Goodbye my friend, goodbye now," and with that he returned to the drawing-room.

There he was embraced and kissed by three distinct *monsignori* who'd tucked their dangling crucifixes into the black satin sashes with which their waists were swathed; and he was hugged paternally by Father Rosario. Everyone present was shouting and drumming their coffee-spoons on their saucers. A myriad of sounds met and clashed between room and room: the radiogram, the piano and (since it was nearing Christmas) the shepherds with their bag-pipes, who must have made their way up the back stairs, and perhaps even ensconced themselves in the kitchen. Rain had already arrived to lash at the windows, and low clouds scudded over the roof of the lawcourts, masking Mount Etna.

When the clock on the lawcourts announced the hour of seven, Barbara cried, "We simply have to go up and visit grandpapa! It would give him so much pleasure, poor old dear."

A small platoon, composed of the notary himself, Signora Agatina, Father Rosario and the betrothed couple, clambered the dark stairway and all but tiptoed into the tiny chamber.

Backed up against the wall, they stood in total silence round the old man, while he, propped up on his excuse for a bed, kept head bowed and eye fixed on his own two hands, crouched like two dry crabshells on the turn-down of the sheets.

Antonio waited for someone to say something or do something, to give him a cue. But no one either spoke or moved: they might have been looking at a funerary marble.

All of a sudden in swept Signor Alfio yelling "But what the..." (he lowered his voice abruptly) "what the devil are you up to here?"

The nonagenarian baron raised his eye towards the newcomer, painfully forced his lips apart, and croaked, "The trees!... Alderman, you!..." Whereat he keeled over as if at a puff of wind. In the person of Signor Alfio he had recognized one of the aldermen at the time the Town Hall had presumed to plant plane-trees in front of his house.

"Off with you, off with the lot of you! Back downstairs!" urged the notary. "It's a mere nothing. I'll deal with it. Agatina and I will deal with it. The rest of you, and especially you young people, be off downstairs and have fun."

They left, shoved along by the notary muttering, "It's nothing!" over and over again. And the word "nothing" pursued them the whole length of the corridor, right to the threshold of the reception rooms, where it was swallowed up in the whirl of the dance.

The plain fact was, the old fellow was dead. But the sad tidings were not disclosed until the following day.

Antonio, on his father's advice, immediately donned a black tie, the which bestowed upon the pallor of his face an old-fashioned gravity. To the extent that a bunch of anti-Fascists, seeing him pass their café table, grumbled to one another in undertones, "He's got the looks of a Brutus, but he doesn't mind emptying the potties of ministers and Party Secs. If I were in his place I'd wangle an audience with Mussolini and plant half a dozen slugs in his belly!"

Two days later a long procession followed the baron to the cemetery. Antonio and his bride-to-be were for the first time seen together, at the head of a funeral procession and followed by a host of relatives buttoned tightly into suits and overcoats, with hats, stockings and shoes all as black as ink; in their wake, two straggling rows of orphans from the "Sacred Heart" with mouths agape in the execution of the *Miserere* and eyes darting curious glances at the shop-windows, at the balconies; then by a retinue of carriages laden with wreaths which the wind fluttered with a sound much resembling a patter of rain; and bringing up the rear a crowd of friends and acquaintances chatting about their own affairs, who now and again in twos or in threes sidled off into a side-street or found refuge in a café.

All this because the dead man, by the simple fact of being a nonagenarian, exempted even the most dyed-in-the-wool hypocrites from wearing long faces or coming over all sentimental, leaving them free to beam at Antonio and his bride-to-be, and the young girls to focus their binoculars on the head of the bridegroom, on his right arm with Barbara's ring-laden hand slipped through it, and on a corner of the pall-covered coffin which willing hands were hefting along shoulder-high.

Antonio was conscious of the touch at his back of his mother and father's hands pretending to straighten his coat-collar as an excuse to give him a bit of a fondle. His mother, clasping the left hand hanging loosely at his side, pressed it firmly upon the hand of Barbara. But then, discovering that she had thereby concealed his fiancée's battery of rings, she hurriedly plucked it away, and blushed as if she had committed a gaffe. From time to time he heard voices speaking into his ear from over his shoulder, uttering tender whispers, such as "Put on your hat!... Don't catch cold now!... Silly of you not to bring your topcoat!... Now don't go staring around at the balconies, remember you're ENGAGED!... I think the Prefect gave you a smile just then: smile back for goodness' sake!... And, why ever is the mayor not among us today?"

Brusquely the notary thrust his way forward between Antonio's parents and stationed himself at the young man's side.

"I want you to write to Count K!" he hissed in an undertone.

"The mayor must have a really guilty conscience where I'm concerned, since he didn't have the face to show up!"

"I'll write tomorrow, papa. But please don't run away with the idea that I'm..."

Signor Alfio, eavesdropping behind the backs of the pair, here gave Antonio a pinch on the bum that shut him up at once.

"This son of yours," he proceeded in a mutter to his wife, "is his own worst enemy. If I hadn't been right on his heels he'd have gone and told the notary that he scarcely knows the minister."

"He's just modest," murmured the good lady.

"He's a cretin!" declared the father, waving his arms so wrathfully that he dropped his hat.

"Do behave yourself. Every eye is upon us," said the signora, halting beside him as he bent to pick it up. Fatal hesitation! A phalanx of Puglisi females overtook them and, stiff and wooden as a rank of Madonnas in procession, formed a palisade between parents and son.

"Maybe you had better write to him this very day," continued the notary, clinging to Antonio's side. "We'll send an express registered letter, and I shall post it with my own hands at the railway station. You know his home address, of course?"

"I know where he lives because he's asked me to lunch a couple of times."

"What!" exclaimed the notary, taken aback. "Did you not dine with him practically every evening?"

"Well, no..."

"Ah, then I imagine he came to your place?..."

"We met in various places," said Antonio, to put an end to this discussion. And he took a deep breath.

The cortège had halted in a small piazza near Porta Garibaldi, where an orator was already to be seen erect upon the church steps in the act of hauling a hanky from his pocket to dab his lips with. The costermongers flogging prickly-pears trundled away their barrows heaped with empty husks, hefting them in close against the walls to make room for the mourners irrupting among them. A tram came to a halt, crammed with passengers thronging the railings of the platforms and bulging with parcels, shopping-baskets and suckling infants.

"Who is the speaker?" enquired Antonio of his father-in-law.

"Avvocato Bonaccorsi, a friend of my father's."

"Why 'ave the old baron seen off by an anti-Fascist?" came an unknown voice.

"Because he's the number-one lawyer in Catania, and a gentleman who has never given the least bother to any living soul!" was the notary's spirited reply.

"'e wos a Socialist!" was the voice's comeback.

"He was... he was... We were all... Dammit, you have to look at what a man *is*, not what he *was*!"

"Twenty years it is, since the baron of Paternò decided to take leave of his friends..." began the orator meanwhile.

"I'm surprised," went on the other voice, "to 'ear a Socialist pronouncing the word 'baron' with such respect!"

"You're never satisfied with anything!" retorted the notary sharply, suddenly aware that the person he was talking to was a skinny eighteen-year-old, the son of a tenant of his, a tenant who some day or other would find his belongings out in the street, for non-payment of rent.

"Just see what's come of it!" continued the petulant voice. "Down there, look, near the tram."

At the spot indicated by the young man, they observed the Prefect cramming his otter-skin hat violently onto his head, turning his back and stalking away, followed by five or six other persons.

"This is very vexing!" exclaimed the notary, "very vexing indeed... Antonio, what do you advise me to do?"

"Nothing," said Antonio.

"Do you not think we may suffer some unpleasant consequences?"

"We have sunk very low," said Antonio, "but not to the

point of having anything to fear from a paltry pen-pusher in Catania, when we have friends in Rome."

This because at that particular moment he was undergoing one of those sudden bouts of euphoria to which he had been subject since becoming engaged to Barbara.

"Oh, heavens!" he thought. "If I'd wanted... How silly to be afraid of..."

Then and there all his recollections of Rome, in his memory as frigid and stiff as geometrical figures on a blackboard, were flooded with light, with colour, even with pungent odours, ranging from that of the dried fruits which in December pervades the alleyways around the Trevi fountain, to the sharp stench of the foxes in the zoo.

"Why," he asked himself, "does Barbara's hand resting on my arm affect me so much every time it draws free of the grip of my left hand? It makes my blood hammer in my temples... And when she blushes, if I am not mistaken, the odour of her skin is enhanced..."

Attended by this happiness he reviewed his years in Rome. Now, he could aim defiant looks straight in the faces of those before whom he had previously lowered his eyes; and he was mentally in the act of perpetrating a highly brutal act upon the person of the Countess K, when he realized that the orator, his voice hoarse, his beard streaming with tears, was bidding the last adieux to the coffin already mounted on the hearse. The cortège dispersed. Barbara was packed off home as were the in-laws, while the notary and Antonio climbed into an open carriage to accompany the baron all the way to the cemetery.

Need we say that in the course of this journey, while the walls of the cemetery of Acquicella came looming above the black plumes of the pair of horses, Antonio was the happiest of all Sicilians under thirty years of age. From time to time he cast a glance at the austere notary seated beside him, and thinking that that austerity, translated into shyness, chastity and innocence, bestowed upon the beauty of Barbara the warmth of an August sun, stimulating as it was to all the wonderful happy-go-luckiness and derring-do which drift through the dreameries of an afternoon nap, he gave thanks to God for creating not only blackguards but men of honour, and not only your wives of Count Ks and your Luisa Drehers, but the daughters of notaries. Had his father-in-law not been a man most respectful of legality, and above politics, Antonio would instantly, out of gratitude, have embraced the notary's political party, so greatly did opinions, solemn oaths, and the motives for which one either went to gaol or was licensed to rob and steal with impunity, seem unimportant compared to a certain feeling firmly implanted in his heart.

The old baron descended into the family vault beneath the eyes, sparkling with happiness, of this handsomest of "grand-children" who never once, as the coffin vanished into the dark chamber, gave a thought to the fact that there was a man in that box.

The notary gave the custodian a ticking-off about the messy state of the cemetery: "The paths are awash with tangerine-peel and wrapping paper. I'll have you know, friend, that every month we pay a kings's ransom, and have a right to insist that our dead are properly cared for!"

This said, he looked around as if hoping for a nod of approval from those faded faces gazing forth from the head-stones on every side, pictured on porcelain, set in marble.

"Let's get on home," he added, addressing himself to Antonio. "Barbara will be on the lookout at the window for you!"

And they climbed back into the carriage.

Reaching Piazza Stesicoro, Antonio immediately raised his eyes to the windows of the Puglisi residence, but saw no face there; indeed, all was shuttered tight.

"What a scatterbrain I am!" said the notary. "I clean forgot that we're in mourning."

The street door was ajar, heavy with black ribbons and notices bordered with dense black, still damp, with black crosses in the middle and inscriptions such as: TO MY FATHER, TO MY FATHER-IN-LAW, TO MY BELOVED GRANDFATHER.

Black-clad was the porter, and even the visitors hovering in the dim carriage-entrance were deep in mourning.

"Looks like I'm going to have to wear black along with the rest," Antonio ruminated as he climbed the stairs.

"I regret," said the notary, climbing at his side, "that your joy has been impaired by this misfortune. But they say it brings good luck. I can scarcely wait to throw open the windows again and let in some fresh air... This afternoon we must write that letter to the minister."

Antonio got down to it and wrote the much solicited letter. The notary had it typed out in duplicate and read it over a hundred times, each time disgruntled by the fact that Antonio did not address the minister familiarly as *tu*. The letter, express registered, was duly posted at the station.

"Will I get an answer?" muttered the notary again and again until Barbara got huffy and came out with a simple, yet stern, "Daddy!"

A week later the minister replied, announcing that the mayor, "for this and for other far more serious reasons", would be sacked and replaced.

Our good notary was beside himself with joy and, conquering his natural caution, took his good tidings off to the Law-courts.

"Very strange," scowled the Prefect, "I have not been informed of this. Am I to believe that the minister communicates his decisions to private citizens?... In saying this I do not wish to cast aspersions on your son-in-law, whom I know to have excellent connections in the Capital. But after all *I* am the person who represents His Excellency and enjoys the honour of carrying out his orders... No, my dear sir, I doubt very much that the decree to dismiss the mayor has as yet been signed... It may, perhaps, be something the minister has in mind, that might be put into effect in the more or less foreseeable future... but as things stand today... To put it mildly, I have my doubts."

Our notary blushed.

"What if this were the case?" he thought to himself. "How utterly imprudent of me to count my chickens before they're hatched. I've never done anything so silly before in my life! If he's right, I'll shut up shop and move to another town. It's my own fault for getting into cahoots with young people. Go to bed with a babe and you wake up in wet sheets!"

However, it came about that three days later the Prefect received a telephone call from the minister, and after the following aside ("What's up in Catania? What are the police *doing* at night? I have been informed that in a urinal in Via Pacini someone has written a rhymed couplet about me that's now going the rounds of the whole of Italy, and those nitwitted egg-heads in the Caffè Aragno are already bandying it back and forth!"), he received the news that the mayor of Catania could start packing his bags.

This information spread like wildfire the length and breadth of the city, and procured for Antonio respectful salutations from people he didn't know from Adam. As he walked along the street the word whispered behind his back was "potent..."

"He's a potent youngster," everyone repeated. "Count K would give his right arm to be in his shoes!"

The one time this chit-chat came distinctly to Antonio's ears, he flew into a rage, drew himself up before the old gentleman who had uttered it, and stared him squarely in the face. The old man blanched and shook like an aspen.

"I only said that you were a potent youngster!" he stammered. "D'you call that an insult? I'm a friend of your father's. In fact it was Signor Alfio who told me..."

Antonio turned on his heel and left him standing. But from that day onward he began to check up on his father and was rewarded, through a half-open doorway, with the following peroration: "He's inherited it from me and his grandfather! Old boy, I tell you with us Magnanos women go weak at the knees if we touch them with a fingertip... I know nothing about my son's relations with the *contessa*: but I do know that when a woman has been with him, she goes licking her lips for the rest of her life."

Antonio waited for his father's friends to take their leave, then shot him a fiery glance.

"What's up with you then?" demanded Alfio. "Why are you glaring at me like that?"

"I overheard what you said just now."

"So what? What did I say wrong? Anything to be ashamed of if you're a good stallion? Why, you'd be ashamed if you weren't!"

Antonio stamped his foot with vexation and burst out, "But don't you understand that..."

"Oh ho, my friend," broke in his father, "I understand very well indeed. What matters is that *you* should understand that I am entitled to talk about my own son when and how I please!"

Antonio bit his lip and said nothing, though the following morning, perhaps in search of comfort, he rang up his cousin Edoardo.

"I'm very anxious to speak to you too," replied his friend. "Wait for me there at home, and I'll be with you in a brace of shakes."

He came, huffing and puffing. His eyes were red about the rims and he had every appearance of suffering from the pangs of unrequited love. They went out together onto the terrace.

"I'm disgusted with myself!" said Edoardo, leaning on the railing that overhung the sun-drenched Corso. "We've really hit rock-bottom!"

"Who's *we*?" asked Antonio.

"All of us... you, me... but specially me."

"But why?"

"I tell you I haven't slept a wink for six nights or swallowed a morsel. Yesterday in the street I had to prop myself on a beggar's shoulder because the ground was reeling beneath my feet. And what's more, I've got an itch I can't get rid of...

I'm always shunting off to the "Pensione Eros"... Today I laid hands on the charwoman – who's all of fifty – and rammed her against the wall..."

"Why on earth?"

"Listen here, Antonio! I've got to be made mayor of Catania. Me, and no one else! It's a debt of honour I've taken on with myself and the entire bunch of my relatives, who regard me as pretty small beer. You've got to write to the minister! If necessary we'll go up to Rome together. I'll pay the fares and everything. But I've simply got to be made mayor of Catania! In any case," he added, raising his face, with half-closed eyes, and filling his lungs with moist February air, "this dud show can't last, if it's true they're gearing up to invade Abyssinia. You need to be as dimwitted as a schoolmarm if you plan to do today what the English already did three centuries ago! Listen to what Croce has to say, for godsake."

"Come again?" queried Antonio.

"Benedetto Croce. Never heard of him! He's the only reason we can claim that Italy's a country fit for human habitation, and not just a sheep-pen..."

And drawing forth Croce's *History of Europe* from where he held it, secreted under his arm, he read aloud a number of pages peppered with such comments as "No!... The man's mad!... No, No and No again!" in case the book should fall into the hands of a Fascist fanatic or a policeman in mufti.

Edoardo read aloud with great fervour. The little terrace, abud with leaves dappling the rosy sunlight with violet shadows, heard the word "freedom" pronounced in the most devout and desperate manner possible, by a man of thirty-two who knew only too well that he lacked the fortitude and courage not to let the whole thing slide.

Antonio was on the point of feeling genuinely moved when a venomous thought darted into his mind. "And how often have you been to the 'Eros' lately?" he blurted out.

"Yesterday, three times!" replied Edoardo, breaking off his

reading. "The day before – you're not going to believe me – four!"

"And whatever happened with the old char?"

"Oh nothing... I squashed her against the wall as if I was about to strangle her, said *boo* in her face and passed the whole thing off as a joke. So I beg you, Antonio, dear boy, to write a letter to the minister here and now!"

Yet another letter Antonio wrote to the minister, but this time his missive met with no success. In his courteous reply, Count K declared himself regretful that he was unable to comply with the request of his friend Antonio, because the appointment of Edoardo Lentini as mayor of Catania did not meet with the approval of the local Party Secretary, Calderara. The Town Hall would be administered provisionally by a commissioner, in the person of the Deputy Prefect Solarino, fifty years old and a decent fellow, though for thirty years deprived of the joys of life; the author, what's more, of a number of sonnets inimical to France and to Russia.

The moment Edoardo learnt that the chief obstacle to the chief aim and purpose of his life was Lorenzo Calderara, he set to work to butter him up, and began to pay daily visits to the headquarters of the Fascist League (a charming palazzo designed by Vaccarini, at the portal of which two sentries stood at ease with a blend of apathy and insolence, clasping across their stomachs enormous rifles weighing more than they did themselves, while in gruff, drawling voices they would bark out a "Take yer 'at off comrade!" at the backs of all who crossed the threshold). And Edoardo put so much vim into sucking up to Calderara that eventually he came to regard his own actions as being intelligent only if they were of the sort that appeals to a positive cretin...

Antonio, for his part, wrapped himself up entirely in his private life, and spent five happy months in the company of a girl who only on Sundays, on returning from Mass, allowed him to run up the stairs with her, leaving her parents puffing behind; and, near the frosted-glass window on one of the landings, to kiss her on the mouth.

He had also tried to snatch a kiss late one evening in the drawing-room, when the notary's hand fell from the arm of his chair along with the newspaper it was grasping; but Barbara put all her strength and craft into freeing herself from the embrace without making any noise about it, sprang from her chair, ran from the room, and instantly leant her back against the closed door... so weak did she feel at the knees.

When she re-entered the room those lovely green eyes of hers, which so overawed the Lenten homilists, had grown the more severe as the countenance surrounding them had darkened. Antonio's mind reeled: he found that heady mixture of sensual ferment and moral inflexibility so irresistible that he was compelled to take his leave half an hour earlier than usual. This due to a rapture that made him tingle from head to foot.

On leaving the Puglisi household he began wandering through endless streets, and avenues, and courtyards, aware all the time that in the most austere palazzo in Catania, in whose wardrobes hung the clerical attire of her monkish uncle, herself defended by crucifixes steely as swordblades, slept a girl pure as spring water, destined for him alone.

Accompanied by these thoughts he walked the length of Via Etnea, which loomed the larger in the stillness of the night, passed the ebony-dark Bellini Gardens, and turned into Viale Regina Margherita, a long straight incline flanked with suburban villas serried with terraces, palm-trees and godwottery, until it petered out, lofty and free, up there near the stars.

Reaching Piazza Santa Maria di Gesù, he took the road for Cibali, and after a loud tramp of boots, some bouncing back as echoes, others squelchy with mud, he gained the tiny piazza of that little town, swathed to its roof-tops with sea-breezes. From this vantage-point, on moonlit nights, the sea lay calm and still, except for that glittering quicksilver path on which the city printed the ink of its chimney-pots, or now and again the dome of a church.

Eventually he made his way back down a deserted road, all but a country lane, skirting a public wash-trough redolent of soap-suds, and sundry kitchen-gardens with their lettuces and cabbages, re-entered Catania through a maze of winding alleys still hot from the swarming bodies of urchins that jam-packed them the livelong day. And throughout this ramble he held his chin high and his eyes fixed upon the heavens – upon that warm, live, multitudinous sky of the south which, at the very point where rooftop, terrace, tree-tip end, there she bursts forth! No vague, ambiguous, half-hearted sky is this, as in the cities of the north, but immediate, utterly dense and teeming; majestic and silent as perhaps she is at one thousand light-years from this earth.

A shudder of chill brought him home again both weary and happy, and plunged him at once into a long sleep from which (or so it seemed to him) certain dreams that before his engagement to Barbara had distressed him night after night were now banished for ever.

One afternoon in March Barbara took it into her head to arrange a visit, along with Antonio and his parents, to the Magnano property in La Piana, the great alluvial plain to the south of the city. A decrepit carriage, swaying this way and that and crushing the life out of poppies and daisies, bore them at a snail's pace into the heart of this delectable plain, flanked, in the chrome-yellow light of the sirocco and the sandy soil, by the skittering wavelets of the Ionian Sea.

This fertile expanse is bounded to the east by the finest of golden sands; to the south by the heights above Syracuse and Lentini; to the north by the outskirts of Catania, the very last houses of which straggle up the lower slopes of Mount Etna, from here looming in all its vastitude: startling, solitary, unequivocal, as is the retaining rampart of an ancient temple when the rest of the masonry has all but crumbled away. A twelve-hour cloudburst suffices to submerge this plain completely, mingling the waters of the River Simeto with those of the Lake of Lentini; but conversely a single day of sunshine will bring it to the surface again, dripping and verdant, its lanes muddily odorous and its birds all skin-and-bone from their long, strenuous flights over grasses viewed through a window-pane of water.

On March afternoons this landscape shimmers with the most limpid light imaginable. Depending on the wind, a wind which seems to hammer at the heavens themselves, and to draw swift veils of cloud, red, yellow, brown or blue, across the sun. This wind whirls furiously about all points of the compass: now we see it, passing in the puff of dust that veils the lush lower slopes of Etna, now to the east in the mantle which suddenly darkens the surface of the sea, now in the plain itself, all around us, close around us, in the wheat-fields that sway low their heads, to rise again dispensing from their bosoms glints of gold and silver.

As soon as the party came within sight of the gate of the Magnano property, and beyond, the long drive leading to a knoll topped with a cluster of buildings, Signor Alfio doused his pipe with a stab of his thumb, wiped his mouth and burst out, "That's him! There's the fellow who sucks my blood! Now we're in for a mammoth dose of his belly-achings!"

The person thus referred to was the share-cropper, a lean old figure in fustian trousers and a pleated shirt, white though grimy with dust, the rolled-up sleeves of which revealed two leathery arms as dark as a negro's. His face rough-hewn and wrinkled, with two little light-coloured eyes so weighed upon by the pouches above it seemed impossible that they should move. A red handkerchief was knotted about his neck in such a way as to leave two ass's-ear ends dangling onto his collarless shirtfront.

He straightened up from his work and rested his hands on the handle of his mattock; then, with his right, hampered in his movement by its very massiveness, he grasped the peak of his cap, made a clumsy effort to raise it, pushing it this way and that across a forehead to which it appeared to be glued, until finally, with a furious twist that might have been sheer anger, he wrenched it off and held it in hoverance above his head; onto which, after a brief moment, he curtly returned it.

"Hey there, Nunzio!" shouted Signor Alfio, poking his own head out of the window of the carriage, come to a halt in the middle of the driveway. "You call *that* the way to work?"

The labourer lowered his eyes and shook his head, biting back a grumble.

"When did you start that piece of digging?"

"*Stamatina*" (first thing this morning) replied the other, lowing his eyes again.

"And how's it going?"

"*Malamenti.*"

"Badly? Why?"

"*Pirchí va malamenti.*" ('cos it does)

"And just you tell me, brother, what'd you do if you couldn't be forever bemoaning your lot?" Then, in a quite different voice and dropping the dialect, "I have come to show my daughter-in-law my orange-grove."

"*E unni su', st'aranci?*" (where's these oranges, then?)

Signor Alfio thrust open the door and descended grumbling from the carriage, needing for his arms, which felt a furious desire to wave about, the requisite space to do so.

"Listen here, in God's name don't make me lose my temper! I've brought my daughter-in-law here today, and it's got to be a happy occasion for all present, so I don't want to get hot under the collar. Signora Agatina, Barbara, Antonio," he proceeded, poking his head back into the carriage: "Get down, do!" The two women and Antonio climbed down from opposite sides of the carriage, blinking in the dazzle of light from the sea which, beyond the green fields and the sands, rose brave and bristling with wind in a half-moon of horizon.

"How lovely it all is!" exclaimed Signora Agatina. "Good for you, friend Alfio, really and truly! I never imagined it was so lovely here."

The corn was high already, pastelled with an inkling of wheat-ears and gorgeously emblazoned with poppies great and small, their cups spilling scarlet light into the air, in among the cornstalks and into the very furrow. Olive trees, their windswept leaves a-sheen with silver, stood at regular intervals, like human figures halting their steps at a holler from someone left behind. The drive led up the knoll on which stood a small yellow house with green-painted shutters, flanked by farm buildings – dirty-white walls riddled with the black rectangles of doors and windows. Verdant and shining on the right of the drive, brightening the air with the breath of cool springs, the lemon groves swept to the top of the knoll; and beyond again, as far as a second knoll atop which, constructed dry-stone fashion out of blocks of lava, stood an imposing well-head.

It was towards this well that Signor Alfio immediately, and with pride, raised the ferrule of his stick.

"Look there, friend Agata! That is *my* well! All these local numbskulls," and he swept an accusing arm which embraced not only the share-cropper but also a number of peasants dotted about the landscape, "day and night repeated we would strike salt water. But I stuck to my guns and said No, the sea belongs in the sea and not under the earth! Dig, and we shall find fresh water!... If I hadn't been so stubborn about it these splendid orchards before your eyes would still have been in the mind of the Almighty... But everything here, dear lady, every single scrap of it, is the fruit of my obstinacy. Every single tree is a death sentence hanging over my head, for I had to use a hundred fearful oaths before getting it heled in. Now come this way: look there!"

Rejuvenated by the very sight of his farm, Signor Alfio set off up the drive at a brisk pace. The share-cropper, preserving his disgruntled look, kept pace with him on one side, Signora Agatina on the other, with a firm grip on her hat, the feathers of which were ferociously tugged at by the wind. In the rear came Barbara, one hand clasped between Antonio's two, her

72

eyes fixed shining and joyous on the farm that would one day be hers.

"Here we are, here's the orange-grove. Just look what beauties!" exclaimed Signor Alfio, pointing his stick towards a patch of land where the lemon-trees ceased abruptly and densely massed, warmly glowing, began the oranges.

"Hey, my fine sir! Hey, you dolt!" he yelled at the peasant. "I suppose you're going to tell me these aren't oranges!"

The man pulled a face and stared at the ground.

"You can't answer that one, eh." insisted Signor Alfio. "Have you lost your tongue?"

"*Ma unni 'i vidi, st'aranci?*" grunted the peasant.

"What d'you mean, where do I see them? Here, look, and here, and here, and here. Come with me! Open your eyes man! What do'you think I'm touching with my stick?"

The peasant pursed his lips and continued to look at the ground.

"Speak up, for pity's sake: give it a name!"

The man repeated his performance.

"What is it? A potato?... a tomato?... or a shrivelled up old cucumber like you?"

"*Chistu è 'n'aranciu. E chi vordiri?*" (OK, it's an orange. So what?)

"Eh? So what? So there *are* oranges growing here!"

"*Unittu!*" (Call that a crop?) sneered the peasant, wagging a forefinger. "*E pi' unu! . . .*" he added after a pause, as if to say, "And you're making all this fuss about one measly orange?"

"But there, there, there again, can't you see others?"

"*Picca ci n'è... nenti!*"

"Nothing worth mentioning eh?... You must be blind!"

"*Nun sugnu orbu. A tia, ti fanu l'occhi stasira, Alfiu!*"

"You're not blind? So it's Alfio who's not seeing straight this afternoon, is it? Let me tell you brother, the only time I didn't see straight was when I gave you the right to share-crop this cursed piece of land. Oh, if only an angel had tapped me on the shoulder and told me how bitterly I was going to regret it! What we need is Communism, by God, and I'll die laughing when I see how you come out of that!"

"*An, macari 'u communìsimu avi a véniri ora? Sintemu st'autra.*" (Ah, now it's Communism is it? That's a good 'un).

"Yes, what we need is Communism!"

Signora Agatina turned in bewilderment to the two young people, hoping for an explanation, but Antonio merely winked at her.

"*E iu chi ci perdu?*" asked the peasant. (What've I got to lose?)

"Being able to do as you please, and to steal – that's what! Because they'll put a chain around your neck like a dog, and make you work until you drop dead!"

Meanwhile they had climbed the hillock and the dogs were giving tongue on all sides, shaking the palings and kennels they were tied to; the hens, wings outspread, fled in the wake of the shrilling cockerels, trampling a tumble of yellow chicks.

"*Ma 'a terra ci 'a perdi tu!*" put in the peasant.

"All right, all right, it'll be me who loses the land! Yes, I'll lose it, and with pleasure, because this cursed property does nothing but fill your belly!"

"*Pirchí 'a chiami sempri svinturata, sta terra ca ti desi 'u Signuri? nun è di giustu!*"

"Yes, cursed, this land God gave me, because it's had the bad luck to end up in your hands! What do I ever see out of this cursed soil? Not so much as a bite of greenstuff for my salad! I suppose you think that when Communism comes you'll get your hands on my land? You're mad. With that lot in power no one'll have any land. Only place to find it'll be the cemetery! And you'll have to toe the line and sweat blood, because if you don't sweat blood they hang you from a carob tree for the ants to eat. D'you imagine these Communists are anything like Alfio Magnano? My brother, I tell you, that lot bury you alive with your head sticking out and then jump up and down on your eyes!"

"*Iu nun sacciu nenti, Alfiu. Stai parrannu ammàtula. Iu nun vogghiu né comunisimu né autri nòliti: vogghiu sulu travaghiari.*" (I don't imagine anything, Alfio. I don't want Communism or any other of your innovations. I only want to work).

"Little work and a lot of thieving: that's your motto!"

"*Iu non arrobbu, Alfiu.*" (I'm no thief, Alfio).

"You'd gobble up even me."

"*Iu nun mi mangia a nuddu!*" (I'm no cannibal).

"Hold your tongue man, d'you hear? I won't have you speaking to me like that!"

"*Ma ch'avìti, ch'avìti? Sempri ca facìti battarìa, vuatri dui!*" shrieked an old hag from the farmhouse doorway, gesturing with a huge, gnarled hand at the end of an arm totally withered by the years. "Stop that now! Always quarrelling! *Dui fratuzzi di latti, signuri mei, can nun avìssirua vìdiri di l'occhi unu pi' l'autru, e talìati comu s'accapiddìunu!*" (Two foster brothers, and they only have to get together and they tear each other's eyes out).

"Mamma Tanina," said Signor Alfio, drawing closer to those ancient orbs which saw everything as shadows, and in which white and iris were mixed like the white and yoke of a shattered egg. "Mamma Tanina, after sucking at the nipple allotted to him, my foster-brother here had the rotten habit of taking over mine. Is that true or isn't it?"

The old girl's face seemed gashed by the blood-red of her gums and the rims of her eyes: she had smiled.

"Come on, Mamma Tanina, don't deny it! That's what he did, the louse!"

"*Veru è, veru è*, quite true, quite true," conceded the nonagenarian, still smirking that smirk and shaking her fist in the direction of her aging son Nunzio and her aging foster-son Signor Alfio.

"There now! He robbed me then and he robs me now!"

The old girl, tucking her chin on her shoulder like bashful sixteen attempting to conceal a laugh, "*Oh, Alfiu, Alfiu!*" she exclaimed, "you're always the same, you are, when you've a mind to have a joke."

"On the contrary, Mamma Tanina, what you ought to say is '*Oh, Nunziu, Nunziu!*'"...

Since things were now taking a more cheerful turn, and everyone was all smiles, Barbara laid a hand on Antonio's chest and: "Come on, take me as far as the well!" she said.

"To the well?" returned Antonio quaveringly, peering in the direction of that part of the landscape totally immersed in the sparkle of the wind.

"What an idea, Barbara! Did you say *to the well?*" put in Signor Alfio. "That chap doesn't know how to get there!"

"Doesn't know how to *get* there?" repeated Barbara with an incredulous smile.

"It's the truth. He hasn't a notion how to get there. I, with the sweat of my brow, have set up this heaven on earth for him, and he hasn't the faintest idea how to get about, or what path leads where."

"Not true dad, not true at all," said Antonio; and having by then worked out the quickest way up to the well he gave Barbara's hand a tug: "Come on, let's go."

"I'm coming with you!" cried Signor Alfio.

But the two young people were off and away, running up a path along the edge of a terrace wall with a tiny stream trickling beneath it; and they were on the other knoll in no time at all.

Up there the wind was fearsome, buffeting against the lava slabs of the well, which gave back hollow groans.

Barbara, hair breaking free from its pins, bent a regal brow upon the olive-groves, the lemons, the wheat-fields stretching out on every side, all stamped with the name of her Antonio; and in its midst, tiny in the distance and worn out from plodding the damp terrain, they saw the person who had purchased and nurtured them with so much sacrifice.

"It's gorgeous!" Barbara burst out, turning to Antonio. "It's an absolute gem!"

And since the rest of the party were still far off, she threw her arms round his neck, and for the first time it was she who put her mouth up to his and gave him a long, long kiss.

"Darling," she murmured. "Darling, darling. . ."

The dazzle in Antonio's eyes as Barbara kissed him with a vigour now cool, now fiery, now as if she had ceased to breathe, now gasping as if in unbearable ecstasy, became one in his memory with happiness itself; a happiness that held him in thrall throughout the time that elapsed before the wedding, happiness that yet vouchsafed him, in its rich and generous dominion, room for some spells of anguish and unrest; short-lived albeit, and always bound up with *her*, as precious stones are to the gold wherein they are set.

This happiness suffered a serious setback during the wedding ceremony. There he was kneeling on the velveteen hassock, hearing at his back the bizz-buzz of the most influential men and the loveliest belles in Catania. It suddenly appeared to him that the church walls soared out of eyeshot, that quilted curtains, black and heavy, had unfurled before the doors, pinning themselves to the floor with every appearance of permanence, and that the very notes of the organ, cascading from the oak-panelled organ-loft together with the crash of anthems, had cut him off for ever from the streets, the piazzas, the trains, the sea, like the thunder of a waterfall in spate that rends and pulverizes any vessel that may happen beneath it.

Then it was that, over his shoulder, he cast the look of a hunted beast at bay, and the faces there, rather than reassuring him, threw him into a still greater funk. Especially those of the lovely belles, which seemed to harbour a malicious inquisitiveness, a derisive challenge, almost an air of smugness. Towering above them all, black-clad, bent forward in his agitation, stood out the figure of his father, Signor Alfio, a tear in his eye...

It was but a passing moment. At the rustle of Barbara's dress as with the aid of a hand on her right knee she rose to her feet the familiar thrill mastered him again, and his throat tightened with joy.

It was July the 5th of 1935. That day, the sheer beauty of

Antonio touched even the priests (even the one who had denied absolution to the Archbishop's niece because she had too often committed the sin of attempting to draw the outlines of Antonio's body on a baluster). One poor lame half-wit, who had managed to worm his way in amongst the elegant throng cramming the nave, cleared himself a path ahead of Antonio, dancing in jubilation and uttering inarticulate cries, so greatly did the bridegroom remind him of processions and banners, fireworks and the town band – all that for him smacked of festival and splendour.

Many were the young women who kissed Barbara, all the while casting languid glances athwart her nose at Antonio and keeping up a stream of resounding smackers on her cheeks and mouth, those places where her husband's kisses would shortly rain.

Meanwhile, our spinster Elena Ardizzone stood aloof beside a pillar, a revolver in her crocodile handbag, savouring the bitter gall of witnessing the minute-by-minute survival, at the side of a rival, of that beauteous youth whom she could have felled with a touch on the trigger. Big tears rolled down her porous cheeks and she let herself dwell on how good she was, how generous, and noble, and superior, not to use the weapon she had in her bag – which in any case had never been loaded.

The men, to distract themselves from the jealousy that brought bile to the mouth whenever they looked at their women and found them flushed and flustered as if every one of them had wedded Antonio and was entering with trepidation upon a day that would lead to its evening, and thence to the mysteries of the night, well, the men talked politics, not without having glanced furtively around to see if they might mention the Head of Government – not abusively, of course, but with somewhat tempered respect and without the cant phrases. The stand-in mayor maintained that in the autumn there was to be a large-scale military expedition against Abyssinia, as stated in a sonnet he had composed the previous day.

This sonnet, which he recited without further ado, sent Notary Puglisi into a fit of rage.

"No mention of war, for goodness' sake!" he burst out. "Today of all days, no mention of war! No point in asking for trouble! We'd do better to leave church... follow our newly-weds out."

This exhortation was promptly acted on.

Outside the church a platinum sky dazzled a street crowded with people shading their eyes and pointing out the bride and bridegroom, come to a halt on the bottom step.

Antonio, blinded by the glare, screwed up his eyes, causing the delicately blue-tinged skin of his chin to pucker, and producing, perhaps involuntarily, an expression as of someone caressing a beloved face.

The girls on the balconies across the way were all of a flutter. The one who succeeded most thoroughly in not seeing the bride, the crowd, the steps and façade of the church with the sun hanging plumb above it, the one who best managed to conjure up a picture of herself and Antonio framed in that intimacy and us–two–togetherness which perfectly matched his expression at that moment, more in a flutter even than the others, shrank back against the wall as if afraid of toppling over the rail.

At long last the vehicles stationed in the side-streets of Via Etnea drew up at the foot of the church steps, and the newly-weds, relatives and guests disappeared within, to become visible a moment later through the car windows. The procession got under way, and having proceeded a few yards, stopped: for it had already arrived at the Puglisi residence in Piazza Stesicoro. A number of girls took the short stretch of Via Etnea between church and residence at a run, and succeeded in catching a second glimpse of Antonio and bride in the act of climbing back out of the car hampered by an enormous bunch of carnations.

It was just then that the Marchese San Lorenzo, halted in the middle of the piazza, fist on hip, straight-backed, wasp-waisted as a riding master, had a notion to denounce all those relatives of his whom he found to be wearing morning coats despite the Secretary-General's orders to the contrary. And it was at just that moment that one of the girls exclaimed, "I'm sure we'll never again see Antonio promenading in Via Etnea until two in the afternoon. It's really true – our youth is over!"

Nor was the girl mistaken. After the wedding Antonio and Barbara lived a retired life; and seldom indeed were they seen in the streets of Catania. The whole town knew they spent their days either at the house on La Piana or in the one at Paternò, immersed up to the eyebrows in happiness. Principe Di Bronte, who lived in an old, dilapidated country house two kilometres from the Magnano farm, declared that he had been investigating the curtains of the newly-weds with his powerful spy-glass, and caught them in each other's arms every time. This information led to a lot of daydreaming, and when the March wind rattled the shutters, not a few women's thoughts flew to the lovely rustle of the corn on La Piana, and the pleasure of watching through the window the swaying ears of wheat while in the arms of such a man as Antonio.

In this way passed two years, during which, at the end of every month, Edoardo Lentini sent his friend some books. Freud, Einstein, Croce, Bergson, Mann, Ortega, Gide: they all took the road to La Piana or to Paternò, though it was never known whether Antonio read them.

"What are you sending him? Books?" exclaimed Signor Alfio one day, when he met Edoardo in Via Etnea. "I rather fancy that chap spends day and night with his pestle in the mortar!"

"And children? Any in the offing?" enquired Edoardo.

"Not a one," snorted the old man.

"It's a bit of an enigma," pondered Edoardo, "but when one overdoes it, children are not forthcoming. It has occurred to me that only methodical husbands, the ones who lose a night's sleep once a week, succeed in producing children one after the other."

"Come to think of it I only had Antonio after four years of marriage. I waited for him like the Messiah, that ugly little imp!"

"Come off it, I really can't believe he was ugly!"

"Hairy as a monkey!... Though I have to admit, he turned out all right in the end."

"Too darned much so, if you ask me!"

The old fellow put his chin in the air, as was his wont when he wished to conceal his gratification, grasped his stick in both hands behind his back, and went off without further ado. Of a sudden he turned, shaking his stick in Edoardo's direction.

"You there!" he shouted at the top of his voice. "Are you never going to get yourself made our mayor?"

Edoardo blushed to the roots of his hair and hurried home thoroughly put out.

"That old nitwit will throw a spanner in the works," he stumped about the house muttering to himself. "If a statement like that comes to Calderara's ears, which isn't at all unlikely with all the spies hanging around in Via Etnea, not even Christ himself returned to earth could get me the job of mayor!"

But he was not destined to suffer any such disappointment. A week later Calderara was appointed Deputy Secretary-General of the Party and moved to Rome, relinquishing his place in Catania to one Pietro Capàno, a coarse-grained twenty-five-year-old with eyes like marbles that bulged from a close-cropped head. One who dreamt of nothing else but striding – as a feared and respected figure – into the classroom at the *liceo* where his father, his uncle and his brother had all studied before him, and where over and over again he had heard, "Ah, so you're *all* cretins in your family are you!"

No sooner in Rome than Calderara went to pay his respects to Count K. who, to show how well up he was in Catanian affairs, mentioned Edoardo Lentini, a name fresh in his memory because he had rediscovered it in Antonio's letter of 1935, which his son had been using to conceal a diamond he had stolen from his mother. Calderara got the impression that

Count K really was a friend of Lentini's, and before taking leave he casually suggested that the latter should be appointed mayor of Catania. The count raised no objection, and five days later Edoardo, returning home, found two workmen up on the balcony with hammers and wire in their hands.

"The Town Hall is installing a telephone for us at its own expense," explained his wife.

Edoardo dared not believe his ears, and in a fit of feverish shivers wrapped himself in a shawl to await the completion of the installation.

No sooner had the workmen said "Well, that's that job done!" than the instrument started to shrill and a hundred voices came in a steady stream over the line, from humble office and noble mansion, showering congratulations on the be-shawled young man for his appointment as mayor of Catania.

It was the 2nd of January, 1938.

Three months later Antonio and Barbara returned to Catania and set up house in a wing of Palazzo Puglisi. That same evening Edoardo invited the couple to the mayoral box to see a performance of *Norma*. Not a pair of opera glasses but was trained in their direction.

During the intervals, in the corridors, Antonio was greeted by his friends. "How do you do it?" they demanded of him. "You get younger and younger and slimmer and slimmer, while we were no sooner married than we got pot-bellies like bran-sacks!"

"It means that for *him*," said Luigi d'Agata slyly, "marriage is no rest-cure!"

"Poor cousin Barbara," murmured Edoardo Lentini between his teeth. "She never sees the light of day, with that immovable object always on top of her."

The following day invitations to lunch poured in, as did also the relatives.

Signor Alfio, walking along Via Etnea between his son and daughter-in-law, would stop every few steps before the café windows, ostensibly to study the sugar lambs transfixed by their little red flags, but actually to observe the reflections of Antonio, himself, and Barbara all lined up as if for a family portrait.

"They're in love," he would say of an evening to the relatives who had come to call. "They're in love, and that's all there is to it!"

"It doesn't take much to fall in love with Antonio," commented one black-clad aunt.

"Well it doesn't, but it does," retorted Magnano senior, fishing for further compliments. "You have to rub my son up the right way, or else he scratches like a cat."

"Now listen to me," said his wife one evening, after their visitors had left. "All this upheaval in the house makes my cheeks burn as if I had the fever on me. We'll be the target of all tongues if we go on in this way about our Antonio. A little bird tells me that people are laughing at us behind our backs."

"Are you dreaming?" burst out Signor Alfio. "The man who can make a fool of me has yet to be born! In any case, all these people swarming about the house, scratching the floors with their hobnailed boots like the clodhoppers they are, I tell you I don't like it either!"

For some time thereafter the two old people received nobody. But around the beginning of May they were obliged to offer a cup of coffee to Cousin Giuseppina, a person in her fifties and practically deaf, who talked for a couple of hours without pausing to draw breath, the feathers of her headgear nodding like a trotting horse's, and who as she was finally taking leave enquired of Signor Alfio: "Is it true that Barbara Puglisi is marrying the Duca Di Bronte?"

"*Now* what are you cooking up?" yelled Signor Alfio, his nose not an inch from her hair. "Barbara Puglisi is my daughter-in-law!..."

The elderly cousin's answer was to rock her head from side to side, wooden-faced, mouth sagging, saying nothing.

"Antonio's wife!... My son's wife!" he added, bawling louder than ever.

"Exactly," was the reply.

"What d'you mean, *exactly*? Did you grasp what I said?"

"I perfectly grasped what you said, and my answer was: 'Exactly'."

"So it *is* true that you've lost your wits?"

"Believe me, Cousin Alfio, I'm the only one in the family with a decent head on their shoulders.

"Sara," said old Magnano to his wife in an undertone, struggling to overcome his wrath, "kindly see her out, because if I escort her to the door, I swear to God I'll throw her down the stairs like the dirty-minded old bag she is! And tell her to get to work on herself with a curry-comb before visiting human beings again!"

Signora Rosaria saw their relative to the door, gave her a perfunctory kiss and went back to her husband.

"Well, what d'you think of this, ladies and gentlemen?" the old fellow was grumbling on. "I explain how things stand, and tell her that Barbara can't go off and marry anyone at all, because she's already married, because she's my daughter-in-law, because she's Antonio's wife, and what does she say? 'Exactly', she says. And she then goes on to make *me* out the old dotard!"

"But Alfio," said the wife, "you really *are* going a bit soft in the head."

"And why, pray, am I going a bit soft in the head?"

"What on earth were you thinking of, sitting there arguing with a half-wit who'd just told you something with neither rhyme nor reason?"

"Maybe she meant to insult me."

"What sort of an insult is it, to say something that makes not a scrap of sense this way or that."

"I don't know, but she may have meant to insult me."

"Keep your hair on, Alfio. Let's swallow the bitter pill and get to bed."

84

The pair of them sat opposite each other in the dining-room, and chewed their boiled greens in silence.

"D'you know what she was implying?" burst out Signor Alfio when he had lit his pipe. "That. . . when it comes to. . . well, er. . . that kind of thing. . . Barbara and Antonio don't get on."

"Well, just look what you're fabricating now! Those two are inseparable all day long. . . They can't bear to leave each other's side. Why on earth shouldn't they get on?"

"How do I know? But here in Catania nobody keeps their trap shut – their tongues are itching to wag. D'you know what they're saying? That your son is overtaxing his wife!"

"What do you mean, overtaxing her?"

"God in heaven, do I have to spell everything out? Your son is randier than a ram, and if he has a woman to hand he never gives her a moment's peace."

"Antonio is a husband like any other husband!"

"You know very well that's not true. Antonio has a face like an icing-sugar angel, but when it really comes down to it he's a randy ram! In Rome he had three or four mistresses at the same time, and if now he's putting all his eggs in the one basket, may the Lord have mercy on his wife!. . . She has a right to be fed up. . . In any case, tomorrow I want to have a word with Notary Puglisi."

"Very good, tomorrow have a word with whoever you please, but now let's get to bed. You never think straight when you're sleepy. And don't waste time peering under the beds! Thieves don't pay visits on paupers like us. . . They know well enough where the money is."

V

"YOU SEE, YOU SEE!... I was right!... It's just as I said!..." yelled Signor Alfio, resting the receiver on the desk he was sitting at and twisting his head, snail-like, towards the passage. "Come and listen to this! Sara! Rosaria!... Hullo? Hullo? – He's rung off!"

Signora Rosaria appeared in the study doorway, red-faced and panting with the effort of having removed from the wall a large picture of Sant'Agata, which she still had in her hands.

"Can't you ever stop carrying saints around? Leave 'em in peace! Even they have... ahem!... their little troubles... So did you hear that? I was right! Puglisi rang me up this very moment, in a voice like a mother superior's, and told me he wants a word with me, that things aren't going well, that we must meet at once!"

"Lord save us! And what did you say?"

"I told him I'd expect him here, and asked him to pick me up two cigars on his way past the tobacconist's, since my wife," he added in a severe and meaning tone of voice, "forgot to remind me to buy them this morning."

"What a thing to bring up at such a moment!"

"Hang on there! Am I supposed to go around in mourning because *your* son plays the turkey-cock? Has the penny dropped? He likes to scratch and I pick up his fleas... And on top of it all, that whatsit... that Mr Notary, with his prissy little voice and his long, long face... What's he expect? Does he want Antonio to carry abroad the very thing that ought to stay at home? Does he want him to keep a mistress, or father children on chambermaids? If my son has such a yen for his daughter, Mr Notary shouldn't poke his nose in! Every man should be master of his own house. Does he think their marriage was blessed in dirty dishwater?"

"Holy Mother of God, what are you saying?"

"I'm telling you – let him leave them be! He knew my son was a man with some spunk to him!"

"Hush! That's the doorbell... Mother in heaven, help us!"

"Don't drive me round the bend, Sara. What are you scared of?"

"I don't know, but it's better if things like this don't happen."

That very moment rang out a voice in the passage: "Kindly announce the notary!"

"Show him in, show him in at once," Rosaria hastened to call. "What are you thinking of, leaving him in the corridor? Come in, come in. No standing on ceremony, dear Signor Puglisi. Consider yourself at home."

Signor Alfio heaved himself out of his chair. "Have you brought the cigars?" he asked.

As if such a futile question was unworthy of an answer, the notary entered the study with set lips: black jacket, pinstriped trousers, black felt hat in hand. His face was the epitome of gravity, the hair of both head and chin were arranged as neatly as the numbers on a balance sheet, and firmly fixed in his two little eyes was the look with which he drove dying men to unseal their lips and speak for the very last time of the things of this world.

Signora Rosaria's smile melted away on the spot, and Signor Alfio himself hadn't the heart to repeat his question on the subject of cigars.

"Sara," he growled. "Leave us alone for a while. Send us in a couple of decent coffees, put that picture of Sant'Agata back where you found it, and look sharp about it!"

Signora Rosaria lifted the dusty picture, dropped a jittery little curtsey, and scuttled off down the passage, bending her head every two steps to kiss the glass protecting the sacred image.

"Now then," said Signor Alfio, "what's the problem?"

The notary seated himself in an armchair, waited until his host had plonked himself down on the settee with the little pots, statuettes and dangly knick-knacks at its back; waited until these trinkets, shaken by the thud of Signor Alfio's body, had ceased to tinkle, and then, lowering his eyes and twisting his hat in his hands, said almost in a whisper. "The problem is that things are not going well between our two children."

"My friend," was Signor Alfio's instant reply, "to tell you the truth, I was intending to telephone you today on this very subject."

"Indeed?" returned the notary, raising his eyes and planting, full in Signor Alfio's face, a look as stiff as a poker.

"Yes, because I too... recently, I mean... have got wind of... Well, you know how here in Catania nobody gives a damn if he's a cuckold, but he has an itch for where the grass grows greener... So I got wind that Barbara was upset..."

"That's not possible!" snapped the notary.

"What's not possible?"

"That my daughter has uttered a word on a matter of such delicacy. You know her upbringing, her character, her manner of comporting herself!"

"Come, come, sir! Nobody said they'd heard a single word about this from Barbara's lips. But this is the way we Catanians are... we read things in people's eyes. One gesture, one sigh, and people imagine they've cottoned on."

"I would hate to think that your son has been talking!"

"Ah, now *you* are making a mistake, my dear sir. You don't understand Antonio, truly you don't. You don't realize what a treasure you have for a son-in-law."

"I am the first to admire the good heart, the refinement and the intelligence of your son. But unfortunately, in married life, as you know better than I do, there are other things of major importance."

"Oh come, important yes, but not as important as all that! We mustn't push 'em too hard otherwise we'll see 'em carried out feet first! . . . But the main thing, if you want my opinion, is that where their offspring are concerned parents have as much to do with such matters as Pontius Pilate with the Apostles' Creed!"

"What precisely are you trying to imply?"

"That parents have nothing to do with it and shouldn't meddle."

"Only up to a certain point."

"Only up to a certain point, of course. If matters were to become really serious, if they really overstepped the limits, then, I agree, a word from me, a word from you, and we'd be able to make Antonio realize that. . . in short. . ."

"My dear Signor Alfio, in cases such as this words are of very little use."

"Now now, my dear Mr Notary. We are not brute beasts, we are Christians, baptized, confirmed Christians! If Barbara is suffering, Antonio will be the first to worry."

"Barbara is suffering only morally speaking."

"Can't see why she should be suffering morally speaking. It's no shame for a wife if her husband. . . well, in short. . . is a very ardent lover."

There was a pause. The notary knitted his brow unhappily, without shifting his gaze from his host's eyes.

"What did you say?" he murmured at length.

"I said," repeated Signor Alfio, rather irritably, "that there is no shame involved for a wife if her husband shows that he desires her more than is usual."

"But that's not the problem at all!"

There followed another pause.

"What's that?" stammered Signor Alfio. "What's that you said?"

"I said, 'That is not the problem at all.'"

"Then. . . what *is* the problem?"

"Ah, I was persuaded that you had some suspicion, but on

the contrary I now see that you are very far from divining how things stand between our children. I assure you that this will make it very difficult for me to explain myself, and very distressing."

"Come, come, sir! Don't keep me on tenterhooks. What's the matter? Is my son ill or something?"

"I do not know whether one could say that he is ill, but. . . his condition. . ."

"Then what's wrong with him? What's wrong?" demanded Magnano senior, masking a shudder of fear with gruffness of manner. "What's wrong with him? The suspense is killing me! What's wrong?"

"Calm yourself, I beg of you! His health is in no way endangered."

"Rosaria," bellowed Signor Alfio. "Send me in a glass of water!"

"Calm yourself," repeated the notary. "I assure you that Antonio is perfectly well. It's just that. . ."

Whereupon in came Signora Rosaria, delivering the glass of water with her own hands in the hope of reading, on the faces of her husband and his guest, a serenity that might allay her apprehensions. But what she saw was the notary's face clamped tight like a mechanism given an extra wrench with the spanner, and her husband's a blotchy yellow and red, with one wandering eye that seemed almost to dangle down like a loose button.

"Mother of God, what's the matter!" she burst out as soon as she saw him.

"Stop jabbering!" retorted her husband. "Stop jabbering, put the glass down on the table and get back to wherever you were."

She hurried away, though not without turning on the two men, before closing the door, a face stricken with terror.

"Mr Notary, sir," said Signor Alfio, when he had gulped some water and several times smacked a tongue clogged with bile, "let us speak plainly, let us not beat about the bush. What has happened?"

"What has happened is that my daughter, after three years of marriage, is in exactly the same state as she was when she left my house."

"What's that? Who?" burbled Signor Alfio; mildly enough, for he was completely baffled. For some little time he fixed upon the notary a pair of eyes that appeared as calm as they were drowsy, so entirely were his wits befuddled and adrift.

The notary sighed, realizing that his words, which he had taken great pains to render unequivocal, had not lured Signor Alfio one step nearer to the truth; and the two men sat there looking at each other, the one in distress, the other in perfect tranquillity.

Until suddenly came a flash in Signor Alfio's face, as if something had exploded in his brain and left its drastic reverberations in his eyes.

"No!" he cried, "what the devil are you saying? No! No!"

"I am very sorry, my dear friend, for my own sake and for yours, but matters stand exactly as I state them."

"No, no, I'm not going to take *that*!" cried Signor Alfio with a bitter laugh. "Not for love nor money! Not for anything in the world! Not even if I saw it with my own eyes! No, no, I'm *not* going to take it!" He got to his feet to laugh the louder, but with the agonized expression of one staggering up to gasp for air. "Ha, ha, ha, how could you be so simple-minded as to be taken in by such poppycock? Who told it you?"

"Not my daughter, you may be sure! Left up to her things might have gone on this way until the two of them were both in the grave. Barbara went into marriage as innocent as a toddler in kindergarten. For three years she believed that her husband was behaving like every other husband in the world. You will excuse my saying so, but your son has taken advantage of the artlessness of his wife. Indeed, if you wish to know what I really think, Antonio has shown himself to be utterly irresponsible."

91

"Hey now, sir, let's watch our words!"

"Utterly irresponsible, I say; because a young man does not get married when he knows his problem..."

"Problem, Mr Notary? What's the problem with my son? What's Antonio's problem, eh? Something that puts ants in your... Lord alive, help me to hold my tongue!"

"By all means do so. It is I who must speak: and I say that if Antonio has been irresponsible, then you have been doubly so, because a father ought not to encourage his son to marry when he is aware of the state of affairs."

"What state of affairs, sir? My son's state of affairs is that he's pestered the life out of all the women in Catania, Rome and the rest of the universe! That's my son's state of affairs!"

There was a pause, during which the notary tugged his beard skywards and twisted it about a good deal.

"Listen to me, dear friend," he said at length, in a voice as level as his face was pale, "we must not go on in this fashion. Otherwise all we shall achieve is to confuse the issue and never find a way out of the quandary. We are two unfortunate fathers struck by the same calamity. Do you imagine that it is not extremely distressing to me to place the most intimate affairs of my daughter, of my Barbara, on the lips of all and sundry? No, my dear Signor Alfio, this catastrophe has dug a grave beneath my feet, and though you may see me dry-eyed at this moment, when I am on my own I cry like a child."

"But sir, my dear sir," began Signor Alfio, and all of a sudden himself burst into tears, with a squeaky kind of a sob so faint and far away that the notary thought he was coughing.

"How *can* it be true, what you're telling me?" he continued brokenly, once the sobbing in his poor lungs had died down. "I know Antonio. He's played fast and loose with women. Why *now*... with his wife... with a girl like Barbara who would make the blind to see... Why? Answer me that!"

"I do not know why. But I assure you that the situation our children are in has become humiliating for both of them, and can continue no longer."

"What do you advise me to do?"

The notary raised his palms in a disconsolate gesture, then lowered them again onto his knees.

"The most important thing," Signor Alfio put in hastily, "is for us to act in such a way that this matter remains between the two of us, and that no one, I repeat no one, not even my wife or yours – not even Jesus Christ who hears us this minute! – knows anything about it whatsoever. You understand me, Mr Notary? Nothing whatever!"

The notary shook his head, raised his palms once more in a gesture wider and slower even than before, and held them poised. "How can it be done?" he sighed.

"What do you mean, sir, by 'How can it be done?' This is scarcely like you! We can do it by sealing our lips and not blabbing to a soul!"

"And then?"

"Then. . . we'll see how things stand. I'll have a talk with Antonio, – it's only right I should talk to my own son. . . I know you for an upright man, but who can tell? You might have got the wrong end of the stick. . ."

The notary smiled an acidulous smile.

"Well anyway," pursued Signor Alfio, "do you allow that I must first talk to Antonio?"

"By all means. Indeed, it is your duty to do so. You are honour-bound to defend the interests of your son, as I am those of my daughter."

"But Mr Notary! The interests of my son and your daughter are identical!"

"They would be identical, I agree, if Antonio and Barbara really were man and wife; but as it is. . ."

"What d'you mean: 'as it is'? Are you trying to tell me they weren't properly married?"

"You are well aware, dear Signor Alfio, that in circumstances such as these a marriage is as if it had never been. It is null and void."

"And who says it's null and void? Why've you taken it into your head to say so just today?"

"It is not I who say it, but the Church."

"Church? What Church? And when, may I ask, did it say so?"

"It has not yet said so. But it will."

"Mr Puglisi, you are being about as clear as mud. Speak plainly, sir. What are you cooking up in that head of yours and keeping us all in the dark about?"

"Listen, Signor Alfio, if you're going to start taking on like that again I shall bid you farewell and be off."

"Be off with you then, be off!" shrieked Signor Alfio, beside himself once more. "Go away and stay away!"

The notary had risen to his feet and was buttoning his overcoat, stiffening and drawing himself up to his full height, more austere, more curt, more beetle-browed than ever; but Signor Alfio was not impressed.

"And I'll have you know, Mr Notary, I don't believe a word of what you've told me! I shall speak to Antonio instanter, and learn the truth!"

"Do so by all means," said the notary. "Have a talk with your son. I, in the meantime, shall concern myself with the interests of my daughter. Good day to you! My regards to your wife."

This said, he threw open the door, and there, head lolling against the wall and white as a corpse embalmed, was Signora Rosaria in person.

The notary performed a low bow before the swooning woman, and vanished into the penumbra of the passage.

"Sara!" cried Signor Alfio, dragging his wife into the study "Did you hear? Did you hear all that?"

"Yes," gasped his wife, in a whisper as cold as the draught through a window in an icy February, "yes... Let me sit down, Alfio my dear."

The old fellow helped his wife onto the settee, raised his half-finished glass of water to her lips, gave a few vigorous pats to her cheeks to bring her round a bit, and started pacing up and down the room.

"The damned liar!" he bawled. "Damned liar, damned slanderer!... With that holier-than-thou look on his mug... damned liar! Just imagine," he proceeded, planting himself in front of his wife and shaking a fist ceilingwards, "just imagine Antonio... my son... Antonio... not being able to!... No, no, Mr Notary, go tell that to the blockheads in your office, who hang upon your every word whatever rubbish you tell 'em, but don't try that one on me!"

Up and down the room again, stamping the floor at every step as if crushing venomous reptiles. Then, "If our Mr Notary ran a risk in bringing Antonio into his house, it was that my son would cuckold him from tip to toe, along with his brother and all his precious kith and kin!"

"Alfio, Alfio, don't say such things!"

"Just you let me say what I like, let me get it off my chest, for God's sake! He has the nerve to come here and tell me that my son... that Antonio... can't make it... Can't make what?... My son... What can't he?... Well, you've got to laugh, eh? In this family everybody makes it! Even I, an old man and with diabetes to boot, even I, if I get on top of a woman, I'm of a mind to have my cock coming out of her ears!"

"Alfietto, child! Don't talk that way!"

"Can you imagine? Eh? Eh!" went on the old man, bunching his fingertips and shaking them next his nose in a gesture of furious disbelief. "They're driving me mad!"

"Alfio, listen to me, will you," said his wife, in the pleading tones of one whose strength is at a low ebb. "There's something fishy in this business, something devilish. Ever since that Cousin Giuseppina said what she said, I've been down in the dumps."

"Cousin what? Who on earth? What did she say?"

"Alfio, don't you remember what Deaf-Adder Giuseppina said? She was right there where you are now, and she said: 'Is it true that Barbara Puglisi is going to marry the Duca Di Bronte?'"

Signor Alfio struck himself a mighty blow on the forehead. He struck himself another. He struck himself a third. "You're right!" he cried, "You're right! By God you're right! That snake in the grass knew... It's as plain as a pikestaff! D'you expect that old pest to leave home, stinking as she does, unless there's someone else's troubles for her to get her teeth into?" Then, suddenly horror-struck: "So this means that the whole town is prattling about us!"

The very thought sent the floor spinning beneath his feet. He had to sit down.

Now it was the wife's turn to get up, to clasp his head to her bosom, to stroke it gently.

"No, Alfio," she said. "I don't imagine the deaf old pest knows all that much. The notary is a man of honour..."

"A bloody Jesuit!" croaked Signor Alfio, his mouth enbosomed in her blouse.

"All right, call him a Jesuit. All the more reason he should know how to serve his own interests – and he also knows as well as we do that when people's tongues start wagging the loser is the woman, not the man."

"True," said Signor Alfio, pushing away his wife and perking up a bit. "Yes, true enough, but only when the case is the opposite of what he's maintaining. In that case yes, it's the woman who takes the rap. But he's out to look after his own interests, and he's picked on the most poisonous, the most malicious, the most loathsome of slanders to the detriment of my son, and my son alone!"

"But Alfio, Alfio, here we are tearing our hearts out and not doing the one thing we ought to be doing."

"What's that?"

"But Alfio, surely – to have a word with Antonio."

"You're right, you're right! I'll give him a ring at once!... What's the number?"

"Alfietto mio, you know it perfectly well: 17420."

"I don't know it! I wish I'd never heard it! One-Seven indeed!"

He got up, crossed to the desk, and began prodding at the telephone dial.

"I can't see the numbers, I can't see the numbers," he shouted a moment later. "Get me my specs!"

"But Alfio, they're on your nose..."

He put a hand to his eyes and had to admit that the specs were already in position.

"All the same, I can't see!" he moaned. "Come here and dial this wretched number for me."

Signora Rosaria trundled over to the desk, removed the specs from her husband's nose and put them on her own; then she had a bash at dialling the number. But her sobs broke her.

"I can't see the numbers myself," she wept. "They've robbed us of ten years of our lives, curse them!"

The old people fell into each other's arms; and the cheeks of each were wet with the tears of the other.

"We'll have to call in the maid," said Signor Alfio. "But let's dry our eyes first! No one must suspect a thing..."

"Lend me your hanky, Alfio."

"Here... Give yourself a good mop... there, on your nose... And you've made your blouse all wet."

"No harm done, Alfio, blouses wash. If only that was the worst trouble in life! Rosina!" she called when she had patched herself up as best she could. "Rosina! Come along here please."

The maid appeared with wet, red hands and, half-illiterate as she was, had no little trouble in dialling the number. But at long last she did it.

As soon as the ringing tone started, Signor Alfio tore the receiver from her hand, while Signora Rosaria bustled her post-haste out of the room and firmly closed the door.

"It makes me sweat cold, having to telephone that house!" grumbled Signor Alfio, the receiver to his ear. "I wouldn't care for Mr Notary to answer, or that wet rag of a wife of his.

97

I swear to God, I'd tell 'em something they'd not forget in a hurry!"

But Antonio answered.

"Who's speaking? Oh, is that you, dad?"

On hearing his son's cheery voice, old Magnano put a hand over the mouthpiece and sobbed, as if he had woken that moment from a frightful nightmare. "Antonio!" he blabbered. "Antonio!"

"What on earth's the matter?" asked his son, somewhat perplexed.

"You can say that again! Antonio!..." And, beside himself with joy, he again covered the mouthpiece. "He's thoroughly mystified," said Signor Alfio in a hurried whisper to his wife. "It's all a lot of tosh, you'll see! Imagine there being a word of truth in it!... Antonio," he resumed, unsealing the mouthpiece, "any news, dear boy?"

"None at all, as far as I know."

"Postively none at all?"

"Dad, I don't follow you. What sort of news?"

Old Alfio started windmilling his left arm around to give his wife some notion of his elation.

"In a word," he went on, "you've nothing special to tell me?"

"I really don't follow you, dad. What could there be to tell you?"

"Well in that case," declared Signor Alfio in a voice both resonant and solemn, "your father-in-law is the worst blackguard ever to besmirch the face of the earth!"

A pause ensued. Then: "What makes you say that?" asked Antonio, some sudden trouble creeping into his voice.

"He was here this morning. Didn't you know?"

"There with you?"

"Yes! Here with me, trying to break my heart by telling me things that... well, if you'd heard them!... Are you alone?"

"No," said Antonio faintly. "But say on, anyway."

"How can I, if the things I have to say just stick in my

gullet? He's as mad as a hatter, my boy! As soon as he gets home, put him in a strait-jacket! And gag him as well, because every word that comes out of his mouth covers us all in shit!... Do you know what he had the nerve to tell me, right here in this room, and the only reason I didn't stuff his silly little goatee down his throat was that I was his host?... What he said was, 'Barbara...' Oh, it makes me sick just to say it!... He said, 'Barbara, after three years of marriage is just exactly as she was when she left my house...'"

Antonio replaced the receiver.

VI

THE COLOUR HAD DRAINED from his cheeks and his teeth were chattering. Droplets of chill sweat trickled down his chest and flanks. From the waist down he felt a weight, a density, as if the full rush of his blood had flooded to his feet in its haste to sink into the earth and vanish. But from pit of stomach to crown of head he felt diaphanous, all but a vacuum, with thoughts flitting through his mind as swift as tremors of wind in a dead leaf. Filled with the insensate fear of one who stands aghast at seeing his crime revealed after years of deceit and duplicity, and is unspeakably woebegone, he was none the less appeased by the ineffable consolation of the truth.

His first impulse was to tiptoe away and conceal himself somewhere in the country, to hide between two stones like a lizard; but a number of women's voices, and the flap of the monkly uncle's sandals, and the chimes of the Lawcourts' clock (who knows how?) told him that the last word had not yet been spoken, and that he might still save some coals from the fire.

He hastened from the house – not even a word to his wife – and having done the length of the sun-dazed Via Etnea made a beeline for his father-in-law's office. He thrust aside the heavy curtain shielding the doorway and, seeing nothing and no one, blinded as he was from the dazzle of the street, stepped into the ground-floor room.

But the notary, in that flash of brilliance through the curtain, had seen Antonio clearly silhouetted. He rose from the desk at which he was seated with pen in hand and pencil tucked behind the ear, surrounded by peasants clad in corduroy.

"One moment!" he told the said peasants, whose massive hands were firmly implanted round the rim of his desk. "I wish to have a word with this gentleman."

He took Antonio swiftly by the elbow, as one does with someone plainly about to go off the deep end, conducted him down a narrow, low-ceilinged passage where old documents gave forth the odour of bergamot snuff-boxes, and drew him into a room at the back.

This room boasted a lofty vault. Dozens of chairs stacked one upon the other in a corner showed, between the curvy legs of the top row, a glimpse of the portraits of all the Mr Notary Puglisi's who had been lords and masters of that office over the last two centuries. The mid-May sun was ablaze in a small round window.

Antonio put a hand to his brow, aware that his face was bloodless, whereas into the visage of his father-in-law seemed to flow and concentrate those of all the other notarial visages enthroned among the chairlegs.

Incapable of opening the conversation, Antonio set himself to stare at his father-in-law, fixing on what was apparent through the hairs of his beard: the thin, red, straight-set lips that showed no signs of parting.

"My boy," said the notary at length, having left his countenance for a considerable time at the mercy of those moist, ardent, desperately questioning eyes, "you must take into account that no other course of action was open to me."

"But why?" cried Antonio. "Tell me why!"

And he cast a half-hearted glance over his shoulder, as if searching for something.

The notary extracted a stool from the pile of chairs and placed it behind Antonio's knees. He slowly sank down on it, once again stammering "Why?"

"Now Antonio, you are a man," said the notary, and the blood at once came rushing to his cheeks as if he had unwittingly uttered a word that the other might consider sarcastic.

Hypersensitive as he was to catching peoples' reactions on this subject, to following its tortuous course in their innermost thoughts, Antonio caught that blush on the wing and turned more wan than ever.

"You are a man," repeated the notary, since it seemed to him that the only way to avoid giving Antonio offence was to treat the phrase he had just pronounced as inoffensive, "and you must take it like a man! A tragedy has occurred, and that's all there is to it. There are thousands of tragedies, and this is just one of them."

"Tragedy... what tragedy...? I don't understand..."

"Oh, tut, tut, Antonio! That's not the way to set about it! No indeed! You rely too much on the fact that your wife is a girl who's worth her weight in gold, and would rather die than unseal her lips. But this is scarcely fair on your part! Don't put too much faith in that. No indeed, no indeed!"

"But heavens alive," pleaded Antonio, "*what* would Barbara rather die than talk about?"

"Antonio!" burst out the father-in-law, highly incensed, "it is I who am asking *you* what Barbara would have said, had she spoken! Do you follow me, Antonio?"

"No, I don't," replied the young man weakly, "I'm waiting for you to put me in the picture."

"Perhaps it will suffice," said the notary, weighing his words, "that I should mention one name?"

"One name?"

"That of Giovanna."

"Giovanna?" repeated Antonio cluelessly. "Who is this Giovanna?"

"In November of last year you gave notice to a maid. Her name was Giovanna..."

"So?"

"So... nothing!" replied the notary irritably. "In the name of suffering do you want to crucify me, by heaven! Giovanna talked! As soon as you'd dismissed her she went to my wife and let the cat out of the bag." The notary gave him a frosty stare, and added. "I request you not to ask me what she said."

Antonio passed his hand hard across the corner of his mouth where a tic had developed, and managed to quell it.

"I, on the other hand," he mumbled, "would like to know."

The notary drew forth from his pocket a solid gold cigarette-case – he opened it – he extracted a cigarette – he closed it again – he put into each of these gestures sufficient force to crush that gadget to pulp, and equal energy into restraining himself – he lit a match – he raised it to his lips with the tremor of one at the nth degree of tension – he noisily puffed it out – and, staring at the floor, began to smoke. Then, with the same extraordinary effort, he raised his eyes and riveted them on Antonio's face; and, still weighing his words: "One day," he began, "Barbara had a dizzy spell, and the maid asked her whether she might not be expecting a baby. Barbara replied 'I think I am.' The maid had five children of her own, and, in order to calculate the date of the happy event which Barbara had just announced, she asked a few further questions. In this way she learnt that according to Barbara, who had learnt it from you, babies are born as the result of chaste and fraternal embraces which, after midnight. . ."

"Stop!" cried Antonio. "That's enough!"

"By God you're right!" exclaimed the notary, hurling down his cigarette and stamping on it. "Quite enough! More than enough! I should think so too! You hoped that. . ."

"I hoped nothing!" retorted the young man. "But this kind of thing. . . instead of going to my father with it, why didn't you come to me? We could have done. . ."

"Done what? What do you imagine we could have done? I am older than you, and know about such things. I know that when relations between husband and wife turn out this way, the only thing to do is split – split up at once!"

Antonio closed his eyes and rested his brow on the palm of one hand, forcing his faultless eyebrows upwards and revealing in full the delicate tissue of his eyelids.

Then he raised his head.

"At once?" he queried. "But November is six months ago! What made you wait so long, if you already knew?"

For the first time, the notary's face betrayed a flash of discomposure.

"True," he replied. "Six months have passed. That is true. I cannot deny it. But I first had to make sure... to talk to Barbara..."

"Do you mean to say," cried Antonio, "that for the last six months you've been talking to Barbara – about *this* – behind my back?"

"Wait a moment!" cut in the notary, re-injecting the stern quality into his voice. "'Talking to Barbara' is not exactly a precise way of putting it. We attempted to speak to her, we attempted to persuade her, we..."

"Persuade her to what?"

The notary narrowed his eyes, as one taking good aim before delivering his broadside. "To persuade her," he said, "to think of herself as what she actually is: a virgin who never married anyone!"

"In heaven's name!" cried Antonio. "Are you out to create a scandal? To set everyone gossiping about me, about her...?"

"We are in the hands of the Almighty," replied the notary.

"No, no, I beg of you!" Antonio burst out. "Think, before you act! Consider the dreadful consequences!"

"Is there anything all that satisfactory in the present state of affairs?"

Antonio bowed his head, but after a moment's thought he looked up. "Neither you nor I should be judge in this matter," he said. "Only Barbara."

"Barbara is a young woman of good judgement."

"What are you implying?"

"I simply say that Barbara is a young woman of good judgement. She will judge wisely!"

"But... does Barbara know you were going to discuss this with me today?"

"Antonio, it was you who called on me!"

"Then does she know that today you were going to discuss it with my father?"

"I am of the opinion she does not."

"Does she know or doesn't she?"

"I am of the opinion she does not!"

Antonio realized that he was up against a brick wall. He hesitated a fraction of a second, then thrust aside his father-in-law, who was blocking the doorway, flung out into the corridor without giving the other so much as a nod, stalked through the office filled with hands raised in amazement, clumsily tore aside the heavy curtain, and gained the street.

He had to talk to Barbara! Now! Not a moment to be lost!

He re-did the length of Via Etnea, barging into the hundred sun-baked backs of persons stopping for a word every other second, whipped round into Piazza Stesicoro, bounded into the doorway of Palazzo Puglisi, and flew up the staircase with a din as of someone tumbling down it.

He found Barbara in the bedroom, ensconced in an armchair with a piece of crochet-work on her lap. The moment he saw her, a bitterly ironic notion occurred to him, one which he himself was bound to bear the brunt of: a young wife preparing little things for her firstborn.

Daunted by these freakish ambiguities and allusions coming at him from all sides, and in need of some miraculous support, Antonio raised his eyes to the wall where hung a picture of the Madonna... But there too a thought of similar stamp awaited him, though gilded, perhaps, with some measure of comfort – the Madonna had borne her Son without having recourse to that act...

He sat himself down on the floor at his wife's feet, and "Barbara," he said, "my darling Barbara..."

He squeezed her shapely hand and felt, as ever, the most fervid emotion, compounded of desperate fantasies and longings for a pleasure that no one in real life has ever tasted.

His wife reddened, colour gushing into her cheeks like blood from a severed artery, and spreading in waves over her forehead, into her hair, behind her ears.

"Barbara!" cried Antonio. "Why are you blushing so?"

"I'm sorry," she said, as a more crimson tide than ever swept across her cheeks. "I'm sorry... I just can't help it!"

He looked up at her, carried away by the wondrous beauty of that lustre of blushes, and sorely wounded by the thoughts he imagined to be at work behind such tides of blood.

He pulled himself to his knees and grasped his wife by the arms.

"Barbara," he said. "Something really serious happened this morning. Do you know about it?"

Her blushes ceased, she seemed on the point of fainting. Then looking her husband straight in the face she answered: "Yes."

"Yes?" he said. "You're telling me you do? You know that your father called on mine this morning?"

"Yes. I know."

"Since when?"

"They told me afterwards."

"Heavens! Are you telling me your father took such a momentous step without consulting you?"

She set herself frantically to pick up the stitch she had dropped in her crochet, and said nothing.

"Barbara," pursued Antonio, tilting up her chin with his fingertips, "Barbara, tell me the truth. Do you approve of what your father did? Come on, give me an answer! Do you?"

She remained silent for a full minute, letting her chin rest on Antonio's hand, her eyes cast down. Then, "Yes!" she said.

Antonio leapt up. "You approve?" he demanded, horror-struck. "You think he did right?"

Faced with the wordless silence of his wife, a silence he dared not think about, a silence that cut him a blow across the face and tore at his flesh, he covered his eyes with a hand and murmured, "Oh, God in heaven, the shame of it! The shame of it."

Barbara, in silence, took up her crochet-work again, an almost imperceptible tremor on her set lips.

"But Barbara," Antonio went on, "why is it that suddenly, after three years of marriage and for no apparent reason, you and your parents decide..."

"Antonio, you're being unfair," broke in Barbara, pulling herself together. "You know perfectly well that it was only last November that I learnt from that woman..."

And she lowered her head in such a way as to cause several locks of hair to mask her face and her blushes.

Antonio gulped, then said, "Perfectly true. But even after that, didn't we vow to each other to live together and love each other all the same, even more so in fact?... How often have you told me you were happier that way than... and that God's blessing was on our house in which we didn't..."

"But now," said Barbara, twisting thread around the fingers of her left hand, "I have learnt that the Church does not bless our house!"

"But why?" cried Antonio. "What harm do we do to a soul?"

"We do no harm to anyone, but our marriage does not exist in the sight of God!"

"And how long have you known that our marriage 'does not exist in the sight of God'?"

"For some little while."

"How long? I insist on knowing exactly!"

Barbara hesitated. Then she said: "Since it was explained to me by the Archbishop."

"What!" blabbered Antonio, left almost speechless. "You mean you've been talking about these things even with the Archbishop? So you've all been discussing me. You've thrown me to the town dogs, eh?... And while I," he added, a tremor in his voice, "was living with you in complete trust... and you seemed so happy and so tender towards me. But as soon as I turned my back you all rushed off, did you, to prattle to priests and archbishops?"

"It only happened a week ago!" broke in Barbara. "Only a week!"

"But how did it happen? And why? What was so special about a week ago?"

"I don't know what was special about a week ago, but my dear Antonio I have my duties as a daughter, as well as those of a wife, and I had to obey my father!"

"I see. So it was your father who took you a week ago to see the Archbishop?"

"Yes."

"And why, such an upright man, does he begin to concern himself with our affairs only a week ago, when he had known since November?"

"Antonio," said she irritably, "are you criticizing him for what he did, or for being so hesitant in doing it?"

"I'm not criticizing him at all, but no one can convince me that he hasn't got some secret scheme up his sleeve for you."

"I have no idea what schemes my father may have for me, but in any case they could never be other than honest and affectionate. My father is a man of principle, who goes to confession and takes Holy Communion far more often than you do, Antonio. And my duty is to obey him."

"Barbara," he shouted "look me in the eyes!... You know the truth, Barbara!"

"I know nothing," she replied – and her face ceased its spasms of blushing and paling, taking on that severe and lofty inscrutability which made the Puglisi clan, terrifying when they spoke, more terrifying still when they were silent.

"So Barbara," continued Antonio, a pleading note in his voice as he sat down again at his wife's feet, "so what's become of all the love you once had for me?"

"I do still love you," said Barbara gently, "but no longer as a wife loves her husband!"

"Why this 'no longer'?..."

"Because we are *not* man and wife!"

"Since when aren't we man and wife?"

"Oh, Antonio, we never have been... And I didn't know... But now I do!"

"And this is the reason why you can't love me any more?"

"But I do, I do! I do love you – how can I explain? – I do love you, but no longer as your wife. It's... another kind of fondness," she insisted, tearful-eyed.

"I don't know what kind of fondness you're on about," said Antonio, "but I certainly know that no one could do me down more foully than you're out to!"

"An even fouler thing, Antonio, would be for a man and a woman to go on living together without being properly married!... Don't you realize," she went on in a queer sort of voice, "that since they explained it all to me I haven't been able to be with you without blushing scarlet?"

"But we're not doing any harm by being together."

"Indeed, we are doing nothing, and that's what makes me blush so!"

"We can sleep in separate beds... split up and live in two different rooms!"

She shook her head.

"In separate flats..."

She shook her head.

"If you want, I'll leave. I'll pretend to be going on a trip, then never come back... I'll go and work in Africa... I'll stay there for the rest of my life!"

"And wouldn't that make matters worse, Antonio?"

"No, it wouldn't. Nothing could be worse than what they're cooking up for me!... Listen!" he added, in the voice of one who has found some unhoped-for lifeline: "We'll go to America and get a divorce."

"No!" she replied firmly. "I am a Catholic, and would never get divorced, not even if you'd murdered our child!..." She bit her lip and blushed again, realizing that she had stupidly stumbled upon one of the half-dozen words she had sworn to herself never to utter in her husband's hearing. "My dear," she went on, passing a hand across her eyes, "ask what you like of me, except things that go against my conscience."

"But if our marriage is judged to be null and void by the Church," said Antonio, "well then, why not think of it the same way ourselves? I'll go off and live in the back of beyond, we'll be living apart, we won't see each other – or else from time to time we'll meet like two strangers... And it'll all be all right!"

"No," she said. "You know as well as I do that that's not enough!"

"Not enough?" gasped Antonio. "Is there more to come?"

"We have to confess our error to the Church, and the Church will rectify it."

"*Rectify* it? How?"

"By annulling the marriage contract with which we virtually swindled the Church!" burst in impetuous the voice of the mother-in-law from between the curtains of the dressing-room.

Signora Agatina made her appearance clad in a flourish of plumes and furs, feathers, fineries and gauzy veils, with a rustling of silks between her hefty knees and at the armpits, while plumes and featherages merged and parted by turns, casting upon her shoulders, her bosom, her countenance itself, their sheen and shadow.

Antonio shot to his feet and took a few steps backwards, shedding fearful glances at another couple of doors which might at any moment exude further figures.

"Were you in there eavesdropping on us?" mumbled Antonio.

"Not eavesdropping," replied that lady, tartly. "I just happened to be in the dressing-room, fetching myself a looking-glass, and I happened to overhear..."

"It was wrong of you to listen, Mamma!" cried Barbara, rising to her feet in turn. "You ought not to have listened! Really you ought not..."

And having thus delivered herself, she burst into tears and hid her eyes in the crook of her right arm.

It was a minute or two before anyone spoke. Antonio followed each of Barbara's sobs, accompanying it with a motion of his lips, as we do when carried away by the words of a speaker who convinces, persuades, and has our entirest approbation.

The mother-in-law kept her eyes on Barbara, but turned her face towards Antonio, so that in that indicative swivel of the eyes he could read the thought in her bosom: "Now just look what you've done!"

Suddenly Barbara burst out, "I can't stand it! I can't stand it any longer!" And hurling her work and crochet-hook onto the double bed, she left the room head bowed, still sobbing.

Antonio and the elder lady heard, throughout the length of corridors and chambers, those retreating sobs, recalling for both of them the silvery tones of the girl.

Then the mother-in-law spoke, and said: "As you plainly see, things cannot go on like this!"

Antonio made no reply. He was quite at a loss; the ebbing of his strength left him with a sense of being entirely soothed and coddled. His face, reflected in the circular mirror on the wash-stand, and in the square one on the wardrobe door, exuded sensitivity; and on his lips there appeared to hover words such as even to a noble spirit it is given but once in a lifetime to pronounce.

Signora Agatina could not restrain herself from seizing one of his hands and clasping it to her bosom.

"Dear boy," she said. "You must not lose heart. You're still so young."

And, more taken with him than ever, she wrapped her fur-draped arms around him and hugged him with intensity, resting her cheek against his.

"My dear boy!" she repeated. "My dear Antonio!"

"But... but..." mumbled the young man, lacking so much

as the breath to puff away the monosyllable that seemed glued to his lips, "but..."

"Speak up, dear boy, tell me all! You can say what you like to me!" urged Signora Agatina, hugging him still tighter. "I'm an old woman... I've seen a bit in my time! You needn't be afraid of telling me..."

"All I wish to know," continued Antonio in a voice so faint that the lady was obliged to draw very close to his lovely, parched lips to read his words.

"Come now, tell me! What do you wish to know?" asked the lady, also in a hushful whisper and almost mouth to mouth.

"What I want to know is why your husband the notary has for seven months been pretending ignorance about all this, and then suddenly, without first coming to me to hear... to find out... makes up his mind to talk Barbara over, makes her discuss it with the Archbishop, and then goes off to my poor old dad..."

"Ah me, Antonio," sighed the mother-in-law, again pressing her cheek upon his. "Antonio, my love, you have to *understand*!"

"But understand what? I'm prepared to throw myself on my knees before your husband and before Barbara herself, if without meaning to I've given them offence."

"No dear, no no, my love, that's absolutely unnecessary! Why should a young man of your stamp go on his knees before anyone? He mustn't kneel to a single soul in this world, my lovelier than the sun itself, my own Antonio! With you and Barbara, the will of God was not favourably disposed. So be it! This can only mean it was writ in heaven that you should marry another! The behests of heaven are known only in heaven, and when a marriage is not written in that Book, it's of no avail for us poor wretches to scribble our names side by side in the parish register... Such a marriage stays only there on paper!... Have patience, my lovely boy! You are both young. Life hasn't even begun for you yet. Just you see, you will find your real, true spouse, the one the good Lord has destined for you; and Barbara, she too... I scarcely think you'd like her to be left a spinster!... She too has her rights... No harm done if she too finds the mate destined for her by the Lord!''

The conversation had proceeded in tones so hushed and low that a slight movement of the lady, provoking a rustle of silks, more than sufficed to drown her last few words.

"Is Barbara likely to be married soon? Who to?" enquired Antonio, with a mildness that matched the grief he felt able to hold at bay thanks to the torpor so entirely overwhelming him.

"You'll never guess who's fallen in love with her," purred the mother-in-law enveloped, she too, by a peculiar sensation – it may be by a dream of pleasure that caused her tongue to wag. "And so madly in love that he'd tear himself to pieces for her and relinquish all his billions? The Duca Di Bronte!''

"Ah, the Duca Di Bronte? Him, eh?" said Antonio in a low, slow voice, adding: "But isn't he already married?"

"His brother the prince is married, but not the duke!"

"I thought I'd heard it's a tradition in that family for only the eldest son to marry."

"So it is. But this time the eldest son is childless, so they are allowing the younger son to get married."

"Ah well, so it's the Duca Di Bronte, eh?" said Antonio huskily. "But he's so fat!... Or so it seems to me... Could I be wrong?"

"He's been to Paris and done a slimming cure. Cost him a packet!... And you, sweet boy, who would you marry, if you had your choice?"

"What, me? Oh, leave me out of it!"

"How d'you mean, out of it? Tragedies happen once in a lifetime, not over and over again."

"No, no, me... leave me out!"

"Love of my life, why so?"

"Leave me out, leave me out!"

And thus saying, his thread of a voice by now reduced to a

113

faint murmur – such as persons of inflamed imagination fancy they hear by gravesides – and his face having acquired an almost lustrous pallor, Antonio closed his eyes and swooned away.

"Caterina! Graziella!" shrieked the mother-in-law, as she felt the young man's whole weight slump into her arms. "Caterina! Graziella! Come quick as you can!"

And meanwhile, having hauled Antonio to the bedside, and laid him athwart it as best she could, she hastily straightened up, under the impression (or was it a dream?) that she had kissed him, and more than once, full on the mouth.

VII

COMING ROUND FROM HIS SWOON, Antonio had no wish to stay another minute under his father-in-law's roof, and ran for cover in Via Pacini with his parents. There he shut himself up in his room and for three days remained alone, allowing admittance only to his mother, who had the goodness to sit at his bedside watching in silence as he slept, and smiling from time to time should his eyes be half open.

After these three days he began to venture into other rooms and passages, but by no means all; and as he absolutely refused to set eyes on the maid these sorties of his were frequently preceded by shouts from Signor Alfio and Signora Rosaria: "Rosina, go into the lavatory and lock the door! Don't come out until I tell you!" He consented to see his father, but only if his mother was present, never alone; he took good care to keep well away from the windows in case he should be spotted by the neighbours: above all he feared the barbed glare of the Spinster Ardizzone, whose head he imagined sticking out from the wall of the house opposite like that of a harpy; and when darkness fell, before turning the switch of his bedside lamp he would dispatch his mother to close the shutters securely. Likewise, he gave door-handles a rattle before opening them, because whenever he padded silently in his slippers from one room to another he always stumbled on his father in the act of beating himself on the temples – though checking his fists an instant before impact – or on his mother pressing a handker-chief to her mouth, and sighing into it her spasmodic sobs.

Friends (even Edoardo, who every morning sent round a

municipal policeman with a bag of fresh fish), were told that Antonio had gone down with measles, a serious illness for a grown-up, and dangerous for Barbara and her family, who had not had it in childhood; consequently he had been conveyed to his father's, and would not be receiving anyone until he had completely recovered. . .

'I want a promise from you,' said Signor Alfio to Notary Puglisi, "that by the love you bear your daughter neither you nor any of your family will for the coming fortnight let out the least hint as to what has occurred!"

"You have my word," returned the other.

"Remember, sir, that an ox is judged by his horns and a man by his word."

"We Puglisi have always been gentlemen, and known where our duty lay. For a fortnight it shall be done: we shall not even go to confession, and our tongues will not know the sufferings of our hearts!"

But the fortnight was fleeting by and Signor Alfio had as yet not been able to steel himself for a heart-to-heart with his son. Time and again he passed to and fro along the corridor outside Antonio's door; sometimes he rubbed a fumbling hand across it; but when it came to knocking he would find himself, knuckles poised, waiting expectantly for his wife to come hurrying out of the living-room crying, "Alfio, what are you doing? Leave the boy in peace! Haven't you noticed how thin he's got?" And should it happen that his wife did not come hurrying out he slowly lowered his fist and began pacing up and down again.

But just before the two weeks ran out, he took his courage in both hands and, bursting open the door, entered.

"You've got to tell me just this one thing!" he said without preamble, making full use of the modicum of resolution that spurred him on: "Is Barbara the same as every other woman, or has she got some defect?"

"What defect could she possibly have, Alfietto! We women are all made in the same way," put in Signora Rosaria who, on seeing her husband enter Antonio's room had bustled along from the living-room and set the door ajar.

"Silence, you!" roared Signor Alfio. "Let me talk to my son!"

And he pushed his wife from the room, half following her out into the passage to make sure she really went away. Then he came back and locked the door.

Antonio had leapt from the bed on which he'd been lying prone, and gone to rest his brow against the window-pane, though shielding himself from view with the lace curtain.

"Well then?" demanded Signor Alfio.

"No, dad," answered Antonio, without turning. "Barbara has no defect."

"Then in God's name, why?... I'm going round the bend!"

Antonio answered nothing.

"Did you do it on purpose perhaps? Did you deliberately not..."

Silence. The nape of Antonio's neck, waxy beneath the back hair now grown long, but none the less bewitching for all that, stirred no more than that of one asleep; but into a fold of the lace curtain fell a drop of blood from a bitten lip.

"Yes," he groaned out. "I did it on purpose."

"Enough! That's all I want to know!" yelled Signor Alfio, leaping from his seat. "Not a word more! I've got it. All I want to know! God be praised! I've got it, I've got it, all I want to know!"

Then Antonio did turn, longing to eat his words and to put things right, but his father, flourishing his hands on high, had already left the room.

"Ah, sweet Jesus!" exclaimed the old man, making at the top of his speed for the living-room. "I told you so... He made up his mind not to... And he'll have had his own good reasons. That we can find out later... But it's taken a load off my mind... Now just watch me settle the hash of that billy-goat-bearded scrivener!"

"What's happened Alfio?" asked his wife, full of apprehension.

"What's happened is that my son has restored me to life, that's all... God's bones! Come here and dial that awful number for me, the one with One-Seven in front."

"What on earth are you up to?"

"I want you to dial the number with that foul One-Seven in front!"

Signora Rosaria put on two pairs of spectacles, one on top of the other, and dialled Notary Puglisi's number.

"Hullo, is that you?" demanded Signor Alfio into the instrument. "Listen to me then, there's something that simply must be done!... Yes, yes, it's me, Alfio Magnano speaking... Listen here... There's something that must be done, by the three of us, you, me, and my son... go to some woman... wherever you please... even a brothel... and you'll stand there and watch the whole proceedings from beginning to end!... Eh? What'll you have to watch?... Why, my son's performance!"

"But Alfio, Alfio!" cried his wife, stretching out her hands in an effort to stop him.

"You are mad," replied the notary witheringly from the other end of the line. "Therefore to hell with you!"

"Mad? Not a bit. Don't try and pull that one on me! And get this well into your thick skull: that before spreading your iniquitous insinuations you're going to come along with me and my son, whether you like it or not, because otherwise, old as I am, I'll haul you there by that beard of yours and rub your nose you know where!"

"The day after tomorrow," replied the notary in tones of ice, "the matter will be out of our hands and in those of our lawyers."

"No!" bawled Signor Alfio, his eyes bulging fit to burst. "First you must see for yourself!... at the whatsit... at the brothel! I'll haul you there by the snout!..."

"Dad, dad!" came a cry at this point. "Dad, what ever are you up to?"

Antonio, who had overheard the end of the sentence, wrenched the receiver from his father's hand and banged it back on the apparatus where, sizzling like a red-hot ember in water, the notary's reply was quenched.

"Dad, do you want to be the death of me?"

"No, no, it's me, it's me I want dead!" burst out the old man, collapsing into a chair and fanning himself with one hand. "Bring me a drop of whatsit... yes... water!"

The following day Signora Rosaria went off to pray in the little church of the Madonna in Via Sant'Euplio.

While she was kneeling before the altar of Santa Rita, a voice said, "I know all too well what is going on in this poor head."

And the hand of a young priest was laid lightly on the grey plaits knotted at the nape and held in place by countless almost invisible hairpins.

It was Father Raffaele, Signora Rosaria's new confessor, who had stepped into Father Giovanni's shoes since the latter's heart had abruptly stopped while he was contorting himself with rage during a sermon on the misdeeds of certain "damned souls" – whom some Fascist spies kneeling in the congregation, heads bowed, assumed to be the Nazis.

"Father Raffaele," quavered Signora Rosaria, turning on him the eyes of a frightened child, "then you *know*?..."

The priest took her by the elbows and assisted her to her feet. "I know, alas, I know..."

"But whoever could have imagined such a terrible misfortune?"

The priest smiled ruefully.

"Can it be true," she went on, casting terrified glances one after another at the saints looking down at her from niche and chapel; "can it be true that the Church is really against us?"

"What are you saying!" murmured the youthful priest paternally. "The Church stands for truth and justice."

She looked searchingly into his face, in an effort to understand why the young man's eyes were so mild and reassuring, while his words were so abstruse.

"What about Barbara?" she asked. "You know your Barbara. What's your own judgement of that blessed girl?"

"I cannot judge her. A pastor's duty is to guide his flock, not to judge them. But I have to confess that. . ."

"That?. . ." Signora Rosaria egged him on.

"That I have found in her a hardened heart."

"Father," begged the poor lady, tortured by her incapacity to grasp the meaning of a man in whom she must repose so much trust. "What do you mean by 'hardened'?"

"I mean," replied the priest, tortured in turn by the impossibility of using the words which sprang most readily to his lips, "I mean a heart created by God to perplex us poor priests, a heart impossible to make head or tail of! All her mental attitudes are in order, and we can only approve and admire them. But all the same," he continued, turning suddenly scarlet with a rush of true peasant blood, "all the same, if you want to know my feelings, and not my judgement, that girl. . ." – and here his voice rose almost to a screech – "I wouldn't allow her into church even in her coffin!"

The young priest's face had lost its habitual tint, the wan hue of a tired man living in twilight. His endless meditations and studies fled from his cheeks, which lost their hollow look as true Sicilian anger blazed darkly in his wide-spaced, slightly squinting eyes.

"That girl's heart is like the octopus," he went on. "The longer you cook it the tougher it gets. The more you talk to her the less you convince her, and in matters of religion she knows more than the devil himself! Shall I tell you what she told me? – not in confession, of course, because in that case my lips would be sealed. . . She told me that ever since they explained to her that the Church considers her marriage null and void, she has no longer permitted herself to love a man who is not her husband! Can you beat it! She no longer permits herself... It's a convenient heart to have, hers is (God forgive me, tomorrow I'll make confession myself). It's so constructed as to make suffering impossible for her, except with full advantage to herself and satisfaction to her parents. And never, never will she run the risk of losing either her head or a brass farthing!"

The priest's rage threw Signora Rosaria into ecstasies. Though she did not understand every word, she had no doubt about the general drift.

"Father," she asked. "D'you think it would be possible for me to have a word with that dratted girl?"

"Do so, if you want. But you'll be wasting your breath. Her nostrils are already quivering with the scent of money."

"Scent of money? What ever do you mean?" muttered Signora Rosaria, the happiness that had put new heart into her swiftly slipping away.

"I mean the scent of money! The Duca Di Bronte, who is to be Barbara's husband when her marriage to your son has been annulled, possesses three hundred million!... Now watch this coincidence: the moment this gentleman expresses his regret at not having married a down-to-earth girl like Barbara, her father happens to meet the Archbishop and, after considerably beating about the bush, asks his advice on how he should conduct himself regarding his son-in-law *vis-à-vis* his daughter..."

"But for seven months!..."

"Indeed, for seven months he had known how things stood between Antonio and Barbara but, as it happened, during those seven months he never came across the Archbishop! 'But,' you may say, 'did he not have *you*, the humble parish priests? And in his own house did he not have a Dominican with a whopping great cordon round his waist?' Ah, my dear lady, you are really ingenuous! It needed an Archbishop, if not the Supreme

Pontiff in person, to unseal the lips of a Notary Puglisi on a matter of such delicacy!"

"But Father, do you think this marriage will definitely be annulled?"

"I'm afraid so, dear lady. Cherish no false hopes on that score. If matters stand as they're said to stand, the marriage will be annulled."

Signora Rosaria began to weep quietly: "Just think, Father! My Antonio... Father Giovanni used to see him come into church of a Sunday and give him a nasty look, because all the women's heads swivelled over their shoulders and stayed that way... My Antonio, Father, who when he was in Rome committed so many of those sins which young men are bound to commit!... Sometimes I beat myself about the head when I think that the Lord took me literally when I prayed to him to calm my son down and make him less of a lady-killer. 'Calm him down, you ask?' replied the Lord. 'Right then, I'll cool him off good and proper!' Father, do you think the Lord wished to punish me by sending us this shame?"

"But it is far from being shame, Signora Rosaria!"

"Oh, it *is* shame, it *is* shame!... Believe me, it *is* shame! Why, even the Church puts us in the wrong, and the Archbishop – forgetting all the favours my husband has done him – is all for Barbara and against my Antonio!"

"Oh, dear God, how can I make you understand!" exclaimed the priest, giving a vigorous wipe to his forehead with the back of his hand. "The Church puts no one in the wrong. It simply annuls the marriage."

"*Simply*, Father? The Church simply annuls the marriage, does it? It does the bidding of Barbara, of the notary, of the Duca Di Bronte. If it didn't mean to put us in the wrong it would do what *we* want, it wouldn't annul the marriage. No, Father, no... God has seen fit to chastise me because I (better my tongue had fallen out!) have prayed to Him all too often to cool my son's passions. I see now that a mother should never pray such a prayer even in her sleep, that she should

leave her sons to go their own way, to sow their wild oats. . .
But it was Father Giovanni (God rest his soul!), Father Giovanni himself, who struck terror into my heart by saying, 'If
your son goes on this way he will create havoc in Mother
Church, and the Church will take stern measures with him.'
Next thing that happens, my son becomes a perfect angel,
behaves like a little angel descended from heaven, the living
image of St Joseph with the Blessed Virgin. And the Church
takes stern measures with him all the same – worse than stern,
in fact! – and is prepared to do something that will at any
moment take our whole family and rub our noses in the dirt!
What has the Church got against my son? What harm has he
done it? What harm have any of us done?"

"What a muddle in this poor head!" murmured the priest,
patting her greying hairs and thoroughly discouraged. "How
can I ever explain?"

"But Father, aren't I right? Aren't I making sense? I admit I
made too much fuss when I realized that other women fancied
my son. But who should we expect to take a fancy to a boy,
eh?, if not the women. . . Silly fool that I was, instead of
moaning and groaning why didn't I thank the Lord with all
my heart for having granted me a son so beautiful that the girls
tore him to shreds with their eyes? . . . And look at me now,
no one to help me – not even you, Padre Raffaele!"

"No, Signora, you are unjust," said the priest. "I am prepared to kiss your son's feet, if you wish, sinner that I am."
And he thought of how, many an afternoon, after attempting
to keep his passions cool as the dew with a diet of milk and
chicory, he had been thrown into a state of fever by the image
of this same Barbara. . . whom perhaps, for this reason
amongst others, he condemned too severely. . .

"It's Barbara who ought to kiss my son's feet," declared
Signora Rosaria. "Not you, Father Raffaele! That Barbara has
cut us to the quick with poisoned steel. . . Father," she added
after a pause, "this favour you must do me and don't say no!"

"What favour, Signora? Tell me."

"Arrange for me to have a talk with my daughter-in-law. But not at the house of that sly lot! Here in church in the sight of the Lord Jesus!"

"It shall be done, dear friend. Come at five o'clock on Saturday afternoon, and I will see to it that you meet your daughter-in-law."

Two days later, at five o'clock precisely, Signora Rosaria returned to the church of the Madonna in Via Sant'Euplio.

As she entered, who should rise from the grille of the confessional but Don Luigino Compagnoni, a man who in his youth had terrorized the surrounding countryside with acts of brigandage. (Five girls had, through his agency, lost their innocence beneath a tree in no more time than it takes to say knife). But what sweet mildness now, in those eyes of his! What respect for modest middle-class customs in his mode of dress! Not for many a day had Signora Rosaria received so comforting and sympathetic a greeting as she was accorded in the middle of the church by this gallant bandit, who bowed to her deferentially while his right hand made the gesture of sweeping off the hat he was actually holding in his left.

Passing abruptly from the gentle eyes of the repentant bandit to the glacial ones of Barbara, whom she found kneeling before the chapel of Santa Rita, Signora Rosaria felt her hands trembling. Was it anger or fright?

"Good afternoon," she said faintly.

"Give me your blessing," replied Barbara.

The two women knelt side by side in silence, each making a show of reading in her missal.

"Shall we go into the sacristy?" said Barbara after a while, deftly crossing herself.

"As you wish," replied Signora Rosaria.

In a cubby hole in the sacristy, from which Father Raffaele made a soundless exit, Barbara and Signora Rosaria stood for a moment face to face with lowered eyes.

All of a sudden Barbara threw herself at the elder woman's feet, clasped her round the knees, and wept.

Signora Rosaria made an attempt to stroke her hair, but her hands kept jerking away, they were shaking so much.

Barbara's sobs started quietly, then grew in strength and frequency; they were swelled by a kind of inchoate cry, which turned into a tumble of words and sobs, sobs that sent the words spinning, overwhelmed them, crushed them.

What Signora Rosaria thought she heard was, "Forgive me! I beg your son to forgive me for the harm I have done him! I must make amends at once!"

Signora Rosaria felt a softening of the heart and pressing Barbara's head more firmly to her knees, began to comfort her.

"There, there," she said. "Enough of that. Pull yourself together, my dear..."

But imagine that lady's consternation when Barbara, having indeed pulled herself somewhat together, and one by one disentangled her words from her snuffles, repeated her tear-strangled statement after this manner: "Forgiveness, forgiveness is what Antonio must beg of me, for the harm he has done me, and he must make amends at once!"

Woe and alas, were all those tears, then, nothing but the tears of self-pity?

Signora Rosaria simply gaped, unable to fetch out a single word from a bosom dumbstruck with horror, but at last a burst of anger thrust half-a-dozen words into her mouth:

"Say that again, if you please!"

Barbara did not think it necessary to repeat the sentence which she had just pronounced all too clearly.

"But how has Antonio harmed you?" pursued the poor old lady. "What wrong has he done you?"

"Signora Rosaria," said Barbara, hiding her face in the lady's black skirts, "when I married Antonio, and I swear it here in the sight of God, the head I had on my shoulders was the head of a three-year-old. If I had died that day – the Lord should have taken me! Oh, would he had taken me then! – I'd have gone straightway to Paradise! Every word from Antonio's lips was for me the truth and the law. In heaven, God! On earth, Antonio! That was my religion... I loved him as I love my own soul! And I thought he too loved..."

"What are you saying? Wasn't it true?"

"No. It was not true!"

Barbara began to snivel again, but very quietly, almost to herself.

"I am no longer the three-year-old girl who trusted in Antonio's every word as in those of the Gospel," she continued. "I have now found out!"

"But... what have you found out?"

"What any married woman ought to know."

"But child, explain yourself. Don't leave me in agony!"

"Antonio never loved me. He slighted me from the very start."

"But... if his eyes lit up whenever he looked at you?"

"True. He was kind and affectionate. He couldn't sleep without holding me in his arms..."

"You see, you see? You were his treasure, his all-in-all!"

After a pause:

"He slighted me!" repeated Barbara sharply.

"Until you have explained to me why he slighted you, I shall conclude that you are just making excuses!"

"Excuses?" exclaimed Barbara, her eyes hardening. "Did you say *excuses*? Then why did he treat me like a log of wood? Do you think he ever treated *other* women that way?"

Signora Rosaria's mouth drooped. "Barbara," she said, "you are still a babe in arms. You think you know it all, but you've a long way to travel before you understand life. What has happened to Antonio is sheer bad luck, simply a bit of bad luck, dear child. It could happen to anyone."

"I know that too," replied Barbara, still on her knees but straight-backed now. "I know that such a misfortune can happen to a man."

"And you know when it happens?"

"Yes, I know."

126

"It happens when he is head-over-heels in love with someone, when his emotions are too strong... when he thinks that
person is an angel from heaven..."

"Yes, I know... But that could happen for a day or two...
it could happen for a month! But with calm, and confidence,
and seeing that his wife is a flesh-and-blood woman like every
other, he gets over this... this bit of bad luck."

"What if a young man never loses the feeling that his wife
is an angel from heaven, and his heart never ceases to..."

"Leave his heart out of it! In the early days, I do admit, I
heard his heart beat on my pillow and even shake the bedhead.
But later on, not even on the side where his heart lies, when
at night he was clasping my hand to his breast..."

"You see, you see!" interrupted Signora Rosaria, in tears.
"Don't you see how much he loved you? He slept with your
hand clasped to his breast, as he did mine when he was a little
child! Because when you come down to it he's still a child..."

Barbara threw up her chin with an air of irritation and almost
of exasperation.

"Possibly," she said. "But when he used to sleep with your
hand clasped to his heart, mother dear, that meant that he loved
you. When he slept clasping *my* hand, it meant something quite
different – that for him I might have been a log of wood!"

"Off you go again with this log-of-wood business!" exclaimed her mother-in-law with some asperity. "Really, Barbara... here we are, two married women, and you've got a
few years behind you, you're no chicken. I had a son of twelve
when I was your age."

"If I am childless," said Barbara in high dudgeon, "it is no
fault of mine!"

"Now then, young lady! Kindly mind your p's and q's! I'm
good-hearted and gentle, but that sort of talk, with the poison
of the Puglisi in it, doesn't go down with me... Just a glance
at you and I can count the money in your purse!"

Barbara rose to her feet.

"Now then, young lady," said Signora Rosaria, "don't think

you'll make any impression on me! You may stand up, sit down, lie on your back or stand on your head for all I care. Such goings-on leave me absolutely cold. But here we stay until we've put a finger on the truth!"

"Well let me tell you..." began Barbara, in a rage.

"Pull yourself together," interrupted the elder woman. "For your own sake you'd do better to control yourself... I mean to have first say, and I'll start by telling you that I refuse to listen to that rigmarole about Antonio slighting you. No, no, young madam! You Puglisi can't pull that one on me – I can read what's going on in your heads before you have time to turn round... I know your lot inside and out, so just you drop all this carry-on about slights. You know as well as I do that Antonio doesn't slight you, because he has no earthly reason to slight you. In fact he loves you like the very heart in his body. Ask me how I know it? I only have to hear his footsteps coming and I know what he's thinking. And ask me how long I've understood him for? For ever! Since he was a little child, and I only had to hear him turn over in his sleep to know what he was dreaming about. So this business of his slighting you – just you leave it be. What reason has he?... Tell me that!... You're as lovely as a rose, you've got health and to spare, green eyes, jet-black hair, skin as white as snow... in short, Antonio's dish with all the trimmings!"

"Possibly, but..."

"Possibly nothing! Our boy had a bit of bad luck, that's all. God has not willed..."

"And if God doesn't will..." interrupted the girl.

"Hold your horses, my fine lady! Let me finish... God has not so willed, up until today. But tomorrow, who knows? Don't leap before you look! Things weren't so awful that they couldn't wait a little longer."

"What good would waiting do?"

"How do you mean, what good? Something that doesn't happen today might happen tomorrow. Antonio's a young fellow any woman alive would be glad to have after her...

This time the devil's put a halter round his neck, but so what? Ropes can break. You could have waited, my sainted girl! You had all the time in the world."

"Signora Rosaria," said Barbara coldly, "I don't like the turn this conversation is taking. I had hoped that you, informed of how I have suffered these last three years, were here to offer me comfort."

"Come now, Barbara, suffered?" cried her mother-in-law. "You come here telling *me* things like that? Exactly what *have* you suffered? One can very well get on without that side of things. It doesn't kill you. Three weeks after we were married my husband was called up, and I waited two years for him without a murmur. Who gave a thought to all that? God save us, who on earth gave it a thought?"

Barbara's face burned red, her pupils dilated.

"Well really!" she cried, "the Lord didn't send me into this world to be insulted by the Magnanos! Your son casts me aside like an old rag, then you outrage my feelings... I won't have it!"

"Take it or leave it, my girl. If I don't get everything off my chest I swear I'll have a heart attack!"

"Listen to me then. That side of things you tell me about, I've never even had a whiff of! Until seven months ago I didn't even know such things existed. I've never been the flighty, flirtatious type. As a woman I consider myself just about as cool..."

"Cool, cool, cool!" shrieked Signora Rosaria, also rising to her feet. "That explains everything, and you're saying it yourself! Then you've only yourself to blame if what's happened has happened! I've always thought you were as cold as they come and would put a damper on the lustiest chap alive. So take the blame yourself!"

"*Goodbye*, signora!" snorted Barbara, abruptly turning her back and, having halted a moment at the door to steady her still-quivering lip, turned the handle and disappeared down the passage, at the end of which, opening another door, she issued forth into the nave and was on the instant illumined, from a stained-glass window, by a shaft of multicoloured light. Then she vanished, leaving Signora Rosaria smarting to the very marrow of her bones with the bitterness of one forced by a skilful adversary to act clumsily. Not only bereft of her just redress for the provocation received, but also racked with chagrin.

The poor thing gnawed her handkerchief and wept.

A little later Father Raffaele accompanied her to the church door and, "We shouldn't have been so rash," he said. "No one can get the better of that girl. What she says has the fire of truth and the infernal slickness of cool calculation. She's only sincere when her sentiments are to her advantage. She is, in good faith, unaware of the fact that all her feelings have been well rehearsed."

"Do you remember, Father Raffaele, seven years ago, when you brought me the holy oil because I was at death's door?"

"Dear friend, I remember as if it were yesterday..."

"Well then... while you were giving me Extreme Unction I prayed to Our Lady to grant me this grace: that I should live to see my son a married man. Oh, Father Raffaele, what a foolish prayer! How much better if I were not in this world today!"

"Oh dear lady, how wrong you are! Your son has committed neither theft nor murder. Think of how many poor women are the mothers of thieves and murderers."

"Can't think of any other way to put it, Father Raffaele. I'm losing my faith... I think the Lord never cursed anyone else on earth with a disgrace such as ours!"

"What you say is blasphemous, dear friend. In time you will come to realize that your son is neither a disgrace nor a dishonour. It's all that Barbara's fault!" he added, assailed a second time by resentment against the image of the girl that troubled him all the more brazenly the more cold and spiteful he conceived her to be, until he himself no longer knew whether his was harsh criticism or a way of wooing her...

But he took a hold on himself. "Barbara is what she is," he said softly. "Maybe she's no worse then many others, and she's certainly better than I am, standing here talking like a fool... The important thing is not to mention this to your husband. We men are apt to get up in arms. So goodbye, dear friend, and God be with you!"

But Signora Rosaria could not resist confiding in her husband.

"You did the wrong thing!" said he. "You shouldn't have behaved so openly with her. Now, I've studied how to behave towards the Puglisi. Watch me: like this – compressed lips, like theirs. I've thought up a few frigid little phrases too, and as God is my witness the first of them I happen across I'll freeze his blood for the rest of his born days! We'll see whether Alfio Magnano himself can't play the Jesuit!"

Two days later, in Via Etnea, he came across Barbara's uncle, Father Rosario.

The friar attempted at first to give a wide berth to old Magnano by stopping to gaze into a shop window devoted, as luck would have it, to fashionable lingerie; but he soon realized that it was scarcely seemly for a Dominican to be ogling the corsets and brassieres with which the window was chock-a-block, and, turning abruptly away, he found himself face to face with the very man he wished to avoid. But picture his surprise when, instead of the irascible old rogue he was expecting, he observed an unruffled gentleman who spoke to him through tight, half-smiling lips...

"I am anxious to enquire of you – you who know about such things," said Signor Alfio straight off the bat, "why it is that the Church considers a marriage null and void simply because the husband and wife do not commit carnal acts."

"Ah, dear Signor Alfio, I wash my hands of all that! I assure you I have no wish to get involved in the tangles of the young! They make their beds and they must lie on them. Nothing to do with me, nothing, nothing!"

"I am perfectly aware of that," replied Signor Alfio,

sweating from head to foot with the effort of maintaining his calm. "But I would be grateful for information concerning the question, as you might say, in general, not simply as regards my son. I am very curious to learn how these things work..."

The friar cast a sidelong glance at his interlocutor, and seeing his face as white and tranquil as that of one who a moment since passed serenely away, he shuddered slightly. Such serenity was far from normal in Signor Alfio, and if one of the pair of them was to retain his calm, the friar much preferred to be the one.

"Listen to me, dear friend," he said cordially, "let us speak as Christians and as relatives: I appreciate to the full your grief and indignation."

Signor Alfio suppressed a growl that rose from deep down in his chest, and again succeeded in stamping a tight-lipped smile on his face.

"No no no!" cried the friar, having slunk a glance at him. "I quite understand. You are a father, and your son is the apple of your eye, and rightly so..."

"Get in through that doorway!" exploded Signor Alfio, overwhelmed by an access of wrath that gushed up past his shirt-collar, and set fire to his face. "We can talk there."

They made their way into the damp, deserted courtyard of a well-to-do residence.

"Right, this is what I want to know," demanded Signor Alfio in his usual voice, and permitting his face to contort at its own sweet will: "Just explain me this, will you! Why does the Church annul a marriage simply because the partners do not commit acts of carnality? What does the Church want? Wants them to stick at it day and night, does it?"

Seeing Signor Alfio with foam on his lips the Dominican heaved a sigh of relief and slipped easily into the pristine cool which the other had now abandoned for good and all.

"Matrimony, my dear Signor Alfio, is in all respects a *sacrament*. Indeed, I will go further: it is one of the most solemn of sacraments."

"That's exactly what I'm saying, that it's a sacred thing.

Something that can't be broken from one moment to the next just because the husband (and he'll have had his reasons) decides not to mount his wife."

"I'm sorry you feel it necessary to put it that way. Matrimony is a sacrament. . ."

"Like hell it is!"

"Kindly do not swear, because if you do so I shall feel obliged to take leave of you."

"You'll do nothing of the sort, reverend sir, you'll stay right here! So on we go: marriage is pot luck. . ."

"No, no, no! Marriage is not pot luck! Matrimony is a sacrament! And you know who are the officiants in this sacrament? The bride and groom! The priest merely consecrates, he does not officiate."

"All very well and good. But so what? Where is it writ that the sacrament can be annulled simply because the husband, for reasons of his own, I repeat – not being of a mind to probe further – doesn't make the beast of the two backs with his wife?"

"I *must* beg you not to speak in such terms," exclaimed the friar, losing a fraction of his composure. "What more can I say?. . . I am at a loss. . . Matrimony is composed of two elements, the one spiritual and the other material. . ."

"Very good! Very well and good! But if one party in this marriage decides to make it consist purely and simply in the spiritual side of things – I say this quite hypothetically, since we Magnanos always stay on the job until the cows come home – but be that as it may. . . if one partner, according to his own lights, wishes to make this a purely spiritual communion, what does the Church have to say about that? It ought to be as happy as a sandboy, seeing the way it bores us to death with its sermonizing against the evils of the flesh."

"But in matrimony, Signor Alfio, the material act is as sacred as the spiritual! *Caro una, sanguis unus*. . ."

"Speak plain Christian, Father, and I might be able to follow you."

"*Caro una, sanguis unus*: one flesh and one blood."

"Aha, *now* you come up with that one, now that you've got your eyes on the Duca Di Bronte and all his wealth! But when my son in Rome... and me too, here, until the day before yesterday, made ourselves one flesh and blood with a woman, why did you confessors in your wooden kennels squeak and squeal so loud that anyone'd have thought we were choking the life out of you!"

"But Signor Alfio, you are not even attempting to think straight. You were making *caro una sanguis unus* with women who were not *your* women!"

"Have it your own way, they weren't 'ours', but they came along with us all the same, and were perfectly happy about it. When a man's wife falls ill, or let's say he's a bachelor, where d'you think he finds the flesh to cleave to, if not on the other side of the fence?"

"Dear Signor Alfio, do you know what a man ought to do in such a case? Practise chastity! Are you under the impression that chastity is harmful? On the contrary, it benefits both the health and the intellect! Chastity, sir, is the greatest of the virtues..."

"Bloody hell... You'd squeeze swearwords out of a dumbbell, you would! Now tell me, if chastity is the greatest of the virtues and a man practises it in his own house and home, why do you lay your curse upon him, anathematize him, and annul his marriage?"

"The Lord grant me patience! Matrimony, I repeat, consists of two elements, the one spiritual, or intentional, and the other material. If the consummation of the material act does not take place, it clearly follows that the intention also is invalidated. Increase and multiply and fill the earth, said Our Lord to those who wed..."

"Surely, monks and monsignors, windbags and crows of ill-omen the lot of you, aren't *you* enough to keep the birth-rate on the rise?"

"I would ask you again, Signor Alfio, to moderate your language."

"I shall speak as I please!"

"In that case I shall leave you."

And Father Rosario made a move to go.

"If you shift a peg," bawled Signor Alfio, almost demented, "I'll run after you and show you up in the street!"

"Anything you can say to me, dear friend, is water off a duck's back!"

"What if I shout to all and sundry that the flesh of the Puglisi is sold to the highest bidder?"

At this the friar flew completely off the handle. "You're making the biggest mistake of your life, Signor Alfio!" he yelled, his eyes darting fire.

"No I am not!"

"Yes you are!"

"No!"

"Yes!"

"No!"

"You're pissing away and missing the potty!"

"I'm not missing the potty!"

"Yes you are, you're missing the potty!"

"I'm not missing the potty!"

"Yes, by God, you're pissing away and missing the potty!"

"No, by God, I'm not missing the potty!"

The friar gave two resounding slaps to his cheeks, then two more, and then another couple, to vent and to restrain his wrath, to hit out at someone and to mortify himself. Then, his face buried in his hands, muttering inaudible words and quite possibly shedding tears, he hurried out of the courtyard, turning left.

Signor Alfio made no move to follow him.

VIII

MAGNANO SENIOR lacked the courage to report to his wife what had passed between him and the friar. He spent his days in the living-room watching Signora Rosaria at her mending, and each time she stopped to wipe her spectacles, blurred with unheralded tears, he threw up his hands and brought them down thwack on his knees.

"I'm going out of my mind!" he declared. "The more I think, the more unlikely it seems. . . How could it be true? . . . How did it happen? . . . What sense does it make? . . . What did he think he was doing? . . . And why? Why? . . . Has he said anything to you?" This last in a more gentle tone of voice.

Signora Rosaria shrugged without raising her eyes from her work.

"By rights it ought to be me to talk to him. After all I'm his father. . . But how's it to be done? I'd rather have a talk with the Lord of Hosts in person than with my own son! That's what I'm reduced to!"

But it so happened, at the very end of June, after an absence of twenty years, that who should turn up in Catania but Signora Rosaria's brother, Ermenegildo Fasanaro. Back from a long sojourn abroad, he looked worn out, emaciated, older than his years. His skin, with no meat beneath it, hung slack on him as if no longer attached to his person. His teeth, always on the long side, by nature protruded a little of their ivory even when his mouth was closed, though this had been if anything the defect of a good-hearted man whom nature had gifted with an irresistible smile forever hooked on his projecting incisors; now, however, these tartared, gum-shrunk teeth were as evident as those of an old horse, and where once flashed so fetching a smile a mass of crevices predominated, in which, at the conclusion of every meal, lodged morsels of salad or fruit. What had become of the elegant belly, the vigour of the chest, the smooth clean cut of the features? Walking along Via Etnea, trying to keep up a good pace, as in the days when people used to cry "You're as good as a breeze, Don Gildo!", he was compelled every now and then to halt in mid-pavement, as if a wall had suddenly barred his way, or some wild beast sprung up before him; then, clasping to his side the ebony stick with the silver knob which in 1918 he used to twirl nonchalantly in the fingers of his right hand, he appeared to hug it to himself as if it were the love of his life, such was the effort of bearing its weight.

In the cafés he used once to frequent, which he now entered surreptitiously because, poor thing, he was mad about cream puffs, he would at once attract the attention of the woman behind the bar.

One good woman stared at him blankly and repeatedly: then came a spark of recognition. Her jaw dropped almost onto her chest and she started to shake her head. At last she plucked up courage to say, "Pardon my asking, but aren't you Cavaliere Fasanaro?"

"Yes," replied he, with a smile smothered in confectioner's custard and an air of a man wondering whether the impression he is giving is quite so bad after all, and in any case full of apology.

"You're sure you're Cavaliere Fasanaro?" queried the woman again.

"Ye-es," faltered that gentleman.

"You! Jesus, Mary and Joseph!" She crossed herself three times. "Praise be to God, now isn't nature naughty!... Carmelo!" she cried, "Carmelo, come here quick and see what's become of Cavaliere Fasanaro! Quick, Carmelo, and tell me if the good Lord isn't sometimes 'orrible naughty."

Cavaliere Fasanaro hastened to wipe his mouth and leave the

premises before the owner of the place had washed his hands and hurried in to scrutinize him.

His sister Rosaria and Signor Alfio were alone in noticing nothing of this deterioration, so engrossed were they in their own calamity.

"*You* try, Gildo," said Signora Rosaria immediately after they had recounted their afflictions. "Try and see if he won't talk to you. Us lame ducks, we're too timid to ask him anything!"

"I'm beating my brains out, wondering what the devil really happened," muttered Signor Alfio.

"Antonio's always got on well with you," resumed Signora Rosaria, addressing her brother. "See if you can't bring us off this miracle, Gildo my love! All we want is to know what really happened and what he wants to do about it. Surely that's not asking too much? Then our worries will be at an end, and no more need be said about it."

"*You* may say no more about it, but I will!" asserted Signor Alfio roundly. "I'll talk about it as long as there's breath in my body! I'll have their guts for garters! I'll give 'em the hiding of their lives, the low swindlers! *I'll* teach 'em what sort of a person Alfio Magnano is! Alfio Magnano, he'll haunt their dreams! Whenever they catch sight of Alfio Magnano they'll feel the urge to leg it. Every morning I'll take my stand outside their mouldy old palace, and if one of them tries to leave I'll put on a stentorian voice and yell, 'Get back to bed you rotten infidel, you Judas you! That way you won't plague your neighbour! Get back to bed on your own two feet, or I'll kick you there with one of mine! Get back to bed, you Di Bronte lackeys, you who sold 'em your daughter!"

"This princely family of Di Bronte," began Ermenegildo, pressing on his emaciated cheeks to assist a yawn, "I have known since childhood, my parents and I having lived in a wing of their palace. But you must remember it too, Rosaria..."

"No, I was born in the new house."

"Ah, of course, so you were..." And Ermenegildo sank into reminiscence with the rapidity of one overwhelmed by a powerful narcotic. "Heavens alive, how the memories crowd in!" he exclaimed. "In the new house, eh?"

"Don't start blathering on!" broke in Signor Alfio. "Let's stick to the point."

"Well, the point is this: they're rich, rolling in the stuff, don't now what to do with it all. And d'you know why?"

"Because they're sons of bitches, every one of 'em," answered Signor Alfio, "and sons of bitches have God on their side."

"For the last three hundred years," pursued Ermenegildo, "they have never permitted their estate to be split up. Whenever there are several sons, only the eldest marries, and if he fails to produce issue, the relatives secretly gang up and get the wife to have a go with the second barrel. That's their name for it."

"Their name for what?" enquired Signora Rosaria. "Second barrel? What's that mean?"

"What does a hunter do when he's missed with his first barrel? He fires his second, doesn't he? Just so the princess. If she has no children by her husband, she fires her second barrel with her brother-in-law."

"Lord save us!" commented Signora Rosaria. "And then they have the impudence to open their mouths for the consecrated Host?"

"They have indeed," continued Ermenegildo, "for they maintain that the flesh of a brother commits no cuckoldry... And who knows, they may be right. The second brother always used to be an abbot, but for quite some time now he's been simply a bachelor. When I was a nipper I used to spend hours and hours on the balcony with my face through the railings..." He broke off, then continued, "Heavens, how the memories crowd in! Did I really have such a tiny face that I could poke it out through the railings?"

"Stop waffling and get on with it," grumbled Signor Alfio. "Hours on end waiting for what?"

"For the prince's brother to appear – the Little Duke."

"With his mother?" enquired Signor Alfio sarcastically.

"Mother, be damned! He was fifty years old. They called him the Little Duke because he was the younger brother. He invariably dressed in black, with a stiff collar, cravat complete with diamond pin, and bamboo cane under his arm. In his breast pocket, instead of a handkerchief, he sometimes had a couple of eggs. I'd see them from up there above, for they stood out against his black suit like a brace of billiard-balls."

"What was this infernal loony doing with two eggs in his pocket?" demanded Signor Alfio. "Who did he think he was? Did His Senility think that because he was the Duca Di Bronte he could carry eggs around in his pocket just to show off to everybody?"

"On the contrary, he had no wish to show them to a soul, and only kept them in his breast pocket to prevent them being crushed."

"You don't say! Then briefly, what was he on about with these eggs?"

"He was, as I learnt later, on his way to visit his mistress, one Donna Concetta by name, the widow of a waggoner. He was as stingy as a Jew."

"A Jew, forsooth! Worse! Far worse!" declared Signor Alfio, though he had not the remotest acquaintance with that duke.

"Well anyway, he was stingy. For a mistress he had selected a working-class woman, whom he rewarded with a couple of eggs each time she did for him what the princess no longer wished to do – having given birth to two sons, the present prince and the present duke."

"And Mr Notary Puglisi," bellowed Signor Alfio, "would go around picking up spare change with the cleft of his arse just to take his daughter away from Antonio and give her to *that* scum!"

"The present princess is as barren as a mule," proceeded

Ermenegildo. "No one had any luck with her: not the first barrel nor the second. It's as if she'd been salted and dried. That's why the relatives have given the second son permission to marry and have offspring into the bargain."

"Offspring! What, him? That suet-belly!" cried Signor Alfio. "Why, I've heard that whenever he visits a... certain house... they bolt the doors and don't allow anyone else in, because he comes over all wheezy and you can hear him puffing and blowing in all the rest of the rooms and on the staircase too."

"And you, Alfio," put in Signora Rosaria bitterly, "for the sharpness of your tongue, and having a bad word to say for everyone, have been punished by the Almighty! And now the blight has been visited upon our son."

"Blight? What blight?" shrieked Signor Alfio, quite beside himself. "So now *you're* taking their side, are you? *My* son has a cock that could drill a hole through stone!... Gildo," he continued, in tones of supplication, "after lunch tomorrow I'll take this one out and leave you alone with him. Gildo, you'll be Christ returned to earth in my eyes if you manage to get him to open up that clam of a mouth of his and tell you the truth, the whole truth, whatever it may be."

"I'll have a shot at it," returned that gentleman. "Though I'd do better to go straight to hospital, rather than try such treatment!"

So after lunch the following day the two old people left the flat, accompanied by the maid, who went ahead of them down the dark staircase perpetually muttering, "Take care, madam, there's another step to come."

Uncle and nephew were in the house alone.

"Now look what I've let myself in for," snorted Ermenegildo, left to himself. "Don't I have troubles enough of my own, what with this rat gnawing at my guts, and the way I can't breathe, and the spots before my eyes, and the rest of the devilish crew that's getting at me?... Oh well, chin up!"

He approached Antonio's door, and finding it ajar he gave it a gentle prod and poked his head in.

Antonio lay propped on the bed, visibly relieved at having heard his parents go out and the house divesting itself of people suffering on his account.

When Ermenegildo entered, Antonio's face clouded somewhat.

"I stayed in," his uncle hastened to say, rather apologetically, "because that pain in the neck Marraro has taken a month's leave from the Town Hall and at this time of day doesn't know what to do with himself, so he stands there on the pavement like a rooster on a dungheap, all poised to bore the pants off any acquaintance who happens to pass by. There's a strong chance the Party Sec. will descend on Via Etnea too, along with all those skunks who lick his boots, and if I so much as set eyes on them it poisons my bloodstream. I'll go out later on. . . Can you bear my company for a while?"

"Of course, dear uncle," replied Antonio. "You're welcome to stay as long as you like."

"In that case, with your permission, I'll take a seat in this comfy chair."

Antonio gave a slight nod of assent and smiled weakly.

Uncle Ermenegildo reached over to the table, picked up a hefty volume and started leafing through it. Then, laying it down again, he asked, "Would you object to my smoking my pipe?"

Antonio raised his head, gave his assent, and smiled weakly. Then he closed his eyes and, abandoning himself exclusively to the care of that prematurely aged gentleman, received the comfort which an afflicted person feels in the company of another whom he judges to be in an even worse state than himself.

"The world's an ugly place," began Ermenegildo, sensing that the more he made of his own demoralization the more likely he would be to gain Antonio's confidence. "Yes, it's an ugly place. . ." He broke off, as the latter still kept his eyes closed.

"I'm not asleep," said Antonio, without opening them. "In fact it's a pleasure to have someone to listen to. Tell me where you've been."

"Where've I been, eh? I've been where I never ought to have been. To Spain, for my sins. And I've taken stock of my contemporaries and mankind in general. They're an ugly lot, Antonio my lad, and believe me, by the love you bear your mother, they put the fear of God into me!"

He waited for his nephew to open his eyes, but as this did not occur he relit his spent pipe and continued.

"Don't ask me who's right and who's wrong, or which of these two principles will win out in the end. People hide their opinions in their heads, so I didn't see them. What I did see was that both sides were quite ready and willing to butcher, burn and make mincemeat of Jesus Christ in person, and that if you get on the wrong side of them, then prepare yourself to scream a scream of pain such as you never thought the bowels of a human being could bring forth!"

He crossed to the window, opened it, spat outside, closed it again and returned to his seat.

"You simply can't conceive the sort of suffering they are capable of inflicting on a man's flesh. A square centimetre of your skin suffices them to let all hell loose in you. There's no courage on earth could withstand it, my lad. I'm no coward, but I assure you no courage could withstand it. Christian Culture, Social Justice: fine words! Both the one and the other of inestimable good to mankind. But take a look at the contorted faces of the carcasses they leave to rot for days on end in pot-holes, or drive lorries over to obliterate all traces of their features, and tell me if that's the way to provide for the good of mankind! Even these carcasses were once men, for God's sake, and that's all they got for their pains. Now, you'll tell me it's all being done for posterity. . . But even the men of tomorrow will think of the future, and want to do something

143

for *their* posterity, so they'll butcher each other like our own contemporaries. To this type of do-gooding there is no end. No, Antonio, believe you me, mankind gives me the jitters and nightly nightmares too."

"You've got a nervous breakdown for *your* pains," said Antonio affectionately. "You ought to take sleeping pills so as not to dream at night."

"Call it what you will. You can even call it a nervous breakdown. But as for dreamless slumbers, I can't manage them any more, not even with doses of veronal verging on suicide. My brain doesn't close off well any more – like an old shutter hanging loose on its hinges that lets through hundreds of threads of light. And would it were only light! But there's the din as well, and the talk – pandemonium in fact... Why did I have a mind to see them for myself, those abominable creatures? Did anyone force me to go, for God's sake? No, I simply wanted to know who was in the right and who in the wrong, and all I found out was that they're an abomination, every striking one of them! What a handsome profit I made from my travels! Handsome's scarcely the word for it! Three cheers! I congratulate myself!... By good luck my heart is enlarged, my lungs are shrunk, and everything leads me to believe that next Sant' Agata's day you'll watch the fireworks without me."

"Come off it, uncle, don't go on like that. I'm convinced it'll be you to walk us all to the graveyard," murmured Antonio, though without opening his eyes.

"No, no, don't rob me of my only comfort. If I'm going to get off to sleep at night I need to think that death is sitting at my bedside. It's the only thought that brings me a little peace of mind. Without it all is anxiety, terror, insomnia and cold sweats. No Antonio, I'm telling you: in a few months' time I shall be the lucky one. Revolution will touch me no longer, any more than Reaction will. Fascism, Communism... they already leave me cold. Whichever wins, neither of those bully-bullies will be able to get at me again, to rob me either of bread or breath. No one will ever again wrench my guts into that scream which many a time, when at home and alone, I have sought to imitate in front of the mirror, hoping perhaps to solace myself with the thought that it *is* within human capacity: sought to, yes, but always in vain. From which I have deduced how bestial the suffering must be, which instructs a man in it all at one fell swoop!"

Antonio opened his eyes, feeling a tender affection for this man so mellowed by the yearning for death.

"But let's hear about you now," said his uncle. "What's up with you? Although, to be perfectly honest, I know what's up with you. Easy enough to see. . . I know perfectly well what's up with you. . . But everyone here's wondering why? how? what happened? . . . Well it's not hard to guess, and I don't need you to tell me. I really don't. Anyway, you're not letting on – so I'll do the talking."

Ermenegildo broke off, to see if his nephew would decide to spill the beans; but as Antonio remained silent he continued:

"I'll do all the talking. . . I'll give you the whole picture with all the trimmings. All you have to do is listen. You've been going it too hot and strong, my lad. I remember you in Rome – that air of burning the candle at both ends. The way they used to come and go in your flat there might have been a corpse laid out in the parlour! But every single visitor to the catafalque was a woman, and there on the catafalque were you, stretched out like a dead man, I'll grant you that, but as lively as sin and always ready to start again. Those girls, passing at the hall door, regal as queens, every one of them – and you could scarcely fob them off with an 'I like your pretty face', could you now?

"I remember that coming down the stairs one day I passed one of them going up, and the mere fact that I stopped to give her the once-over made her turn away as if she'd seen a heap of sicked-up spaghetti. But she wasn't snooty for long, I'll warrant! Aha! She was at your feet ready and willing to have you trample all over her sweet innocent features. . . But then, you saw more than your fair share of that... Always so abstracted, always gazing towards the window as if you were meditating on the souls in purgatory... You'd yawn, and sometimes turn them down and their pants got hotter than ever, and who knows what endearments and caresses and sacrifices you had from them. They led you into bad habits. They spoilt you... And one fine day, when you found yourself with a wife who was a bit stand-offish, a bit stiff, a bit on her high horse, well you got it up your nose, and turned your back on her, and slept for three years with your face to the wall, thinking of the girls in Rome."

Antonio cast a lightning glance at his uncle's face, then once more lowered his lashes.

"So now, tell me: have I put my finger on the spot?" continued his uncle. "I envied you, of course, very bitterly, at a time when I still fancied women. And Lord, how I fancied them! How I fancied them! But the day came when I got sick even of that. 'Is it possible,' I thought to myself, 'is it possible that I have to go on, after so many years that I barely recollect the first time, is it possible that I have to go on and on, mindlessly filling holes in flesh with other flesh?' And, for crying out loud, it's always same thing! Even if you go to bed with the queen herself, it's the same thing. It starts the same way and it ends the same way. And if you go with an unwashed hunchback, no difference whatsoever: it starts the same way and it ends the same way. Apart from the fact that now I haven't even strength enough in me to die... But anyway, leaving aside my troubles, which are as they may be, tell me honestly, haven't I just given a picture of you stripped and flayed?"

"No," said Antonio.

"No, eh?..."

"No!"

"Well then, let's hear it. What *is* the truth?"

Antonio sat bolt upright on the bed and wrung his hands.

"The truth?" he said. "The truth?... You really want to know the truth?"

"Certainly I do!"

"Then what?"

"Then nothing in particular. Stop wringing your hands like that, will you! Well... then we'll see."

"Uncle... uncle..." stammered out Antonio, rising from the bed and pacing to and fro, pale as a ghost, "you're not going to believe it, but I..."

"But you?..."

"I... I... I wish I'd never been born!"

"*You* say such a thing, Antonio? You, of all people? Leave that sort of thing to me, it's right up my street."

"Why's it up your street? Because you've seen what fiends men are, seen them cut each other up and kill each other. I couldn't care less if they do go on like that. There's something else they do that I... that I..." Again his voice rose in a shrill crescendo on the word he couldn't tear himself away from: "That I, that I..." then falling to a barely audible whisper... "something I have never done!"

The old gentleman shook like an aspen.

"Never done?" he quavered. And getting to his feet he went over to Antonio, whose back was turned, and tried every which-way to turn the young man round and get a glimpse of the splendid visage which he had so often envied for the effect it had on women.

"Never done?" he repeated. "Did I hear aright? Did you say *never done?*"

Antonio made no answer. His whole body was rigid with agony and his uncle failed to force him into turning.

"Antonio, I beg of you, look me in the face! I'm your uncle, for God's sake, and a reasonable person. You can't be afraid of an old man like me!"

Antonio wheeled slowly, and slowly, as the sunken cheek, the sweaty, pinched nose, the hollow eye-sockets were sketched in the glimmer of light from the window, the old

147

gentleman felt all hope of having got the wrong end of the stick, or having been misled by an overstatement, freeze in his breast.

"But Antonio," he declared, "I feel as if I'd been pole-axed! Can you be telling me the truth?"

A deathly pallor, spreading over the young man's face, made answer for him.

"Never?" Ermenegildo pressed him. "You really mean *never?*"

Antonio knitted his brows as if to concentrate all his scattered wits into a single look, and said, "Hardly ever."

Ermenegildo was taken aback, but then on the instant leapt heart and soul at the morsel of hope contained in those two words.

"Hardly ever is a different matter from never!" he burst out. "It's a different thing altogether!"

Antonio said nothing.

"Hardly ever, eh?" resumed Ermenegildo with increasing vigour, perhaps trying to encourage himself, "hardly ever can mean a whole heap of things. 'Never' is one thing and 'hardly ever' is another. I must confess that even I, on occasion... I don't say always, or even often, but... well, in a word, sometimes... You can't eat without dropping crumbs, as they say... If you're always in the saddle you must expect to take a tumble sometimes."

"Uncle! Uncle! Uncle!" cried Antonio, first angry, then desperate, and finally beseeching. "*Please* don't say any more!"

There was a pause.

"All right, I'll shut my trap. But you do a bit of talking instead. Come on, my boy, speak up!"

There was a second pause.

Antonio couldn't get a word out; but from between clenched teeth he let out a soft, continuous hiss, as if he had inhaled enough air to pronounce a non-stop speech of a thousand words, and was giving it forth all skeletal without a single syllable. In that hiss were exclamations, cries, questions, and even sobs; but all stifled and voiceless.

"No, dear boy, no," said his uncle. "You've got to speak up clearly, frankly and straight-forwardly. And waste no more time about it, because around seven o'clock my head begins to spin so awfully I can't tell the floor from the ceiling."

"I mean by 'hardly ever'. . ." Antonio suddenly yelled at the top of his voice, "that in that business, I. . ."

"Softly now, softly," broke in Ermenegildo in alarm. "We don't want the whole town to know!"

"Let 'em know! Let the whole town know!" shrieked Antonio, writhing and squirming as one trying to struggle free of his bonds. "I, I, I. . ."

And having gnawed his hands, a wrist and the crook of an arm, he threw himself full length on the bed, clenching his teeth and panting.

His uncle seated himself at the bedside and began to stroke the lad's forehead, waiting in silence for him to calm down.

Twilight was falling, and the little light from the window no longer succeeded in prevailing over the darkness in the room, when the old gentleman became convinced that Antonio must either be asleep or have fainted away.

But just then a calm voice, a voice entirely bereft of feeling, inflexion, human warmth, a voice which truly seemed the voice of nobody, a dead, impartial voice, rose from the pillow where Antonio's head was laid, eyes closed.

"Hardly ever. . . yes," said the voice, coldly repeating the words that had previously been sobbed and screamed. "Until I was eighteen I used to do it in my dreams; then, once, I half did it in a brothel in Via Maddem, and that evening I vomited. That was the 3rd of May, 1924. After that I didn't do it any more, even in dreams, or even half way, because every time I set out on that path, or when my thoughts, routing around among memories, happened upon that 3rd of May, I had spasms of retching, like seasickness. I remember one day, on a marble table-top in a café, I found two scrawled figures engaged in the act. I went as white as a sheet and had to rush to the lavatory and splash water on my face. All this time I was madly in love with all women, especially with their faces, their eyes, and their feet. Sometimes, when I spent the night at my grandfather's – it was on the first floor – I only had to hear the tapping of high-heels fading out of earshot to start writhing between the sheets like a deportee locked in the hold of a ship and listening as the harbour-sounds of his home town, sweetest of serenades, die off into the distance. . ."

Uncle Ermenegildo closed his eyes. He was gaining from his nephew what his nephew had shortly before received from him: the powerful distraction of an anguish other than his own.

"As regards women," continued Antonio in the same chill voice, "my situation was this: with all my heart I wanted to throw myself at their feet and roll on the floor begging for mercy."

"But my dear boy. . . I don't get it," said his uncle, venturing his words into the dark. "If I am not mistaken, the women themselves were mad about you!"

"So you all say," went on the voice, "but I saw things in a different light. For me, in the eyes of every girl there dwelt an almost sarcastic come-hither, a challenge to get together with her and to be a man. They'd step up flaunting their bosoms with the laughing, swaggering air of approaching an adversary who has them covered with an unloaded pistol. Maybe I got it wrong. . ."

"You certainly did!" declared his uncle, less to provide comfort than simply to interrupt that frigid, monotone voice.

"In Rome, in 1930 it was, a strange thing happened to me. The evening of the day I arrived, after having a larger dinner and drinking more than usual, I went to a brothel, and before I'd had time to feel frightened or nauseated I succeeded in being a man. . ."

"You did? Ah, good, very good, by Jove!"

"It seemed too incredible to be true, and I left the place reeling around for joy, and kissing all the walls and the doors between the scene of my victory and Piazza San Silvestro. That night I dreamt I was doing it over again, and let out such a cry that the landlady came running in her dressing-gown. Then it was I realized that the smiles bestowed on me by women, which I had thought to be a sardonic challenge, were, on the contary, signs of the most genuine rapture. And now I understood the expression I had seen on the landlady's face twelve hours earlier (and interpreted as one of disagreeable, sneering curiosity) to be the very evident effect of a desire conceived the moment she saw me, to meet me on terms of greater intimacy. This I knew from the flush of pleasure that spread over her cheeks as she came into the room, and the promptness with which she'd scurried there, as if the desire to accomplish that act had put her in a condition to get down to it there and then... I'm not going to claim I was very enterprising that night. I was sated, and had to wait at least six days for this to wear off. A week later, in fact, I was able to pleasure both my landlady and myself. The following day I had to feign illness, not being able to think of any other way to justify breaking off our relationship.

"That was the most glorious period of my life. I was twenty-four, the women were besotted over me, and I, once a week, was able to make one of them swoon with delight. The very next day began the lies and subterfuges because at all costs I had to avoid going back and sleeping with the lady... How many times I fled to Naples and a hotel on the sea-front, to be tormented by the mandolins outside the restaurants and the smack of kisses from behind closed doors, while I waited for my desire, spread so evenly throughout my body as to seep placidly from my hand whenever I shook that of a woman, to condense into the place which is made for it... I have never mentioned these things to anyone, but I've written them down and copied them out countless times on sheets of paper which I then burnt: by now I know them by heart. And I must say that when I did ever think of a person in whom I could confide, that person was you."

His uncle silently squeezed Antonio's hand.

"I was happy that year," continued the voice. "I was even arrogantly full of myself. Once a week? So what! I felt like a bull! What's more, that sensation, though rare, was so powerful that the day before experiencing it I got into a state of excitement unknown to most, be they even in the act of undressing the object of their desire for the first time; and for two days afterwards I still had the taste of honey in my blood, and if I saw, or touched, or heard anything truly throbbing with life, it held such sweetness for me that I nearly fainted. Ah, how lovely was life! how lovely it was!"

There followed a pause which Ermenegildo did not dare to intrude on.

"That May," continued the voice, "I happened to set eyes on a German girl with her fiancé, a young Viennese officer, sitting at a café in the Villa Borghese. Both were of such beauty that the couples around them had an air of humiliation and mourning: not a man or woman among them dared hazard a caress, or even hold hands, for fear it might seem that by so doing they entered into some pretentious and ridiculous rivalry with those two sublime foreigners."

"Well, in point of good looks," put in his uncle, "you didn't leave much to be desired yourself!"

"Yes I... well anyway... But if you'd seen that Viennese officer you'd have gone weak at the knees."

"To tell the truth, I'm not in the habit of giving men the once-over. But let that go. What was *she* like?"

"She was tall, with rose-coloured hair..."

"Rose-coloured? What the devil?..."

"It would have been reddish in anyone else. But hers was so ravishing it seemed rose-coloured. Her eyes were azure, but her gaze was as if dusted over by the finest of fragrant powders, and I could scent the perfume of it..."

"What the blazes is he on about?" muttered Ermenegildo under his breath.

"... Fine, firm breasts, perfect legs, long, with knees that made themselves apparent through any garment as if they were luminous. Luminous her belly too, it seemed to me... and that recess between the legs which in the past had made me vomit, but appeared to me now to gleam like a priceless treasure."

Ermenegildo felt a tremor run down his spine.

"Here's a fine thing!" he thought to himself. "Even at my age, just the mention of it... while this unfortunate youngster..."

"Every afternoon without fail I went to the café, the Casina Valadier, and there I always found the German couple. I affected to be admiring the panorama of Rome spread at my feet, but my shoulder-blades saw her, the hairs on the nape of my neck saw her, and my heart felt as if it had done a right-about-turn, so that the view below me acquired a positive feeling of pathos, as might a landscape before the eyes of a corpse.

"After a couple of weeks I found the German girl alone. Almost slouched in her wicker chair, her hands in her jacket pockets, sun glasses on her nose and half an inch more leg showing than usual. I plucked up courage to look at her, though very shamefacedly because her fiancé, now that he was absent, seemed to me a veritable god, and the deep blue shadow immersing the empty chair beside her to be projected by that gentleman from some seat in the heavens."

"The way you do go on!" exclaimed Ermenegildo. Then he stubbornly repeated: "In point of good looks, you didn't leave much to be desired yourself, by Jove!"

"There you go again! I tell you that girl's fiancé would have made the carved image of a saint swivel on her litter and the whole procession behind her too!"

"Oh all right, have it your own way," grumbled Ermenegildo, bitten by his long-standing resentment against any man who began to get on his nerves. "So you gave her a look..."

"I looked at her, yes."

"And what about her? Did she look back?"

"She did more than that. She spoke to me!"

"Damn it!" muttered Ermenegildo, under his breath, feeling his heart miss a beat, as it was wont to do when he still had his health.

"She said, 'Excuse me, signore. Are you coming here alvays?' I answered 'Yes', hardly believing my ears. Christ alive, I thought, is it really possible this girl is interested enough in me to speak the first word? And with a fiancé before whom she ought to light votive candles night and day?"

"Skip all that. Get down to brass tracks."

"Her name was Ingeborg, but at home they called her Ing; and as she'd been in Paris her French friends pronounced this Ange... The result was I called her Angel."

"The way you do go on!" repeated Ermenegildo, this time to himself.

"Her fiancé had gone back to Vienna, and she sat near me reading his long letters, reddening as if someone were kissing her before my very eyes. 'Good news?' I asked, and she gave a ghost of a smile and thrust her hand into her pocket, letter and all. I was so dominated by that vision-of-a-man that I would have preferred to talk to her of nothing else, but she changed the subject every time."

"All well and good," broke in his uncle, "but didn't you try to get somewhere with her?"

"No I didn't, in spite of the fact that, as I said, I felt full to the brim with lust, like a ram. Every three days I spent the afternoon with one of the girls I had already formally abandoned – who'd be overcome by an out-and-out fit of hysterics at unexpectedly finding my head on her pillow again. I don't know if you noticed I said *every three days*, but indeed this miracle had happened: I no longer needed to wait a whole week for the tastiest of fruits to ripen on my bough. My happiness was so naïve that I attributed this miracle to the fact that I was in the papal city; and one day, when I went with Ing to a public audience in the Vatican, while we were kneeling before the Pontiff and Ing was praying aloud to heaven to grant harmony between herself and her fiancé, I silently thanked the Vicar of Christ for the boon which his city had bestowed on me.

"When we left the Vatican I remembered Ing's prayer. 'What's this?' I asked, 'don't you get on with your fiancé?' 'Oh yes,' she replied. 'Ve see the same vay about everything. Ve like the same books, the same miusic, the same peektures, the same strheets, the same bloomps, and he is ver' good and kayind. And he is zo beautifall. . .' At this point I read on her lips a *but* as sombre as the tomb itself."

"Well then? Did you get your end away or not?" cried Uncle Ermenegildo, losing patience.

"One evening we'd gone for a ride in a horse-drawn cab," continued the voice, as cold and unruffled as that of an automaton, "and I couldn't see her face, and not seeing her face, nor did I see her fiancé's, which until then, in my mind, I had always envisaged close to hers. . ."

"How he does drag on!" thought Ermenegildo to himself.

". . . I kissed her fervidly, and, although I'd spent the previous afternoon with a girl, I again felt all the honey in my veins rush to concentrate at that point where I most loved to feel it. . . I didn't say a thing, but in my heart of hearts I cried a cry that surely must have reached the heavens, a cry to all those saints who had at last taken pity on me! A week later we had a tryst at the opera. On reaching our meeting-place I realized at once from the way she offered me her hand that Ing had decided to give herself to me that very night. On the stage, the tenors and prima donnas carried through their roles in *Don Giovanni*. . . and all the while I was thinking, 'But what about the fiancé? How *can* she betray him? What goes on in these women's minds? They're twisted, they're really twisted!' After we'd left the theatre and reached her door, she was so well aware that I was aware as to be frankly amazed at my moment of hesitation before crossing the threshold and going upstairs with her. A little later. . ."

"No, don't jump! Tell me everything in order! What room did she take you to?"

"Her bedroom."

"Like that, right off?"

"Yes. And I, weary but happy, stretched myself on my back on the bed. She disappeared into the bathroom and returned a minute later in her night things, her face streaming with tears."

"Don't believe those tears!" cried Uncle Ermenegildo as if actually present at the scene, an excited public cheering on its champion. "Wham it in there. Don't believe those tears!"

"She sat down on the bed and began telling me the story of her life... She came from an influential German family and had been sent to study in Paris. There she fell in love with a Spanish architect from whom – surprised by joy – she learnt what until then she had not entertained even the remotest curiosity about. This Spaniard was squat and ugly, but he enflamed her with the fire of his passion..."

"Of course!" exclaimed Ermenegildo. "He was a Spaniard, which is like saying a Sicilian!"

"But her family opposed the match. The architect was a foreigner, and they considered him to be of inferior race. Ing returned to Berlin to try and talk her parents over, but they were deaf to all entreaties..."

"Germans!"

"Enraged by all this shilly-shallying and opposition, and wounded in his pride, the Spaniard wrote Ing a farewell letter which he signed with all his family's titles of nobility. She returned to Paris determined to throw herself in the Seine. During the journey she met a childhood friend, the beautiful Viennese officer of whom I told you, who was also contemplating suicide on account of a misfortune which he dared not speak of; not even when, having crossed the frontier into France, and having both rid themselves of the strange feeling of oppression which arose from knowing themselves to be on German soil, they confided their sorrows to one another and fell into each other's arms. A month later they were engaged..."

"Women!"

"They telephoned to her family in Berlin and were greeted by a chorus of compliments and congratulations. They agreed to get married, and then... Well, you know how it is with these northern women..."

"Well, a bit, yes..."

"Once they were going to become man and wife, they shared a bed."

Antonio stopped.

"All right, all right, they shared a bed. So what?"

"And there..."

"And there?"

"He..."

"He?"

"Nothing!"

"What d'you mean, nothing?"

"Just that – nothing."

"By God, that strapping great chap?"

"Yes, that strapping great chap."

"Well! And they always say... but did they try again?"

"Yes."

"So?"

"Nothing."

"Still nothing?"

"Still nothing."

"Good Lord alive."

"Ing confided in her mother, who told her there was no need to worry, they should get married anyway, and then, with time... But Ing had already succumbed to a fear that the fault was hers, that she wasn't fit for anything, that she ought to have known how to... When I heard all this – conceited and full of myself as I was at the time – I burst out laughing. 'You?' I said. 'No need for you to move a muscle. Why should you? A girl as beautiful as you, she doesn't have to do a thing.

She's already done enough with the mere rustle of her skirts!'
Ing threw her arms around me in a rapture of joy and gratitude.
Evidently her ears had been burning for ages to hear such
heart-warming, undreamt-of words. When next she spoke she
confided in me that this was the reason for certain tearful out-
bursts which I couldn't understand, this was the misfortune
for which the Viennese officer was contemplating suicide on
the journey to Paris, and this the lack of harmony she had
besought Pius XI to set to rights... We spoke no more, but
switched off the lamp and hugged each other tight. Soon she
was near fainting with pleasure, opening little by little like a
rose to the sun. As for me, I was beside myself with a joy even
greater than hers, and already warning myself to smother the
cry which I felt in my throat and which soon would escape
me, when..."

He broke off. His uncle, on his part, held his tongue, but
felt his right eye twitching like a fly in the clutches of a spider.

"When..." continued Antonio, and broke off a second time.
"When a sudden panic and chill came over me, and precisely
in that part of my body which, if I'd had to die that instant of
frostbite and paralysis, I would have wished to be affected
last!"

He fell silent.

Uncle Ermenegildo drew a long, deep breath, accompanied
by a mournful wheezing of the lungs, but when it came to
letting it go he opened his mouth and breathed out noiselessly.

"She was still lying on her back, lips parted, eyes closed,
and I, frozen with shame, slid down at her side, pressing my
trembling mouth into the pillow. It was the end of everything.
Everything died a sudden death for me! The blood which so
lustily and zestfully had converged in one point of my body
was fled not only from there, but seemed to have vanished
entirely from my veins, dried out by an icy wind that circulated
in its stead; and I knew without a doubt that, even if blood
should return to my veins, from that particular part of my
body it was for ever deviated, as if *there* began the territory of

some alien being into which my thoughts, my yearnings, my impulses, could never again in any way penetrate. With this certitude in my heart, confirmed by two hours of silence beside that perfectly motionless woman, who lay as if crushed by the sum of my shame and her own, two hours of silence during which all my efforts to regain the condition of happy manhood were doomed to failure, doomed to render me ever more incapable of that kind of happiness, and the few moments I had known of it in the past to seem almost incredible and unreal; after two hours which seemed to me brief but static, like the split second the bullet takes from a rifle-muzzle to the condemned man's heart, I got up from that bed, that bed which I no longer saw, even the shape and size of which I had forgotten, and I left the room, and within it a woman I also could not remember the look of, so greatly did the warmth of the joy she had formerly given me, and the glacial iciness she transmitted to me that night, combine to render her image split, divided, unfocused, and, in the last analysis, terrifying."

IX

U NCLE ERMENEGILDO'S HEAD drooped and he shook it almost inperceptibly, causing his dewlap to quiver.

"And then what?" he asked.

Antonio was silent.

"And then what?" reiterated his uncle.

"Shut the shutters," said Antonio.

Ermenegildo crossed to the window and closed the shutters; the room on the instant became a sudden blaze of electric light.

Antonio, sitting on the bed, his back against the wooden bedhead, still had in his hand the switch of the bedside lamp. He looked as if worn to a shred by long illness; but his face, chiselled by its very gauntness, could scarcely have been more beautiful.

"After that," he resumed, resting the nape of his neck on the bedrail, thereby increasing the tension and fine-drawing of his nose and cheeks. "After that... I never again saw light!"

"Meaning?"

"I stayed for a fortnight holed up in my room. Then I found the boarding-house intolerable, and rented a small flat overlooking the park of the Villa Borghese. My father shipped me some furniture from home. When I saw it there, arranged around the room, it made me weep wrathful tears, because it reminded me of the times when I suffered that nausea, though desperately in love with every woman I set eyes on. A month later I made another sortie to Via Mario dei Fiori, to the brothel where I'd been restored to life the evening I first arrived in Rome. As I followed the woman up the spiral wooden stair the frost in my loins froze anew; and as she – ushering me into a room heated by an Aladdin stove and closing the door – unbuttoned her bodice and slipped off her clothes, I thought I'd play the smart alick. Still fully dressed, leaning against a chest of drawers laden with photographs, I produced a smile: 'Look, I've got a suggestion to make.' The woman had already relaxed naked on the bed, hands clasped behind her head, and was looking me over. 'What is it?' she asked, adding in honeyed tones: 'You know, darling, you're really really easy on the eye.' 'Fancy me?' said I. 'Yes,' said she, extracting a hand from behind her head and excitedly massaging her throat while giving me a meaning look. 'When I've done my stint in this house I'd like to spend a fortnight with you in Venice! You just see what a good time we'll have! A single caress from your Caterina here can make a man wake from the dead!' 'I bet you're exaggerating!' 'Not a bit of it, my winsome laddie.' 'All right, I accept, but on one condition.' 'What's that?' 'That if I manage to keep cool beneath your famous caresses, you'll pay for the trip to Venice. If not, OK, the jaunt's on me.' Her shining eyes looked at me squarely. 'Done!' said she. 'The wooden effigy of a saint couldn't resist *me*.' 'Right then,' said I, stripping off quickly in the hope – you never know! – of losing my bet."

"And did you?"

"Five minutes later the hapless Caterina was pouring sweat into the sheets, hair plastered to her cheeks, breath hissing through her teeth. . . But I remained unmoved, a malignant smirk on my face. Ten, fifteen, twenty minutes, half an hour. . .

"'Listen here,' said that hard-working lady, 'you've won and I don't deny it. This means I'll pay for your trip to Venice. But now, for goodness' sake relax and let nature take its course.'

"On this I rose from the bed with a sarcastic laugh, dressed slowly and with deliberation, twice re-tying the knot of my tie, chucked some money onto the woman's bosom as she lay mortified on the bed, and took myself off into the street. I made a rush for the Café Aragno, had them unlock the gents' for me, and once I'd slammed the door gave vent to a long and agonized flood of tears."

"But you should never have pitted yourself against such a challenge," declared his uncle. "Better to have bided your time."

"I'd already waited six weeks!"

"You should have waited longer. It's a mistake to hurry matters of that sort."

"Well, after that visit to Via Mario dei Fiori I spent three months steering clear of so much as speaking to a woman. One afternoon – the best of hours in times gone by – who should turn up but an old tootsy of mine who'd been searching for me like a needle in a haystack and had finally run me to earth. I allowed her to lie down beside me, kiss me, and practically take the skin off my face, rubbing her palms over my cheeks, slow, rough, loving, furious by turns. 'You've got a heart of stone!' she burst out... But oh I was not stony-hearted, Ermenegildo. I was simply praying that death, the old body-snatcher, would snatch me out of there!"

"And then what?" prompted his uncle.

"Uncle! And then, and then... Is that all you've got to say?"

"Now hold your horses. Don't drive me up the wall. I may be on the verge of second childhood but, believe me, I'm not there yet!"

"What are you on about, uncle?"

"What d'you mean, what am I on about? Is it or is it not the case that your place in Rome was always chock-a-block with women? Is it or is it not the case that they were all beside themselves about you? Is it or is it not the case that the Countess K... what was her name?... you know who I mean... would come rubbing up against your door like a cat on heat? Is this the case or did I dream it?"

Antonio grasped his uncle's hand and drew it to his lips.

"What's this! Kissing my hand, eh?" said Ermenegildo, putting on a bluff manner to fight tears down. "Kissing my hand? Where do I come in?"

Antonio gently deposited his uncle's hand on the bed.

"What a fag," he murmured, "all the lies and cheats and shams and excuses and pretences and deceptions!"

"On whose part?"

"Mine."

"Why's that?"

"Not to give myself away... to women, to my parents, to my friends, to you... I even went so far as to go to church and confess all the sins I wanted to commit but couldn't, praying from the bottom of my heart for the Lord to make me capable of them. How pleased I was when the confessor shook his head over some of the yarns I spun him, and grumbled, 'My son, you've gone too far. Don't you realize I can't give you absolution?'"

"You ask me to believe this?"

Antonio expressed a wry smile by snorting delicately down his nose. "Countess K", he proceeded, "is the only one who must have suspected the truth, because one evening she said, 'Antonio, tell me frankly, wouldn't it be convenient to be able to possess a woman with your eyes?' I don't know if she meant that I had the eyes of certain Sicilian shop-window rapists whom she'd been going on about the previous evening..."

"Ah, the strumpet!" burst out Ermenegildo. "Just let her come here and they'll be in and out of her like the door of the lawcourts... And not just with their eyes, you may be sure!"

"Or maybe she meant that with nothing but my eyes I could..."

"Ah, strumpet, strumpet a hundred times over! Strumpet like her mother, her grandmother, her sister and her daughter before her!... However, listen here, Antonio: there are some things I simply can't swallow, even to save my life. Your being able for years and years to pull the wool over the eyes of all those women around you... no sir! that I can't swallow, I can't get it down, it sticks in my gullet, here!"

And he vigorously thwacked his Adam's apple.

Antonio raised his eyes to the opposite wall, projecting the shadow of his brow onto the wallpaper beside him.

"No," resumed his uncle. "No, never!"

And in a different tone of voice: "Why are you trying to deceive me, Antonio?"

"Until yesterday I was deceiving you, uncle. Today is the first time I've told you the truth."

"But hell and dammit! Women, I tell you, they're not so easily duped... And about this matter, what's more – the thing they care most about in all the world! Not even Beelzebub himself could bring it off! Not even some soi-disant kingpin of tricksters!"

"I brought it off," said Antonio, with a smirk of ironical pride.

"But let's be reasonable! The first time, with a woman, you can kid her that you've taken an oath, or got a tummy-ache, or have to be in a state of grace to go to Communion. But what d'you tell her the second time? Out with it! What d'you tell her?"

"Uncle, I always found an excuse."

"*Always?*"

"Always."

"But I ask you, did nobody, nobody ever, absolutely nobody ever smell a rat in all this?"

Antonio raised his head and shook it.

"No?"

"No."

"You think I'm such a fool as to believe you?" shouted the old gentleman.

"Uncle Gildo, do you really want me, over a matter like this, to swear on the life of my mother and father, who at this very moment don't know which way to turn, as they're elbowed around by the crowd, half-blind as they are? What

164

d'you want me to say – that if I'm lying may they never come home alive?"

"No!" cried Ermenegildo, in a fright.

"Or 'may I lose the sight of my eyes'?"

"God forbid!"

"Or 'may I get shot down in a narrow alley'?"

"No, no! I believe you!"

A pause.

"Well then," resumed Ermenegildo, "after that time with the German girl, nothing more, nix, not even some pit-a-pat, some loosening up, some something, half-something, how can I put it?..."

"In 1933, in August..."

"There you are, you see?" exclaimed Ermenegildo with a sigh of relief. "So – in August?..."

"I happened to be in Collalbo – place near a town called Soprabolzano. Ever heard of it?"

"Collalbo... Yes, of course, naturally! A town. Summer resort."

"It's a town in a manner of speaking: a handful of wooden buildings, all of them boarding-houses, a hotel or two, a public garden with a tennis court..."

"Yes, yes, I know, I know. Collalbo."

"And then there's a mass of woods all round..."

"Yes, woods, of course, of course," put in Ermenegildo pressingly, as if to second Antonio's welcome inclination to talk about something less depressing.

"It's there on a mountain one thousand two hundred metres high. To the north you can see even higher mountains."

"The Dolomites."

"Yes, the Dolomites."

"So, in Collalbo...?"

"I was there with Luigi d'Agata, Turi Grassi and the Pertoni brothers. They were all rolling around in the grass like a bunch of nincompoops in their lust for a woman, hunting every-whichway and at their wits' end because they couldn't find one. At night they were so frantically randy they rushed off into the woods and howled loud enough to wake the whole neighbourhood, 'What shall I do, cut it off? Holy Mother of God, if it goes on like this I'll cut it off and throw it to the dogs!' Hour after hour, baying and wailing like werewolves, 'What shall I do, cut it off?'"

His uncle had to smile – a relief to the oppression which for quite a while had been weighing on his heart.

"One evening," proceeded Antonio, "a hypnotist turned up at the poshest of the hotels. You know, one of those fellows who puts people to sleep."

"Yes yes, a hypnotist."

"He was a poor half-starved individual who did his act in evening dress along with a wife, most *décolletée*, whom he referred to as 'the lady wife'. This wife, either because she had undergone less hardship, or managed to filch something from the larder, or else because the good Lord was rooting for her, was as fat as any butcher's bitch, slabs of beef under her belt, a bottom that would burst apart the most capacious of skirts, half of her two boobs bulging out of her bodice, and a pair of olive-black eyes that appeared to ooze from under lowered lids.

"Having produced doves, flags, confetti and silk handker-chiefs from his top-hat, the hypnotist put his wife into a trance, turning her as white as a sheet, and while she was in this state, with imperious gestures which her eyes could not see but her flesh felt like whiplashes, he had her walk stiff as a ramrod out of the lounge, along the corridor and into a little room where she remained standing motionless, eyes tight shut. Ten minutes later, in thunderous tones, her husband demanded to know what numbers had been written by three gentlemen in the audience on three little scrolls of paper which he had that instant unrolled. And the woman, still in a trance, rattled off the numbers to a nicety, as if they'd been right in front of her nose."

"Queer goings-on those," mumbled his uncle.

"Well, the second evening Turi Grassi and Luigi d'Agata, guess what they did! They hid in the little room, and when the poor woman got there, eyes shut and arms outstretched, one of them, I forget which, without so much as by your leave slipped her a length as calm as you please."

"You amaze me! I am flabbergasted. And the woman didn't wake up?"

"I tell you no lies! She didn't wake up: either she pretended to remain in a trance so as not to create a scandal and not lose her livelihood, or else she lapped it up."

"Very possibly... And what about you?"

"The whole thing threw me into fits of agitation. It was like a drop of liquid fire on my flesh. God, what a ferment I was in! That night I went off into the woods on my own. The moon lit up the Dolomites, the trees smelt sweetly, and from down there beyond the wood came the receding sound of a band on the march as it left Collalbo for a nearby village. Something seethed in my blood, and my very sight and hearing felt as if they'd recovered the happiness of times when the least note of music or ray of light brought me to the brink of ecstasy..."

"Go on!" pressed his uncle. "Don't stop!"

"But that's exactly where I have to stop, because everything stopped there. Nothing else happened. That's all that occurred. My hopes were not fulfilled. My blood froze again, and again I felt as if between me and that part of my body there was a great knife fixed."

"Hell's teeth!" cried his uncle. "Hell's teeth I say!... But after that? Forgive me, dear boy, if I keep on repeating this question, but I'm too fond of you not to, and I'd give these last few months of my life to be told that, afterwards, things went well."

"Dear uncle," said Antonio, squeezing the old man's hand again, "things went as badly afterwards as before. Impossible for you to understand..."

"On the contrary, I do understand."

"No, you can't understand what it's like, that agony. There's a dead man in the midst of your life, a corpse so placed that whatever move you make you're bound to brush up against it, against its cold, fetid skin."

"I know what you mean. Indeed yes, I know very well! You're wrong to think I don't understand such things... But forgive me," he burst out, as one suddenly plucking up courage to jettison a weighty burden, "forgive me for saying it, dear boy, but if you knew things were tending this way..." And here, joining the tips of the thumb and forefinger of his right hand he applied them to his forehead, "if you knew, I repeat, that – at least for a period – the beast which God gave us for our torment fell to its knees when it should have stood upright and, well... to cut a long story short, was inclined to flop a lot more than was proper, then why, I ask of you..." And here, having joined the thumb and forefinger of his *left* hand, he applied them too to his forehead "... why, in heaven's name why, you blessed son-of-a-gun, did you have to go stepping into that nest of priests and vipers – by which I mean get involved in marriage (and what a marriage!) with a self-seeking girl, offspring of a self-seeking breed, colder than marble, prickly as a porcupine, probably touchy too – one of the sort you couldn't say 'What lovely eyes you've got' to –, with a crucifix on her breast which when the time suits she flashes like a dagger at you, armed with the counsels of a confessor who forbids her to do this and do that, until you feel the honest fellow is right there in bed with you managing your affairs, and you watch every word you say because tomorrow they'll be the property of the confessional; a woman quick to turn her back on you at the least friction and bundle herself up in her portion of blanket as in a sack, by day forever with a bad smell under her nose and the keys of all the drawers hanging from her belt; who keeps count of every mouthful you swallow, can't stand perfumes because she says they stink, refuses to shampoo her hair because she says it makes it fall out, has a bath only once a week because baths are debilitating;

who gets huffy if you read the paper at table, answers in mono-syllables if you talk to her, and if you don't – never utters a word; who if you're warm towards her grumbles that you're taking her for 'one of them', and if you're off-hand accuses you of neglecting her; all agog and willing like the dumb cluck she is to grow old and grey and swell up all slovenly fore and aft, to get swollen feet and hobble around as if a brick had dropped on her big toe – yet if you wear better than she does, she'll wish you all the ills in the world... not mortal ills, I need hardly say, but uncomfortable ones none the less, that make you once and for all drop the pretence of being still young."

"No, no, no, no!" cried Antonio.

"What do'you mean no, no, no? Aren't I right?"

"You're miles from the truth, my dear uncle!"

"I'm as sure as eggs is eggs of what I just said."

"You're miles off the mark."

"D'you realize how well I know that type of woman? Like the back of my hand. It's quite right of you of course, to defend someone who has been, and in a certain sense still is, your wife, it shows your good breeding, but kindly let me speak as I please, let me vent my bad temper, otherwise I'll fret myself to pulp."

"You're miles off target, Uncle Gildo."

"Then you tell *me*. Explain to me who is this Barbara Puglisi, why the devil you married her, and what happened between you and her. For crying out loud, the truth must be somewhere. If I've got it wrong, it's up to you to tell me. I'm prepared to stand corrected."

"In 1934 I returned here from Rome fed up to the back teeth with my own lies. I'd contrived to infer that I was the lover of Countess K, of the daughter of an ambassador, of the wife of a Party supervisor..."

"For the love of God I can't imagine how you managed to abide all those Fascists."

"Uncle, that kind of thing crosses Party barriers. The rub

was not that the women I knew were married to Fascists: I didn't give a damn about that. No, the hell of it was that with those women I had to confine myself to acting a part, because in real life I couldn't do a thing. If I could have been any more enterprising with the wives of the anti-Fascists, I can tell you, uncle, the Fascist Youth, Workers and Militia put together wouldn't have prevented me from paying court to them."

"What are you thinking of! Anti-Fascist wives are highly respectable, dear boy, and wouldn't have given you much rope."

"I could tell you a thing or two. . . But let's leave politics aside, Uncle Gildo. It's always politics politics with you. Politics has nothing to do with this."

"All right, all right! Go on with the story: in 1934 you came back from Rome."

"And I came back like a poor brute bound for the slaughter-house, and what a turmoil of emotion my head was as I tried to drop off in the sleeping-car. Rome, you see, was the city that had given me my greatest, my only delights in life. I was putting miles between myself and the Pope, to whose proximity in 1930 I had attributed the miracle of those ineffably halcyon days, when happiness besieged and beset me on every side. Memories of those endless hangings about in Naples, with the sound of mandolins boring into my flesh, and the lies of those times too, and the farewells, and the flights. . . all cancelled out! What remained with me was the taste of mulled wine that the world had then, a world I drank in at every pore, and the memory of the celestial moment – all the more celestial with the passing of these years bereft of it – that moment of fire, of honey, of paradise. . ."

"Take it easy, take it easy," urged his uncle. "It's a moment like any other. . ."

"Could be I've been making too much of it," admitted Antonio mildly, "since I ceased being able to repeat it. But don't say it's just a moment like any other!"

"It can be an awful let-down," said his uncle, digging his

heels in. "But don't let's argue. Get on with your story."

"Rome, the city of my few and far-between delights – and I was leaving it, perhaps for ever, and in store for me was Catania, the ghastly town were I had known only the one woman, and that only once, and then not all the way; the town where I'd lie on my bed at night trying to pick out the high heels among the footsteps of passing night-birds, and follow them furiously in my mind's eye until, little by little, as they grew further off and fainter, and finally eluded me, I tasted to the full my desperation as the useless husk of a man. In those endearing sounds fast fading away I heard the very echo of my own destiny; and so, having saturated my mind with bitterness as with a narcotic poison, I lost consciousness for an hour or two."

There was a pause during which his uncle dared not utter his usual "Get on with it then!"

"The moment I arrived in Catania my father spoke to me of the girl they wished to make my wife. Just imagine! Some chance of my being in a position to think of marriage! But one day, as I was standing on the pavement in Via Etnea lending an ear to Salinitro the chemist relating a judgement of my friend Angelo's – and I remember it all as if it were yesterday – I saw Barbara Puglisi passing by with her mother. My dear uncle, the Almighty must have fancied a joke at my expense! For as Barbara drew close, and I saw her green eyes and the flush on her cheeks, I was so overcome I had a rush of blood to the head. I was rooted to the spot."

"You don't say! After all this?"

"Yes, after all this. I don't tell lies, you know that. The same evening I went to my parents' room, sat on the edge of their bed, and announced my resolve to marry Barbara. I can't tell you how happy they were..."

"What a mess!" sighed Ermenegildo. "What a bloody awful mess! On the other hand, you're right... If merely setting eyes on her... The good Lord certainly pulls a fast one sometimes, there's no denying it... Forgive me for asking, though, but while you were engaged, when you were together, and a kiss or something of the kind was bound to crop up – although in a house like theirs, stuffed with monks and crucifixes, I'm sure *I* wouldn't have the courage even to go to the lavatory... As I was saying, during your engagement, that is, while you were engaged, didn't you have a chance to, er... see how things were shaping up for you?"

"Uncle, in that house stuffed with monks and crucifixes, as you put it, in the presence of the notary and his wife, who never took their eyes off us, beneath the scrutiny of so many other dead notaries and monks glaring down from their frames, and several curious stains on the walls and ceilings that also gave an impression of being the eyes of the house, and the saints, gaze upturned to the heavens, but who none the less saw us as in a mirror; in that atmosphere pregnant with respect, devoutness and high principles, where every Sunday the maids kissed the hands of their employers, the children those of their parents, and the parents that of the monkish brother, and no one entertained a thought that was not irreproachably upright... and the clothes in which the women were encased looked at you with buttons like the eyes of rabid dogs, and you really thought that if you dared unbutton a single one of them your hand would be bitten, lacerated and torn to pieces; well, in that house..."

"In that house?... For goodness' sake get a move on!"

"In that house I was almost always in a state of feeling ashamed of myself. But it was not a crestfallen, gloomy kind of shame. On the contrary it was of the glad, proud sort. And the fear that this might be found out closely resembled a hope and a desire that it would be... and the shiverings, the queasy turns, the dizzy fits, the shooting pains that stabbed at my back and the nape of my neck around midnight with their stiletto sharpness forced something deeper and deeper into my flesh, something that glittered and shone like a diamond and stayed within me all night long, flooded my dreams and my blood with light... Uncle, I tell you, it was happiness!"

"Very good, very good, this is excellent news. Tell on."

"Barbara is the most beautiful girl in the world."

"You really mean that?"

"Barbara is the most beautiful girl in the world!"

"If you say so..."

"When we were married, and I saw those arms of hers, and a bit of a knee, and all the other beauties that stirred beneath the lace of her nightdress... and when I saw the ineffable light cast upon her face, and even her eyes, by the modesty of those first moments of intimacy with a man, and I harkened to that serious head of hers, and heard a little girl's thoughts going round inside it, all the more naïve the more we were left to our own devices, well you can't imagine, uncle, how exciting it can be to a chap..."

"All right, all right, it's exciting. Get a move on then. What happened next?"

"Dear uncle, what happened next is what had happened five years before with Ingeborg."

"You stagger me!"

"That's the way it was, uncle."

"You mean... *exactly* what happened five years before?"

"Well, not exactly. This time it wasn't a total freeze-up of my body... It was more as if at the moment of climax everything evaporated and went up in smoke: as if my flesh complete with blood and nerves and all had arrived at boiling point and then dissolved in sweat and steam."

"Ah, what tricks the good Lord has up his sleeve, indeed he has! And so, poor boy, you're telling me that this time too..."

Antonio stared at the opposite wall without the flicker of an eyelid.

"But tell me, dear boy, why didn't you take immediate measures?"

"Measures? What sort of measures?"

"Leave your wife at once, before she got a whiff of the truth. Dear boy, you should have taken the initiative!"

"But how?"

"Well, for example, made off with a peasant girl, or a woman hoicked out of a brothel."

"I can't think that would have been the proper way to behave."

"Absolutely not. It would have been the conduct of an out-and-out blackguard."

"So you see my point? But apart from that I was really happy with Barbara. I was full of all sorts of curious delights and hopes."

"Even after. . . ?"

"Yes, even after that."

"I can't understand you."

"Barbara was not Ingeborg. As far as Ingeborg was concerned, after what happened happened, I was left with a feeling of terror, and if I'd ever come across her again I would have fainted away as surely as if I'd seen my own corpse pass in front of me eyelids closed and all. But it wasn't that way with Barbara. No. I felt her moral sense to be positively majestic – she instilled in me respect for all the churches she had frequented before her marriage. But as far as relations with men were concerned she was spotless as a clean sheet of paper. She knew nothing, she asked nothing, she blushed continually, and whenever I put my arms around her she clung tightly round my neck so that I should be the one to defend her from what I might be about to reveal to her. Like a stubborn child, she went on turning her back on a fact that she had never even encountered. Well uncle, it was a fact *I* was not in a position to reveal to her, but I pretended to believe that I was behaving that way because Barbara was begging me to do so. At the same time, by her side I was neither frigid nor frightened, let alone disgusted. My blood boiled and my head seethed with intense excitement, but this, at a certain point, leaked out through the pores of my skin and was lost in the air, leaving me with the sort of dispersed, ineffectual pleasure that children have in dreams, shortly before they lose their innocence."

"Pleasant and pleasurable, certainly, pleasant and pleasur-

174

able. . . but for a day, or a week, or a month – not for three years!"

"But uncle, I was always hoping that things would buck up. I got more and more excited. I was like a car revving up faster and faster but never able to budge."

"So what then? You threw in the sponge and cocked a snook at the lot of them?"

"Not a bit. As I got more and more worked up, so I grew happier and happier. I could already feel the first inklings, the first real seethings, dawning in Barbara's mind. This girl who, without committing the least misdeed, always in herself irreproachable and upright, was allowing the forebodings of sin to encroach upon the sacred images that filled her thoughts; this girl who, when she got into bed with me, blushed redder and redder every evening and remained for hours on end with a face of flame upon the pillow. . . uncle, what could I do? This girl made my head spin. Though it's a fact," he added at once, "that her turmoil became particularly noticeable after the maid – a stupid woman whom we were forced to sack – had explained a good few things to her."

"What?" burst out his uncle. "You mean to say you *knew* that Barbara was in the know?"

"After her conversation with the maid I took my courage in both hands and confessed everything in the minutest detail, as I have to you, uncle. I then asked her if she wanted to go on living with me or to separate."

"And her answer?"

"She threw her arms around my neck and kissed me in a way I shall never forget. She said we ought to continue to live as close in each other's embrace as two angels. But when she came to bed that night she was scarlet in the face, and I could read her heartbeat in the ribbons knotted on her bosom. Thus started a new period. She found it hard to get to sleep at night, and lay there, as I told you, with her face aflame on the pillow, turned towards me but with eyes tight shut. Every so often she would open them and look me straight in the face, and they were shining with love, curiosity and joyous premonitions: at which I really and truly began to think that the miracle of 1930 might be repeated, since it was this devout girl who asked it of me nightly in the purest and warmest manner possible. So life slid by very happily and lovingly until suddenly her father, her mother, and she herself, I don't quite know why..."

"No," cried his uncle, leaping from the easy chair, "Don't say another word! You know why, and so does everyone else. I've been patient and let you talk, but at this point no, that's enough, I refuse to appear any dumber than I am. You know why Barbara decided to cut and run, you know it very well. I bided my time while you were painting that glowing portrait of your wife. 'No doubt she is as he says,' I thought to myself, 'beautiful, chaste, innocent etc., but what price the avarice, the coldness, the calculation she's inherited from her family? Let's see what he says about that! He won't dare deny that she's a self-seeking girl, a girl who well knows which side her bread is buttered, prepared to sacrifice everything except financial advantage. When she sees wealth it dazzles her, as a fish trapped by the light of a jack-lamp rises to the surface as good as gold and can be caught in the palm of the hand. He won't dare deny this, by God! If he does, it means that he takes me for a nincompoop, and I don't have any truck with people who take me for a nincompoop!'"

Antonio allowed his uncle's tantrum to subside with the indolent air of someone who has foreseen a tiresome event and then sees it happen.

"Uncle," he murmured at length, "you speak the gospel truth: Barbara is a self-seeking girl, a girl with her head screwed on. So shall I tell you something? That I like even this side of her..."

"Well, in that case," snorted Ermenegildo, "it's useless to go on discussing it. But how come," he added, stabbing at him with a finger and raising his voice wrathfully, "how come this woman promises to live with you like a cherub with a seraph, tells you that you'll be as happy together and as close as two peas in a pod, hugs you and kisses you and gives you loving looks all night long, and then kicks you out on the spot like a mangy dog?"

"Uncle, please! No one kicked me out, I left of my own accord. Barbara didn't take her decision on the spot, as you say she did: she's a true, honest, scrupulous Catholic, not one of those who claim to be Catholics and then go their own way. When she promised to go on living with me she didn't yet know that the Church considers a marriage like ours null and void: she hadn't yet spoken to the Archbishop of Catania. . ."

"Fool, fool, fool," bellowed the old man. "Such a fool it needs me to tell you you're a fool! Don't you realize you're behaving like a babe in arms, the way they're exploiting you? All your fine perspicacity they're ready and willing to gobble up in two mouthfuls. The Archbishop, the Church. . . What you ought to say is the Duca Di Bronte, the Duca Di Bronte, the Duca Di Bronte with the buttocks of an abbess and broad acres in La Piana!"

Antonio heaved his legs off the bed. He seemed to shrink into himself. In the opening of his pyjama jacket his chest looked skinnier; the delicate whites of his eyes were shot with red.

"Well anyway," he said, "I love Barbara, I always have loved her, and since I've not been seeing her I've been going mad with love for her."

"In that case," broke in his uncle disgustedly, "why not crawl under her door and implore her to do you the favour of allowing you to stay in the kitchen to keep the mice down, instead of the usual old grass-snake they use."

Antonio shrank into himself still more. All his nobler qualities (not noticeable in what he said or, to be honest, in his manner of comportment), shone forth in his face.

"You don't understand me," he said. And restoring his legs to the bed he lay down again.

"Not understand you? Why d'you think I'm calling you fool, fool and fool again, if not because I *do* understand you?"

"I would not go back to Barbara, not even if she came licking the ground right up to my door in front of the whole of Catania. I'm in love with her, yes, madly in love with her, and behind her back I'd kiss the ground she walks on, but from these lips speaking to you now Barbara will never hear her name again."

In due order his uncle repeated to himself these last words of Antonio's: "From these lips speaking to you now Barbara will never hear her name again."

"Fine!" he cried, "That's as fine as could be! That's the way for a man to talk! It's absolutely essential not to give those chisellers a chance to crow!... Instead," he added after a pause, "let us think about what to do next. What shall I say to your father? The poor fellow believes that matters went quite differently. Who's to tell him that?..."

He broke off.

"What gets my goat," he resumed, "is that tomorrow people will be making a meal of our private affairs. They won't credit it in one of our family, who have always been the cuckold-makers and never the cuckolds, and no one, thank God, not even the fellow who prides himself on being cock of the roost, can brag about having got a foot in *our* door. And even you, for heaven's sake, the women were scrimmaging to get at you, you had them on such tenterhooks... or so at least I thought, and so did everyone..."

His whole frame suddenly slumped. He sat down again.

"Hmm," he said, clicking his tongue and leaving long pauses between one exclamation and the next. "Hmmm... yes... unfortunate..." And after a deep sigh: "Well, what's to be done? These are things that can't be helped... On the other hand there *are* worse things in life: I'd almost forgotten my own ailments... It's quite true that when your mind's taken off them... My head's been spinning for an hour now, and I haven't given it a hoot... How I'd like to make a present to Notary Puglisi of the hound that's clamped its jaws on me – right here!" And he rapped his stomach. "Lord, it's half-past seven already! Your parents'll be back any minute. What's to be done? What shall I tell them? The truth? Not on your life, I haven't the nerve... A lie then? Don't trust it... short-legged things, lies are, and wouldn't carry us very far... There always comes a moment when we have to open up and spit out the mouthful we're hiding in our cheek. Then again I don't feel up to telling your father... or your mother either .. even less than him in fact... I know my sister too well: she seems as solid as a rock, but actually she's the fall-to-dust-if-you-touch-me type. Then again, have I got the brass to hide it from Alfio? Or try and act so that he doesn't... or leave him to understand that... or better, put a damper on the whole conversation... or better still, lead it onto another tack?..."

And with these *then agains*, *howevers*, *what's to be dones*, *or elses* and *or better stills* he carried on for half an hour, without noticing that at every word Antonio grew more wasted and wan, until it appeared that he must surely flicker out, like a candle which, as we talk and drink and wave our arms about, we inadvertently douse with water.

Signor Alfio and Signora Rosaria, preceded by the maid, reached home shortly before eight.

They found Ermenegildo in the dining-room, sitting lonesome at the table on which he had flung his stick and his panama hat.

Signor Alfio, quite done up by the effort of climbing the stairs after that long, anxious peregrination, apologized with a wave of the hand for not expressing himself in words and with another wave of the hand ordered the maid to leave the room, close the door and shut herself in the kitchen.

This time without her husband requiring it of her, Signora Rosaria retired, with the excuse of taking off her hat in front of her dressing-table mirror.

In the dining-room silence fell.

Seeing that man across the table, his cheeks sunken, bereft even of speech, Ermenegildo so raged against the iniquities of

179

destiny that he quite lost all tact and prudence, even towards the victim of that destiny.

"Alfio, my friend," said he, "you'd do well to pull yourself together, turn over a new leaf, and not give another thought to that... what the devil's her name?... that Barbara."

Signor Alfio made a long, intense effort to unglue his lips, with the sole result of further deepening the hollows in his cheeks; then he turned his hands, at rest on the table, palms uppermost, as if to say, "I never have thought about Barbara, I think only of my son."

There was a conspicuous silence between the two men.

At a certain point a wheezy groan took root in Signor Alfio's belly, a distant, barely perceptible groan like a tummy-rumble. It rose into his chest and then, infinitely slowly and with prodigious difficulty, clambered in among his vocal chords, and at long, long last, breaking through the glutinous pastes of tongue and palate: "The truth!" he glugged.

"Well, the truth is that Antonio hasn't been too well recently."

Signor Alfio sank his chin onto his chest, lowering his head to mask his contorted lips.

"I must know," he murmured in a faint, hoarse voice, "whether Antonio did it on purpose or not."

"He didn't do it on purpose, Alfio. D'you imagine he'd do anything so wishy-washy on purpose, and for three long years on end?"

"So what's the answer?"

"He was unable to do otherwise. He finds Barbara attractive, but with her... in the old you-know-what... he never manages to make the grade."

The bitter droop of Signor Alfio's mouth increased, as he turned one corner of it down so very far that his nose had no option but to follow suit.

"Craziest thing I ever heard! A young man, when it comes to you-know-what, doesn't manage to make the grade, as you put it? And a young man like him, what's more, who's spent more time on top of women than he has on his own mattress. Stuff and nonsense! So you're implying that even if he took it into his head – not from choice, mind you, but as a sort of slight, as a bet, or because he was required to do so by me or his mother – if he took it into his head, I repeat, to show that bitch there... what's her name? Barbara... to show her what a Magnano is capable of when he wants... you're saying that he, debilitated as he is, wouldn't have the spunk to do a thing?"

Ermenegildo bent his head and began stroking his chin and his cheek, each time leaving a furrow which was slow to return to its natural shape.

"But there's one thing he's got to do!" blurted out Signor Alfio. "This he must do, by God, or I'll cut him off with a shilling! He must take a mistress, two, three, four mistresses, and without delay! I'll sell the orange-grove, I'll sell this house, I'll sell the clothes off my back and give him all the money he needs, but he must take four mistresses!"

Ermenegildo continued to stroke his face, but with such force that the flesh of his right cheek moved round under his chin onto the left, and one eye seemed to slip half-way with it.

"Eh? Well? Don't you agree?" demanded Signor Alfio. "Isn't that the right answer? In that case what *do* we do? Fold our arms and do nothing? Stand there like so many Christs with mock sceptres for all and sundry to spit at? Become the sewers of the city? Let them shit in our mouths?"

"That's not what I'm saying," murmured Ermenegildo.

"Then what *are* you saying? Come on, spit it out!"

"I'm saying it's better not to add fuel to the fire."

"Why? What d'you mean? Add fuel to what fire, if my son takes four mistresses? After the dirty trick they've played on him, hasn't he the right to parade in an open carriage with an entire brothel on board? Who's he got to account to? Tell me that!"

"Alfio, do as you please," replied Ermenegildo. "Give him

four mistresses, give him a hundred for all I care. But for my part I do not advise it."

"Why not?"

"If I were in Antonio's shoes I'd leave Catania and go travelling somewhere... what the devil's it called?... ah yes, abroad."

"Why?"

"For a year I should like not so much as to hear the name of Barbara, or Luisa, or of any other woman on the face of the globe!"

"Why not?"

"Alfio, I've got to say it..." For a long moment Ermenegildo looked his brother-in-law straight in the eye, then: "And if what happened with Barbara should happen to him with some other woman, what would be our next move? We'd be tying a whatsit... hell and dammit, I can't find the right words either... a millstone, that's it! We'd be tying a millstone round our necks and then – join hands, all of us here in this house, and straight off with us to the far end of the jetty!"

Signor Alfio thereupon began brandishing a hand at his brother-in-law and stammering frantically. The word which refused to rise to his lips, and for which he felt an impelling need, was Ermenegildo's name.

"What the devil's your name?" he burst out.

"What, mine?" quavered Ermenegildo.

"Yes, yours. What is it?"

A brick whammed into Ermenegildo's brain: what with his haste to give the answer, the fear of having forgotten his own name, and the rage that all this was stirring up in him, he began babbling disconnected syllables, repeatedly coming close to the word Ermenegildo and fluffing it every time.

"Come on, what's your name?" bawled Signor Alfio.

"..." replied the other.

"What is it? Spit it out! You're even worse than I am!"

"..." replied the other again.

"You don't even know your own name!" Signor Alfio taunted him.

"Ermenegildo!" exploded the other at last, leaping from his chair quite beside himself and thrashing the table with his stick. "By God, this is getting a bit thick! Ermenegildo, Ermenegildo, Ermenegildo!"

"Ermenegildo," demanded Signor Alfio, "what did you mean by what you said just now, that my son... that it might... what's the word?"

Ermenegildo made not the slightest effort to help him out, he simply remained mum.

"What's the word? What's the word?"

Ermenegildo kept his sulky lips hermetically sealed.

"...happen!" exploded Signor Alfio. "That what had happened to my son with his wife might happen with some other woman. What did you mean by that?"

"I meant that it's better not to tug too hard on the old rope," replied Ermenegildo, picking his words and keeping an eye on where every phrase he hazarded was going to land him, for fear of falling into another lapse of memory, "especially when the rope isn't as hefty as it might be."

"Not as hefty as it might be..." repeated Signor Alfio. "And what d'you mean by that now? Not as... as it might be..."

"I mean that Antonio ought to rest up for a year or two."

Signor Alfio drew a large handkerchief from his trousers pocket, half unfolded it and held it in front of his mouth, in the manner of one about to spit out something disgusting.

"Oh, the disgrace of it!" he murmured.

He then carefully refolded the handkerchief, first into four and then into eight, and pocketed it again.

"For a year or two, you say. But don't you realize I'm so old they'll soon be able to scoop me up with a spoon. Have I really got to spend the last years of my life knowing that neither I nor my son have what it takes to go to bed with a woman? Or rather, that he doesn't, my son doesn't, by God, when at his age he ought to be able to lift rocks without using his hands!... Lift rocks, I say!"

"And so he will," said Ermenegildo in conciliatory tones. "When he's rested for a year or two he'll lift rocks without... what did you say?"

"I said what I said," muttered Signor Alfio in frenzy. "Anyway, what are you on about?" he resumed out loud. "After a year or two, eh? What's he going to do after a year or two? The older you get the more uphill it is. Do at forty what you can't do at thirty-six? Ermenegildo, what are you trying to kid me into? Get along with you, we must resign ourselves and say no more about it. It just means I no longer have a man for a son. He died, my son did. I had a son, but he died."

Not a sob had escaped Signor Alfio, nor apparently had his eyes shed tears, and yet his old cheeks were streaming and shining with them, and some ran down onto his collar like drops of sweat.

"He died, my son, he died. I had one, but he died."

The old man slapped a hand down on the table. Then, leaning on it, he made to rise. But he realized that his legs had turned to jelly inside his trousers. So he sat down again.

"A year or two, you say... But come off it, for goodness' sake, we're not here to tell each other fairy stories. It's no use crying over spilt milk. Until just now I had a man for a son, a son in Rome who was the apple of my eye, and I kept him on a pedestal, and everyone envied me, and that woman whatsit... what *was* her name? Ermenegildo, help me!"

"Who?" queried his brother-in-law, raising his brow from the palm of his hand.

"The wife of that feller who felt he'd been made a fool of."

"Yes, yes, I know who you mean," replied Ermenegildo, reassailed by the cold sweat of amnesia: "ca... ca... Oh holy mackerel!"

"Relative of Mussolini's."

"That feller, yes I know... hell and dammit!"

"All right, let it go. You know who I mean. That feller's wife..."

"Countess K!" burst out Ermenegildo with profound relief.

"That's her – Countess K! She tore her fingernails out on his door, and he didn't open up because..."

Ermenegildo gave Signor Alfio a look.

The latter stopped, jerked his head back, stared his brother-in-law straight in the eye. A black cloud plummeted into his brain.

"Because..." he attempted to continue, but "Oh my God!" he murmured, without having formed a thought or made any supposition whatever, but already half-dead of fright as if the suspicion of the truth had filtered unobserved through his consciousness and seeped into his bones.

"Ermenegildo," he said, as faintness swept over him, "call my wife at once! Hurry, hurry!"

Ermenegildo shot out of his chair and rushed to the door to shout his sister's name, but having gasped like a fish once or twice and realized that his memory had snapped shut on him again, and that the more he tried to clear it the more fiercely it clung to the word he wanted to wrest from it, he closed the door behind him, scurried down the corridor into the bedroom, seized Signora Rosaria by the hand and said, "Quick, he needs you!"

"Who?" she asked, thoroughly scared.

He was about to answer "Alfio", but fearing that the name would get lost in the brief journey from his brain to his lips he prudently confined himself to saying, "Your husband."

X

THE NOISE OF THIS SCANDAL was heard all over Catania like an eruption of Mount Etna.

Antonio Magnano, son of Alfio, nephew of Ermenegildo, the beauteous youth who made even the devoutest of girls raise her eyes from her missal, Antonio with that perpetually sleepy look in his eyes (ah, who did not know him? They would raise a hand above their heads to indicate how tall he was, or pass their fingers caressingly over their cheeks to imply that his face was perfection itself), yes, that very Antonio, exactly that Antonio and no other, well – between him and his wife... nothing happened! Absolutely *nothing*! Barbara Puglisi, after three years of marriage, had still not tasted the greatest gift of God.

"What did her husband do with her all these years?"

"Brushed the flies off her."

"Is it possible?"

"It's the fact of the matter."

"What, Alfio's son doesn't find fresh bread toothsome?"

"He does not."

"Come off it! You expect me to swallow that?"

"Strike me blind if it's not the truth! On the wedding night they went to bed together and... nothing happened!"

"How in the world...?"

"How? Just like that. I wasn't there, friend."

"So, a flop?"

"An utter flop, friend."

"Nothing but a flop for three years?"

"Nothing but a flop."

"Every night a flop?"

"Every night a flop."

"How on earth?"

"Go and ask Our Father which art in heaven, he's the one who cooks up these things."

"I could understand it once or twice, or three times... I'll be generous – five times. Which of us hasn't done a flop?"

"I tell you no lie, friend. *I* never have."

"Never?"

"Never!"

"In a certain sense, in the sense of a complete and hopeless flop, neither have I."

"May the Lord send me death rather than such a misfortune! What's a man got in life if they take even that away from him? I tell you I'd go jump in the lake."

"Why ever does he go on living?"

"Better dead!"

"A thousand times better dead!"

"What d'you mean, a thousand times? A million times better dead!"

"If ever I found myself reduced to such a condition, better a hundred yards underground, as you say, or at the bottom of the sea being eaten by the fish. I'll go further: better to be imprisoned for life with my hands and feet manacled like Christ's, but my honour as a man intact, by God, worthy of commiseration, maybe, for steeping my hands in the blood of my neighbour, but at least not a target for sniggers and nudges as I walk down the street, because if anyone dares to laugh or stick his elbow in his companion's ribs I can always yell 'What're you laughing at, pieface? Why not send me along your sister or your wife and then we'll have a really good laugh!'

"And who can blame you? Jesus, Mary and Joseph! If I had such a useless thing just dangling there, God knows, I'd hack it off and toss it to the dogs! What's more Our Lord himself said much the same thing: If one of your members offends you, cut it off and throw it away."

"Fair enough, but not everyone has the guts to do it."

"Ah, I would! In fact I can't understand how Alfio's boy hangs on to such a bit of bad news without doing something berserk."

"How do we know he won't?"

"Not a chance, friend. He's let too much time slip by already. If he hasn't done it so far there's no reason for his doing it tomorrow. I don't know what stuff young people are made of these days, but they soon throw in the sponge."

"Let's wait before jumping to conclusions."

"As far as I'm concerned, you can wait as long as you please. But listen here now, has he always suffered from this raw deal, or did it come over him after he got married?"

"Honestly friend, I won't tell you a lie: I simply don't know."

"Rumour has it that in Rome this lad gobbled up so many women he lost count of them, and that when he was in Catania he constantly needed a woman to tickle his elbow for him. One evening I was at the next-door table in a café, and I assure you that at least ten times I heard his friend – the one they've now foisted on us as mayor – ask him (and he was pretty persistent), 'What's next on the agenda, Ninuzzu? Shall we nip down and get our ends away?'"

"That mayor gets his end away, and how! Seen all those pretty secretaries he's taken on at the Town Hall? But as for Alfio's son, he's a different kettle of fish. Can you swear to it, in all conscience, that he managed to get his end away that evening?"

"I can assure you in all conscience that later on – might have been elevenish – I heard him say these very words: 'All right, let's nip off and get the old end away!'"

"But friend, it's one thing to talk and another thing to act. Were you there in the bed while he was trying to have it off?

What do you know about what went on there? It's dark in bed, mate, and you never know what goes on."

"Christ alive, the women talk!"

"That depends. I once met someone who paid a whole heap of money for the woman to keep her mouth shut."

"Are you suggesting that Alfio's boy paid a heap of money for women to keep their mouths shut?"

"I'm not suggesting anything. What's it matter to me, whether he makes it or not? That's his problem. Nothing I can do to help him... That is... If he'd called me in on his wedding night I'd have given him a helping hand very willingly."

"Not much effort needed there, friend! *There's* a girl to bring the dead to life."

The conversation grew moist with lustful slaverings and roguishly laughing mouths sprayed forth saliva. A minute later and it was time for back-handers on the belly and shoving each other about. Enough, in short, of solemn discourse; perfectly possible at this point that even a Justice of the Peace, barged into by a friend, might go thumping, as on a big bass drum, against some great resonant door already barred for the night.

The ones who were utterly crushed and annihilated were Antonio's friends.

These men, all in their thirties, were unable to master their emotions, and for several days the eyes of the envious were able to feast themselves upon their pale, drawn faces. It seemed as if the honour of the whole crew had suffered a blow, and some of them, in their eagerness to compensate, behaved atrociously even towards the wives of their relatives.

"I don't turn anything down. Opportunity never knocks twice," was Luigi d'Agata's maxim.

"But really! Your uncle's wife..."

"Stop getting on my tits. Let me fend for myself."

"But... your uncle's wife!"

"No go, old boy. I won't listen to reason. What I find, I

take. It's not my fault is it, if the beastly thing keeps rearing its head and won't stay quiet for a moment?"

"But really... a little consideration!"

"The beastly thing has no consideration for anyone. Is *this* a time to start standing on ceremony and let others walk all over us with their boots on! Let everyone take care of his own. As far as I'm concerned, when I come across a woman I don't give a hoot whose daughter she is or whose wife she is. She's a skirt? Right then! That's all I want to know."

"But what's it all lead to?"

"One underneath and one on top."

"And what would you say if I did that to *your* wife?"

"I'm not married."

"But you've got a mother... a sister..."

"Kindly don't drag in my mother and sister. My mother and sister have nothing to do with it!"

"But aren't they women too?"

"Certainly they are, but I'm telling you they have nothing to do with the matter."

"How can they have nothing to do with it? If they're women..."

"I said they have nothing to do with it. Do I make myself clear? Or do I have to tear a leg off the table?"

"Ah, so that's your kind of logic is it?"

"Yes, that's my kind of logic, and if anyone doesn't like my kind of logic he can piss off... Before I start in on him with a table leg!" he added from between his teeth.

"OK, OK, let's drop the subject."

"Dead right! Let's drop it."

The group fell silent, but here and there could be heard a foot tapping nervously on the floor, a rhythmic leg banging the rung of a chair, fingers drumming on the table-top.

All of a sudden one of those present, struck by who knows what unspoken thought, clapped his hands sharply together, making everybody jump.

"What the hell's up with you?" they demanded.

"Take it easy!"

"Steady now!"

"Scarcely good manners!"

"Ah, my poor little diddumses!" countered the aforesaid, abashed at having been caught red-handed thinking his most intimate thoughts, and annoyed at having to apologize for them. "Did I scare them, the little duckies? Mamma's pets, my sweetie-pies, did I give them a fright? Did I give them goose-pimples?"

A gloomy atmosphere of bickering closed in around Antonio's friends.

The gloomiest of all was Edoardo Lentini. Grief over his cousin's catastrophe and hatred for Hitler had made him the most despondent man to tramp the streets of Sicily in the midnight hours.

"My respects, Your Worship." Some passer-by emerging from the shadows of a tree would recognize and greet him, raising a servile hand in the Fascist salute right under his nose.

"Goodnight," Edoardo would reply, and then in an undertone, "Up yours!" in response to the "Son of a bitch!" or "A pox on you and your bloody bosses!" which the passer-by had undoubtedly added under his breath right after his respectful greeting.

Then Edoardo would turn and good-naturedly watch the other disappear into the darkness under the trees – he had a liking for anyone who insulted him as a representative of the regime.

But the THING, the SHAPE, that made him writhe with revulsion, and toss and turn at night between the sheets, and spit in drawing-rooms to the consternation of the ladies (who had admired his *savoir-faire* in former days), was the face of Hitler with its moustache like that of a hyaena its trainer has been trying in vain to teach to laugh. Ah, that face, that face! It was inconceivable! Intolerable!

When Hitler claimed the Sudetenland, and the war-scare started, and certain gas-lit alleyways in Catania filled with the scuttling of thousands of men incited by fear and by the thought, "So, seeing we are about to die, we'd better 'do it' as often as we possibly can," on the 5th of August, in the hall of the Fascist Headquarters, while Party Secretary Pietro Capàno was hammering his fists on the table in an effort to instil a mite of martial quality into those black Supervisors' uniforms within which (out of prudence, vanity or self-interest) so many bourgeois nonentities had been hiding for years, Edoardo asked to be allowed to speak; and, all eyes upon him, he asserted that war would not break out.

Edoardo's bloodless face had the Party Secretary worried.

"On what do you base your claim that war won't break out?" he asked.

Edoardo paled still further, from the exquisite pleasure of the risk he was about to take, and from the fact that at long last he was giving vent to a hitherto hidden animosity.

"Hitler," he said, "barks, but does not bite – like all men who have no balls."

Pietro Capàno felt his head spinning with fright at the mere sound of such words.

"Eh?... What?... Whassat?" he babbled.

"It's not the Führer's fault he's in that condition," continued Edoardo. "Indeed, it's to his credit as an ex-serviceman. You will yourself be aware, Mr Secretary, that in the last war Hitler was invested by a cloud of poison-gas which shrivelled his... whatever it was it shrivelled."

"I know nothing about it!" gabbled Pietro Capàno, thumping the table with alternate fists. "I know absolutely nothing about it!"

"Come now, Mr Secretary. It's common knowledge."

"To tell the truth," interpolated a particularly ingenuous Supervisor, "I too was unaware that Hitler had been affected by gas in that quarter... To judge from the way he goes on, however, I would not say that he is a man without balls. On the contrary, I am of the opinion that his are of the sort that reach to the ground and churn up the dust!"

"Of course," yelled Capàno, this time giving the table not a thump but a wallop and then drawing himself up to his full height. "He has a pair of balls that churn up the dust! All the men in his family have balls that churn up the dust! What's more no relative of his, so far as I know, has ever been repudiated by his wife!"

The allusion to Antonio was plain enough. Edoardo rose to his feet, half his face flaming red and the other still bloodless.

"I repeat," said he, "that Hitler lost his balls in the war."

The enraged Secretary grasped the corners of the table.

"If that's the way you think," he hissed, "you have but one duty!"

"And what might that be?"

"To cease to serve a regime led by men without balls, you, who have balls yourself, as do *all* your relations!"

"Leave my relations out of it," growled Edoardo morosely. "Just leave them out of it!... And as for your insinuation," he added almost in a shriek, "my answer is that I do not serve the Nazi regime but the Fascist regime which is led by a man with all the balls you could wish for!"

"You know perfectly well," said Pietro Capàno, biting his lip, "that the Duce and Hitler love each other like brothers, and anyone who insults the one insults the other."

"Mr Secretary, come to the point: are you saying I ought to resign? Very well then, I resign, I resign, I resign!"

And with this Edoardo, already on his feet, plucked from a chair his beret with the gilded-eagle badge, adjusted it painstakingly on his head before the mirror – pretending to be absorbed with his appearance but in reality giving his face time to moderate its red and yellow blotchiness; then, saluting the Secretary and the other comrades with a highly stylish Fascist salute, he left the room.

Once outside Palazzo Vaccarini he took a deep breath.

"Phew!" he said to himself. "I'm free! I've got free at last!"

As soon as he reached home he recounted the whole occurrence to his wife.

"Very well," said she. "Can I use the official car today, or shall I take a taxi?"

"Use the car, for goodness' sake. Until I'm replaced I'm still mayor of Catania!"

After lunching in silence with his wife and his five children he sat down at his desk and penned the following letter to Count K:

Your Excellency,

I wish to inform you promptly of an episode which occurred today at the headquarters of the Fascist Federation, an episode in which I behaved intemperately. In the course of a discussion on foreign policy, of which you are etc., etc., I perhaps yielded too much to the feeling of intense admiration which I have for our LEADER.

As you know, I cannot permit that the Führer be considered as of the same moral and intellectual standard as the DUCE. Whenever I think I perceive some such intention in the pronouncements of others, I, Your Excellency, lose control of myself and react with violence.

Today, at Headquarters, I seemed to discern that the officials of the Party ingenuously considered Hitler to be the main protagonist of present events. I say "ingenuously" because the comrades here in Catania are attached by profound devotion to the DUCE, to your own person, and to His Majesty the King and Emperor. But their ingenuousness wounded me deeply. Your Excellency, I could not restrain myself, and I reminded them in no uncertain terms of the mutilation of which the German leader was a victim during the late war, in which (let it be said) our own superb troops were resplendent for their valour – a mutilation in itself glorious, but which sets the Führer, even physically, on a level below that on which soars the figure of our DUCE.

I will not say that the Secretary denied the difference in stature between the two men, but he was too warm in the defence of Hitler, so that at a certain point in the discussion he stooped to the use of strong words offensive to family honour.

Your Excellency, I am not accusing anyone! I will go further: I excuse them all and accuse only myself.

Thinking over what was said, and the whole course of that dispute, I am obliged to recognize that I am suffering from nervous strain, and that my love for the DUCE renders me so liable to irritation that I am unable to serve him with serenity at a time when HE has seen fit to take to his bosom another leader a fraction of himself in stature, but at whose side he has declared he will march *to the very end*.

For this reason I make so bold as to offer you my resignation as mayor of Catania, and offer it to you, Your Excellency, rather than to the Minister of Internal Affairs, begging you to consider me the most grateful and devoted servant of the DUCE and of your own person.

With Fascist respects etc.

This letter was reckoned by Edoardo's relations to be a model of diplomacy. The manner in which he expounded the facts was the only one which could save him from expulsion from the Party and maybe even banishment.

But no sooner had he posted it than he fell a prey to gloomy thoughts.

"Is it fair that I have to lie in order to tell the truth?" he grumbled to himself, slipping down a side-street in an attempt to hide his tracks from some fellow who had been tailing him for three days, who switched his eyes skywards, adopting the air of a lover or a contemplator of clouds each time his quarry turned to observe him. "Is it fair that to show how much Hitler disgusts me I should have to choke back everything his crony arouses in me? True, I've achieved my aim: I've resigned as mayor. The position I so set my heart on I've thrown to the dogs. But in order to reject this honour which would make millions of Italians delirious with joy I've had to demean myself as if I were a toady. Evil times indeed, when even pride has the vile taste of its opposite!"

Once more he took to tramping the empty avenues in the midnight hours, and to the rare passers-by who flashed an open palm in salute before his eyes with a "Your Worship!" he replied, "I'm no longer the mayor. I've resigned."

His step was impatient, and he turned over strange and terrible things in his mind... Tomorrow, at dawn, he would send a second letter to Count K: "Dear Sir, You will doubtless have realized that my previous letter was written in the style of convention and stupidity. But to prevent any misunderstandings arising between us, I will tell you the real reason which induced me to resign as mayor of Catania. It is that Fascism, the Duce, the Führer, and you yourself, Count K, provoke in me a profound sense of nausea which at long last I have the strength not to fight down. For years I lacked this strength, because the very air we breathe infects our lungs with fatalism and falsehood; for years I have gone about in my mayoral uniform, and the people, seeing me through the windows of the official car, with the gilded eagle on my brow, have been at liberty to salute me with the most servile of salutes and to preserve an image of me to carry home and scoff at at leisure and with impunity. But those times are over. The man now writing to you is no longer afraid, as you see, to call you lei* and address you as plain Sir etc., etc... "

At this point the voices of his wife and children screamed in his ears... No, such a letter would be useless folly; no paper would publish it, no one would think it credible. He himself would be thrown into prison on a charge of having, say, demanded three hundred thousand lire from an engineering company to allot them the contract to build a road... His imagination changed tack, and he was a man three thousand metres high, exactly the height of Mount Etna. Each stride of

* The Fascists banned the use of the polite third-person form of address lei as being of foreign origin (from Span. usted). They used Voi instead.

such a man would be two kilometres long. Two hundred and fifty strides and he is already in sight of Rome. The guns thunder against him, their shells barely prick his skin, he squashes the aircraft between his palms like bothersome mosquitoes. Sweeping a foot to right and to left he tramples and scatters the army attempting to bar his passage. Now he is bending over Rome, inserting one hand with difficulty into the narrow crevice of Via Nomentana in an attempt to catch a car dashing hither and thither like an ant, carrying within it an insect even smaller than itself. At last he manages to grasp it with thumb and two fingers and, straightening up again, lifts it to the height of Mount Etna itself, on a level with his eyes. He removes from it a tiny little kicking figure which he immediately places under a vast magnifying glass. He makes out the insignia of the Chief Marshal of the Empire, absolutely minute and totally invisible to the naked eye...

A voice broke into his reverie: "My respects, Your Worship!"

His heart jumped into his mouth.

"Goodnight," he replied, "however I am no longer..."

Disgust and discouragement pulled him up short. What was the good of telling a night-owl that he had resigned? That poor fellow, stunned with lack of sleep and years of hard work, long since incapable of believing in the courage and altruism of his compatriots, would he fancy cudgelling his brains in order to understand that the administrator of his city had really and truly resigned, had not been kicked out, and that the futile reason which he had given for resigning hid another and far more profound one? Certainly not. So how *was* he to behave? Edoardo struggled and strove like a tunnyfish trapped in the nets. What ought he to do? What ought he to say? Was it possible that in this damned society even an act of the most magnanimous wrath ended up as bowings and scrapings?

Even before receiving Count K's answer to his letter he considered himself a private citizen and no longer went to the Town Hall. When secretaries telephoned him at home he invariably replied, "I am no longer mayor."

"But Your Worship..."

"No longer, I tell you!"

"For me you'll always be my mayor."

"I order you not to think of me as mayor!"

"But Your Worship..."

To settle the matter once and for all, he began to frequent the apartment of the Socialist lawyer Raimondo Bonaccorsi, around whom gathered a group of anti-Fascist "non-cardholders" who had left their thumb-prints in the police files.

His host was a man who, except at meetings and in the lawcourts, had always spoken in a hushed voice, as if destined from birth to be the opponent of a regime with flapping ears. This thoughtful, hesitant man dominated his listeners with wisdom of the old school, rummaging at length in his beard before finding a yes or a no, and making it understood that beyond the obvious and facile arguments of his restless friends there were others; to be found not in the books and newspapers they were in the habit of reading, but in more venerable newspapers, and books exceeding rare, on the extremely distant fringes of culture which his mind alone was capable of embracing.

The first evening Edoardo went to Avvocato Bonaccorsi's apartment the company kept their eye on him as a suspicious character. But within three days he had won all hearts.

The old anti-Fascists had been reduced to a sorry plight by endless disappointments. The habit of failure had engendered in them a bitterness that was little by little benumbing them, to the point of slowing down their pulse rates. Their host appeared to be afflicted with this malady even more than the rest of them, and some said that he was so attached to his gloom that he would have relinquished the pleasure of victory rather than that of his despondency.

Lifeless voices filled the Avvocato's study when Edoardo

burst on them with his implacable hopefulness and his rugged assurance that the things he hated would soon be dead and buried.

Apart from erstwhile Socialist and democratic Deputies, the study was frequented by the ex-bandit Don Luigi Compagnoni, always fretting because his honesty and mild temper, which had by an unfortunate coincidence come over him in 1925 – the year in which the ruling tyranny had killed off all strength of character both in good and in evil – might seem to be attributable to funk. "Bless me!" said he. "Oh for the times when a man performed his devotions with his knife! Oh for those times!" He hoped to see such times again in order to flaunt his integrity in the midst of a multitude of daggers unsheathed anew.

But for some years now, in fact since the exploit in Ethiopia had ended successfully, disheartenment reigned stagnant in the Avvocato's study. It seemed as if their host piled the grate high with blocks of ice, rather than with the fires of hope. And the one to suffer most from this was the good ex-bandit Compagnoni, and along with him a young architect, Pasqualino Cannavò, a fanatical hummer of modern popular songs, and one who until 1936 had also been a fanatical supporter of Fascism. That was the year he fought as a volunteer in Africa, singing *Faccetta nera*, but as this song about little black faces was subsequently banned he marched into Addis Ababa with sealed lips and a heart heavy with the suspicion that he was not a free man. Three months later the suspicion had become a certainty, and robbed him of his sleep. In 1937 he was sentenced to two months internal banishment, and on his return to Catania he began to visit Avvocato Bonaccorsi's study – where he succeeded in doing so much damage to his liver that in the summer he had to take the waters at Chianciano.

It was only natural that the advent of Edoardo should be greeted by these two – by the others also – like the dawn of a new day. The Avvocato's premises rang with shouts, with the thump of fists on tables, with Neapolitan songs; the hopes of the old campaigners shook off the hoar-frost, and stretched forth wings made stiff by the long night.

"They won't start a war! They won't do it!" cried Edoardo. "I'll bet anything you like they won't!"

"Excuse me, but why not?" asked Avvocato Bonaccorsi.

"Because their little fannies are all of a tremble, the pair of them."

"I have my doubts."

"And you, *maestro*," stormed Don Luigi Compagnoni irascibly, "tell me, could you live without doubts?"

One evening their host waited until Don Luigi had finished printing kisses on Edoardo's forehead because he had announced that "Hitler would chicken out," and then said very quietly, "Avvocato Lentini. . ."

Edoardo tucked his tie back inside his jacket, whence it had sprung in the tumult of the embrace, and said, "You want a word with me, *maestro*?"

"I think you should know that in Palazzo Vaccarini they are spreading a malicious rumour about you."

"Why should an honest man take any notice of what they say at Party Headquarters?"

"Even the saints fear false report, you know."

"What are those brigands saying?" demanded Don Luigi, his great hands grasping an invisible neck and wringing it. "What are they saying?"

"That you," resumed the Avvocato, turning to Edoardo, "resigned as mayor because in the course of one session, or assembly, or meeting – I don't know what these gatherings are called – the Party Secretary made an allusion to the business of your cousin, Antonio Magnano."

Edoardo thrust out his lips disdainfully: "My dear *maestro*, no one will believe what they say. One of the exhortations in the Party membership card is in fact *Believe!*, because each and every one of the things they say is, without distinction, unbelievable. In any case, I should like you to know that the incident which took place at Party Headquarters was provoked by me. It was I who declared, in front of all the Supervisors, that Hitler's balls had been shrivelled by gas."

"You said that right there at Party Headquarters?" cried Don Luigi, rising from his seat with wide-open arms. "I must kiss you again!"

"Yes, I said it and I repeated it," continued Edoardo, once he had broken loose from the embrace. "*Maestro*, please forgive my curiosity, but who gave you this information?"

"Avvocato Targoni. An excellent young man."

"The Party Supervisor?" exclaimed Pasqualino Cannavò. "Are you, *maestro*, on familiar terms with a Party Supervisor?"

"He is an extremely courteous person, from whom I have received nothing but kindness."

"*Maestro*, you astound me! There is no such thing as an extremely courteous person on that side of the fence."

"My friends, I was brought up in times very different from yours. In my day political ardour did not prevent us from recognizing good qualities even in an adversary."

"Hell, that lot aren't adversaries," shouted Edoardo, "they're a bunch of thugs out to treat us like slaves! I'm not prepared to recognize any good qualities in any one of that crew. I refuse to believe there's a decent sort to be found among them!"

A burst of applause drowned Edoardo's last words, and he was in danger of being embraced a third time by the reformed bandit.

When silence was restored Avvocato Bonaccorsi, his face very pale, turned to Edoardo and declared: "That is because you are still a Fascist at heart."

It was as if a bucket of cold water had been thrown over the only log burning in the grate, and the frost of old had taken possession of the room once more.

Edoardo rose and went to get his hat. "If that's how you feel," he muttered between set lips, "I shall take my leave at once."

Everyone leapt to their feet and rushed after him. Avvocato

Bonaccorsi himself attempted to detain him by grasping his arm. "No, no, no," he cried, "Avvocato Lentini, listen... What I meant to say..."

But Edoardo, politely but resolutely, removed his host's hand and left the apartment.

"What I meant to say," persisted Avvocato Bonaccorsi, craning over the banisters towards where Edoardo's hurrying steps had reached the last flight, "was that you and I have been brought up in different times... naturally you cannot feel as I do... and I may well be mistaken... indeed, I am most certainly mistaken..."

But his last words fell into an empty stairwell, with the result that Avvocato Bonaccorsi, with his friends on his heels, dashed to a window overlooking the street.

"Forgive me!" cried the good man to the swiftly receding figure of Edoardo. "I beg you to forgive me!"

All the regulars were thrown into consternation. The young man who had shot round the corner of the house opposite would never again return to put new heart into them...

But as luck would have it, two days later Ermenegildo Fasanaro paid a visit to Bonaccorsi. They seated themselves in a circle about him.

"A veteran anti-Fascist, what? Tried and proven!" said Avvocato Bonaccorsi, identifying the gentleman to his friends by a thump on the back.

"No longer either Fascist or anti-Fascist," replied Ermenegildo.

"What-what-what? Everyone's *bound* to be one or the other!"

"Show me the law that says so."

"There isn't any law, but... Excuse me, but what party *do* you belong to?"

"I belong to the party of the worms who will shortly be eating the meat off my bones; or, if you prefer, it's my fleshless skull that thinks that way, and I'm certain *it* will stay intact until a time when Fascism and anti-Fascism no longer mean anything to anyone."

The company pulled long faces. Their political hatred had by now become an unassailable hide-out wherein happiness could not hope to discover them – but no more could the thought of death. Ermenegildo's words had rudely intruded on them.

They at once changed the subject by imploring their guest to intercede with Edoardo and use all his authority to persuade him that Avvocato Bonaccorsi was not one to offend anyone, least of all Edoardo, whom he esteemed, respected, admired, and so on.

Ermenegildo promised he would try and see the ex-mayor of Catania the next day. The promise was kept, and Edoardo was obliged to meet one of Antonio's relations, something which up until then he had taken good care to avoid.

Naturally, the main subject of conversation was not the incident at Bonaccorsi's – dealt with in a few words and declared forgiven and forgotten – but Antonio's disaster.

"Why have you never looked in on him?" asked Ermenegildo.

Edoardo lowered his eyes. Then he said, "I don't feel up to it."

"Why not?"

"The moment I saw him I'd burst into tears – like setting eyes on a corpse – and that certainly wouldn't do much to pep him up."

"To be sure, it would not! But couldn't you avoid bursting into tears?"

"Look!" said Edoardo, pointing to a tear running down his cheek. "If this happens just from thinking about it, imagine seeing him! You know we love each other like brothers."

"All the more reason. One doesn't leave one's brother in the lurch when he's in trouble. Come on, take the plunge and come and see him... When will you come? This evening? Tomorrow morning? Tomorrow afternoon?"

"Make it this evening!"

And indeed that same evening Edoardo was there at the Magnanos.

Antonio, a silk handkerchief knotted at the neck, was in the dining-room, sitting at the long table (already laid) on which he had rested a book.

The two friends sat facing one another for several minutes in silence. Then Edoardo stretched across the table and firmly grasped his cousin's hand, already in the act of sliding towards him.

"Edoardo!" came a shout at this juncture. "Edoardo, come here!"

It was Signor Alfio calling from the bedroom, where for the last week he had been laid up with a temperature.

Edoardo made his way down the corridor, followed by Antonio, but when Edoardo entered his father's bedroom he stayed outside, propped against the wall.

Once in the room redolent of pipe-smoke, Edoardo was hugged hard and silently by Signora Rosaria and then impelled by Signor Alfio's red-hot hand to take a seat at the bedside.

"Can you believe it," the old man started in at once, "Nello Capàno's son has the nerve to insult us, taking advantage of the fact that they've stuck that Secretary's bauble on his head. Who does he think he is? What's he think he's doing? Where does he keep his brains? Alfio Magnano, just as soon as he can unstick his old bones from this bed, will go and winkle him out, even if he's hiding under God-the-Father-Almighty's nightcap, and ram these two fingers right in his eyes!"

"Do go gently," urged his wife. "If you don't keep calm your temperature will never go down."

"You must do me a favour," continued Signor Alfio, addressing Edoardo. "You must persuade Antonio to write to Count K and tell him to rid us of the son of that cess-pit that Nello Capàno always was. Here, take my pen and pass it over to your cousin. Off you go, and come back with that letter. If you don't, sure as God is my witness, I'll throw off the sheets and walk to and fro stark naked at the window. Here's the pen, get along now!"

Edoardo took the pen and dashed back to Antonio who, yielding to his cousin's urgings and his own wish to do something to please his old man, wrote a long letter to Count K.

Signor Alfio had it read aloud to him and heaved a sigh of relief. "If the count comes to meet me on this," he said, "I'll be a well man again in two shakes of a lamb's tail."

But Antonio's letter reached Rome two days after the news of his fall from grace, and was greeted by a universal shout of laughter.

"I've always said, and even committed it to writing," declared Party Deputy-Secretary Vincenzo Calderara, "that Antonio Magnano never had the stuff of a true Fascist." And addressing Count K, who was reflectively prodding his nose with a thumb, he added, "Has he never confided in you, Your Excellency?"

"Why on earth should he confide in *me*?" demanded the count huffily.

"He always boasted of being a friend of yours."

"We met in the Rs' drawing-room... he came to my house three times... no, only twice... On one occasion I asked him to lunch... I hardly think that constitutes a friendship."

"If we are to believe his father, it seems that with you, Your Excellency, he shared..."

The count sprang irritably to his feet, leaving Calderara with the rest of his sentence still on his lips. But the next day he dictated to his secretary the following letter in reply to Antonio's: "Dear Comrade, His Excellency Count K has instructed me to remind you that the rank-and-file of the Party may present their grievances against their superiors only through the official channels. Fascist greetings..."

At the same time local Secretary Pietro Capàno received orders to publish the following communiqué in bold type in the Catania newspaper: "**ACTS OF THE F.N.F... I have imposed on Comrade Edoardo Lentini the withdrawal** of his Party Card, on account of his lack of Fascist sentiments. He is therefore relieved of his post as mayor."

All wind of this was kept from Signor Alfio to give him a chance to get better. But when he was quite recovered and able to leave the house, after a mere half-hour the streets hurled him back home again as white and limp as a rag. He had been told the lot, and in the worst possible manner. On his way upstairs, feeling on his last legs, he had furthermore learnt from Avvocato Ardizzone that the Duca Di Bronte, thanks to the backing of a powerful big shot in the Party who was close friends with a highly influential big shot in the Vatican, would very soon obtain the annulment of Barbara's marriage.

It was all quite enough to send the old fellow back to his bed; and indeed he immediately suffered another attack of fever and delirium, during which it was necessary to keep untrustworthy people out of his room, and even to replace his doctor, who was a Fascist official, with an old Freemason. For at the height of the fever Signor Alfio seethed with foul oaths at the expense of Capàno, Calderara, Count K and the regime in general – for to them he attributed all his misfortunes. The result was that on the evening he first began to feel better he found seated in his room, with hats in hand and walking-sticks on their knees, all the friends of Avvocato Bonaccorsi – the ex-bandit Compagnoni, Pasqualino Cannavò, Cacciola the pharmacist, Professor Rapisardi, Marletti the engineer, Speranza the navvy, and Avvocato Bonaccorsi in person.

Several of these had sat with him on the City Council, in the happy times when a man could spit on the ground while a city Prefect was passing, and he would lift up Antonio's little frock and proudly display to all and sundry that there was a manchild beneath it. In order to back up this son, who had made friendships of all kinds with the new powers-that-be, he had drifted away from his own real friends... And lo, that evening, with tears in his eyes, Signor Alfio insisted on kissing them every one. He had them repeat the names of each of the younger generation, the first time listening with scrupulous care, and the second – after a pause – commenting on it, with a "Good! Excellent! Good lad!"

To Compagnoni he said, "And do you, Don Luigi, still have the unfortunate habit of leaving your fly-buttons undone?"

The good bandit glanced at Signora Rosaria and blushed like a schoolboy; then he turned his back and ran his fingers over the buttons which that evening too, the devil knows how, had indeed remained oblivious of their buttonholes.

"And how is your son?" enquired Bonaccorsi.

Signor Alfio braced his head firmly on his shoulders and met his old friend's gaze. "So-so... as God disposes... Raimondo," he added tremulously, "do you know what has happened to my son?"

The Avvocato joined the fingers and thumb of his right hand as if grasping something, then flicked it back over his shoulder, in a gesture of discarding a worthless trifle; intending in this way to divest the business of Antonio of all gravity and importance.

"No," insisted Signor Alfio, "no, it's not that way at all, alas!"

The Avvocato repeated his gesture, accompanying it with an expression of contempt for all those who attached importance and gravity to such matters.

"No," insisted Signor Alfio a second time. "Alas not, Raimondo!"

The Avvocato repeated his throwaway gesture a third time, accompanying it with such a shrug of the shoulders that for a minute his neck was swallowed up in his jacket.

"Really?" queried Signor Alfio, perking up a bit.

"No doubt about it!" asserted the lawyer.

Old Alfio asked him to step up to the bedside because he wanted to give him another kiss.

At the end of the corridor furthest from the bedroom, Antonio and Edoardo sat secluded in the dining-room.

"Please do come and meet my friends," urged Edoardo, in an attempt to drag his cousin to Signor Alfio's room. "I assure you they're people of quite another stamp. They look at things from a very exalted viewpoint. Avvocato Bonaccorsi has read three hundred books of philosophy and goodness knows how many poets; Professor Rapisardi has at his fingertips all the pictures in all the museums in Rome, Florence and Paris; Engineer Marletti knows Bach and Beethoven like the coins in his pocket. . . They never poke their noses into other people's business. How can I put it? All that matters to them is a person's moral qualities. . . They're exceptional men – they don't make them like that any more. You can read in their faces that their mothers were pure, strong women liable to blush at the slightest thing."

"What about our *own* mothers then?" muttered Antonio irritably.

"Oh, our own mothers are saints. Who ever would imagine we were their sons?"

Antonio cut him short: "I won't come, Edoardo. You're simply wasting your breath."

"All right. Have it your own way."

All evening long the two cousins sat in the dark, near the window. Every now and again, just to fill the room with any sound whatever, Antonio would cough, and Edoardo, almost in reply it seemed, would clear his throat.

In this way many an evening passed. Lacking the courage to speak open-heartedly about the terrible thing that had happened to one of them, they spoke not at all. Any other subject of conversation would have aggravated the magnitude of the one they were avoiding. So that the immense events of that September, the order to black-out the cities, Hitler's bellowings filling the darkened streets from loudspeakers positioned in the windows, the call-up of recruits, Munich – all failed to cohere into a single word on those two pairs of lips twisted with bitterness.

XI

FOR TWO MONTHS Antonio never left the house, consoling himself each evening with the mute affection of his cousin Edoardo. Towards the end of November he yielded to the counsels of a friend of Bonaccorsi's, Engineer Marletti, who two years previously had been abandoned by his wife and, a year later, by his mistress: he therefore had an intimate knowledge of all the alleyways, the times, and the techniques that might enable a man whose honour had been wounded to begin, slowly and cautiously, on his task of making a re-entry amongst people long since accustomed to never setting eyes on him while discussing him all day long.

The engineer was clad in a mack, Edoardo walked with his stick tucked under his arm and a scowl on his face, directing his short-sighted eyes wrathfully at the street-lamps which he mistook for men pausing to gawp at them; between the two, one hand on his cousin's arm and his jacket collar turned up, proceeded Antonio with downcast eyes. The night was far advanced and the windows, from which so many glances had rained down upon our Sicilian Adonis, seemed firmly closed for the night. If, however, the glimmer of a lamp showed through the slats of the shutters, Antonio's heart began a subdued thunder, almost a churning, like a propeller under water. He immediately divined those sweet, enkindled things that are the eyes of women, even now at the slats; he imagined plaited hair falling onto naked bosoms, one shoulder of a nightgown slipped down to the elbow; he imagined bare feet arched in effort to stand on tiptoe; he imagined elegant shoes, smart umbrellas, slippers, petticoats, powder-puffs, mirrors, ear-rings, buckles, trimmings, combs and ribbons; and all these things delivered a rebuke, and gave rise in his breast to an inkling of fear. Antonio quickened his pace and his two friends, as at the release of a spring, put on a spurt along with him.

Needless to say, during these walks Edoardo and Marletti were extremely careful to give a wide berth to Palazzo Puglisi, and at the same time Antonio himself appeared to have acquired a wooden neck from the care he took not to look in the direction of Piazza Stesicoro.

When, however, at two in the morning, he got home and went out onto the terrace, his eyes roved off at once to a certain roof, black and glistening like the scaly back of a fish: the roof beneath which Barbara was sleeping, chaste and alone, her mouth a little open against the pillow, a delicate scent of fresh dough emanating from her skin to her nightgown, her right hand palm-downwards with the fingers ever so slightly curled. Leather-bound, and encircled twice by the beads of a rosary, a missal lay blackly on the bedside table, resembling a revolver. A small lamp shaded with blue cloth gave a look of marble to the pillow where once his cheek had lain, and caused Barbara's black hair, sunk along with her head between one pillow and the other, to resemble an abyss of shadow.

Antonio knew that in that head everything worked like clock-work, that the hands regulating her thoughts revolved rigidly over images dictated by duty. Never, never over the image of himself! Cold sweat broke out all over his body as he realized that his own image could never have found an entry into those girlish thoughts, even when relaxed in sleep. He established, with the meticulous precision of a madman, the point in space where Barbara's brow was at that moment resting: that white, severe, secretive brow whose thoughts he no longer had a chance of fathoming, not even at night... Ah then a fretful restlessness seized hold of him; he would wander up and down the terrace, stopping every now and then, squeezing his temples and pressing his eyes: then shake his head, again and again, and, between clenched teeth, make desolate moan.

He would go to bed and lie there open-eyed, minutely examining the darkness spread before him. Towards daybreak, when his father summoned the maid – no longer with the fine, irascible voice of yore, but in a flat, listless whine – Antonio closed his eyes and at long last drifted into sleep.

But need we say it? Need we say that this man, this thirty-five-year-old, godlike enough in his youthful and happy times, had now through insomnia, humiliation and anguish become more exquisitely godlike still?

Edoardo would look at him time and time again, with dolor-ous astonishment: never had all the marks of manliness been so patent, so disconcerting; never had desire for women been so strongly expressed by so desirable a male face.

"It beats me completely," mused Edoardo. "Or maybe I'm not qualified to judge, being a man myself."

But the women thought the same as he did.

Since that February of 1939, when he began to leave the house even in the daytime, Antonio was forced to concede that women darted him glances of such profound tenderness that he was obliged on each occasion to slacken his pace, as if something warm and debilitating had brushed against his flesh.

One day on the staircase he saw the Spinster Ardizzone standing stock-still at the bottom of the second flight, prepar-ing to hurl herself down on the steps to prevent his passing. He attempted to slink by along the opposite wall, but, as he sidled down, the poor spinster had the opportunity to speak with her eyes the very uttermost in words of love and devotion; and when he came within reach she threw her arms around his neck and clasped him to her heaving, burning bosom, spurting a gush of hot tears onto his cheek.

Antonio detached himself roughly and fled away down the stairs.

When he got out into the street he was in a frenzy of rage and perturbation. The thought struck him that the news of his plight had freed the opposite sex from all shyness and reserve towards him, and that they were treating him with the very masculinity they knew he lacked. He walked his habitual route as red in the face as a slapped child; so flushed was he that in one deserted piazza he stopped at a drinking-fountain to bathe his cheeks and forehead; and bumping into Edoardo two hours later he was still scarlet, as if the spinster's clinch had occurred just a moment before.

Edoardo endeavoured to coax him to Avvocato Bonaccorsi's study, but Antonio would have none of it. "So far I've done everything you've asked," he said. "I went out at night, and now I even go out in the daytime. I go to church on Sunday, I venture into cafés. . . but don't ask any more of me. As soon as I set foot in anyone else's house I feel suffocated."

His cousin did not insist.

"Well, I must be off there anyhow. Be seeing you."

Antonio continued his walk alone, looking up at the roofs and the terraces of his own beautiful city.

Leisurely the eye seemed to penetrate that Sicilian air and absorb the sweetness of everything it lighted on. From inside a building with balconies piled with mattresses, carpets and potted palms, between the thwacks of a carpet-beater came the sound of a woman singing, while a little cloud of dust, emerging sluggishly from the dark of the window, halted in mid-air as if dazzled by the sun. . . Liberty, Beauty, Kindness: to which of these three deities might he have directed his deep sighs, if he could but have freed his breast of the boulder that was crushing it? What act would he not have performed willingly, if he had first been able to perform *that* one? Out in La Piana, while he was living in hope with Barbara, he had read books that had sent him into ecstasies. At dusk, his forehead pressed against a window-pane, he had mentally seen his Century, his Time, this personage whom some reckoned to be happy, others horrendous, some to be tyrannical, others free; he had seen it garbed in grey, with neither eyes nor mouth, and the outline of its face embraced half the sky. Then it was, aided by the philosophers he was reading at the time, that he too was on the verge of making a judgement about his Times. And who knows if he wouldn't have fastened on it some epithet or even nickname that would have stamped it for ever and a day? The age of Liberty-Tyranny? Liberalism-Socialism? Idealism-Materialism? Immanence-Transcendence? Heavens, how many choices were open to people not shackled by his particular bondage!

He returned home with a bad headache. It was a fact that the very idea that he might begin to think again was exhausting to him.

The following day the postman delivered a scented envelope. He retired to his room and opened it. It was a letter from a woman, and the reading of it made him blush and sweat.

My very own Antonio,

No scorn is sufficient to repay that notary's daughter whom you chose to honour with your name! If I could have her to myself in a locked room I'd tear her to shreds with my nails!

Is this what she learnt on the red velvet and mahogany prie-dieux at home? Did she imagine she heard *this* in the words of the Mass? I too was a Daughter of Mary, and the Madonna taught me quite a different thing. She taught me to love you, to love you eternally, to love you as a faithful and devoted spouse, to love you with head held high, with all the power of my purity!

When your marriage is annulled, remember that at the second corner along Viale XX September lives a heart which has for years been brimming with love for you, a slave prepared to spend the rest of her life (which may be a long one – I am only eighteen) at your feet, like a dog which (if you so wish it) will not even raise its eyes to look you in the face, content to see you tread the same floor where it rests its muzzle. . .

★

This was the first warning of a storm, a veritable cloud-burst of letters of every shape and kind, signed and anonymous, lengthy as confessions and brief as dispatches, some so imperative as to appear to threaten, others imploring; the handwriting upright, sloping or falling over backwards, the script clear or horribly messy, uneven as the writing of a medium in a trance or uniform and proportioned to a nicety. One said, "As soon as we're behind closed doors your blood will seethe!"; another, "One night on my breast and you will be all ablaze!"; a third, "Pass a hand over my skin. Try it: I have worked miracles."

But the majority were letters from mere girls: "To live solely on spiritual love, on glances, words, mutual understanding, has always been my dream"; or else, "One afternoon at Taormina, in the garden of the Albergo San Domenico, my fiancé seemed to me to have been stricken with a malaise that, rather than pity, gave rise to terror and disgust. It was explained to me later that this was love of me, or rather the love of men for women in general. I was appalled! I broke off my engagement and vowed to take the veil. Any place, even the darkest, the dampest, the gloomiest, the one buried deepest behind the highest walls, would have seemed to me paradise simply because no person of the opposite sex could ever gain admittance there. But now I feel heart and soul that I am able to forswear my vow in order to marry you, you, Antonio my precious love. Last night St Catherine appeared to me in a dream and told me that the Sacred Heart of Jesus considers me free from every obligation. Let us be married, Antonio! Let's marry very soon..."

Or again: "Antonio, don't you remember the fifteen-year-old girl who held up Barbara's train on your wedding day? That girl is now a grown woman regretful that she didn't throw petrol and a lighted match on the train in her hands, to burn to ashes that infamous creature who dared in the sight of the Lord to pronounce a deceitful *Yes*. Oh how I envied her that day! How willingly I would have changed places with one of her eyes or one hair of her head, to marry you myself just a little! How willingly I would have changed places with the hand you then clasped! Whereas I ought to have despised her, and demanded from her the respect which liars owe to honest folks!... I have torn up all the photographs in which I figure, standing there all meek and modest behind that monster – after I had cut out your likeness, of course, which now I carry next my heart. Antonio, might it not have been the will of God that placed me so near you at the moment you took to yourself a companion in life and in death? Did this not in truth make *us* just a little bit married? Did I not with all my heart cry out in answer to the priest's question, 'Do you take this man to be your wedded husband?'; did I not answer with a *Yes* that soared far higher than the one which Barbara let fall from her lips like a rotten apple? And did God not hearken to my *Yes*? And what other *Yes* could have reached heaven if not mine, springing from a heart hectic with adoration of you, anxiety and trepidation for you, desire for you?... etc., etc.".

And yet again: "During your wanderings at night along Viale Regina Margherita, maybe you thought everyone slept in the buildings as you passed. But I was not asleep. My room is a semi-basement, and my window, when unshuttered, is a pandemonium of shoes, skirts, trousers, dogs, cats, carriage-wheels, horses' hoofs, a medley of things passing this way and that, or sometimes stopping and blocking out the light. From my bed against the wall under the window, at exactly one o'clock each night I used to hear a special sound emerge from all the other vague and distant sounds which fill the city at that hour – mostly from the main thoroughfare, which cuts across the end of our avenue only a few steps from my home. My heart recognized it immediately, and gave a bound: and I gave a bound with it, right out of bed! And then that sound left all the other sounds behind, entering on the quiet of the avenue, reverberating from one pavement to the other. At night I always have in my mind's eye a picture of the trees along my avenue, their shapes and their great height; and the sound of your footsteps gradually became more and more a part of these pictures, and so gently and sweetly that my heart would drop into the pit of my stomach. Swaying as if just about to faint I would go to the window, lift the slats of the Venetian blind and peep out. One more minute and – there! your beloved feet were before my eyes... I could have reached out a hand and made you stay! Hundreds of visions crowded into my mind, hundreds of ways things might evolve: I saw you stumble, but not clumsily, I saw you cry out, I saw you shake your foot free and hasten on... I saw you bend down and smile at me, I saw you sit down by the window and talk to me, imagined you kissing me, I saw you drag me by the hair out into the street, I saw you jump down into my room... And these hundreds of imaginings came all at once, in a single flash of thought, so I was stricken to the quick with my face against the blinds, while the sound of your footsteps died away among visions of plane-trees far vaguer than my picture of the trees near my house, for these were still as crystal clear in my mind as your beloved footsteps as you passed them by... O my darling, O Antonio of my heart, why did you marry that woman? Why did you cease your bachelor walks by night? I have no desire to marry you, I have no wish to shut you up with me in my semi-basement. All I ask is to hear you go by at night, to hear you always, with that youthful step of yours, the step of a man not bound to any woman, your step so sweetly linked to the night of my twentieth birthday, when I deluded myself that as you passed my window you paused for a moment, as if you knew that behind that Venetian blind was a girl now celebrating her twentieth birthday for your sake, for your sake alone, Antonio my life, my soul... etc."

These letters, which would have sent any other man into ecstasies, rather than calming Antonio exasperated him to the Nth degree, as clumsy caresses can be unintentionally offensive and painful. In his state of irritation, which increased from day to day, he fancied that he provoked in women an abnormal voluptuousness, something unnatural and slightly monstrous: the so-called entirely spiritual love in which, in his opinion, devotion and naïveté masked a ferocious male aggressive streak. Women behaved towards him as men behave towards women: they thought they had a right to address him, to write to him, to sugar the pill for him, to conceal the truth from him with crafty euphemisms, to act so as to allay his fears and finally to persuade him to place himself confidently in their hands. Were these not the very means employed by the most consummate Don Juanism? He had become the quarry of pure hearts, of noble spirits, of creatures superficially weak and feeble, but in reality hair-raising. He sensed their voracity, which had nothing in common with spirituality except that it was infinite, irrepressible, uncontrollable and insatiable, he sensed it hungering for him from windows high and low, from tiny chinks hardly above ground level, from eyes with half their attention on books of prayer or still moist with starry skies long dwelt upon; he felt an intolerable molestation all over his skin, assaulted as it was at every turn by the thoughts of unknown women, thoughts that made his cheeks burn for shame.

Gradually, as the existence of a devoted heart was revealed in this street or that, he altered the route of his perambulations, and on reaching home immediately cast a glance full of revulsion at the desk where a strewing of letters unfailingly loomed white against the dark surface. Thus it was that so many transports, so many deep and delicate stirrings of ardour and benevolence and devotion, were rewarded with anger and aversion. Never were girls so modest and enamoured so heartily detested.

In the meantime Antonio's calamity came to a climax.

The legal proceedings, referred by the diocesan court to the *Sacra Rota* in the Vatican, and at which the Magnanos (terrified at the idea of having to discuss such a subject) raised no objection and did not even have a representative, had been concluded in June 1939 with the annulment of the marriage.

Antonio had learnt that in society Barbara was publicly and persistently addressed as *signorina*. One day, as he was crossing

Viale Regina Margherita from the south side to the north, in order to give a wide berth to Miss Semi-Basement, he saw about a hundred men at work on the façade and roof of Palazzo Di Bronte; and as he was staring in alarm at the doyen of these workmen, tied head downwards to a pole with his feet in the air, and labouring away to cover the happiness of Barbara and her future husband with a loftier roof, Antonio suffered a violent attack of dizziness, accompanied by a roaring in the ears. He had to go home in a hackney cab. Next day he learnt that the wedding of the duke was to be celebrated in a fortnight's time.

"Good Lord, so soon?"

"Yes, a fortnight!"

Thanks to powerful relatives in the Party and the government, the Di Bronte princes and dukes obtained anything they wanted in the briefest possible space of time, with a prod here and a prod there, in places high and low, administering a shock to every rung on the ladder of bureaucracy, since the billows of their power, deafening in Rome, were with the last of their infinite ripples able to winkle out and waken the sleepiest and most benumbed of bureaucrats at the end of the darkest corridor in the most dilapidated and worm-eaten office in any one-horse town. Documents which, for others, crept at a snail's pace from one desk to another, for them simply darted from archbishop's palace to law court, from law court to ministry, from ministry back to parish office.

The Duca Di Bronte (of whom we have not reported that his name was Nené), overcome by what had happened as by heart flutter – a flutter very grave in his case, since the gay and beautiful things of life were not balanced out by exertions or worries – put on so much weight that his neck disappeared: and what was seen passing down the street, bearing his name and being the recipient of deep bows and a host of smiles, was a remarkable contraption of human flesh composed of two bundles alternately distorted, now the upper one towards the right and the lower one towards the left, then the upper one towards the left and the lower one towards the right. But who dared to judge that man solely by his physical appearance? Behind him, in everyone's eyes, there lay always the majestic background of his vast properties which a horse at full gallop could not traverse between sunset and sunrise; and if he himself was ridiculous, solemn and severe were the mountains within the perimeter of his estates, so exclusively his property as to be untouchable even by the birds, at whom wrathful field-watchers loosed off guns and the dogs chased at breakneck speed up the crags, giving tongue the while: and if he himself was no beauty, most beauteous were his orchards of shining dark-leaved lemons and his wheatfields ruddy with poppies.

He was certainly no genius, and perhaps not even remotely intelligent, but how can you tell a man he hasn't got a brain in his head when he can come back at you with the lowing and the barking and the bleating and the neighing of the thousands of head of livestock he owns: beasts feeding on the grass in his meadows or dying in the slaughterhouse for his sake; or at the mere sight of him cringing beside their dog-kennels, though a moment ago they tried to snap their chains to assault some dust-covered trudger-by?

At the same time he was a sweet-natured man, devoted to St Antony of Padua: a man who on New Year's Eve would kneel among the elegant throng in the midst of the collegiate church and, after a long spell with his brow resting on his hands, would raise towards the altar two cheeks streaked with tears. He gave handsomely to charity, both in secret and in public, he supported orphanages, hospitals, football teams, fencing-schools, parish churches, the local Party and the beggars' almshouses; during the summer months he provided accommodation for officers' wives in one of his country houses, he built mountain refuges, gave gold to the motherland, railings to make guns out of, sheets to the Red Cross hospitals, gift parcels to the municipal police, flags to submarines and scholarships to grammar-schools. He was prepared to help anything just so long as it was favourably viewed by the government, it being inconceivable to him that any single person, with a single head to think with, could disapprove of things sanctioned by the Ministers, the Prefects, the Chiefs of Staff of the Armed Forces, the Presiding Judges, the Top Brass of the Carabinieri, the King, the Cardinals, the Bishops, and all those who have no need to run into debt to keep themselves and their families. In addition to this he was a modest, courteous man, whose wide-eyed look expressed constant wonderment, so that anyone who conversed with him received the pleasing impression of interesting him exceedingly much. "Ah, is that so?" said the duke every other moment. "Ah, is that really so?" In a word, one had to take one's own poverty and hardship altogether too seriously, to set about hating so mild-mannered a man.

The duke's wedding to Barbara was attended by the flower of the nobility of Catania, Palermo and Messina; also by a number of Roman princes, a Florentine marquis, and a Spanish baron on a visit to Taormina. The Di Bronte palazzo – to which those hundred workmen had added a turret – looked like a ship against which beat unceasing waves of Fascist uniforms (both the black and the white), of military full-dress tunics of every hue, silken dresses and flowers in bouquets in *pot-pourris* in bundles in bunches in sheaves... The balconies and verandas were crammed with people, glass in hand; the piazza below and all the side-streets resounded with motor-horns and klaxons, the clatter of hoofs, the shouts and insults of coachmen and chauffeurs, some of whom were thumping on their doors to drive away the inquisitive. The humble crowd thronged round the gates, their penurious, envious faces reflecting back the light of all that gaiety and opulence, and mirroring on embittered lips those myriad smiles. At sunset the crowd grew denser, it having been announced that the duke and his bride would shortly make an appearance before departing on their honeymoon.

Taking advantage of the rout and the semi-darkness, his shoulders planted against the trunk of an oleander, pressed upon in front and on both sides by women young and old who constantly turned towards him as if seeking approval for their smiles, approval which they naturally did not obtain, or managed to elicit in a form very weak and soured, Antonio Magnano watched with wild eyes which that day seemed created rather to express terror than to see with.

At twilight, when the street-lights are still unlit, and wings which have carried swallows to their nests attach themselves to mouse-like forms and raise the squalid bat from its cavern (bats fly, but their fate denies them song, and abashed by their squeaky voices they flutter to and fro in ignoble silence, climbing irefully into those levels of the heavens where the swallow has left off its twitter and the lark its trill), at twilight, I say, the great doorway of the palazzo lit up, the garden flanking it blossomed with tiny lights of every hue, and the bride and bridegroom appeared at the top of the steps.

The city was in darkness – only that garden was aglow. Antonio had a clear view of Barbara's face in a glitter from a tree teeming with lights, he saw her hand pass over her ear to smooth the surge of black hair at temple and nape of neck, he saw the impression of her knees beneath the silken dress, and finally, when she stepped down the topmost step, he saw her foot, as white as if bare, encased in a dainty black evening shoe. His excited eye aroused the other senses, and he again inhaled the odour of her powdered skin and that freshness he always noticed on his cheek the instant before it brushed hers, he heard her voice slowly enunciate the name *Antonio!*, while from his outstretched hand he felt hers disentwine, the knuckles snagging one by one, the catching of the rings, the fingernails... Barbara was on his breast, his mouth, his eyes, but at the base of his body, at the point which by this time he thought of as "down there", this many a year the kingdom of ice and death – there ice and death reigned ever undisturbed.

In the meantime Barbara and the corpulent Nené climbed into the motor-car. A gaga aunt appeared at a window clutching a hand-warmer long gone cold, and at a tiny window high up appeared the mad uncle, who stuck out his tongue and was immediately jerked back out of sight by a striped-jacketed manservant. In attendance at the car door were the bridegroom's elder brother, Prince Sarino, and the wife who had failed to give him an heir, and yet invariably wore the expression peculiar to pregnant women suffering from morning sickness. Down in the crowd index fingers poked between other people's heads to point out the firstborn of that ancient family. But it was when the municipal police in full-dress drew up on either side of the gateway, and down the steps paraded the new mayor of Catania, the Prefect, the Police Chief, Party Secretary Capáno, Deputy Secretary-General Lorenzo Calderara, and lastly the Archbishop (who turned back in a fluster waving his hands about because he had lost his skull-cap on the way downstairs), that an old man's voice was heard to bellow:

"Body-snatchers, blood-burglars, thievish infidels, you've bought up justice and religion with your cheesy stinking money! Yes, because you found another mob of delinquents tarred with the same brush, that ravening gilded-eagle lot, out to gobble up this stricken country to the last crumb, if the Lord God doesn't get a move on and exterminate them like vermin! You've all ganged up and rigged this situation to suit yourselves, you soulless bunch of cynics, you pisspots you! But we'll have the last laugh yet! We're going to hawk up and spit freedom in your faces, by God! The time will come, for honest folks! So what I say now is *Down with the king!* I say, *Down with the . . . !*"

At this juncture a hand clapped over Signor Alfio's mouth, impeding further speech.

"Don Alfio," whispered his captor into his ear, "do you realize that if I didn't still remember your kindness to my father, remember you paid good money for him to go to Salsomaggiore for his health, I'd have to take you in double quick, and you'd be lucky to get away with banishment?"

"I don't care," spluttered Signor Alfio through the rozzer's hand, which smelt of tangerines into the bargain. "I'm ready and willing to go into banishment. *Down with the . . .*"

But the rozzer tightened his grip and stifled the Name on Signor Alfio's lips.

"You'd better come quietly," he said. "Get moving. . ."

"Let's get moving by all means. Let's waste no time. That way I'll be able to give your Chief a piece of my mind!"

"Come along quietly now, *if* you please."

The Force pushed Magnano senior ahead of him out of the thick of it, hoisted him into a cab and clambered up after him.

Antonio recognized his father only when he saw the crowd make way for the cab as it turned into the avenue. He started to give chase, but after a stride or two he lost sight of it among the palm-trees, refreshment kiosks, and black-clad pedestrians of Via Etnea.

The rozzer luckily did no more than take the old man home. There, having kissed Magnano's hands, much moved because in the circumstances he felt that "the sainted spirit of his father" must be showering its blessing on him, he advised the old man both calm and caution, then sped off down the stairs without accepting so much as a glass of wine.

"Swear to me on the heads of your ancestors," he begged from the doorway, "and by the love you bear your wife and son, that you'll never allow That Name to escape your lips!"

But the wrath of old Magnano had by now taken a political turn.

"They'll start a war and they'll lose it! Sure as God is my witness they'll lose it!" he announced sententiously in the living-room to Signora Rosaria who, seated in her usual chair with her mending in her lap, looked at him and shook her head as if to say, "So that's what we're reduced to is it? – it's subversion now!"

"You just wait and see," continued her husband. "Wait and see how they've made a rope to hang themselves, these two who right now are acting all hoity-toity. They're threatening to bust up half the world, like a pair of lions with their hackles up, but what sort of lions are they, eh? Stuffed lions, that's what they are! Ever seen a stuffed lion? Well that's what they are, no more and no less. So listen to what Alfio Magnano has to say this day, the twentieth of July 1939: those two barnyard bandits are upsetting everybody's peace and quiet, but you know how it's all going to end?"

His wife raised her eyes and looked at him over the rim of her spectacles.

"It'll all end with savages, black men and yellow men and cannibals, men with rings in their noses and feathers stuck in their hair!"

"Where, here?" murmured Signora Rosaria in some alarm.

"Here in Catania, right here in the main thoroughfare where now there's a host of cuckolds as quiet as lambs, not realizing they've been sold to the slaughterhouse, every one of them!"

"But Alfio, what are you talking about? You've gone off your head."

"No I haven't, I'm telling the truth. I wish I were as sure of going to heaven as I am of what I'm saying now. Here, in Via Etnea," and he strode to the window to indicate that stately thoroughfare chock-a-block with people overflowing from the pavements and in among the trams and carriages, "there'll be savages with rings in their noses, and they'll pillage the shops and strut around like lords and masters. . ."

"God forbid!" was his wife's muttered prayer.

"They'll parade along Via Etnea with feathers in their hair and rings in their noses. And as for you," he bawled, wheeling on Avvocato Ardizzone who had emerged onto his balcony, "you with a face like an old boot, you'd better get the Bar Association to jettison that portrait of you with all that Fascist junk, because if *they* find it they'll make you pay for it with a good few kicks up the arse!"

"All will be ours! All will be ours!" was the Avvocato's jubilant comeback, spreading his arms in the air, along with the ample courtroom-type sleeves of his dressing-gown.

"Who's us? What's everything?"

"They'll give us everything, Corsica, Tunis, Malta, Nice, they'll give us everything we want without any war... All will be ours!"

"Who'll they give it to, tell me that now!" cried Signor Alfio in exasperation. "To you, d'you suppose, for having a face like a putrescent egg-plant? And why should they give us everything, answer me that! D'you think they're scared of you and your precious Senate, which isn't ashamed of getting to its feet and singing *Giovinezza* when it's told to, like children at kindergarten – and which in any case you'll never get into, never! Mark my words – not even to serve the speechifiers with a glass of water!"

"I make allowances for you because you have your troubles," replied the lawyer with spiteful solemnity, "and you therefore do not know what you are saying."

"Go to the devil!" hollered Signor Alfio. "You're a nitwit with knobs on!"

And he slammed the window shut.

"But Alfio," observed Signora Rosaria meekly, "if you go on this way we'll turn everyone against us! If we're ever in need, we'll have no one to put in a word for us."

"I don't give a damn for their words," retorted Signor Alfio. "There'd be poison in 'em anyway."

And he went on pacing the room from end to end, making a show of puking every time he drew near the window and observed, through the holes in the lace curtains, Avvocato Ardizzone as puffed up and red as a turkey-cock.

"And why all this?" he added, more in sorrow than in anger. "Why all this? Because the good Lord has it in for Alfio Magnano – Alfio Magnano who's just an ordinary poor sod who's never given cause for alarm to anybody, least of all God Almighty."

"Alfio, that's blasphemy."

"It's not blasphemy, I'm telling the truth. God Almighty has it in for me – for me, who've never killed or robbed a soul or sent anyone to prison, or stirred up trouble in families or taken the bread out of people's mouths; in fact, when I've had a chance, and you can vouch for it, I've robbed myself of it to give to others."

"That's true, Alfio, that's true."

"And the good Lord rewards me with the worst, blackest, most venomous tragedy it's possible to saddle a man with. No enemy of mine could have thought up one more perfidious if he'd racked his brains for a thousand years. Why, a tragedy of this sort, the Almighty must have had it in mind since he created the world, such a nauseating, such a murderous tragedy – and who for? For Alfio Magnano."

"That's blasphemy, Alfietto!"

"No it's not. I'm telling the truth. A tragedy, I tell you, that gouges the brains from your head just to think about. My own son, my only son, my pride and joy, my life! to see him reduced to less than a boot-rag, less than a boot-rag because at least with a boot-rag you can clean your boots. But a man in his condition, what use is he? What kind of good is he? What's he alive for?"

"Alfio, Alfio, you're breaking my heart!"

"And whose son is he, look you? He's the son of Alfio Magnano, Alfio Magnano who in his time... Well, well, we won't go into that... Alfio Magnano who had only to walk into a drawing-room for all the husbands to pull long faces and start nudging their wives and telling them it's time to go home."

"And for this, in his own due time, the good Lord..." began his wife severely.

"Nothing of the sort! I'm only sorry I can't still do it, by heaven, and not to be, I won't say forty, but sixty, even sixty-five, and have what it takes to cock a snook at some fresh beardless bridegroom. And if you want to know, two years ago, when I was sixty-five, I did father a son!"

"You, a son! Who by?" demanded his wife, her hands all of a tremble.

"By a... whatsit... a typist at the lawcourts."

"And where's the boy now?"

"Dead!"

The good lady shook her head, her face full of sadness and reproach: "Alfio, Alfio," she murmured.

"Surely you don't imagine I've only fathered Antonio? Lots and lots of cuckolds have brought up the sons of Alfio Magnano at their own expense!"

"You ought never to have done such things, Alfio, and now you ought not to boast about them."

"I'm not boasting, I'm telling the truth."

"Personally, I sincerely hope you're lying!"

"Very well then, we'll name a few names. Bertolini," he pronounced solemnly.

"What! Bertolini?"

"Bertolini the magistrate, surely you know him?"

"Of course I know him, God bless us. I'm sure he's the worthiest person on earth, but *so* disagreeable. . ."

"Well, his second son, the naval officer. . ."

"That funereal specimen?"

"Yes. Well. That funereal specimen is my son! Another son of mine is headmaster of the secondary school in a town near here called Regalbuto. Another one is a veritable half-wit, but the luckiest of the lot, because he owns a thousand hectares of land in the heart of Sicily, and on the death of that poor cuckold whom he imagines to be his father he'll be a baron into the bargain. . ."

"But Alfio, you tell all this to *me*? To me who. . ."

"You who what? Forget it! I had these brats before I married you."

"It was very wrong of you just the same."

"Is that so? In that case, please to note I also had others afterwards!"

"Alfio, I hope you're not serious."

"Not serious? Why, one time in Florence a chip of a young bride on her honeymoon left the bridal chamber and came to my room. . . I left my mark on women, I did! And you know it! Here in Catania a whatsit... what's the word? Well, in short, a tart, wanted to leave the brothel and become a plain, respectable housemaid, and come into service with us – not a penny to pay: all for love – just so as to see *me* all day long!"

"But Alfio!" wailed Signora Rosaria through her tears. "Why are you telling me all this?"

"I'm telling you so that you don't run away with the idea that your son has turned out as he has turned out through any fault of *mine*. Unluckily for him, and also for me, Antonio is not of my stamp – I'd have preferred him to squander every penny I had on running after women than... than..."

Signor Alfio, worn to a frazzle, threw himself down on a sofa.

"And if I'm not still up to it," he said in a washed out voice, "it's because of this disaster, that's robbed the very breath from my body. All I need is to see a scrap of light, just a tiny little scrap of light, and I'll be at it again..." And after a full minute, between clenched teeth he added: "By God!"

Next day, as one hastening to his confessor to unburden himself of a mortal sin, he sped to Avvocato Bonaccorsi's.

"You've seen it all now," he began tempestuously, right there in the middle of the study, "you've seen how they've insulted me? You've seen how they've all clubbed together to do me down? What's become of religion, what's become of justice, what's happened to the world? Ah, now listen to me, allow me this or you'll lose my regard, even you: the day this foolery finally gets its come-uppance I want to be Public Prosecutor in the People's Courts. I'll be no respecter of persons, I can tell you. Let my own brother be brought before me clutching our mother's portrait, and if my brother has worn that gilded hen on his hat I'll have him shot! Yes, dukes, notaries, Party Secretaries, archbishops, counts, ministers... I'll give 'em the chop!"

"Come now, there's more good in you than you give

yourself credit for," murmured Avvocato Bonaccorsi. "You wouldn't hurt a fly."

"You're wrong there, Raimondo," retorted Signor Alfio. "When good men rise in wrath you have to watch your step. Place these men in my hands, and see me hang them up on hooks like so many scalded pigs!"

"You're a good man and don't know it," insisted the lawyer.

"I'm *not* a good man, and I know it."

"You're a good man, Alfio."

"Raimondo," growled old Magnano, planting himself squarely in front of his friend, "are you out to provoke me? I've been telling you I am *not* a good man!"

"Dammit!" burst out ex-bandit Compagnoni impatiently. "Why shouldn't we believe, for the time being, that Signor Alfio is not a good man? I've had long experience of human nature, and I know that when good honest people see red they spit more fire than the devil himself. The only time I was really scared, in the days when I was wicked, was in a café once when I began taunting a seminarist as weedy as a reed and yellow as a lemon. First thing I said he kept mum. The second, mum. The third, mum. The fourth, mum... But the fifth time, Lord alive! A rabid cat! A hyaena! He bounded about till he looked like busting the ceiling with his head: he came at me from all sides; he bit me in the wrist – just look, the scar's still there. No sir! Never again will I pick a bone with the virtuous, because when a virtuous man sees red he's worse than the devil! And you know me – I play rough."

"Wise words," commented Signor Alfio. "Better the devil himself than a good man when they drive him too far. And they've driven me too far, Raimondo. They've trampled my heart underfoot."

"You're right, you're right," muttered Compagnoni. "And as far as I'm concerned, the day this foolery finally gets its come-uppance I won't think twice about appointing you Public Prosecutor in the People's Courts."

"Who will gainsay you?" agreed Avvocato Bonaccorsi.

"You will be both judge and jury. Who has ever denied Alfio's right to act as Public Prosecutor in a People's Court? It's just that. . ."

"None of your 'just thats'!" broke in Signor Alfio.

Compagnoni winked one of his outsize eyes at the Avvocato to advise against his persevering, and Bonaccorsi silently spread his arms wide as priests at the altar do over the Mass-book.

"None of your 'just thats'! If even you deny me justice, I'll pack you all off to buggery yourselves!"

"Come now, come now. . ."

"Hell, I want to be Public Prosecutor! Is that any skin off anybody's nose? I want to expose all their life and works in public, I want to take their cuckoldry and rubber-stamp it for them!"

"And you will have ample satisfaction, Don Alfio."

"Yes by Christ!"

"All the satisfaction you could wish for."

"I should think so too!"

"It'll be entirely up to you to say, 'Stop now, I've had enough'."

"Too true, by God!"

And the old man, chest heaving, threw himself back into an easy chair.

However, it so happened that two days later, as he passed along Via Etnea, he heard the following, muttered in an undertone: "It's only fair for them to get their ends away at the expense of those emasculated anti-Fascists. . . They've certainly played fast and loose among the wives of that bunch of geldings. . ."

Signor Alfio wheeled round in fury. He raised his stick. But he encountered nothing but faces engrossed in private conversation, or in reading the placards, or in daydreams worthy of the angels.

"There's someone in this town who's tired of life," he said, simmering with rage and causing the two or three people who caught what he said to turn his way in astonishment.

"I'm not mad," he pursued. "I'm not talking to myself, I'm not drivelling. I'm talking to that fucking cuckold who spoke just now and hasn't got the guts to repeat what he said."

The bystanders pulled faces as if to say "You're off your rocker," or "D'you think I'd deign to tangle with a poor old sod like you?"

Their expressions drove Signor Alfio to the point of paroxysm.

"Once again," he bawled, his stick still hoisted above his head, "I'm telling that fucking cuckold to repeat what he said, and I'll take this stick and snap off his horns for him!"

"Go home, go home!" was all the reply he got from this side and that.

"Toddle off to bed!"

"To bed with you!"

"Go take a nap!"

The voices reached him from afar, from round the corner, and drove him clean off the handle.

"Come out of there!" he bellowed. "Come here if you dare! You lousy yellow-bellies, I'll squash you like cockroaches!"

"Toddle on home!"

"To bed with you!"

"Come out of there you sons of stinking whores, you limp cephalopods you, and I'll plant the toe of this boot in the cracks of your bums!"

"'O *cúrchiti*, to bed with you!"

"Shit, I'll catch you one!"

"'O *cúrchiti*!"

"With this boot, you hear me? Shit!"

"'O *cúrchiti*!"

"Shit on you – and your mothers – *and* your fathers!"

"'O *cúrchiti*!"

"Shit, I'll catch you one – shit and dammit!"

"Signor Alfio," came a kindly voice. "This isn't like you!

What, taking notice of a couple of gutter-snipes who wouldn't show respect to their own fathers on their deathbeds?"

"Shit and dammit, let me kick their arses for them, friend!"

"Forget it. Calm yourself. Don't lower yourself to the level of that riff-raff. You'd be the loser, believe me: they've got nothing to lose. That sort wash their faces in the muck every morning. Take my advice and come away. I'll walk you home."

The old man was hard put to it to drag himself away from the scene of such insults, and all the way home never spoke a word to the kind friend beside him. He halted now and then to thump his right hand down on the pommel of the stick which his left had planted stubbornly on the ground.

Once home, he uttered not a word for the rest of the day.

His wife, not hearing him hawk, or so much as clear his throat, went frequently to peek at him in the study, as heart-in-mouth as one nursing an invalid who seems to have stopped breathing.

But the old fellow was invariably there behind the desk, staring fixedly at the green baize top, and whenever he became conscious that his wife had tiptoed to the door, without moving his head one whit he pointed a finger back the way she had come.

"What's up with your dad?" she demanded of Antonio. "In all the forty years we've been together I've never known him so silent."

Antonio reddened and clasped a hand over his heart, feeling it unroll and unravel from his breast as when a spindle drops. These days, anything that happened made him expect his humiliation to take on some further and even more repugnant aspect.

"I don't know," he replied faintly, "What *could* possibly have happened to him?"

The next morning the old man woke up yelling his head off. And what do you imagine those desperate cries were all in aid of? Simply that he wanted his coffee brought to him instanter, not a moment's delay!

"It's coming, it's coming," cried Signora Rosaria. "What d'you have to go shouting like that for?"

"Because I feel like shouting. Because in my own house I shout when I want to, and if anyone doesn't like it they know where to find the whatsit... the door! And they're welcome to use it!"

Signora Rosaria's tears began to flow.

The fractious old man swung his legs out of bed, thrust his feet into his slippers and went out into the corridor.

"Antonio!" he bawled. "Antonio!"

His son came running in his pyjamas, his eyes wrenched from sleep by fright.

"Antonio, if you go out today you must do me a favour."

"Of course, dad. What?"

"Carry a pistol."

"Why on earth, dad?"

"No reason. I have my little whims, that's all. But you must do me this favour – carry a pistol."

"But you might at least tell me why."

"Oh, Santa Genoveffa, not again! There's nothing to explain, but will you or will you not do me this favour and carry a pistol?"

"All right, if you say so."

"Good Lord, what a fuss about nothing! I'll do the same: if I go out I'll take my father's old shooting-iron."

Alarmed at this, Antonio left the house earlier than usual and sought out Edoardo. The two friends had very little trouble in piecing together the incident which had befallen Signor Alfio, and this in the most minute detail possible.

Antonio was so upset he felt fit to faint, but as chance had at that moment led them quite near Avvocato Bonaccorsi's, Edoardo managed to persuade his cousin to step upstairs into the study, not least in order to get out of a street full of inquisitive, spiteful eyes.

So up Antonio went, and found the company of friends complete. With the addition of Ermenegildo Fasanaro, lending an ear, head bowed, mouth sagging, like a poor old cow at a standstill beneath a beating sun.

Antonio too prepared himself to listen in silence to those men who never once, in all they had to say, even incidentally or in passing, made any mention of women.

This was a relief to him at first, but after a while it infected him with a fidgety irritation always aroused in him by the words *liberty, progress, dignity, truth, conscience* and so on. Because they were the opposites of other words, words of such intolerable consequence in his life, such as *marry, annulment, wedding night, her, undress, bed, make it, try, flop,* he immediately fell into a state of discomfort which he could only shake off either by once and for all forgetting what tortured him most – for him an impossible feat – or else by fancying the makers of such speeches to be slightly hypocritical. It must be mentioned, however, that the sally which had caused Signor Alfio to brandish his stick in the street had been quoted to Antonio as follows: "They're forever prating about philosophy and freedom because they can't get their cocks up. If they were capable of satisfying their wives, they wouldn't have to fabricate so much rubbish."

Antonio was too shrewd to attribute any measure of truth to such a coarse statement, but it none the less plagued him throughout that gathering. He was utterly and completely oblivious of the tone of vibrant sincerity in their voices, nor did he for one moment notice the warmth which actuated them. In the anguish that gripped him, depriving him of any hope of clear and calm perception, he saw all those present as exemplifying that chastity and abstinence to which he himself was constrained, saw them all without distinction as being useless with women. It slipped his mind that the ex-bandit Compagnoni (to name only one) had, one August afternoon, pursued by peasants brandishing machetes, left beneath a carob tree a sixteen-year-old girl – the same who was to this day his

234

wife – rent by the fury of his effusions as by the claws of a wolf. But as things stood, in Antonio's eyes even this man was tainted with purity.

Consequently, after listening in silence for an hour he shot from his chair, though he quickly restrained himself and checked his impulsive movements.

"I do apologize," he said, "but I must be making a move."

"Wait a jiffy," said his uncle Ermenegildo. "I'll come along too."

On reaching the street, Ermenegildo gave a finishing touch to the look of bitterness and disheartenment which in Bonaccorsi's room had caused him to resemble a poor old cow pestered by flies, and in the course of a terribly laboured sigh he infinitely ponderously pronounced the word, "Bah!. . ."

The tone of voice in which his uncle expelled this monsyllable was very pleasing to Antonio. The first voice for ages which chimed in with the disconsolate sound he clothed his own words in while fantasticating by day, or dreaming by night, of talking to Barbara, or to his father-in-law, or else to other women in his past.

"Bah!" repeated his uncle, and Antonio shivered from top to toe, and half-closed his eyes, and compressed his lips, so as to imbibe that sorrowing yet welcome exclamation to his very marrow.

"Bah! Bah! And bah again!"

They had now wended their way into Piazza Dante, and were passing close to the church of San Nicola with its truncated columns and walls all a whirl of swallows streaking from beneath the tiles of the beautiful monastery next door, launching brief, tenuous cries of the kind which, when accorded to lonely and ancient places, render them more lonely and more ancient still.

"How I love this land, this soil!" exclaimed Ermenegildo. "I could kiss every stone in it; I could kiss even the flies, the bird-shit. What a fool I was to live so remote from it for twenty years! In Paris, in Barcelona, I thought about nothing but these sulky, half-naked urchins with one hand behind their backs to hide the stones they're just about to fling at your head... And look, here's the palm-tree!" He stabbed his stick at a dusty specimen. "This is the palm-tree which I'd have swopped all the gardens of Versailles for... It's the very one, by God! Still here!" He took a couple of turns around the old palm, tapping it gently with his stick, then stood back and eyed it with amorous dejection, shaking his head the while as if reproaching it, though in fact reproaching himself for some mysterious wrong committed against that tree.

"Here she is, the very one!... When I was in Spain," he continued, unwillingly interrupting his contemplation of the tree and resuming his walk with Antonio, "I had bouts of dizziness that lasted a year. A whole year, and I'm not exaggerating. In Barcelona I couldn't take a step without feeling the ground missing from under my feet. But what scared me was not the act of collapsing in itself, so much as the idea of my face colliding with an insipid, odourless soil, a soil that in every respect lacked the tang of my homeland... of *this* soil!" And he stamped his foot hard, not without swaying on his feet, then blanching, and finally smiling at his moment of panic. "Of *this*," he repeated, "which some day soon I desire to kiss so profoundly as to bequeath my carcass to it!"

"Uncle!"

"I know, I'm becoming maudlin. Talk about creaking gates!... However..."

He hadn't the heart to continue. He quickened his pace a little.

"However what?" enquired Antonio.

"However... What I wanted to say... But let's drop it. I'm becoming maudlin."

They left the piazza and turned into Via Di San Giuliano, which plunges straight down towards the heart of the city. From this vantage point, beyond a series of drab *palazzi* bursting with caryatids, pediments, flower-pots, terra-cotta water-butts, portals, jalousies, balconies, dark-hued roofs, all growing smaller and smaller in the illusion of the perspective, they caught a glimpse of a segment of sea, gently shrouded in a siroccan haze.

"However," took up Ermenegildo, of a sudden, "I've never believed in the fact that the human spirit creates the world. That is. . . I'll explain myself better. When I read our Greatest Living Philosopher*, I bow my head and confess myself beaten. There's no denying it, he's right: outside of human thought there is no reality whatever, we cannot get outside our thought, and even the very phrase *outside our thought* is in itself a human thought. . . By heaven, I find no arguments to contravert Croce: I gnaw my knuckles and bite the crook of my arm, but I have to admit that I find no way out. And yet. . . and yet I feel something deep inside me, a protest, an aspiration. . . how shall I say?. . . a madness, something that demands justice against this way of thinking that allows no gainsaying; justice against. . . how shall I say?. . . against the arrogance of our Greatest Living Philosopher. Justice, Justice! Oh may another philosopher come, greater and more gifted even than he, and may he demonstrate, in words refulgent as the sun, that on one hand there is the world, and on the other the thought that believes (note this word!), that *believes* it creates that world but in reality reflects it; on the one hand the body, on the other the soul. Our Greatest Living Philosopher maintains that such a demonstration will never be given by human kind, but (and here I take the liberty of raising an objection against him) how can he count his chickens before they're hatched? How can he decree what mankind will never think and never be able to demonstrate? Has he by any chance become a determinist – a determinist in his own particular manner, needless to say –, perhaps without knowing it? What's afoot? Has he scoffed at prophets one and all, only to come

* Benedetto Croce

237

out now with a thumping great prophecy himself? Eh? What do you think?"

"Watch where you put your feet," said Antonio. "There's a step."

"That truth and fact are one and the same thing," said Ermenegildo, "I've always been convinced... but I've never believed it."

"Come again?"

"What I mean is that it's one thing to be convinced by an argument and quite another to believe it's true. But you can't understand that. When your liver has turned to a stone like mine has, and peeing produces more tears of pain than drops of urine, then perhaps you'll see my point... And what's more, I may be an infant, an ignoramus, an old man who can't see past the end of his nose because he suffers the agonies of the damned, but, in short, what's the sense of saying that life is all very fine as it is, that it's senseless to complain about it and ask for something better? As far as I'm concerned it's a far cry from being all very fine! Once upon a time our men of genius roundly asserted that they wished to know the absolute truth, demanded to know why we are born, and what is the purpose, and whose the pleasure in the sufferings of mankind, seeing that these are cultivated so assiduously the world over: they enquired why we have to know that we will die, but remain completely ignorant of what death is; why, before we die ourselves, we are forced to witness the pitiful spectacle of so many corpses: why our thought is given just enough rope to enable it at one jump to get a sniff of truth, but without the ability to benefit from it; and finally, why we are granted the faculty of asking 'why?' and denied a definitive answer. But today, it's another story! I take my hat off to the idealist philosophers (the others, alas, the ones who in a certain sense might agree with me, are nothing but chicken-shit), and I take my hat off and make a sweeping bow to our Greatest Living Philosopher: but, my dear Antonio, don't you think that this so-called concilatory philosophy, this philosophy which says,

'You are in search of the truth? Very well, the truth is your search in itself. You ask the question, why? Then the essential thing is not the answer, but the fact that you ask why...' Don't you think this philosophy very craftily covers up both resignation and cowardice? And do we thereby enlarge our mental scope, or are we submitting in the face of a mystery which turns out to be impenetrable? Is the serenity with which we say we understand, and accept with good grace, all the contradictions and absurdities of life, is it not by any chance worth far, far less than the desperation with which the great minds of the past cried out that they did not understand and still less accept them, preferring suicide to a life of mediocrity and ignorance which to those souls, truly magnanimous and great, appeared in any case to be ignoble?"

With Ermenegildo gesticulating, vociferating, and clutching wildly at Antonio's arm each time his head began to spin, the pair of them had reached the Quattro Canti, the cross-roads at the very centre of the city. Here they were shoved to and fro by the crowd, and finally hemmed in against a shop window, in which Ermenegildo saw, bearing down on him, the face of a corpse. Hoping against hope that it was not his own, he tried winking one eye; the face winked back; he put out his tongue; the face inexorably retaliated.

"Let's get out of this crowd!" he burst out. "Let's get a move on..."

They stepped out more briskly and reached the gates of the collegiate church, spared by the crowds flooding up and down Via Etnea, ebbing and flowing but without ever quite invading the small recess above which soared the church.

"Of course..." began Ermenegildo; and, after a long pause, as if thinking better of it, "Well, be that as it may..."

"'You're too much in love with your sins'," he resumed after another pause. "That's what that sprat of a Father Raffaele had the nerve to tell me. Me? Too much in love with my sins? What sins, I ask you? The sin of having to make a lot of money, the sin of having the gift of the gab, of envying someone else

239

if he's even quicker off the mark, the sin of packing my bags and being a gad-about, the sin of seducing the maidservants, the sin of bustling around a friend's wife?... I'm sick to death of them! I assure you, Antonio, that if I loved chastity, poverty and the cloistered life purely because they're Christian virtues, and not because they bring me pleasure and relief, I'd ascend into heaven boots and all. But even in this respect, alas, I'm the old sensualist I always was, as we Fasanaros always have been – at least the menfolk, because the women have all been saints. Chastity now appeals to me like a clean sheet, and even death I relish as a potent dose of morphine. *I like it.* Three words which are going to lock me out when I come to Peter's Gate! I like it, I like even death! I can't wait to relish it... Ouch!" he gasped at this juncture, tapping his chest. "This miserable carcass, this accursed cage! Why, the body of a hen is more spry and supple." He now slapped his chest: "Dark prison full of the very same offal you see on kitchen tables when a kid or a chicken is gutted: the same repulsive lungs, liver, heart, intestines... You bloody guts that so often make me shriek with pain and lose the thread of my thoughts, it's about time you went to the devil!"

"Take it easy," murmured Antonio, squeezing him by the arm. "People will think we're quarrelling."

Ermenegildo shrugged.

"Tell me something, Antonio: that stony-hearted woman, have you seen her at all?"

Antonio tossed his head. No.

"She hasn't written? She hasn't asked for a word with you?"

Another toss, eyes shut this time.

"What a way to go on! After a love-match and a white wedding with pages, sung Mass and all the trimmings, after three years of life together, after the entire city has seen you happy in each other's company. How can this woman, without your having done the least thing to her... I mean, the least thing to harm her... just give you a nod and go off with a new husband without so much as a backward glance? And still," he continued in the voice of heartbreak, "still you try to tell me that this world isn't a mean ugly dump?..." A pause in the monologue. Then: "What about it, shall we take a peep inside?"

"Inside what?"

With a glance Ermenegildo indicated the church door.

"But... I was married there!" objected Antonio, blanching.

"What of it? Come on, let's take a dekko."

With leaden feet Antonio trod the nine steps leading up to the forecourt. This he crossed on his uncle's arm, feeling himself under intense observation from the deserted balconies of Palazzo Biscari, from the shuttered windows of the adjoining alleyway, the stones, the statues, the railings like a rank of spearmen... Never as at that moment, and in that deserted spot, had he felt himself more the object of attention. They entered the church.

The ceiling here is painted by the same artist who frescoed the Teatro Bellini, and seems one vast though barely perceptible undulation such as a backstage draught imparts to a drop-curtain. A quantity of sunbeams, striking through the glass, hang like coloured vapours: in their radiance the dust-laden air is visibly in motion; beneath, a seething darkness specked with candle flames... There the high altar, there the prie-dieu, there the carved altar-rail! As if he had taken too large a gulp of the past, Antonio felt himself choking, his breath coming in quick, rasping pants, his chiselled nostrils, drained of blood, flaring wide in an effort to suck in sufficient air.

"Let's kneel," said Ermenegildo. "We'll be comfier."

Mechanically Antonio knelt down beside his uncle, who, clasping his hands on the pommel of his stick and resting his forehead on them, presented the statue of the Sacred Heart of Jesus with a glistening, ivory scalp across which two remaining strands of an almost juvenile blondness were pathetically plastered down.

Antonio, meanwhile, cupped his hands and buried his whole face in them, to spare himself the sight of the high altar stripped now of the purple hangings adorning it on his wedding-day, of the main aisle now bare of the sumptuous red carpet which had muffled the footsteps of relations, witnesses and friends.

He stayed this way for some time, waiting for the waves of blood to stop beating in his brain, the veins in his temples to cease their irksome throbbing.

"Is it possible," began his uncle, raising his forehead from his hands and resting his chin there instead, "is it possible that the words heaven, paradise, divine justice, life everlasting, have no meaning in the sphere of reality? Do these words, the most beautiful words we know, correspond to nothing real? Is it possible that the name Jesus Christ – listen, I'll repeat it: JESUS CHRIST – is simply the name of a corpse, and the saying of it changes nothing in this world or the next? I'll repeat it again: Jesus Christ... JESUS CHRIST... Could this, then, be but the name of a madman living around two thousand years ago, who thought, in good faith, that he was shedding his blood and dying simply out of his own extraordinary, compassionate sympathy for human weakness; that only by struggling to rein in his Omnipotence did he spare the soldiers who scourged him and the towers of the city that witnessed his torment? Jesus Christ, a mere pitiful visionary then, with his face forever upturned towards the heavens, the form, composition and glory of which he was in fact ignorant of, but which he already believed to be his royal abode, visualizing in its midst his own gilded throne on the right hand of a somewhat eccentric Father... So then, that Thursday evening when he prayed in the Garden, repeating this word 'Father' in the tenderest way imaginable, was there no one on the other side to hear him? And when, on the cross, he promised the repentant thief that he would take him with him to paradise – poor thief! how he must have cursed when he realized that after the dark of his death-agony a deeper darkness still had befallen him, and without a ray of hope... In that case for us men, whether our names be Ermenegildo Fasanaro or Jesus Christ of Nazareth, is there naught but darkness and ignorance? Plus, if we have the benefit of a good education, a philosophy of resignation content to bestow the name of Truth on our poor unanswered questions? Well, I deny it! For the third time I repeat: JESUS CHRIST: No, by heaven, I say no! JESUS CHRIST – you have to admit it's not the same thing as saying Ermenegildo Fasanaro. It's a different thing altogether – JESUS CHRIST... And yet, who knows? In twenty thousand years he might be thought of as an irrelevant and practically barbaric moralist; a moralist far from charitable towards the less fortunate of our kind, the sinners incapable of self-redemption, whom he never ceased to threaten with the cruellest punishments... So Jesus Christ is a barbarian, is he? Did you hear what I said, Antonio? Jesus Christ a barbarian! Don't we blush for shame just to hear such words spoken? And what does this blush mean, if not that the truth is the contrary? Jesus Christ, Jesus: the very name of God! Jesus Christ! Jesus Christ! Jesus, Jesus, Jesus..."

Ermenegildo's brow sank back onto his stick, his eyes pressing onto the knuckles clasped around the silver pommel.

"Jesus Christ!" he began to murmur again, still slumped in the same attitude, "the more I repeat that name the more I lose touch with its meaning... But say what you will, how wonderful it would be if one of us men, perhaps this citizen of Nazareth, *had* been the son of God, and were waiting there for us on the other side, his body like our bodies, and he knowing from experience what it means to have had lungs, a liver, intestines, a heart that pumps..."

Antonio felt his mind drawn inexorably towards a certain word, a word that here, in this place, would have sounded obscene. He tried with all his might to exorcize it, but only got as far as regarding it as something dead. He saw all the letters of the word but they had no sense, nor echo in his memory.

"...glands, loins, cerebral matter, spinal cord..." continued his uncle.

And Antonio saw the selfsame letters for a second time.

"...if only he were waiting for us beside our dead bodies, one foot on our corpses perhaps, reassuring us in our fright after the leap we have taken, encouraging us, with the simple fact of his human form, and maybe with a smile... Ah, what bliss it would be, if these worthy priests had always been telling us the truth, the whole truth and nothing but the truth! *I believe in God the Father Almighty, Maker of heaven and earth...* Exactly so: God the Father created heaven and earth... *And in Jesus Christ his only Son our Lord...* Nothing could be truer, could it?... Jesus Christ *is* his only Son and our only Lord... *I believe in the Holy Ghost: the holy Catholic Church: The Communion of Saints; The Forgiveness of sins; The Resurrection of the Body, And the life everlasting. Amen.* As true as true, every word of it: the Communion of Saints, the Forgiveness of sins, the life everlasting... What bliss it would be if these pictures around us faithfully, literally and minutely mirrored the truth: all those angels with wings, the Madonna with her Madonna face, Jesus with his heart displayed on his breast! What bliss it would be if our Pope Pius XII (whose nephew incidentally I happen to know), really *were* the Vicar of Christ on earth; and if the visit the parish priest of Zafferana makes of an evening to our place in the country, lantern in one hand and oilcloth umbrella in the other, were not just a kindly custom, but a visit of genuine utility – more to the point by far than that of any fatuous doctor who looks at you in a proprietary way like an animal he owns, yet knows as much about you from having seen your X-ray as the average Sicilian knows about the China he's seen at the pictures... What bliss it would be, by heaven! How happy I would be if that were the way of things!... But it's not," he went on after a pause. "Christ himself knows, it's not. Son of God, why can't it be true that you exist? Why can't it be true that those who hunger and thirst after righteousness shall be filled, that the persecuted of the earth shall sit on the right hand of the Father in beatitude? And why can't you have *your* way when you threaten unbelievers with hell-fire? Why must the wicked have their's? What's more, if you threaten unbelievers with hell, what must *we* threaten *you* with, we disillusioned lovers? And if you suffered when you sensed that some rejected your teaching, what must our suffering be when we come to realize that your teaching was a cheat, a dream, a blissful dream which the universe takes no account of, the dream of innumerable pathetic humans who hoped even unto death, and died together with their hope? But none the less, and I don't know why, as I utter these words I have a sense of failing in my duty and provoking some awesome response. Unless this is simply the impression of a man who. . ."

"Uncle," broke in Antonio, giving a sudden squeeze to the old man's hand and getting to his feet, "there's a priest in the offing."

"Show him to me!" said Ermenegildo, also scrambling to his feet. "I'll make my confession at once."

They made a move towards a black cassock silhouetted on the steps of the Choir, lifeless as if it were hanging on a hook. At closer range Antonio made out a pallid face attached to the cassock by the black band of the collar.

He halted. "It's Father Raffaele!" he blurted out.

"Fine. I'll make my confession to him."

"Please, not that!" cried Antonio, starting back.

"Why ever not?"

"He's *Barbara's* confessor."

"What of it?"

"I do beg you not to!"

Antonio attempted to turn his uncle right-about-face and hustle him out. A wasted effort! Recognizing Antonio, Father Raffaele himself made to escape – so keenly was that good man's conscience pricked by his penitent's repudiation, an act she refused to accept as a sin, since her attitude had been endorsed by a sentence of the *Sacra Rota*.

Antonio blushed to the roots of his hair. His face burnt worse than ever; it even hurt. The black cassock, now sidling down the left-hand nave, seemed to him charged with the entire mystery of Barbara.

245

"Uncle," he said, "I'm feeling a bit below par. I... I can't seem to focus... Please help me home."

Ermenegildo stepped swiftly to his side and propped him up.

It was in a state of swoon that Antonio left the collegiate church leaning on his uncle who, despite the weight he was supporting, could not help muttering to himself as he laboured along:

"...or even *I'll* become a Communist!..."

"...or an out-and-out Catholic, all faith and devoutness, Family and Church!..."

"...or else I'll turn on the gas..."

XII

FOUR YEARS HAVE PASSED. One August day in 1943, in a little square in La Punta, the village you reach first on the road out of Catania up the slopes of Mount Etna, the good bandit Compagnoni, astride a donkey which, beneath his bulk, looked like a small unruly dog, began bellowing across at the windows of a certain smoke-ridden little house.

"Signora Rosaria," he cried, "Signora Sara, how did your husband get the lowdown? You saw those thousands and thousands of trucks go by? Well, there's no more of 'em to come. The wild men on horseback are right on my tail now, the cannibals... yes, with rings in their noses and feathers in their hair... Just as your husband prophesied! Just as he prophesied, word for word. Savages, cannibals!"

He waved his massive arms about in a frenzy of rage, exhilaration, horror, indignation.

"To think I should ever live to see it! Cannibals in Catania, right there in the main street. And now they're on their way here. Signor Alfio must have had it from the devil himself!"

But where is Signor Alfio? Where is the poor old fellow now?

One night in 1942 he was picking his way slowly homewards, cursing the darkness which every now and then made him start back as if a door had slammed in his face and inveighing against the war and his own old age, when every blessed thing, the cobbles in the street, the carriages drawn up along the kerb, the walls of the houses, the star-flecked sky and the bell-towers all broke out into one long, continuous wail like a flock of sheep sensing the approaching wolf. The air-raid siren.

"Something tells me," muttered Signor Alfio, "that tonight they're not going to leave a stone standing."

And rather than taking the road home he turned into a neighbourhood of smelly alleyways where the noctambulist would as a rule hear on all sides the voices of women cooing, "Come in dearie, make yourself at home..."

But that night, none of the usual solicitings: nothing but the slamming of doors, and these no sooner shut than the loud, hasty clatter of bolts and bars.

Signor Alfio put on a burst of speed, scything about him with his stick and striking indiscriminately on dogs and cats and heaps of refuse. "By God, I'm going to die like a sewer-rat," he thought. Then, "Hey," he cried, "hey, Mariuccia, open up there!"

Mariuccia, who lived down the end of the alley, was a dried-up little morsel whose scrawny chest sported a pair of pale, plump breasts, just as in springtime a chinaberry tree still carries on its bare twigs fruits rotund and pallid.

"In God's name, Mariuccia, open up can't you!"

Signor Alfio, under the impression that he had already reached Mariuccia's door, had halted; but her door opened several paces off, and a face poked out, chalk white in the light from within.

"Oh, sir, you here, on a wicked night like this?"

He hurried breathlessly towards the voice, and stepped into a hovel where the most glittering and precious object was an alarm-clock ticking away the minutes with a cheap tin rattle.

"*You* here, sir!" she cried. "And what'll they be saying tomorrow, if we're found dead together? That Signor Alfio used to go visiting a woman of ill-repute?"

"Just what I want," replied the old man. "I *want* to be found dead here. I want the whole of Catania to know that Alfio Magnano, despite all his seventy years, still goes with prost-

248

I beg your pardon, I mean no offence. Indeed, so little do I intend offence that I've come here to die."

"Mercy on us! And who says we're to die for sure?" cried the girl a trifle huffily.

"Don't ask me. Ask those rogues up there. They're just naughty boys, you know, like the ones you find throwing their weight about at night in Via Etnea, except these do it in the streets of London. *And* they hang about the billiard saloons and have poor sods of fathers who can't get 'em to come home at a decent hour... But tonight they've decided to play billiards with our homes, here a pot, there a pot, and all come tumbling down. Yes, from this minute on every soul in Catania, you, me, the Prefect, the cuckolds and otherwise, Fascists and anti-Fascists, the Duca Di Bronte and that bitch of a wife of his, my son, and my Sara, all of us, and I say *all* of us, are at the mercy of a bunch of madcaps who can snuff us out with a puff, like candles when the party's over."

"Let 'em try," said the girl. "I'm going to call the cat in from the yard."

She opened a small door giving onto a black pit in the centre of which presided a terracotta chamber-pot.

"Hey, don't leave me!" cried Signor Alfio. "I wouldn't care to be found here all alone tomorrow, as if I'd come to say my prayers. I want to die with a woman by my side! I'm jolly well going to take off my jacket, too!"

"Get along with you, we're not going to die," answered the girl without turning round, and shut the yard door again. "*I* know the kind of hiding *that* cat needs!"

Yet die they did. Signor Alfio Magnano, esteemed and respected by the whole town, was found, after a five-day search, under the rubble in an ill-famed part of town. A green shoe with a pink bow, wafted there from a brothel in the next street, lay beside him with its toe resting against his temple. All that remained of Mariuccia was her right hand clutching her broom-handle. As for Signor Alfio, it was not clear what had actually killed him, for he appeared uninjured, his clothes in one piece and relatively clean. In his trousers pocket, tucked into a celluloid cover, he had carefully conserved the note left two years before by his brother-in-law Ermenegildo on the bedside table in the gas-filled room: "This nightmare of life has been endlessly plausible and, even in the midst of its absurdities, has preserved an air of consistency and even of inevitability."

The citizens of Catania, sitting of an evening at café tables in a totally blacked-out Via Etnea, and prattling away as in the good old days despite an impression of masticating gritty murk, found Signor Alfio's death an inexhaustible subject of conversation.

"What an insatiable old fellow! Seventy years old, and on a night like that he has enough pep to go hunting for somewhere to put his pecker!"

"Bit of an exaggeration, eh?"

"Exaggeration? Why?"

"Surely he could have tied a knot in it? D'you mean to tell me that if he spent twenty-four hours without... at his age... it'd have been the death of him?"

"Every man to his own..."

"Ah yes, it takes all sorts... All the same, he wasn't twenty any more."

"No, he wasn't twenty, but he could still take *that* one at a run."

"Lord save us, these Magnanos..."

"The old generation, you mean, because the young..."

"Ah yes, if his son had inherited a single hair of his head, a single hair, I say! Do I overstate it?"

Who knows how much else would have been said and surmised if, one week later, local Secretary Pietro Capàno, filling up his car from a can of petrol in the garage and finding himself unexpectedly plunged into darkness by an air-raid warning that doused the lights, had not seen fit to light a match. A sudden roar in the air, a fierce flame leaping from nowhere, and he was a human torch. Twice he bounded back in an attempt to escape the inferno, but the flame, hugely attracted to his person, followed him hungrily.

Crazed with fear, this thirty-year-old son of doting parents started screaming for mum and dad, for help of any kind, but as no help came he hurtled out of the garage. Not a soul in the forecourt. Ominously flickering, Pietro Capàno made a mad dash into the nearest doorway and up to wherever the stairs might lead – to the door of an enemy, as it turned out. Impellizzeri his driver, whom he had sentenced to internal banishment, and who more than once had mumbled behind his hand "What you need is to be burnt alive, mate!", nearly passed out with terror on opening the door a crack, then flinging it wide and seeing that poor devil trapped in a furnace rapidly lapping up the petrol splashed on clothes and skin and impatient to bite into the living flesh.

"Wait, Mr Secretary, wait there for God's sake. Don't put a foot inside or we'll all go up in flames!"

Rushing to the kitchen he armed himself with a bucket of water.

"Don't panic now, we'll have this lot out in a jiffy!"

So saying, with eager but trembling fingers he started spraying water on Capàno's face and clothing.

"Not water!" shrieked the hapless man. "Water makes it worse!"

Indeed, as if fuelled by the stuff, the flame sprang up with blood-red fervour, puffing black smoke ceilingwards. Seeing the agonized face in the thick of that blind, pitiless conflagration – was it human flesh and blood or a firebrand? – the driver burst into tears.

"Not water! Not water!" howled Pietro Capàno. "You're out to murder me because I'm a Fascist!"

"Fascist or not, we're human! How the devil do I get these flames out?" blubbered the other.

"Your coat!" screamed Capàno, throwing himself headlong

on the landing and dragging with him the flames, which leapt on top of him, gaining in breadth what they lost in height – but losing nothing of their fury.

"Coat! Coat! You're right!" babbled the other. "And carpet!"

He flew to the living-room, blocking his ears to muffle Capàno's screams as he writhed this way and that beneath the flames hungry to attack his back.

Panting and frantic, the driver returned with carpet, rug, overcoat, and threw these over the flames, muffling them. Then flinging himself on top of the pile he pressed down with his whole weight. With a belch the flames died and darkness ensued on the landing. The bundle poured forth smoke more dense and black than the dark itself; and ever more faint came the groans of Capàno.

A girl appeared with a candle. The driver scrambled to his feet a shivering wreck, teeth chattering. With bloodless hand he drew away the covers, exposing a body one mass of burns, blind, mute, blood clotted in the deep lesions scoring it this way and that.

For a moment the driver clasped the girl desperately to him, then knelt beside the man, even more horrifying now than when a prey to those horrific flames, and with no other sign of life than the sound of wounds still sizzling.

Pietro Capàno died next day, leaving vague stirrings of remorse amongst those who had hated him. Only a few – you could count them on your fingers – had the gall to mutter, "He had it coming to him"; but there was always someone to come back at once with a "Hold your horses! Sweet Jesus, are we human beings or aren't we? *He* never burnt anyone alive, did he?"

"What's more," added another. "He was even kind."

"Kind perhaps, but..."

"No, really *kind*!"

"I don't know what you mean by kind."

"When I say kind I mean *kind*. Don't you know the meaning of the word kind?"

"I merely wished. . ."

"You merely wished nothing, keep your trap shut!"

"I merely wished to suggest. . ."

"Drop it."

". . . to explain. . ."

And what of Antonio? His father's death prostrated him for no little time. That tender father, who had loved him more than his own eyes, had made his exit delivering him the most God-awful backhander that ever father welted his son with. The shame was not laid at the old man's door, for having met his end under the rubble of the red-light district and having lain a whole day out on the asphalt with two bulbous-nosed drunkards and half-a-dozen women whom death had scarcely known what to deprive of, so clean had life already picked their bones. . . No, the shame was his: for when he paid a visit to the cemetery of Aquicella three days later, he found on his father's gravestone, scrawled in charcoal by an unknown hand, these blood-curdling words: ". . . died March 6th 1942 to cleanse the family honour sullied by his son." The letters were large, their message unbelievable. He tried to rub it out with his coat-sleeve, shooting nervous glances around him like a despoiler of tombs and encountering the steady gaze of funerary busts and memorial photographs. Never again did he visit the cemetery, and never a night but he was scared to go to sleep; for in his dreams he saw that charcoal scrawl.

Very different was the attitude of Signora Rosaria.

"My Alfio, my Alfio," over and over again she repeated, dressed and draped in black from head to foot, her rosary beads never out of her hand, a black locket on her breast containing a likeness of Signor Alfio (in mourning for his father), her face buried in a black handkerchief: "*Alfietto mio*, Alfio my treasure, breath of my body, dead, among *those women*, under the rubble. . ."

She refused a morsel to eat or a moment's repose.

"How do you expect me to eat or sleep," she wailed to the relatives who patted her hands, some one and some the other, "when my life and soul lies dead under the rubble, and God knows how much he suffered?"

Floods of tears on all sides. The women stole glances at Antonio: his beauty, in his suit of mourning and with the deathly pallor of grief and shame upon him, truly resembled that of an archangel.

Two months later Signora Rosaria, overcome with chagrin at not being able to die, consented to take nourishment and to lie on her bed for a few hours at a time. Antonio no longer dreamt about his father's gravestone. And every so often came a more congenial dream, in which Barbara, touched by the distressing event, wrote him a letter, a note perhaps, or a request to visit her.

But the devil a note did Barbara write, and Antonio took to prowling around Palazzo Di Bronte after sunset, lowering himself, in his agony of spirit, to such a level of oafishness that one night, seeing a glimmer of light through the slats of the shutters, and having hoped in vain that they would be flung wide and She would appear in the window, let out a lunatic cry of "Hey there! Ho you! The gallows is too good for the likes of you lot!"

Out went the light at once and Antonio fled like a petty thief, with such self-loathing that no sooner had he reached the deserted Via Sant'Euplio, there below the wall of the Public Gardens, than he laid his hand on a moss-covered stone and for a long time shed upon that hand hot tears; and since he was in the habit of using the perfume which had been Barbara's, for a little while he had the sweet illusion of weeping not on his own hand at all, but on Barbara's cheek.

Ah, deceitful sweetness! He knew the cheat even in the throes of enjoyment, all the fiercer and more debilitating for the growing knowledge that it could not but collapse into a pit of sour despondency. And indeed the sweetness was already past, already lost! His hand fell from the mossy stone, bequeathing a trace of Barbara's perfume to the green; no more than a trace, the mere ghost of a thing, such as remains of the light of an August day in the flight of a firefly.

"This Barbara," declared Edoardo, "is nothing short of delinquent."

Antonio replied with an ironic smile, almost a conceited smirk.

"I can't help wondering if it's true, what they're saying," pursued his cousin.

"What are they saying?" enquired Antonio, more to hear Barbara talked about than to credit some rumour he knew from the word go would be a lie.

"What they say is... Well, they're saying all sorts of things." Then, catching a glimpse of his cousin's sardonic smile, Edoardo bristled and went on, "And the beauty of it is that I personally believe it! You, of course, don't... Do you?"

"But I haven't the foggiest what you're going on about yet."

"Simply this: that Barbara and her husband don't get on. But when you come to think of it, how *could* a woman get on with that species of cow lacking nothing but a cowbell round his neck?"

Antonio's whole being glowed with pleasure.

"And that's not all. Barbara's cheating on him!"

Antonio scowled for a moment, but then swiftly resumed his trace of a smile and put his nose in the air.

"*You*, of course, don't believe it..."

Antonio sucked in his lips and raised the nose another fraction.

"Well *I* believe it, and I bet you anything it's true."

"And who's she supposed to be cheating him with?"

"The coachman."

Antonio smiled, a smile rising from deep down in his breast, almost his very entrails; and he lofted the nose again.

"No? You don't believe it?"

Nose up another notch.

"It's true though. Barbara has a strong dose of mad blood in her veins. Amazing that after three years with her you didn't cotton on. Personally I saw it at first glance. In that Puglisi family, as you well know, there are two or three crackpots no Mr Notary cares to hear mentioned. Know what you ought to do? Go to your father-in-law..."

Antonio paled.

"...Well, your *ex*-father-in-law if you want, and address him thus: 'Mr Notary, I wish to know the manner of the death of your Uncle Tanino,' and just watch what colour Mr Notary Puglisi turns."

"Why? How did he die?"

"One woman squatting over his face and another straddling him amidships. Beside his bed – where the Puglisi keep their missals – they found a paper twist containing a certain powder... Another Puglisi – an uncle of this Tanino – used to smuggle the stuff after the Great War. He hid the little twists of paper in his hair. Various people I know used to knock at the door of his ground-floor flat of an evening, hand over a sizeable wad of lolly, and buy his permission to scratch his head for him. One fine evening in they stepped to find his wife alone, howling with grief: the poor chap was dead. My friends consoled the woman, calmed her down, then, "I suppose he hasn't left a pinch of magnesia?" "How should I know?" whined the widow. "How should I know if he left any? I don't even know where he kept it. And to cap it all I don't know where to lay my hands on a brass farthing to have him said a Mass!..."

The chaps gently chivvied the woman aside and entered the other room hat in hand. The corpse was laid out on the catafalque, candles burning at all four corners; his head, pillowless, hung hidden by the mound of his chest. One of the chaps stepped up beside him, knelt down, crossed himself, said a prayer, crossed himself again, then ran his fingers through the dead man's hair, extracting a packet. Back in the presence of the widow he took her right hand, clasped it to his breast, and pressed her fingers round the two thousand lire which next day enabled her brother the priest to perform a sung Mass. . ."

"Meaning?"

"Meaning that if Barbara looks around for a drop of insanity in her blood, she'll discover more than one. Also, I've heard that when she was a child. . . But let's forget about when she was a child. Let's talk about today, now, when she's at it lock, stock and barrel with the coachman!"

Antonio rose indignantly to his feet and turned away.

"You're going soft in the head!" yelled his cousin at his back.

Antonio shrugged his shoulders, succeeding with the nape of his neck alone in expressing the most incredulous scorn. Then he walked off.

"All right, all right," murmured Edoardo glumly. "Have it your own way."

Antonio resumed his evening prowls beneath the windows of Palazzo Di Bronte. He glided from the trunk of one plane-tree to another as swift and silent as a hunter, then poked his face between the garden railings, his cheeks savouring the hard chill of the iron like a humiliating caress which Barbara had detailed a piece of her property to bestow on him; the least she could bestow, but a lot to him all the same, filling him indeed with joy and well-being. His heart leapt and thudded at the thought that, unobserved, he was happy, against all the rules of dignity, propriety, decorum. No, Edoardo couldn't have the faintest idea what he was talking about. There stood the Palazzo Di Bronte, as dark and solemn as a church, and from its lofty tower there rose to heaven – taking its place therein with statuesque majesty – the high morality, the pride, the iciness of the woman who wore its keys at her belt.

One day the two cousins espied a carriage with the Di Bronte coat of arms emblazoned on its doors rolling slowly along Via Etnea.

Antonio stopped and nudged Edoardo.

Bowler-hatted on the box, a long whip in his right hand and the reins in his left, doddered the coachman.

"Look at him," exclaimed Antonio. "There's your coachman! Take a guess at his age."

The coachman was old enough in all conscience, but Edoardo gallantly made him out to be a genuine antique, and gave him seventy-five.

"It has to be said," he admitted, "that the chap who regaled me with the Barbara story is a certified liar – believe it or not he told me yesterday in all seriousness that he's positively heard on the wireless that Hitler had put his own eyes out. But I do admit he wasn't the only one to pass the Barbara story on. In any case," – and here he gave a snort of impatience – "let her do as she pleases. Let her treat him as she will: he's hers, after all. There's lots of more important things in the world at the moment than Barbara and her precious Duca Di Bronte. Not long now, my dear Antonio. . ."

The lights are still out all over Europe – ships slipping out to sea by night as dark and lugubrious as hearses – people in many places down to a handful of raisins – but Edoardo none the less catches in the air "the whiff of happiness".

"Not long now," he resumed, "before these twenty years of despotism, brashness and bullying will seem to us like one night's fevered dream. Nothing left of it but the nervous tic of glancing over our shoulders before daring to utter a syllable out loud. . . And we'll be the laughing-stock of our grand-children. 'What's the matter with grand-dad?' they'll ask. 'Why's he always looking over his shoulder?' And our own dear offspring will smile and explain that poor grand-dad lived at a time when every citizen had a cop at his shoulder, and was sent to gaol just for saying that our Great Panjandrum had aged a bit. . . Just imagine, Antonio!" He grasped his cousin by the elbows and shook him with might and main. "Not long now and I won't have to keep saying that Hitler is scarcely knee-high to Our Duce when what I *want* to say is that they're a pair of unmitigated swine. Soon I'll be able to speak the plain truth to anyone's face. Is there such a thing, I sometimes ask myself, can there be such a thing as speaking one's mind out loud, without a qualm?... *Speaking one's mind*," he added almost in a whisper, as if to savour those words to the full, to concentrate on them and grasp them the better: "*without a qualm... out loud...* But you know Antonio," he resumed with emotion, "I can't believe I'll ever make it – ever see that day. I'll die on the eve, for sure. And anyway, would I be up to it? I mean, will I be able to speak the language of a free man? Won't I get tongue-tied, and blush, and commit all sorts of blunders? Won't I make it only too obvious to everyone that I've been a flagrant flunky for twenty years now? Won't I – from sheer habit mind you – won't I break my neck to accommodate someone, to butter up a bigwig, to do the done thing, to be sure to say the politic thing whatever happens... Or will I, maybe, become a rebel for no reason, and end up not paying my bus ticket simply to show I'm my own man? It's enough to drive you round the bend..."

The cousins walked on side by side in silence.

"The only thing that really gets me," resumed Edoardo with a ring of real feeling, "is that the milk of human kindness, times of compassion, of poetry, will return to this earth when we're no longer lads of twenty. That Man there has pocketed our youth, and the day they arrest and search him they'll find our 'twenties on him, yours and mine! Makes me sweat cold, that does – to see a free Europe, a peaceful Europe, a Europe that honours dreams and music, and us no longer of an age to dream as once we did, spending whole days together humming Tosti's latest hit!... But so be it! The main thing is to *see* the happy times again, and above all – freedom!"

Nourishing such sentiments and rhetoric Edoardo spent the years 1940–42, years which for him, in the expectation of happiness, were in fact tenderly, apprehensively, happy ones. In what hues did hope not attire herself? What sustenance did she shun? What tiniest floweret's radiance did she not borrow?

What jingle on the lips of a passer-by did her peerless voice not transfigure into song?

> *E Pippo, Pippo non lo sa*
> *che quando passa ride tutta la citta,*
> *si crede bello*
> *come un Apollo*
> *e saltella come un pollo.*★

Ah, what a song and a half that was to Edoardo! For him it meant the happy times were just round the corner.

And a year or two later:

> Underneath the lantern by the barrack gate
> Darling I remember the way you used to wait,
> T'was there that you whispered tenderly,
> That you loved me, you'd always be
> My Lili of the lamplight,
> My own Lili Marlene
>
> Time would come for roll-call, time for us to part,
> Darling I'd caress you and press you to my heart...

Chin propped on the pillow, Edoardo followed the voice of this noctambulist. This ferocious Europe was weary. It wanted no more roll-calls. It preferred a kiss beneath the lamplight. Here was the return of romanticism, and here the first new-romantic sauntering down the street in the dead of night, right under Edoardo's window: here came the first European with a head full of dreams.

> Orders came for sailing somewhere over there,
> All confined to barracks was more than I could bear...

★ Our Duce thinks he's the kipper's knickers!
When he struts by, with the air of an Apollo,
He's got no idea how everybody snickers...

Sweet European, more than he could bear, eh?

> You wait where that lantern softly gleams,
> Your sweet face seems to haunt my dreams...

Adorable European, needing only the image of a woman in his mind's eye to blot out all the mud and the misery.

Edoardo tossed and turned in bed, snorting with contented expectation.

"Whatever's up with you?" asked his wife.

"Not long now..." replied Edoardo, "not long now..."

"Not long what?"

"Nothing. Wait and see."

And here at last is the day so long yearned for by Edoardo: it is dated the 5th of August 1943. Here it is!... But how black with high explosive and filled with the dull rumble of ruin! The despotism falls, but so do the roofs of the houses, the church-towers, the old bridges over the rivers; atop the public buildings the clocks are stopped, their hands fixed at the time when the bomb dropped in the piazza and killed a huddle of frightened people...

And here, too, is the good bandit Compagnoni, astride a donkey, arriving at La Punta and bellowing in the direction of the little smoke-ridden house where Signora Rosaria and her son Antonio have taken refuge. He yells about the Africans and Red Indians close on his heels.

Signora Rosaria timidly pokes out a beshawled head, crosses herself, pulls it in again.

"Antonio, did you hear that," she asks in the wisp of a voice she has had since her husband died. "Your father must have spoken to the angels, poor soul. Cannibals in Catania, in the main street!"

Stretched out on the divan, the inevitable silk scarf knotted round his neck, Antonio turns his head away. "Here today and gone tomorrow," he mumbles, his cheek against the moth-eaten old sofa-back.

"I pity the poor young girls," sighed his mother. "May Our Lady have mercy on them! They say these savages take it out on the girls..."

Antonio jerked himself upright on the sofa.

"Stuff and nonsense!" he exclaimed. "No difference between negroes and white men."

"Ah, you may think so," returned his mother. "So many rumours... Who am I to judge?..." And she added with a sigh, "Our poor old home, I wonder if it's still standing. Supposing the army have requisitioned it?... Leave me my bed they must, the bed I slept in so many years with your father. They can take anything else they like, but the bed they *must* leave me. If not, despite my years, I couldn't answer for the consequences!"

"You wouldn't have a chance in hell, mother," said Antonio, trying to jolly her along a bit. "Those chaps have guns and they'd take pot shots at you."

"And I'd rip their eyes out with these nails!"

"They wouldn't let you near them, mother."

"I'd get near them somehow all right. *They* wouldn't know I wanted to rip their eyes out, would they? So I'd creep up, I'd creep up, and with this hand... I'd have their eyes out!"

Antonio's spirits drooped. It always happened to him these days. After trying to play the fool he was very soon down in the dumps again. A twinkling of gaiety made him all the more bleakly aware of the gall and wormwood of his habitual state of mind.

"One of these days, my boy," continued Signora Rosaria, "I want you to pluck up courage and get down to Catania and take a look at the house."

"I'll do it tomorrow," replied Antonio, swinging his legs back onto the sofa and stretching out.

Tomorrow came. He didn't budge.

For two whole weeks the sound of the bagpipes which the Scottish troops, billeted in the chemist's house across the way, played day and night every hour on the hour, gave him a kind of ambiguous and paralysing pleasure... What was Barbara up to all this time? Was there any truth in the rumours circulating about her? The notary in La Punta would have it that she had been raped by a German; his clerk swore she had hopped it with a tommy; the local doctor, a friend of the Di Bronte and Puglisi families, who drove his dog-cart every other day to the village where Barbara and her husband had taken refuge – a reliable witness, therefore – reported that on the contrary the Di Bronte establishment had remained unviolated by both Germans and British, and that Barbara, simply by appearing at the window, had dissuaded a body of the soldiery from continuing to demand admittance with the butts of their rifles.

This image of Barbara appearing on high and causing a gang of obstreperous stevedores from Hamburg or London to come over all lax and listless was the one which most appealed to Antonio, and entirely convinced him. This was the true picture, no doubt about it! This was Barbara to a T. His heart confirmed it by thumping fit to burst whenever he contemplated her in that high-and-mighty attitude.

Towards the end of August he shook off his sloth, had a good stretch, put on his black suit and went down to Catania.

What a scene of desolation! In Via Etnea the rubble from the fine *palazzi*, not yet carted away, lay heaped against what walls still stood; most of the shops were closed, their steel shutters wrenched this way and that by the thieves who attempted to force them nightly; mountains of rubble in every corner, licked by half-hearted flames with only a few flakes of dry orange-peel or a scrap of newspaper to get their teeth into, sent a dense cloud of foul odours up to the top floors and the terraces; the swallows, scared by the gunfire, flew high high up as if over an earth submerged by flood-waters, printing on the depths of the sky hazy symbols of woe; conversely, mosquitoes, attracted by army trucks, refugees, and that mysterious vortex which draws insects into the midst of mankind whenever the latter is at a low ebb, pressed in from La Piana to the heart of the city, where they injected malaria even into the heaven-flung arms of the impromptu sopranos – a shabby crew – who sang of an evening in the *Teatro Bellini* for the benefit of the troops; half-naked boys, so thin their shoulder-blades stuck out like vestigial wings, roamed the rubbish dumps in search of scraps; here and there among the ruins, gleaming gold, lay the harp-like innards of pianos stripped of their carcasses, and mournfully in dead of night betrayed the presence of thieves who, tiptoeing off with an item of lumber, inadvertently strummed their strings. Matches, meanwhile, were unobtainable, and the lighting of a fire entailed cajoling a provident friend who might well live at the other end of town.

What desolation! Along Via Etnea placards of all sizes gave warning in English: "Look out for VD!", "Wars end but VD marches on!", "What'll you take home to your girl? VD?" Half-way down the street a long-established café of honoured name had been done over with a coat of whitewash and fitted out with white screens. Over the doorway an illuminated sign exhorted the troops: "Come along in, but wash first – or at least afterwards!" The Public Gardens were one mass of trucks; at twilight the bombed-out among the townsfolk roamed like ghosts haunting the places where their homes lay buried, and the rooms which only a twelvemonth since had rung with New Year toasts and greetings and exchange of kisses. Others, evicted from their apartments and reduced to bumming off hard-up, nagging relatives, hovered in the streets and squinnied in through windows to see what was afoot in the familiar rooms, and saw – on the wall where once had hung the picture of the Holy Family – a nude woman lewdly scrawled, her eye a revolver-bullet loosed off by some drunken soldier.

The harbour area, where the patrician mansions of Catania stand cheek by jowl with working-class dwellings, was fenced off with barbed wire and out of bounds to all civilians – it had been requisitioned as quarters for the hefty but homesick negro troops, some one of whom might occasionally be seen standing at a window, his evicted landlady's hat on his head and her boa round his neck. The old inhabitants of the neighbourhood, rich and poor alike, craned over the barbed wire, peering with all their might, launching the consolation of despair towards their old homes which had fallen, as they put it, into the hands of the Cannibals.

If bricks and mortar were in a state of devastation, no less so were feelings. Resentment was rife between this family and that: greetings unreturned, disdainful glances, political denunciations, had conferred an even more beleaguered air on the buildings still left standing, as if they had been rudely and spitefully slammed shut in each other's faces. The erstwhile Bullies, now deprived of an outlet, were so jaundiced by the poison pent up in them that they couldn't cast a kindly look even on their own children.

And of those who had suffered under them, woe alas, how many were broken by all this! Benevolent old Avvocato Bonaccorsi barricaded himself in his flat and refused to admit his friends, who had begun to get on his nerves. Dressed in black, armed with a handkerchief and seated in front of a mirror as if to console himself with the sight of a man of grief, he wept day in day out. Thus, while some who had beaten up their neighbours, imprisoned or even killed them, went about brazen and insolent, scheming vendettas or putting them into practice, this gentle soul, always on the side of reason and never harming anyone, racked with compassion for his fellow men, had not the courage to show his face in the street.

On the other side of the coin was Engineer Marletti. Appointed mayor of the city, he strutted up and down Via Etnea – dusty and deafening with military convoys – his aquiline nose stuck in the air, pretending not to recognize many an acquaintance and replying (a cheerful smile, a wave of the hand) only to the greetings of the new bullyboys. His authority, it turned out, was nothing to write home about. For one evening a party of drunken British officers caught him off guard on his own doorstep, solemnly declaiming a list of those citizens who were to be permanently deprived of civil rights.

They bundled him into a jeep and whisked him off to an ancient palazzo where, among the leftovers of a banquet, they made him wash up a monumental stack of dishes.

Avvocato Ardizzone was obsessed by a terror as grave and solemn as the airs he formerly put on. One afternoon he dragged some artist fellow along to the Bar Association and there, taking advantage of the fact not a soul was about at that hour of day, had him smother the Fascist symbol on which he was leaning in his portrait with some very thorough brush-work. His likeness, as a result, was left suspended in the void. Unfortunately, be it the fault of the inferior pigment or the work of some ill-wisher, two days later the fasces reappeared, surrounded by a blood-red smudge. An unknown voice came to him over the wire: "Avvocato, the fasces is back again!"

"I don't understand. Kindly explain yourself."

"The fasces in your portrait – it's back again, large as life!"

"I am an honest man and have nothing to fear!"

"I know you're an honest man, but some malicious tongue might..."

"What do you advise me to do?"

"Remove the picture."

"No, no, that would worsen the situation. Who knows what they might not think?... For example... for example that I had once had my photograph taken with that Heinous Criminal, the author of all our misfortunes. Do you understand me, my dear, kind friend, whose name I regret not knowing, but whom I none the less thank from the bottom of my heart?"

"If that is the case, do as you think best."

The avvocato thereupon became delirious, and on several occasions, hearing a knocking at the street door and imagining it to be the British military police with their red tops and white webbing, such was his state of mindless terror that he tried to climb to the terrace and hurl himself down into the street below.

★

266

Antonio got himself down to Catania during the morning, and having no wish to do the length of Via Etnea, where he was more than likely to bump into people altered not only in expression but even in the way they walked, he took a narrow side-turning leading from Via Umberto to his home street. Here his eye fell on a door he knew; which is to say that with a sinking of the heart he noticed, laid athwart a ditch that had yawned open all along the housefronts, a very familiar door now acting as a bridge between the street and a small entrance. A few steps further and he saw the leaf of another familiar door on the ground, serving the same purpose, this time still more recognizable – since it bore the name "Antonio" scratched with the point of a nail in the stiff, upright handwriting he had had as a ten-year-old; and before the alley opened into Via Pacini, lo, a third door similarly placed, the oldest old door in his building, covered with muddy footprints and smashed almost to smithereens under the strain.

"God, the house must be completely flattened!" thought Antonio in panic as he turned the corner.

But the building was still standing. The metal entrance-doors had been hoisted off their hinges, however, and sagged against the door-jamb, immovable. He turned sharply in under the archway. Rubble and wreckage of every sort, pulverized window-panes and mirrors, great mounds of rags and refuse. At the foot of the main staircase, on the step of the porter's lodge, the old caretaker himself, dazed by the horror of events, sat staring blindly into space.

"Don Sebastiano," cried Antonio, "How are things with you?"

The caretaker groped around for Antonio's hand, and having grasped it drew it close to his eyes, then burst into tears.

"They even come pissing right in under here!" he sobbed. "And if I dare say a word it's the worse for me! Come barking into my face like butchers' curs, they do."

"How about our flat? Is it damaged?"

"Not a bomb has fallen here, Master Ninuzzo, but it does seem as the thieves has grown wings these days!"

"Why couldn't you have slept up there yourself?"

"I could never have made the stairs, Master Ninuzzo."

"Give us the keys then, will you?"

"My niece's up there, cleaning around a bit."

Antonio took the stairs two at a time, passing a number of unfamiliar figures on their way down from somewhere he didn't care to imagine, possibly his own home...

"Where d'you think *you're* off to?" said one. "Don't you know the maid's up there?"

"Son of a bitch," muttered Antonio, elbowing the man roughly aside and sprinting up still faster.

From the doorway of his old home issued a cloud of dust as dense as smoke from sodden logs, and in the thick of it swished a broomstick forcefully wielded.

"Leave off a moment, can't you!" panted Antonio as he reached the landing.

The caretaker's niece came to the open door, beating the dust from her broom, and stood in puzzlement. She was fifty or thereabouts, dwarf-like in stature but straight and strong and full of pep, with one rosy cheek and the other entirely covered by a birth-mark the colour of wine-lees.

"...I'm the owner here," explained Antonio.

"Oh, Signor Don Alfio!" shrilled the woman, steadying herself with one hand on the broom-handle while she dropped a deep curtsey.

"Signor Alfio was my father. He's dead. I'm Antonio."

"Oh, oh, Signor Don Ninuzzo!" she cried, more than ever eager to be of assistance. "I'll be off and tidy your bedroom what's all of a mess. If you did but know the job it is to keep an eye on these pesky thieves! Why, they're here every minute of the day claiming they're cops, or Brits, or Yanks, or the devil knows what."

This said, she leant her broom against the wall and bustled off down the passage. Antonio closed the apartment door, the only one in the place still on its hinges, and followed in her wake; but at the sight of his father's study he was overcome by a weariness he hadn't been aware of till that very moment. He flopped down on the sofa, which no longer jangled, the reason being that the back was now denuded of knick-knacks and white with dust. He propped his head on the wooden arm-rest and, letting his eye slowly roam, drank in the portraits, looking sadder now, the sagging curtains, the doorless apertures, the smashed window providing a fine view of the caved-in roof of a neighbouring building all bristling with beams. From the street came unremitting whiffs of stench and clouds of dust and the birdlike acrobatics of half-charred paper. Oh, the pity of it, the pity of it...

A voice from the far end of the passage, unexpected, a breathless voice: "Antonio! Hey Antonio! Where are you?"

The sound of footsteps in the passage, hesitant and slow at first, then picking up speed, and in came a man whom the years had once respected, laying scarcely a finger on him, and then only to caress him, but for whom now they seemed to have lain in ambush on a dark night and bastonaded with sudden wrath and rancour, leaving no part of him unscathed by the daily castigation meted out to him.

"Edoardo!" cried Antonio, struck aghast, flinging his arms wide (though without rising from his couch): "Edoardo!"

His cousin grasped Antonio's hand and shook it: his own palm was dry and callused to the touch. He hooked a stool under him and sat down.

"Edoardo?" said Antonio, "Is that really you?"

"Yes, yes, it's old Edoardo all right," returned the other, pinching the palm of his left hand with the fingers of his right. He looked around him wearily and gave a wry grimace. "Yes, it's old Edoardo. The same old Edoardo..."

The name fell sadly on the air, then silence. "You know where I've just come from, eh?" he added.

"No, no I don't... or rather, yes I do..."

"From gaol."

269

"They told me you'd been sent to a concentration camp!"

"First to gaol, then to a camp, then back to gaol again...
Mind you, I don't take back a single word of what I said! I
haven't changed my opinions one jot. But heavens above, it's
pretty bizarre to have waited so many years for freedom...
and you *know* how I waited!... and when it finally arrives
the first thing they do is shut me in a cell with a steel door,
then it's a barbed-wire compound, then a cell again. It's bizarre
Antonio, bizarre..."

The caretaker's niece poked her head in through the curtains
and asked Antonio if she should make up his bed.

"Yes please," he said. "I'll take forty winks, I think."

The woman smiled, glad to have another job to set her hand
to, and trotted off.

"The more I know of cells, barbed wire, and sentries with
Sten-guns, the more I detest tyranny," continued Edoardo. "I
must admit my sentry wasn't a bad chap, though; a stolid
bank-clerk who'd mugged up a few words of Italian. One
night we had this conversation through the wire about Shake-
speare and Keats, as we looked up at the stars above our heads
and wondered if the world had gone to the bad for ever. Such
a late-night chat between a prisoner and his warder, such
exchanged confidences, the way the same star caught our eye
at the same time, seemed to me a good omen. But every time
a car's headlights swung by, the glitter on his Sten gave me a
sick feeling: if I tried to escape there were bullets in there with
my name on them... And after all... How can I put it,
Antonio? One thing is reason, with its mental processes always
on a tight rein, but quite another is the heart that despairs for
reasons all of its own... No man," he burst out, his eyes
reddening in an effort to restrain his tears, "no man ought ever
to be shut in by another man behind barbed wire or a steel
cell-door. It's a bloody miracle if he gets out of there with
enough human pride left in him to be able to stand on his own
two feet; and even so he'll be left with the wild animal's distrust
of man, instinctively seeking cover whenever humans come

near him. You know, each evening, when it gets to the time of day I was arrested, I go and hide in the attic... Every army truck that grinds to a halt, stops my heart. I'm honestly convinced that the entire Eighth Army is on my track, that it landed in Europe for the sole purpose of hunting me down. No, Antonio, we never ought to hunt men down – never! God knows I've always detested despotism, so just imagine, now that I've experienced it at first hand!... And the bizarre thing is that it's this blessed 'freedom' that has opened my eyes..."

Gently lulled by the doleful drone of this discourse, Antonio nodded off, but a moment later was awakened by the care-taker's niece popping back through the door-curtains, and asking him to step that way a moment as she had something particular to say to him.

Antonio signalled that he'd be with her in a moment, and the woman, all smiles, withdrew.

"Then there's another thing," resumed Edoardo. "Can tyranny really be demolished by gunfire? You know what a cell-mate of mine said to me? 'If you go hating the rich and sticking up for freedom of opinion you're going to be a man of sorrows. Hating the rich will get you in among the Commu-nists, who'll bung you into gaol because you fancy freedom of opinion!' So what's the answer? Do those other Hordes pouring in from the East rebel as much as I do against censor-ship, deportation and imprisonment? Don't you think they might have come to accept these horrors as being in the nature of things? Antonio, we are duty-bound to ponder on these matters and come to a decision that enables us..."

"Excuse me one moment," said Antonio. "I'll be right back."

He rose from the sofa with an agreeable sense of lassitude in his legs, left the study, sauntered the length of the corridor and entered his own bedroom.

The woman was just bending over, putting finishing touches

to the sheets. On hearing a footstep she glanced round and gave Antonio a smiling look from beneath her lashes.

"You wanted me, er. . . what *is* your name?"

"Rosa," she replied, her smile more radiant than ever.

"Then what is it, Rosa?"

The woman straightened up from the bed and turned, took a slight step backwards, staring mistrustfully at Antonio's right hand, raised to his face, as if it might be about to dart in her direction.

"Nothing. . . I just wanted to ask. . ." She hesitated, smiling uncomfortably now, the colour in her cheeks, both the rosy and the vinous, growing more vivid still.

"Come on, tell me. What did you want?"

Another moment of hesitation. "Nothing. . . I only wanted to know would you be requiring anything more?"

A deafening roar in Antonio's ears – a hot flush behind his eyeballs as his vision clouded – on the instant, its own impetuosity breaking the fetters of its steel-hard casing, a wave of passion exploded from the very ganglions of his nerves, shrapnelled his whole skin, pulsed like a heart in tumult in that distant part of his body so many years an orphan.

Reeling slightly he approached the woman, grabbed her under the armpits, hefted her clean off her feet and welded her to him.

"Whatever are you up to?" cried Rosa, emitting the heady odour of physical thrill. "What are you thinking of? I'm gone fifty, I am. . ."

"What of it?" Antonio murmured huskily. "Keep quiet."

And still shackling her to him, her feet dangling, he bore her inch by inch towards the bed.

"Whatever are you up to, what are you *doing*? I want to know!"

"Doesn't matter. Shut your trap!"

"I won't, I won't! Just you tell me what. . .?"

"Shut up!" he repeated.

"Oh my God!"

272

"Shut up!"

"My God, he's shoving me down. . ."

She was flung on the bed, which squeaked and bounced accordingly. Antonio, terrified as of old that the ruttish heat possessing him might come to nothing, though his face was ablaze and every vein in his body pulsing fiercely, hurled himself on the woman, tore off her clothes like a cur clawing at the wrapping of a piece of meat, scratched her, bit her, dashed her to right and to left, rolled her this way and that, panting through clenched teeth, still biting her, fingers digging in. . . until seized by a voluptuousness, potent, double-edged, as of one giving vent to a long-suppressed loathing – and simultaneously receiving a slap in the face which, by paying him back for some sin of his, relieves him of an intolerable guilt. . . A pang in his chest, his bowels, his throat, forced out a sharp cry.

A weight was on top of him, pinning him to the sofa. He awoke – in the grip of Edoardo.

"What in heaven's name's the matter?" gasped Edoardo. "Yelling blue murder and trying to rip all the skin off your ribs! What the hell's up with you?"

Antonio had another spasm, arching his body and pressing up from the sofa with his hands, then fell limply back with a deep sigh.

"So I was dreaming, was I?" he murmured, without opening his eyes.

"You certainly were," retorted Edoardo pettishly. "There I was, talking to you, and instead of listening you coolly went off to sleep!"

"I had a most wonderful dream," said Antonio, the shadow of a smile on his pale lips. "What a wonderful dream I had!"

He sat up and rubbed his eyes.

"Edoardo," he recommenced, a tremor in his voice. "I dreamt that. . . You get my meaning?"

"I certainly don't! *What* did you dream?"

"I dreamt I did it, I really did it. . . I felt such joy I could have died. Or maybe it wasn't a dream, or only the woman in it was a dream, because for me... for me it wasn't a dream at all!"

Edoardo shot to his feet.

"D'you really think this is the time and place to have wet dreams?" he demanded sourly.

"No need to get so hot under the collar about it," said Antonio. "I seem to have rubbed you up the wrong way."

"No you haven't, but there are times, I'll have you know, when a person simply can't stand..."

"You amaze me," returned Antonio. "You've always been so kind, so thoughtful, so... understanding."

"My dear boy," rejoined his cousin, "sometimes *I* need a bit of understanding too."

"Don't get on your high horse, Edoardo. That's not worthy of your intelligence."

"Think I'm offended, eh? Not in the least. But according to you," added Edoardo with a rasp in his voice, "we must always be thinking about that same old thing. Is there nothing else in the world? Would to God there weren't, Antonio! While I was in the camp I did a lot of thinking about things, and you were one of them."

"What conclusions did you draw? Let's hear the worst."

"That you might have been more philosophical about your mishap."

"You call it a *mishap?*"

"Yes I do. I call it a mishap, and a piddling one at that. For anyone in any other country it would have been a piddling little mishap. But for us? Oh, *we* have to make a Greek tragedy of it! And why? Because all we can think of is the one little thing, and that's it! In the meanwhile along comes a despotic gangster. One kick in the pants from him and we go flying into this war, and then all the other countries come charging back at us with another kick in the pants, and the next thing is they've taken us over, lock, stock and barrel. But no matter!

Women, women, women, four, five, six times a day... That's all *we* worry about...

"But," he continued, "has it never occurred to you that there's no dishonour attached to living in chastity all one's life long? You, Antonio, are tall, dark and handsome. You're a fine figure of a man and you've been well brought up. You can master anything you put your hand to. You're capable of understanding anything you care to name, goddam it! Just think of all the things you could have done if you hadn't buried yourself night and day in your one, single obsession, and pined your bloody life away!"

"My dear Edoardo, all I want is one thing and one thing only: to make that dream come true."

"Ah yes, you worship the god of lust, the great god Libido! To what lofty heights do you not aspire!"

"There *is* something else I want, and it's this: to meet Barbara and slap her face for her. I give you my word that if I met her today I'd fetch her such a wallop I'd have the skin off her cheek. And in front of her father and her husband, what's more!"

"Oh, terrific stuff! That's the way to right all the wrongs of the world, be an honour to your country, resolve the social problem..."

"A fat lot I care about the social problem!" yelled Antonio in exasperation. Then, in crescendo, "And still less about my *country*!"

"Naturally! Concerned with matters as life-and-death as you are..."

"Edoardo, if you really want to know, you're getting my goat today."

"And if you really want to know, dearest coz, you're being a pain in the neck yourself. I can't imagine how I've stood your feeble-minded sob-stuff all these years."

"Or I your interminable blathering on."

"In that case we'll call it a day. I'll be off." Edoardo got up, took his hat from the desk. "When your precious dream comes true, just hang a flag out over the balcony. I'll get the message. Be seeing you... Oh, and speaking of flags, hang out another when you've caught Barbara a good hefty whack. 'Bye for now."

In the doorway Edoardo glanced back to see whether he'd got any reaction, but Antonio returned his look with lofty disdain.

"Fathead!" muttered Edoardo. "Man of straw... maniac... layabout... doormat."

In the meantime he had reached Via Etnea and was busy fending off numerous knots of military personnel, some of whom staggered drunkenly in his direction, drawn to him as matter to a vacuum and all set to collapse on top of him.

"Hapless youth... with that bee in his bonnet... always staring past his navel to see if down in the forest something stirs. He's made it his god, his religion. What a fate!"

Thinking these thoughts, and giving muttered voice to them, he reached his own building and turned in at the main door – swung to on the instant behind him by the daughter of the concierge.

"And I *so* badly needed to let off a bit of steam with him... He's left me with all the muck still bottled up inside... It's left a bad taste in my mouth... Hey, Giovanna, what the devil are you doing barring the door? It's not midnight!"

"I'm scared of the soldiers, sir, 'cos I'm alone here. They comes right inside all wild-eyed like, and what they wants I'm sure I don't know."

"You know perfectly well what they want."

"I don't know nothing, sir."

"Get on with you, of course you do."

"Think what you please, sir, I don't know nothing."

"If you don't, you'd better get someone to teach you!"

"No one needs teach me nothing. I don't want to learn nothing from no one."

"Not even from me?"

"Not even you, sir."

276

"Come along now, from me..."

"Not even you, I said – and just you leave my face alone!"

"What a hoity-toity little thing you are!"

"I am what I am. And leave go my hands!"

"Heavens, can't I even touch your hands?"

"No you can't!"

"Not even this little nose of yours?"

"Hands off my nose! Gawd give me patience!"

"Then what *can* I touch?"

"Nothing! You can't touch nothing!... Oh no sir, no!" The poor, dazed girl let out a sudden shriek. "Holy Mother of God, what are you doing? What's got into you today?"

Edoardo acted swiftly, forcefully, never for an instant relaxing his appearance of being in a towering rage.

Having got himself to his feet and mopped his brow, he hastily lowered his eyes, for he had small wish to look the woman in the face: she was making no secret of her smouldering resentment and animosity, tugging her skirt down and dusting it off... He made for the stairs, started up them, but progress was slow up the first flight. The second was no better... but the third he took at a run. Entering the flat, with clumsy haste he flung open the shutters, crossed to the telephone and dialled Antonio's number.

"Yes?" came his cousin's listless query. "Hullo? Who's calling?"

At Edoardo's end, silence.

"Who's on the line, please? Hullo, hullo?"

Silence.

"Oh, stop fooling! Who is it?"

Edoardo burst into blubbering sobs.

For a minute Antonio hesitated; then he said, "Is that you, Edoardo?"

At this end of the line the sobs slackened, grew less incoherent, paused, as if to leave space for a word that just wouldn't come out, and for two or three deep sighs to relax the cramps in the chest. And finally they ceased.

"Yes," said Edoardo, "it's me... I... please, I beg you to forgive me."

"Forgive you? What for?"

"Because I had the impudence to... to tell you off... I... I..." – he choked on another sob – "who am the lowest of the low. I who have..."

"You who have *what?*"

"Next time you see me, Antonio, you must spit in my face! You must stamp all over it and then give your shoes a good clean!"

"But what on earth have you been up to?"

Far in the distance a bomb went off, the window-panes rattled just a little, the sky seemed dimmer...

"Edoardo, what have you *done?*"

Unsparingly self-abrasive, Edoardo told what had happened at the foot of the stairs.

When he had finished there was a pause: Edoardo waited for his cousin to speak. He waited in vain. There was silence on the line.

"Aren't you going to say something?" asked Edoardo, pained.

Dead silence.

"Have you nothing to say?"

Silence.

"Not even a word?"

Antonio still said nothing, though plainly he was listening intently. And another thing he made plain all in a flash was this: that far from condemning Edoardo, or commiserating with him for what had occurred at the foot of the stairs, he envied him. With every throb of blood in his veins, with every least thought in his head, he envied him. Ever more intense, and vehement, and scalding, the force of that envy reached Edoardo over the wire.

"No!" he shouted at the top of his lungs, "no, no, no, no! Believe me, Antonio – I swear by all that's holy – you've got it all wrong – it's not like you say at all –"

"I haven't said anything," replied Antonio; and, drawing in a mighty breath, he held it for as long as he could, filling the telephone wire with all that was utter silence. Until he too broke into weeping.

Between those tears and Edoardo's there was a great gulf fixed. Far more strangled and desperate this weeping was, and ruptured by the rasp of lungs that for many long years had never for one moment breathed freely of the air of happiness.

Edoardo held on for another minute or two; then, realizing that there were no signs of a let-up, he lost heart, took the instrument from his ear and looked at it. For a long, long time he looked at it, depressed, dismayed, as it gurgled forth the sobs of an incurable adolescent.

"Very bizarre, all this," he murmured, wiping away a tear now frozen on his cheek. "Very bizarre indeed. . ."

Then very slowly, very gently, he replaced the receiver.